The Sound of the Sundial

Hana Andronikova

Translated from the Czech by David Short

Edited & Adapted by Rachel Miranda Feingold

Plamen Press

Washington, DC

Plamen Press

1407 Tenth Street NW Washington, DC 20001

www.plamenpress.com

Copyright © Hana Andronikova, heirs, 2014

Published by Plamen Press 2015

Printed in the United States of America

10 9 8 7 6 5 4 3 2 1

LIBRARY OF CONGRESS CATALOGING-IN-PUBLICATION DATA

Andronikova, Hana

The Sound of the Sundial: a novel/Hana Andronikova

p. cm.

ISBN: 978-0-9960722-1-2

Library of Congress Control Number: 2015935563

Translated from the Czech by David Short
Edited & Adapted by Rachel Miranda Feingold

Cover Art by Serena Faye Feingold

Editors

Rachel Miranda Feingold

Roman Kostovski

Editors' Note

The editors' job in bringing a translated piece of literature into the world can be likened to the role of a midwife: we are always mindful that others have done the most important work, and our greatest wish is to augment the experience in every way we can.

In our case, the process was complicated by an interesting conundrum: there were two English translations to work with, and they were very different. The first manuscript was a remarkably comprehensive translation by British linguist David Short, based directly upon the Czech original, *Zvuk slunečních hodin* (Knižní klub, Prague, 2001). The second manuscript, sent to us by the Pluh Literary Agency in the Netherlands (which has a proprietary relationship with Hana Andronikova's family) departed dramatically from the original. But it could not be ignored, either, as it was derived from David Short's translation, and heavily edited and adapted by Andronikova herself, in partnership with editor Ian Miller. Second and third editions in Czech did not reflect these changes, and though she had entered into negotiations with more than one English-language press for publication of *The Sound of the Sundial*, neither of these translations ever saw the light of day.

Hana was quite fluent in English. As an undergraduate she studied English as well as Czech Literature, and later spent a year in the USA on an international fellowship at the Iowa Writer's Workshop, producing several stories in original English with her unique style—striking metaphors, sentence fragments, intense emotional language—all beautifully intact. We were lucky to have these short samples of her writing on which to base our work. Looking at the second translation of the novel, it was clear the author and editor had made some stylistic changes to highlight the lyrical tone of the Czech original, and had removed some sections that slowed the flow of the narrative even beyond what Hana might have intended with her many leaps through time and setting.

Here the question naturally arises: Since Andronikova had worked on this second translation herself, why did we not simply publish it as it was? The answer is: the second manuscript was so deeply cut that we felt important nuances of character development had been lost, and we believed the absence of a published English version pointed to the author's own ambivalence. Yet we had been told repeatedly that it was her dream to bring the novel out in English. Might she have reconsidered if she had had more time?

It would be impossible to convey how often we two managing partners at Plamen Press—one of us a translator of Slavic literatures, and the other a literary editor—expressed the wish to call Hana Andronikova and ask her what she wanted us to do. Sadly, we could not. We marked the third anniversary of her death from breast cancer during the months when we were striving to bring this English version of *The Sound of the Sundial* to light.

Ultimately, we felt that it was incumbent upon us to take all of Hana's original words into account. We decided to go back to the first translation, and—keeping the second one always in our sights—effect an amalgamation of the two. As we have already noted, David Short's work was very thorough, and the changes we made to his English were not a criticism of his linguistic skill, which is undeniable. Rather they were stylistic or idiomatic in nature: our decision--as an American press--to render Short's British idioms more native to the American reader; and our efforts to fully transmit the power of Hana's vivid and lyrical writing.

We decided to honor the choice made in the Andronikova/ Miller version to remove the chapters dealing directly with Anna Vanier's husband, Pete, and his experiences in World War II. As it stands, there are a challenging number of narrative threads to follow, and these cut segments do not intersect materially with the remainder of the story. Pete Vanier still appears intermittently in Anna's own narrative, and following the author's lead, we kept those segments in the book. These deletions required us to renumber the novel's other chapters, but we were careful to preserve intact the brief segments without any numbers, whose headings—"Dusk," "Midnight," "Dawn," and so on—mark the passage of that single day in which Daniel and Anna tell each other their respective stories. We believe these headings were meant to reflect the movements of the sundial itself, Hana's playful little nod to her own preoccupation with time as an architectural element.

It is important to note that Czech is a conceptual language, and tenses in the original novel are often fluid. Short's translation faithfully reflected this fluidity with frequent switches to a historic present—that is, a present tense narrative that is unfolding in the past. But Hana's temporal sleight-of-hand throughout the novel is already formidable, and we were concerned that such shifts of tense could disorient the reader of our far-more-concrete English beyond tolerability, so we rendered almost all of those passages into past tense; the only exceptions were the stream-of-consciousness flashbacks that seemed to call particularly for the immediacy of present tense, and these we set in italics.

In the further interest of narrative flow, we sometimes interspersed sentences from the two translations in a single paragraph; transposed sentences or entire paragraphs; or deleted one of two nearly identical phrases. In every case, we made these changes to reflect the broad linguistic differences between Czech and English, always striving to preserve the author's unique style, and her vision of the boundlessness of time and the capriciousness of memory.

Throughout this process of amalgamation, our esteem for Hana Andronikova's extraordinary creation has continued to deepen. We invite you now to join us in reading *The Sound of the Sundial* and celebrating this love song to the range of human experience, with all of its suffering and cruelty and loss, and its moments of irrepressible joy.

Rachel Miranda Feingold
Roman Kostovski
Editors and Managing Partners of Plamen Press

The Sound of the Sundial

*Whensoever any affliction assails me,
me thinks I have the keyes of my prison in mine owne hand,
and no remedy presents it selfe so soone to my heart,
as mine own sword.*

JOHN DONNE
Biathanatos, preface, c. 1608

I

New Year's Eve

It seemed strange to think I could find something new, a missing piece of the jigsaw puzzle, in a place I had visited so many times before. But as I breathed in the frozen air of Denver, something inside me moved, like the fist of a child.

It was December, 1989. Like every year, we were going to spend Christmas together in the mountains of Colorado, leaving the contours of Toronto behind, its streets sober and rigid, cast in shades of grey.

There were eight of us. At the airport, we loaded ourselves and our ski gear into two rental cars and headed off along I-70 to Breckenridge.

"Turn off here on 203, Dad. Frisco exit."

My eyes rested on the landscape lining Highway 9, and I imagined myself in the streets of the picturesque little town which, a century before, had witnessed the gold rush. The highway merged into Main Street. The tires spun on the packed snow, the wipers creaking across our frosted windshield.

The little roads and houses of Breckenridge were coming back to me, but Alice continued to navigate. My daughter was almost at an age when she no longer needed to make me out to be an idiot all the time. She had become more indulgent lately, and instead of ignoring me, she leaned over and hollered the next instruction

1

right in my ear. "Go left here, Dad."

We turned into Lincoln Street and stopped two blocks down. In previous years we had stayed at the Abbett Placer Inn, but this year we had switched, and reserved all the rooms in Mrs. Vanier's Bed and Breakfast.

Ellen and I took up residence on the first floor, in the "Colorado" room, furnished in a style that recalled the gold rush. Beech-panelled bedroom, old-fashioned bathroom, lamps with batiste shades. Alice occupied the Victorian room, with a bed and commode dating back to the turn of the century and a view of the hillside opposite. Very romantic.

My elder son, Scott, was the spitting image of my father. He was married to the dark-complexioned Frances, the love of his school days; with their little boy, Nicky, they settled themselves into the suite Mrs Vanier introduced as her "Room with a View."

Ross, my younger son, took a remote bedroom at the end of the ground floor corridor with his current girlfriend. "This is the future mother of my children," he would say of every girl he hung around with, replacing them at yearly intervals. He was a sound engineer, though his temperament was more suited to Hollywood: women were drawn to his easy clowning, but once out of their sight, he lobbed verbal attacks and fits of anger like grenades.

Scott was fond of his brother, and sometimes amused by Ross's lack of self-control, but he was unwilling to put up with it for long. Who did Ross take after? Not Ellen, whose family were a bunch of unobtrusive, well-behaved Protestants. No, the answer lay with my side of the family, the side my children knew nothing about. And lately it was becoming clear that some of those hot-blooded genes had passed to little Nicky as well.

Ellen and I were preparing for bed when there was a knock at the door. Scott's mop of hair appeared, and beneath it his imploring expression.

"We were hoping to go out to the bar, but unless you can

step in, there's no chance. We talked Alice into keeping an eye on Nicky, but he only wants you."

It made me feel good. At no time in my life had I mattered as much to anyone as I did to my grandson. And I adored him. I grabbed my bathrobe.

Ellen was smiling. "That's right, Grandpa's the favorite slave."

"You don't mind, do you, Dad?"

"Course not! Off you go."

Nicky, happily ensconced in bed, radiated triumph. "Grandpa, tell me the story your mother used to tell you about the little mole."

"But you must have heard it a hundred times. Don't you want a different one?"

He shook his head emphatically.

Snow fluttered past the window. Nicky had the freshly bathed smell of thyme and oranges, that special scent unique to the bodies of small children before they escape into maturity. Sunk cosily in an armchair by the bed, my feet in the deep pile of the carpet, I began telling him, for the hundred-and-first time, the foundation myth of the Indians of Central America.

"Once upon a time, in the place where Mexico is today, there lived a young man they called the Bowman. That was because even as a little boy he used to shoot birds. He could bring more of them down than any adult huntsman. When he was nearly grown, he stitched himself a magnificent cape of feathers. Day after day he would go off hunting in faraway places until, one day, he found himself at the far eastern end of the land. He reached the steep cliff over which the Sun rose every day, and lay down to sleep after his tiring journey. In the morning he felt a hot glow on his neck. He rubbed his eyes and saw that the Sun had burned a hole in his cape. Wicked Sun! You'll pay for this! But the Sun didn't even glance at him as it went on its way. The Bowman was enraged; he hid in a cave and spent the next two days braiding a strong rope. On the third day, he lay in wait behind the eastern cliff and, as the sleepy Sun rolled up onto the horizon, he tossed a loop over it and trapped it. From that day on the Sun never rose. The world was shrouded in deep black. The Earth was consumed by a bitter freeze, flowers wilted, and small animals shivered with cold and hunger, huddling together and whimpering into the darkness: 'Sun, where are you? Come back to us!' Some of the small animals tried to find the Sun, but they kept tripping over one another because only the owl and the black puma could see in the dark, and so most of them went back to their chilly holes and dens. But the mole persevered. He plodded through the darkness, on and on, chilled to the marrow, his teeth chattering, on and on, until he saw in the distance a light coming from the direction of the eastern cliff. As he approached, the imprisoned Sun tickled him on the nose."

Nicky blurted out:

"Dear Sun, you must come back to us, or we shall all die!"

I stroked his fair hair.

"I would love to come back, little mole, but I'm trapped by these ropes. I can't move. The little mole didn't think twice, but clambered up to the very top of the cliff. As he approached the Sun, he felt a great heat. 'Oh, little mole, little mole, if only I could stop glowing for a moment! I'll burn you to a cinder,' the Sun sighed, when it saw the mole struggling with the rope and growing faint with the heat. 'I must set you free,' cried the mole, and went on trying to bite through the rope. And suddenly, snap! The ropes gave and the Sun hopped up into the sky. On earth, everything sprang to life, trees and plants began to wake up, birds twittered, and animals came creeping out of their holes. And everything was just as before. Well, almost everything. Only the little mole could not see. He could feel warmth and smell scents, he could hear the others babbling, but he could see nothing. The Sun's radiance had blinded him forever, which is why he has hidden underground ever since."

4

The little mole's blindness did not trouble my grandson's immature soul. He was carried away by the mole's courage and endurance, his selfless heroism. When Scott and Frances came home, Nicky was sleeping like a baby bear.

Every morning I was awakened by the tramping of sport-hungry zombies getting ready for the slopes after a night of debauchery and four hours' sleep. Doors banging, brusque commands delivered in cracked voices.

"Don't forget your gloves, Nicky," Scott wheezed in a voice an octave higher than usual.

Ellen was the last to leave; she finished her coffee and waited for the minibus. "Be good here." She winked and gave me a kiss on my freshly shaved cheek. Then silence again.

After twelve days, I had covered the whole area around Breckenridge, crossing it this way and that on foot. I had a pleasant sense of the change wrought by this stay in the mountains: the lobes of my lungs had settled comfortably inside my rib cage and no longer attempted to scramble up to my throat.

New Year's Eve beckoned. Preparations for the start of 1990 were in full swing. It was snowing gently as I returned from my morning walk. I stamped my feet on the metal doormat to clear the snow stuck to the soles of my boots, and opened the door.

In the half-light of the stairway stood the landlady. She was bending down and pouring cat food into a red plastic bowl, talking to her furry darlings in some foreign tongue. "*Pojďte holky moje hladový, jenom pojďte.*"

I realized I could understand that foreign tongue.

"Good morning, Mrs Vanier," I said in Czech.

She jumped in surprise and turned around.

I smiled. "Forgive me. I haven't spoken Czech with anyone in ages."

"Oh, I speak it all the time, but mostly with my kitties. They understand me, but they don't speak it either. American cats."

"I'd no idea you were Czech. Have you been living here long?" I said.

"I should say so! Over forty years. I'd almost given up hope of ever returning home, and now everything's suddenly changed. In March I'm going over for a class reunion with the girls from my school. Imagine, after fifty years!"

"Are you from Prague?"

"Yes. You too?"

"No. Zlín."

Mrs Vanier smiled dreamily. "Will you come in and share a pot of tea?"

I followed her into the large kitchen-dining room where she made breakfast for the guests. The conservatory with its oak table merged easily into the patio, from where you could see the Ten Mile Range. Only a door separated us from the spindly mountains rearing into the sky. The snow-dazzled daylight melted my eyes.

"Have you heard they elected Václav Havel president the day before yesterday? None of it seems real."

Recent events across the ocean were breathtaking. Velvet Revolution.

"So you're from Zlín," Mrs Vanier gushed.

"I was born in Zlín. But my childhood was the Tropic of Cancer."

II

Another World

My father, Thomas, graduated college in 1926 and returned from Prague to his native Olomouc. He started looking for work. A new city was springing up just under a hundred kilometers away—a city of unheard-of opportunity: Zlín, where Tomáš Baťa's factory employed over six thousand people and produced thirty-five thousand pairs of shoes a day.

In the personnel department, they put Thomas through a bushel of tests. A lady with greying hair who looked like a fairy godmother fired a string of questions at him.

"Name?"

"Thomas Keppler."

"One P or two? Single? Any debts? Savings? How much do you want to be earning? What are your monthly expenses? What do you spend most on? What about alcohol? Cigarettes?"

Thomas kept up a smile and tried to reply honestly.

"Prague College of Science and Technology? What degree?"

"Structural engineering," he said.

The fairy godmother pushed her spectacles back with the middle finger of her right hand. She gave him a job in construction.

Hundreds of workers' cottages went up each year. He was given his first task: to make sure that work went smoothly on one of the new batches of cottages at Zálešná. Teams of men

7

with spades, men to lay the concrete foundations, bricklayers, plumbers, electricians. Then plasterers, carpenters, painters. As the groundwork reached completion at the far end of the site, gardeners were laying lawns at the near end. The little brick houses with wooden ceilings and flat roofs sprang up like mushrooms.

He couldn't fathom why the workers' housing wasn't being built more cheaply; bigger units, where more than one family would live under one roof.

Gahura, the municipal architect, explained Baťa's strategy with a knowing grin: "My dear Keppler, the boss operates under the principle, *Work together, live apart.* The man with his own cottage and garden will poke around in the ground instead of in politics, and he'll steer clear of the bars and union meetings."

The construction division grew into a peculiarly nomadic organization, traipsing the length and breadth of the country and putting up shoe stores at an incredible rate. And service centers. Three hundred highly trained and well-paid construction workers in groups, taking their turns at the sites and completing their jobs on time. Assembly-line construction. The architect Josef Gočár maintained that Baťa buildings could not even be described as architecture, but more as "industrial design projects," and the sad fact was that those homogeneous stores, all reinforced concrete and glass, paid no regard to their future surroundings.

After two months, Thomas was transferred to planning and design to complete the blueprints for a new hospital. Gasping for breath, he tried to meet deadlines; exhausted and with little sleep he calculated new variants, weighed new solutions. Detailed drafting, sketches, rolls of tracing paper, and gallons of black coffee. On edge the whole time. Chain-smoking. At the year's end they started construction on the first four units. The main building housed the operating room, maternity wards, exam rooms, and the service block. A few months later, the hospital was admitting its first patients.

A year after that they started on the Market Hall—the first use of a reinforced concrete skeleton in a public edifice. He was personally curious to see what it would be like. In the end, he was thrilled. By 1928, he was running around overseeing the construction of the Masaryk School. He liked Gahura's design, a red brick horseshoe set in a sea of green. It was well thought out, economical but also eye-catching. Fully glazed exterior walls, a spacious gym, the art room upstairs with its own balcony. Generously proportioned classrooms. Heated with forced hot air, which could be switched to cold in the summer.

The factory complex at Otrokovice raised doubts in his mind from the outset. The main thing that worried him was the plan for it to be built dangerously close to the River Morava. They bulldozed the site, washed a hill away with a stream of water, and stabilized the marshland where, in September 1930, they started building the tannery and the settlement of houses for the workers. In Zlín, he witnessed his second flood in late October. One of the greatest mishaps of his career: the Morava burst its banks and construction had to start over again. Later events at the site merely confirmed the folly of trying to command the elements.

By the early 1930s, the Baťa company had branches on three continents. Expansion at a time when the world was in crisis. Worldwide, companies were going bust one after another, unemployment and poverty loomed, but Baťa was hiring new people by the dozen. They called themselves Baťa's Young Men. They spread out across America, Asia, and Africa, heading for exotic regions, primeval forests and jungles, in order to coax modern industrial cities out of the void.

Thomas sorted out all the final details before his departure. Maps, books, and guides. A trip to the hospital. Jarda Bartošík had him examined from top to toe and bombarded him with an avalanche of warnings: beware of the water, don't eat raw vegetables, take quinine every morning to guard against malaria. "Have you seen a dentist? No? So get that done as well."

Then there were the immunization certificates: typhus, typhoid, dysentery, cholera, smallpox. Copies of deeds for the construction sites and his papers of accreditation. Sunglasses.

Late in the afternoon, he stood in a group of twenty-somethings and handed out final instructions. "Check your passports, medical certificates, and all your other papers. Don't forget your medicines. Any questions?"

One of the young men hesitated, then raised his hand. "Yes. I—the thing is, I've got all my papers and certificates, but—I don't speak a word of English."

The knot of men tittered.

Thomas didn't even blink. "So don't forget to take a dictionary! Anything else?"

On the way home he couldn't dispel his fear. It wasn't Rachel he was afraid for; he knew that she would cope without him. But he didn't know how he would cope without her.

She had dinner waiting. "When do you leave?"

"The day after tomorrow."

"And when will I see you?"

"I'll send for you as soon as I can. I expect in about six months. If there are no setbacks."

Six months. Half a year. Now that he had said it aloud, his heart sank. Six months. How innocent it sounded. Why was he feeling so wretched?

"I hope there won't be any setbacks." She half-closed her eyes like a sorceress.

"There are *bound* to be setbacks."

She nodded. The spangles on her earrings danced. She opened a box of matches. Fishing out one redheaded stick, she dashed it against the flint. It sparked into flame between her fingers. Flashes from the earrings entered his eyes and began to circulate in his bloodstream. She lit the candles on the table. In the glow of the flames she looked like a goddess. A nymph. He could sense the molten wax against his skin.

How could he leave her? He got up and walked around the table. Her face in golden rays of light, a pounding in his temples. Kneeling, he sank into the folds of her yellow and orange dress and pulled her towards him, locking his arms. Her skin and the dark red moss of the carpet outlining her raven black hair. That maze of colors stuck in his memory. Sun and blood.

A brief farewell at the station and an endless stream of sleeper cars. The train bore him away from a familiar world to remote and unknown corners.

He embarked. He lost touch with terra firma, the air full of salt, silver gulls and flying fish. The ship like a fish-scale amid the waves, veering from side to side, chairs sliding across the deck. Stewards carrying steaks and wearing obliging smiles, the polite refusals, the loud laughter of a seductive Viennese girl. She knew a trick to confuse customs officials. She had bought eight pairs of shoes, but wore down the soles of each just a little bit, so they couldn't prove a thing. Of course, they would pay back the tax at the frontier if she was only in transit, but there were all those forms to fill in—who would tangle with bureaucrats? She could already imagine herself sipping sherry in Bombay.

Then the sun came up and irradiated the mountain peaks on the horizon. Mainland in sight. Green islands, the shore, port officials on the landing stage checking passports and visas. He disembarked.

The god Vishnu could take three steps and cross the entire universe, but Thomas would need another thirty-six hours by train just to reach his destination.

He wanted to buy something for Rachel. He headed for a tastefully decorated shop with huge window displays. Unique pieces of ivory, all manner of fabrics, amber statuettes, jewelry of beaten bronze, cigars and spices. He bought an inlaid writing box and wrote to her:

They stared truculently at me and shouted something after I refused to take a rickshaw powered by their own bodies. They were gaunt and looked sick. I only understood this bitterness when an Englishman who had just boarded one of these two-wheeled vehicles turned to me and said: "You're new here, aren't you? They get upset when a sahib refuses to let them earn some small change."

In the afternoon I went to the central bazaar in Calcutta. A shocking experience for a well-brought-up European. At every step smart shopkeepers would insist on pressing their wares on me. There were silk saris, men's shirts, shoes, panama hats, a veritable fireworks display of ostrich feathers, live birds, and monkeys thrust in my face. Native men squatted atop mounds of coffee, coconuts, mangos, bananas, oranges. All reaching out to touch me. They caught me by the hand or tugged at the sleeves of my sweaty shirt. Storekeepers, rickshaw drivers, children, the most wretched of beggars seeking alms. Exotic beauties in saris. The scene had a life of its own, assailing all my senses. I drowned in a palette of colors, in a mixture of fancy perfumes and the stench of decay, in the stifling heat of inarticulate noise, arguing and shouting. I let myself be swallowed up in the rhythm of their lives.

Rachel, this city has a soul.

Last evening I was walking along the shore where one of the many arms of the Ganges enters the sea. I spotted a lone diver in a little dugout canoe. A net and two oars, that was all he had. He tucked the net into his armpit and disappeared under the waves. It was over three minutes before he resurfaced. The net was full of shells.

He couldn't waste time. He went about finding how other builders coped with the Indian climate, solved the ventilation problem, and braved monsoons and earthquakes. On the fly, he fitted out workshops for mechanics and carpenters. He had to stock the company shops at lightning speed. There were a hundred shops to set up in Bengal and neighboring Assam alone. In the mornings, he would wake to the heavy fog of Calcutta. That was probably why the English set up here, he mused; it must have reminded them of London. Daytime temperatures gradually rose to 40 degrees centigrade in the shade. He would knock out reports to Zlín until well into the night. Worn to a shadow and sweating profusely, he tried to gather his fragments of thought, interrupted by memories of home, chafing at the mountain of details he had to record. Wooden shelves cost five rupees each, the deposit for an electric meter came to about twenty-five rupees...

He felt trapped. This was a different world. Life in the streets of Calcutta pulsed around him. He met people of every color, from white Englishmen to the blackest of black men, members of every religion and caste, from untouchables to Tibetan lamas in their orange robes.

He walked to the River Hooghly. The city had once settled down like some gigantic beast on its left bank, and ever since had lapped up its turbid waters, spawning countless houses, streets, hovels, and garbage dumps.

The stifling air was riven by some strange, raucous call. *Kalighat! Kalighat!* The voices promised something mysterious, fascinating, something not to be missed. *Kalighat!* The bus drivers cursing the goddess Kali. *Kalighat!* He dithered, hands in pockets, then absentmindedly boarded one of the buses. They drove down the avenue of shop fronts on Chauringi, the main thoroughfare, where he had taken up residence two weeks earlier. Then the right side of the street disappeared and in its place the Maidan opened out before him, a vast plain in the middle of a city. The brown-skinned driver in the white shirt kept chanting his magic spell: *Kalighat! Kalighat!* Like a granite mountain, a white statue of Queen Victoria loomed and the man at the wheel wheezed *Kalighat! Kalighat!* The road, choked with detached houses, drowned in engine noise. The brakes of the bus screeched. *Kalighat!*

A voice announced their destination. He staggered out of the bus. Nothing of note here: just ordinary European houses, boring and severe. Run-of-the-mill vegetable gardens and a battered bus plastered with ads. The other passengers looked neither confused nor cheated. They headed towards a little street running between two of the houses. He followed. The European houses disappeared, and like magic, he found himself walking through a mysterious garden. The sensual smell of flowers in a mass of steam and buzzing insects. The Garden of Eden. Some slimy stuff clung to his soles. A strange slime, squelching and reeking. It was blood. Hot, fresh, running—the air was saturated with it. He was knocked sideways and tripped over some starving stray dogs, licking at the cooling blood with their red tongues.

Above the scene a pulsing, a rumbling, and the wailing of flutes. The Brahmin was ready. The sound of drums filled the yard, reached a climax, the eyes of the pilgrims had a bloodthirsty radiance. The priest approached the sacrifice with a wide sword. A forked wooden chopping block clamped the beast's neck and the instrument of death cleaved the air with a swish. The mesmerized crowd undulated with excitement. Streams of blood jetted from the severed arteries, the lamb's head lay immobile in the pool of red, and the executioner's henchmen carried off the lifeless corpse. All for her: for the goddess Kali, the earth was soaked with the lifeblood of sacrificial lambs. The hordes of pilgrims bought wreaths of marigolds and sacrificed them to the powerful goddess. Reflections of the midday sun in pools of blood. An arboreal cactus in the yard, hung about with the amulets of women who had come to plead for a son.

He did not know how he ended up inside the temple, with the pale blue mosaic on its low tower. Kali's temple. Kali herself was safe within the inner sanctum, but even there the stench must have reached her. It was everywhere. The intoxicating and disturbing taste of blood. The smell excited him.

He went down the steps to the bank of the Hooghly, from which coils of smoke rose into the air. Roaming among the crowds there were sacred bulls, well-fed *zebus* and *sadhus*—holy men whose raiment was dust and whose only property was a bowl for food won by begging. The contours of dead bodies on a funeral pyre and the monotonous murmur of the Brahmins. A burning ghat. Steps descended to the river, where the living bathed.

He would never forget the image that opened up before him.

A stack of wood about two feet high and three feet long, and on it flowers and a girl dressed in white. Her legs deliberately broken and forced back towards her head. Such rough handling saved the bereaved family money. Even the wood had to be paid for. The pyre blazed up, a weary calm around it, no one weeping. The clothes disappeared and the flesh slowly charred, the face and ribcage took on strange dimensions, the body twisted in a dramatic dance. All the moisture was driven off and the body began to carbonize. The pyre and bodily remains disintegrated, and into the ashes the dead girl's father consigned a sacrificial coin encased in the dung of a sacred cow. The fire died down and the pile of residue slipped into the water. The river hissed with pain, and the pilgrims continued washing, passing their sins into the muddy waters.

Unsteadily, he made his way back past the congealing lambs' blood and the dogs with their flicking, saucer-shaped tongues. And suddenly, as if a curtain or the flap of a circus tent had dropped behind him, he was standing in the busy street. The show was over. Show? No, what he had witnessed was no show. The blood was real; the sacrifices, the burning corpses, everything was real. Even the goddess Kali. She had been there, even if she was invisible. He could sense her. He knew that the Hindus' belief in Kali was genuine, even if the Kalighat and its riot of blood looked like madness next to the modern houses. Absurd, almost farcical.

He took the bus back into town, but he didn't feel like bed. He wandered about on the Maidan, that vast area of dry, rustling grass in the middle of the city. He let his faltering legs carry him towards the noise of the harbor, towards the light coming from lamps and fires. Kidderpore. In among the fires were alleyways of scruffy shacks, canals and bridges. A native marketplace in the middle of the night, the turmoil, the crashing and banging, the utter confusion. Betel sellers screamed endlessly *Paan, paan*, and women sold cheroots. The omnipresent smell of roast meat. His head spun.

The damn contract! Red tape, the tug-of-war with officialdom, the usual tricks of middlemen and tactical waiting games. Finally it was signed and the Baťa company had become the owner of a defunct mineral oil refinery in Konnagar that had floundered into debt and never recovered.

Thomas convened a meeting of the construction crew. They bent over a site plan, pencils in hand, dividing up the jobs to be done.

"Josef, you take care of Building 2. That'll be the warehouse. Move the entrance to the corner, but keep an eye on the statics, we don't want it coming down on your head. Knock another entrance through the wall directly opposite."

"And what about the floor? Will it support our shelving?"

"You'll have to cement it over. Vehicles will be using the main corridor, so don't raise it too much there. Line the inside walls with real bricks at an angle. Milan, you take Building 10 and turn it into offices. The ground floor should have room for the telegraphist, the cashier, and some production. Keep the telegraphist close to the entrance, find a space for an "Information" sign, and put Videlka next door. Make sure he's got a window for payroll. The first floor needs to be built out for the reps—Jelínek will tell you what he needs."

Ruda Martinec could hardly wait his turn. He was biting his nails and fanning himself with his notepad. As soon as his boss's eyes landed on him, he blurted out the question he'd clearly been dying to ask. "And what about rubber production?"

Thomas jabbed the tip of his mechanical pencil into the spread-out drawings. "Building 13. We can fit six rings in there. Twelve can be configured for blending. But don't go wild. We'll still need space there for the raw materials storage." He handed an outline sketch for the installation of the curing pans to Martinec. "Everything clear?"

Bat'a's Young Men spread out across the site.

He never had time to eat. He would down gallons of water and lukewarm tea and grab a few boiled vegetables in the evening.

After a few weeks of being a vegetarian, Thomas went to a classy restaurant and ordered some forbidden fruit: a big chunk of meat—a local delicacy. He enjoyed it greatly until the next morning. He squatted in the bathroom, bent double, with a bucket in front of him, disgorging into it at short intervals the half-digested remnants of the previous night's repast. Dinner at a price.

"God," he thought, as he gazed into the bucket of vomit. "This looks like bits of my own brain!"

As if he were dancing he shambled around the room, but nothing was in its place. The furniture kept twisting and changing, and the chairs kept shuffling their feet. The clock was ticking three times faster than normal and it struck the hour with a triple echo that sounded like a dog barking. He tried to bark back at it, but it fooled him by bending over like the leaning tower of Pisa. The savage fever drove him right back to bed. The world was spinning like a runaway merry-go-round.

Rachel wrote that she was pregnant.

I've given up teaching. Amon is miserable ever since you left. He keeps looking for you. He can't get used to not flopping down by your feet in the evening. He spends hours on end watching the door, motionless, just his ears prick up at the slightest sound in case they are your footsteps. I can't get used to not having you here beside me either. It's worst in the evening as I try to get to sleep. Now I tell Amon stories. He lies on guard beside the bed. I'm eating almost more than he does, now that I've stopped feeling sick. It's bound to be a boy. The doctor says he's due in late June.

He'd never felt so ill in his life. He hadn't put in an appearance at the site for a week now. The fever clung to him like a leech and so depleted him that he could barely stand. He was thankful to be able to muster the strength to haul himself as far as the bathroom. He had begun to loathe that room, where he was obliged to spend much of the day and night, and was horrified at the prospect of one day not being able to drag himself back out. "That shit-hole will be the death of me!"

Fortunately, even in India there were specialists. Dr Seagal assured him that he would pull through. "Yes, but when?"

At work they were worried; rumors spread that he was on his last legs. They sent him a nurse. *So there'll be someone to close my eyes,* it occurred to him. Within two days he changed his view. Her name was Shanta: an angel in human form. She reminded him so much of someone else, someone from his childhood who had watched him with the same concern whenever he was ill: his mother. It wasn't any physical similarity—the nurse was dark and slight, with a broad smile on her broad features. Black eyes and the chubby fingers of a child. His mother had been different. Her slim figure slowly took shape before him, her complexion like parchment. She was always pale, almost translucent, as if she did not take part in the world of color around her. No, the similarity lay elsewhere. With his eyes closed, he breathed in Shanta's scent as she bent over him, but that wasn't it either. It was only when she spoke. A strange tremulousness played about her mouth, tinged the air with a warm light. That voice, slightly nasal and deep, permeated and soothed him. That voice belonged to his mother. He could hear her saying: "Wake up, Tommy. Get up. The sun's in the sky. It's a gorgeous Sunday." He would poke his head out sulkily. Sunday? Horrors! He hated Sundays. He'd rather have gone to school, but most of all he'd have preferred to stay in bed until evening, because Sunday—Sunday was purgatory. First there was Mass and then those awful Sunday walks. He used to wish fervently that Sunday didn't exist.

The eternally simpering parish priest with his protruding chin, bleating voice, and hobbling gait was the perfect caricature of a billy goat. All he lacked was the little beard and horns. The one complication of the caricature was his huge paunch, which made him look more like a pregnant nanny goat. Tom had never believed a word the man said. The word of God, supposedly. False teeth bared. He was scarcely twelve and doubted the existence of an Almighty. Neither his parents nor the goat-priest could answer his barrage of questions about God and the divine order, nor could they stir in him even the slightest fondness for Holy Mother Church. And that stench of incense. Ugh! "Repeat three times: I BELIEVE." "I believe, I believe, I believe." But no, no, no. The only thing Tom did believe was that the goat-priest's job was to keep his breadbasket padded. That could be why he imagined God as a squirty little old man with a gaping grin, perched on a cloud and condescending to piss his divine rain on those below.

At confession he pretended he had stolen some sugar lumps from the pantry. It cost him five Hail Marys. How stupid can you get? Hoc est corpus, hocus pocus. He said that five times in a row instead and with relish. He had no idea where such brazen certitude came from, but he simply did not believe.

His mother used to scold him for trying to ride a goat. Which was true. But that had been Aunt Beattie's real billy goat at Uničov, not the goat-priest. When he had visited her for a few days, he had spent most of his time in the goat shed. In Olomouc there were no goats, and here they ranged free, horses and carts drove around the village green, and the neighbor's sons pastured the cows by the forest edge. He tried to make friends with them, but they were a lot older and often made fun of him. When he first entered their yard, he had the shock of his life. You couldn't move for chickens and chicken droppings. In fact it was all droppings, one dollop next to another, with just the odd chicken here and there. He advanced on tiptoe like a ballerina, treading gently, but in avoiding one dropping he couldn't fail to land in another. "Look at the little lady," the boys cried, howling with laughter.

They called him Shrimp. Jeník Kalous was the oldest and once asked him: "D'you wanna try riding a goat?" Obviously he did. He was just five and imagined there could be no greater fun than riding on a goat, except possibly riding on a pig. The whole gang watched as Jeník brought his aunt's billy goat Horace out of its shed, holding it by the horns, then he called the others to shove Shrimp up onto its back. "Hold on tight, Shrimp, hold on," they chimed, laughing until they were hoarse, and waiting for him to come flying off. The goat bucked and curvetted, trying to cast off the unfamiliar burden and flinging its bandy legs out in every direction. But Tom clasped the horned beast around its neck, clinging to it like a limpet, with his face sunk in its smelly coat and his rear end more up in the air than on the goat's back.

As the onlookers' shrieks changed from mockery to

appreciation, Beattie's ancient mother-in-law came hobbling out of her cottage brandishing a stick. "You wicked little heathens! Tormenting a dumb creature like that! Shame on you, you louts!" She launched herself into the rapturous audience, the frantic animal lurched, and he hit the ground like a bird frozen on the wing. The rodeo was over. He was black and blue, but that was nothing compared to the two well-aimed blows from the old lady's stick. Auntie Beattie was indulgent and loved children, although, as she liked to say, the good Lord had not wished any on her and her late husband, Alois. But this old lady was a battleaxe. The boys called her Old Ma Herod. She wouldn't stand for such behavior. She immediately sent his parents a telegram. FETCH SON AT ONCE STOP.

When mass was finally over, he escaped the stench of piety and tried not to think about what would come after lunch. The delicious smell of roast pork, dumplings and sauerkraut wafted through the house. The strudel was turning golden in the oven. The housekeeper's strudel was a work of art, as perfect as she was. Well-rounded, rosy-cheeked, with a smile that nothing could wash off. He liked her a hundred times more than the nanny, who looked like a shrivelled prune, scolded him for next to nothing, and told on him to his parents.

After lunch, Dad would go to have a nap and Mom would take up her sampler with its stretched linen. He could watch her for hours. The metal glinted between her fingers, her needle wove in and out of the fabric to leave a blue mark behind, a tiny cross, then it flew upwards like a bird until its wings were clipped by the length of the thread. At once it changed direction and flew back down onto the cross. It was so soothing—the regular click of the thimble against the needle. He didn't want it to stop. The wheels inside the pendulum clock eased audibly into position and it reverberated with a boom. Half past one. Dad came back out of the bedroom and the peace was shattered. Also wir gehen, he

21

said. They went out: the pièce de résistance on the Day of Rest. They would head for Hejčín or the city center to have coffee and cakes. Respectable families strolled through the center of Olomouc wearing their Sunday smiles and their Sunday best, with a "Good morning" this way, "Good morning" that, and "How do you do?" and "How are you?"

"Go to hell, all of you," he wished, and tried to look indifferent. Ludicrous waxwork figures. Tiny fashion plate kids, little darlings crammed into their Sunday finery, looking like liveried midgets, the playthings of medieval kings and queens. He straggled sulkily behind his parents, who were trawling five-year-old Hilda along between them. She wiggled her butt in front of him, so pretty-pretty in her little pink petticoats and white tights, her legs like pencils, ribbons in her hair. Now and again she turned and stuck her tongue out at him. It wasn't exactly that he didn't like her; he was sometimes even seized by the instinct to be her protector, but mostly he just ignored her. From time to time he had to torment her so that she would know her place. She looked back again and challenged him in a whisper: "I dare you to kick me!"

He tried to look grownup and pretended not to see. She turned around once more. "Go on, kick me, I dare you. Sissy! Sissy!"

He stuck it out for two minutes, but then it got to him. "Stop it, or I really will kick you," he hissed, but she just laughed.

"Scaredy cat!"

"If that's what she wants," he thought, and with a little running start, kicked her so hard through her neatly pressed skirt that she jumped into the air. And the idyll was over. His mother tried to soothe the blubbering Hilda and his father slapped him hard enough that he couldn't eat for two days. And home they went. "How embarrassing," his mother lamented all the way, "For goodness's sake, Thomas, you're old enough to know better."

She always said that. Like the time he had spat in Hilda's face. The memory of that raised a smile to his split lips. He had been kicking his football against the house and it left dirty marks on the siding. She had stood on the balcony and smirked. "I bet you can't spit this high." "We'll see about that! With a loud hawking noise he made himself a mouthful of saliva, bringing it up all the way from his stomach and working it around and around in his mouth, then he bent back and let the thick ball of phlegm fly right into the face above him. He had taken it as a game, but it should have crossed his mind that she would start bawling and go blabbing to their father. "Where is he? Let me get my hands on the little tyke!" Father had unbuckled his belt and Mother had wrung her hands—what was to become of the boy?

He hit rock bottom, couldn't concentrate on anything. His nurse Shanta talked to him in her broken English, her clipped r's and d's flapping against the roof of her mouth, but he didn't mind. Just as long as she spoke to him in that voice he knew so well.

The last thing he wanted was for the work to slow down. Once more he summoned Ruda Martinec to his bedside.

"Everything's going according to plan, boss. You can stop worrying. How are you?"

"Pretty ropy. Rumor has it I've been writing my will."

"I haven't heard it."

"And I haven't written anything yet."

Thomas's ravaged features inspired compassion. Ruda asked if there was anything he could do for him.

As if he'd been waiting for that, Thomas grinned. "It's high time to start on the mass-production building." The unfeigned horror on Ruda's boyish peasant face amused him. "I'm not asking you to commit hara-kiri."

Martinec pulled himself together. "Have you got the plans?"

"They're there on the table. Nothing new about them. Just the standard Zlín pattern. Hand me them, will you? Two aisles, forty meters by twenty, four and a half meters to the roof. Make the walls two bricks thick."

"On the drawing you've put it where number nine's standing now."

"That's right. Take it apart and use the bricks for the new one."

"I get it. And the roof?"

"Iron. And one more thing. Tell Milan that when he's finished the offices, he can fix up sleeping quarters in the buildings themselves...let me see...yes, in one, three, and seven. Eight can be the canteen. If I do kick the bucket, you'll have plenty to do for the next three months."

Ruda's eyes were like dinner plates. Thomas wiped his brow with a weary sweep of his hand and flapped the air with it.

"That was a joke, Ruda, so stop looking as if it's the end of the world."

Baťa's Young Men: guys from all over Moravia, quick-witted and honest, bright and energetic. It wasn't hard to find boys from their rustic background. You could tell they'd never seen the inside of a nursery. In the fancy restaurant on the boat out, they were given little bowls of water to dabble their fingers in, but instead they knocked them back, lemon slice and all, like a shot of plum brandy.

After Ruda's visit, Thomas's head spun with exhaustion. Shanta changed his bedding and sat with him. Her comb ran through his dank hair like a plough, leaving wide furrows. Then washing, shaving, feeding. But he didn't really need any of that. He only needed one thing from her: to hear her voice. He asked her to talk. "Tell me anything, in any language, just speak to me." She smiled her understanding and nodded. Her blurred voice lulled him into a half-sleep.

He saw Rachel, rain-drenched. She was looking into his face, dreamy and faraway, yet closer than anyone. "I know you," she said. "I've always known you. I have known you since before you were born."

And he believed her. She had been with him forever. He recalled the moment when, without knowing she existed, he first knew she was with him.

Lost in the middle of a cathedral nave, the organ pounding like a beating heart. Aunt Beattie's eyes hung on the coffin, motionless and hungry, amid a forest of mourners. But he was afraid to look at the open coffin. He wouldn't have been able to look at it and not cry out, not hurl himself at it, not sob the night away at its feet. Mother!

They were all waiting for his father, expecting him to appear. He didn't. "Couldn't even turn up to her funeral," they muttered in a cluster of heads, "not even to her funeral!"

It was then that he first sensed Rachel. She was there with him. He went outside and felt her touch in the drops of rain that tickled his cheeks. He held out his face and caught her in the palms of his hands. She was the reflection of the light on those little crystals of water, the rustle of leaves, the undulation of birds' wings. Her strength in the gusting wind protected him as he tried to push against it, then raised him aloft and prodded him forward as he moved with it. They thought he'd gone crazy. He was running around outside the church and smiling happily, like an utter idiot.

Father had been a master mason and everyone addressed him as "sir." He had his own company and felt pride in his profession. When he was home, the language was German. But Mother spoke to him in Czech. She was patriotic and wanted them to go to Czech schools. Father didn't mind, "just as long as they learn something," he would say.

And then the war: Father left for the front—disappeared from their lives—and Mother became quite ill. At first they got an occasional card or letter: She should not tire herself out or worry about him. She should write and tell him whether she was getting

25

better. And send him a photo. "Send me the one of us two and the one with the children." Then even the cards with their Bozen or Branzoll postmarks stopped arriving. Mother started praying, she held the pencil in her feeble fingers, running it over a scrap of paper in a frantic whirl of letters and pleas. These would be sent to Vienna, addressed to her sister-in-law, Fanny.

Dear Fanny, if you have any news of him, write to me. I can't take this any more, the uncertainty is terrible, my heart can't take it.

This was a postcard bearing a picture of Jesus, all in white, his palms extended toward heads bowed in prayer. The caption said: "Our Father, who art in heaven, hallowed be Thy name. Thou art our refuge, to Thee we cry. We beseech Thee to succour Thy dear ones, protect them with Thy mighty arm, stand by them and keep them safe in their strife."

In March, Father's name went up at the Town Hall on the list of those missing. Mother took to her bed, gripping pearl after pearl in her thin fingers in a string of Hail Marys. Then Mrs Stejskal, the gossipy old neighbor, came to bring "merciful relief" of the uncertainty: she had heard he was dead. Yes, she was sorry, God knew how sorry she was, but he was out of it now, may he rest in peace.

On April 2, 1916, Mother had written another letter to Fanny in Vienna, read Hildi a fairy story, and stretched out on the sofa with a book. "Tom," she said, "have you done your homework?" He hadn't. Of course he hadn't. He got his exercise book out, dipped his pen in the ink and started dragging the nib with slow strokes across the paper from one side to the other. He propped his head on one hand and pondered. "Mother, how many g's in begin?"

There was silence but for the bump of her book as it fell to the ground, her hand like a broken tulip.

Tom ran to her and then to the door. He ran for his mother's life, ran at the speed of fear. After he got back with the doctor he watched the skillful hands pressing down, then releasing her motionless chest. Will it, won't it, will it, won't it. Please, Mother, please, I beg you. Her revived heart hammered at the closed gates of her brain, pumping hopelessly, tenaciously, driving the blood into the dead tissue. It took three long hours for her body to die again. It was a bleak night: April 2, 1916.

A letter arrived from the Tyrol:

13.4.1916 Branzoll field hospital
  Dearest Marie and children, I have been waiting for news of you every day, but for weeks now in vain. I don't know what could have happened to you. If only I could see you! I've already written 3 letters and 25 cards and have heard nothing for three weeks! I can't stand the torment of not knowing what's happening. Write and tell me the truth. Tom, is Mommy so ill, or worse, that you won't write, or has something happened to you, children? Please, please send me a letter or a telegram. Marie dear, I beg you, write. You too, Tom, Hildi, just a word or two, just sign your names! God preserve you!
  Your loving Rudolf.

Two days after that, another letter:

15.4.1916, Branzoll field hospital
  Dear Marie and children, Happy Easter! I write to you every day, think of you day and night. Oh God, why don't you write? How are you, Marie? And you, Thomas, why won't you write? I've started to believe it's because she is already buried. None of you wants to tell me the awful truth. Now I am only fearful of receiving a letter. How are you, children? Things are not well

with you and I cannot help you.
  Your father.

Thomas could not bear all those "ifs," their bitter burden of reproof. Gastric juices on his taste buds with a tang like sorrel: If he had run faster, if the doctor had arrived sooner, if he only had the touch that could bring her back to life. She was dead.

18.4.1916, Branzoll field hospital
  My dear Thomas, Thank you for your letter. I was so worried for my darling Marie. Oh God, how terrible to think I shall never see her again. I will pray for her, and you pray for her, too, at least say the Lord's Prayer and Hail Mary every day. Be brave and may God help you. I hope Auntie Beattie won't abandon you, that she won't leave us in our distress. I have written to ask her to take charge of you and I hope she will; I know she is good at heart. I've put in for compassionate leave, but haven't heard yet. With God's blessing I'll see you next week. –Father.

She was dead. A true Daughter of Christ. Mother's prayer book, a little ivory cross glued on the cover. He dug his nails into its black leather. He opened it. A prayer for a day of great loss: "The Lord hath given, the Lord hath taken away. Praised be the name of the Lord!"

Curses and the crudest swearwords rang round inside his head, words of disgust and revulsion. But for her sake, he could not say them out loud.

His fingers wrung the leather spine, as if pulling hair, sweaty cowhide. Wretched, beside himself with rage and despair, he flung the book into the corner. Bullshit!

He sat, breathing hard, looking at the prayers spilling out. Aunt Beattie rushed into the room. "What happened, Thomas?" The volume of yellowed pages split in two, God shattered to bits.

Oh, Thomas. Hail Mary, full of grace, bitter tears on fragments of bone, white and cold, she gathered up the sundered prayers between her own sobs and his clenched fists. "She was your mother! My sister! Holy Virgin! What got into you? Aren't you afraid of the wrath of God?"

His steady voice proved his unshakeable certainty.

"I know there is no God!"

She had crossed herself and fled from the room in tears. Two weeks later he got another letter from the front.

Thomas, Why don't you write more? Beattie says you're being difficult, as if the devil's gotten into you. Such behavior is not worthy of you. Don't upset her, don't refuse to go to church. Pray for your mother—that can't be so very difficult. Be an example to little Hildi.

Obey your auntie, there's no one else to look after you, so don't make it hard for her and worse for me. And don't worry about me.

I look forward—God willing—to seeing you soon. –Your loving father

Eventually, Thomas calmed down. He made peace with Aunt Beattie. He promised that he would never swear again or throw holy books if she wouldn't force him to attend church. He became an outsider. People said he was a bit odd. He sealed himself off completely from the world around him. And from God.

Once he was back on his feet, Thomas started thinking about how to bring the new company stores into service. He was well enough to write reports again: "We must adapt. The Indians sell almost everything in their bazaars, on the street or in market halls. We have to do the same."

It was easy to be a cobbler in India! No paperwork, no certificate of apprenticeship, no license to trade. He just sat in the street with a bit of folded canvas under his backside, to be opened out over his head if it started to rain. No tax, no rent, no heating costs. Nothing. Just a modest toolkit that he could easily roll up and take with him to the next street. An awl, a little hammer without a handle, and a gouge for a paring knife. Sometimes he might visit the dump and grab a pair of old boots to give him the leather he needed for patches. It was easy to be a cobbler in India. Except that cobblers were unclean. They handled the skin of dead animals. No one of a higher caste would sully his hands with any such thing. Indian mochees, unlicensed cobblers, despised and unclean, like a medieval hangman or knacker. They *could* rid themselves of the shameful label "unclean," they *could* escape the filth of the street. Yes, they could, but only if they paid to progress to a higher caste, a fee as fat as ten well-fed pigs. The poor street cobbler would never have that much.

Crippling deadlines. Late into the night he would scribble new designs for the facilities, his pencils sticking resinously to his fingers. He used whatever good contacts he had to secure the relevant permissions. Baťa's shoemakers were poised to take over the Indian market.

From February to June not a drop of rain fell, and in May and June the desiccated earth was further parched by intolerable heat. Searing hot streets beneath the perpendicular rays of the sun, pavement you could bake naan bread on. Then, on June 25, the sky opened and it poured and poured, the heavy clouds moving northward, towards the Himalayas, while at home, thousands of miles away, Thomas's son was born. The monsoon was no joke. Calcutta was half underwater, but if the rains failed, life in Bengal would be even worse. The rice harvest was a matter of life or death to hundreds of thousands.

During the monsoon, productivity dropped drastically, among both the natives and the Europeans. The natives were resigned; for them it was a matter of course—unlike the dogged Europeans, who tried to get the better of it. But they could not vanquish the humidity. On the contrary, they were vanquished by it. And the monsoon brought another hardship: you couldn't sleep.

Thomas taught himself to recognize the castes. Brahmins went barefoot, they had a strip of red material wound around their waists, and they led a life of sobriety. People of the upper castes ate no meat. When he was first invited to lunch, he realized that European principles of refined conduct did not apply in the Orient. You ate on the ground, legs crossed, with no cutlery. Brightly colored bowls, vegetarian fare, sauces, chutneys. A feast for the eyes. They used naan or their fingers in place of a knife and fork. They first tested their food by touch, rolled it between their fingers, fondled it, sniffed it, and only then did their taste buds get access. Sight, touch, smell, and finally taste. He came to appreciate the unusual desserts—little balls of coconut and little pyramids of curd cheeses with their bitterish aftertaste.

India had a population of three hundred and fifty million, but only three percent of them wore shoes. The others went barefoot. Their feet did not suffer from frost, but the heat and the sun fired up the ground and the stones underfoot so that their skin fairly sizzled. Baťa knew that he had to produce something cheap enough to be affordable for those who had no shoes. Plimsolls. Lightweight, with soles made from the local rubber and raw canvas uppers instead of leather. Having shoes could be a matter of life or death in India. Deadly snakes lurked in every patch of grass. In India, the number of people without shoes was the same as the number of people who never had a square meal.

In Kharagpur, Thomas visited a Muslim colleague for dinner. He removed his shoes in order not to defile the man's home with his leather footwear, and sat down on the carpet. A servant brought him some water to wash his hands and then brought the food in on a brass tray. None of his Muslim partners ever introduced him to their wives, or even let him see them.

He described his discoveries in his letters to Rachel. *Although physical slavery was banned seventy years ago, even an educated Muslim treats his wife as personal property.*

She wrote back to say she wasn't sure she wanted to join him.

Finally it turned cooler. Down to thirty degrees centigrade in the shade. But the air was still heavy, saturated with vapor, and the Bay of Bengal remained drowned in mist. In the morning he needed a cup of strong coffee and a cigarette to wake him up, and in the evening a decent nightcap to send him to sleep.

At first he assumed he would get by with English. But he was quick to appreciate that the key to success was the local language, so he set about learning Hindi and Bengali. He was surprised to find it going quite well. His teacher would come to the site, which he hardly ever left.

Thomas watched as the gaunt coolies scrambled like ants up and down the bamboo ladders with materials balanced on their heads. Basketloads of bricks or cement, bowlfuls of mortar. He waved to Martinec. "Get hold of a mule."

He personally supervised the construction of a ramp. He patiently explained to the men that it could be used to transport their materials up to the next level. Load it onto a mule and the mule will haul it up for you. They shook their heads. "You'll never get a mule up there, sahib."

The stubborn beast indeed resisted, and Thomas was overcome with exhaustion and the lack of sleep. The air around him was full of the buzzing of insects and the braying of the mule. He remembered Uničov, the goat shed and the Kalous boys. If they could see him now, with these recalcitrant coolies and a mule, they would be laughing themselves silly. He took a few steps, bent down, and tore up a clump of grass. He thrust it at the mule's nostrils and retreated backwards up the ramp. The animal followed. *Hurrah, hurrah,* the coolies cried, applauding the wily sahib. He felt like a clown in a circus ring. He was drained and dirty. Scorched skin and trickles of sweat. He had to push himself beyond exhaustion just to be able to get to sleep in the heat.

In the deep of night, Rachel was in his dream. Milky Way droplets and the taste of her body after lovemaking. She was leaning over him like the palm trees that lined the shore. She was a stream of spring water. He felt the pull of ancient tales in the motionless air, clammy with sweat, his gut gripped with longing. *When did I last taste you on my tongue?*

III

Quest for the Sun

Six months of separation stretched to twenty-two. I was a little over a year old by the time my father came back. He climbed down from the train and went straight towards the wife who was waiting for him with a boy in her arms. What went through his mind when he saw me for the first time? He laughed when he set eyes on me, though later he wickedly pretended to deny it. He claimed to have been devastated because, as he said, I looked like a drooling mealworm.

"Yes, I did laugh," he would tease. "Of course I laughed, I couldn't help it when I saw you. A little bald beanbag with chubby cheeks and an irresistible smile. Two big top teeth with a gap wide enough for two matchsticks. A well-fed, hairless woodchuck."

The next shock had been Rachel, in a white blouse and sailor's trousers, with her hair cut short *à la garçon*. Quite the little rascal.

Tom roamed around the house he had left almost two years before. It seemed bigger and brighter. It was filled with things he had never seen. Scattered toys, a big changing table, and the smell of baby oil in the bathroom. A highchair with rattles attached to the arms next to the dining table. He was at home and he was a stranger. He was looking for something, a reference point, a bridge to carry him to the other shore. In the living room he ran into a rocking horse. The molting wool mane and the cracked, once-black paint, the chewed leather of the stirrups. The poor thing looked like Don Quixote's nag. Home at last. He raised his eyebrows.

"Where did you get him?"

"Who?"

"The horse. That was my horse." He poked at the neatly chiselled nostrils and it started on its rockers.

"Your father brought it over. He thought you might lend it to your son."

"And where is the boy?"

"Asleep. Your son has a nap every afternoon."

He stepped right up to her and looked at her quizzically. He was searching for someone intimate, familiar. He was trying to find that giddy young thing, that frisky minx, that crazy schoolgirl. But he could find nothing of the kind. She was gone. Standing before him was a mature woman. His wife—a mysterious stranger. He touched her cheek as if for the first time.

As she lay in bed that night, she leafed through the illustrated calendar he had brought her from India. It was dated 1854. Eighty years ago. There were times when you could be living in two centuries at once. Thomas had shown her official documents with the double dating pre-printed on the header: the Gregorian calendar and the national calendar. 1932. 1854. Unbelievable. She felt tired. It took an act of will to keep her eyelids from drooping. Finally she gave up. She lay the calendar on the bedside table and turned off the light.

Thomas stood for a while beside the baby's cot, his mind inflamed as he took in the little bundle sunk in teddy-bear-print poplin, and listened to its rapid breathing. Then he tiptoed backwards out the door, reaching for the light switch by memory. In an instant the whole house was submerged in darkness. As he crept into the bedroom, she asked him in a sleepy whisper to leave the door open.

"Daniel wakes up in the night. He's usually thirsty."

In the dark she couldn't see him nod and leave the bedroom door slightly ajar; she only heard him groping for the bathroom door handle. She fell asleep to the sound of the shower.

He stood on the mat by the sink, brushing his teeth. Finally he gargled, whisked his toothbrush in a cup to get rid of the remaining toothpaste, sloshed the frothy liquid down the drain, and spat out the last mouthful. He reached up to the switch by the mirror, and the sight of the sunburnt hulk staring out startled him. He frowned at himself, put a hand to his face, and ran his fingers over his ample stubble. That's not very nice, is it? He reached for the tub of shaving cream and sank his brush in. The razor glided through the white foam on his face like a ship at sea, leaving a wake of smooth skin behind it. In a few seconds he had reverted into the respectable gentleman everyone took him for. Tossing his pajama jacket over his shoulder, he looked back once more at the man in the mirror, switched off the light, and entered the bedroom.

Half asleep, Rachel was only vaguely aware of his presence. She could hear him groping in the dark, shuffling blindly closer. He landed on the bed and lifted a corner of the duvet, then yelped like a frightened animal. Rachel screamed too, thinking that something truly terrible had happened. The light blinded them for a moment. Tom stood by the bedside table with a demented expression while Rachel sat up in bed blinking. She ran her eyes over him, trying to see where he was hurt, looking for blood or a murder weapon. Looking for the killer who must have crept into the house to slaughter them as they slept. They squinted at one another in bewilderment.

"What—what got you?" Only then did she notice the dog sprawled out on Tom's side of the bed. She rolled her eyes, fell flat on her back, and burst out laughing.

Tom returned to bed. "Amon, you hairy monster, scram!

Frightening me like that!" The huge, black Great Dane gave him a doleful look and stayed put.

Rachel prodded him with her foot. "Go find your own bed."

Amon crawled reluctantly from his cosy hollow and ambled towards the door. He paused at the threshold and fired a silent rebuke toward his master, his forehead folded like a harmonica.

Tom grinned. "What? Do you want an apology?" He turned to Rachel. "I'm glad you think it's funny."

Lying in bed, she gripped her stomach from laughing so much. "Poor sweetie, you've driven him away!"

"But you wrote that he's been lying *beside* the bed."

"That was then."

"You could have mentioned that he's been promoted—*sweetie*, indeed!"

The tone in which he uttered the word set her off again.

He pressed the switch on the table lamp and carefully slid his feet under the duvet. In the darkness he could hear her stifled laughter. Just as he reached for her, the house rang with the baby's cry. Rachel shot up and headed for the next room. The alarm clock was ticking away right by his head. It occurred to him that it must be after midnight. He turned the light on and assured himself that his inner clock had not deceived him.

Rachel held a bottle of sugar water to the baby's lips and watched the yellowish liquid go down with every suck. Sleep assailed Tom like a hawker, and he tried to drive it away. He tried to make a deal with it, to resist temptation. His eyelids kept drooping under their burden of lashes.

Meanwhile, Rachel drifted into a mother's sleep, light and fitful, her head buried in the baby's clothes. She dreamed of a white horse darting across an autumn meadow, golden ears of corn beneath its pounding hooves. The gods had created the horse out of the sun and the wind. It ran toward the mountains on the horizon, clambering like a goat up a steep cliff face, its shoes ringing against the rock. As the sun was setting, the horse stood on the top, the world beneath it a minuscule village. When night fell, it spread its wings and flew off into the dark.

She came to when a tongue touched the back of her hand. She pushed the dog's head away and stood up. When she came back from the bathroom, she bent over Tom, who was asleep. She inhaled the smell of his hair and switched the light off.

In the morning he stood half-naked at the sink. He'd imagined the first night back home rather differently, he thought, as he reached for the tap. Rachel snuck up to him from behind and placed her hand on his belly. That gesture was like an electric charge. He felt the blood in his lower abdomen and the touch of her lips between his shoulder blades. She slid downwards. He turned to embrace her but she wouldn't let him. He stood there with an undeniable erection, his arms hanging submissively by his sides. She took him between her palms, drew back the delicate skin, and devoured him. He could feel her hard palate, the cold of the sink pressing on his backside, his fingers weaving through the dark strands of her hair. He shuddered in the grip of her mouth, and she drew him in further, swallowing his life force as her own. Afterward, he seized her under the arms and pulled her up to him, and she wound herself around his thighs like an octopus.

He was struck by the spontaneity of her actions. Her laughter drove away the malaise gnawing, like a woodworm, at his mind. In just two or three days the acrid taste of alienation disappeared, to be replaced by an intimacy he had not known for a very long time. The scent of lemon balm and chamomile, gossamer hair on the pillow, mornings with their bittersweet oneness of mind and body. How quickly he lost the habit of being alone. Countless intimate rituals renewed, and some new ones added. The world of a child: gradually he grew used to the constant presence of a third party.

The entire time he was away, he had been conscious of his son; would think of him, look forward to seeing him, imagine what it would be like when they were all together. But he had barely understood what it meant, this burden of accountability for the life of a helpless creature who had never even asked to be brought into the world. His sense of responsibility for Rachel's life had grown during the course of their marriage, but this was different. Now the full weight of permanency came home to him. *This is my son until my dying day.*

When he couldn't sleep at night, he would sit by the cot in which that little stranger lay, and study his chubby face like a conundrum, trying to understand how it was that nothing would ever be the same again.

Tomáš Baťa was a demanding boss. He expected energy and courage from his people. He didn't tolerate hesitation, couldn't abide wasting time or words. He appreciated those who explained the crux of a matter in the most concise, clear, and comprehensible way. Though Tomáš Baťa didn't drink or smoke, and Thomas Keppler was inclined to take a swig and often had a cigarette on the go, Baťa liked Keppler, who was cerebral, taciturn, and got the job done.

Rachel was interested to know what the big boss was like.

"He's a culture hound," Tom said wickedly.

"You don't say!"

"Except that after seeing a number of museums, he now thinks that *culture* equals potsherds or statues with their arms chopped off."

"And what artist does he like best?"

"Hard to say. But it wouldn't be a landscapist."

"What's he got against landscapes?"

"Landscapes aren't the problem," Tom grinned.

"Meaning?"

"Baťa doesn't want paintings of the sea, or a forest or a still life. A painter ought to be solving some genuine artistic problem.

And a forest—well, a forest isn't a problem, get it?"
"No, I don't. What does that mean, an artistic problem?"
"Like, trying to paint a man's joy at getting some new shoes."
Rachel spluttered, "Well, that's—that's some challenge."
"And he reads a lot. He's interested in Upton Sinclair, but it
bothers him that all the novels end badly. He loves Jack London.
He also reads Tolstoy and Dostoyevsky, but that kind of literature
irritates him, too. He'd rather writers told stories about people
with drive. He can't see the point of bothering with pessimists
and maniacs, and he can't cope with passive heroes. He wants
literature that's packed with practicality: hammering on an anvil,
rolled-up sleeves, sweaty, horny-handed sons of toil. And books
should cost no more than two-fifty."
"So he wants literature to be just like footwear manufacture."
Thomas laughed briefly. "Something like that."
"If only he could hear you!"
"I think he'd agree with me."
But within a couple of days, Tomáš Baťa could no longer agree
with anyone. At four one morning, he emerged out of a dense fog
at the private airfield at Otrokovice, heading for an inspection
tour of the half-built factory in Zurich. He was supposed to
meet his son there, but now he was forced to wait, something he
couldn't abide. He demanded the weather reports from several
European stations, and—always tempted by the most difficult
and unachievable tasks—he swept aside the airfield manager's
suggestion of sending up a small plane to investigate the fog. He
overruled the opposition of the captain, Brouček, a former air
force pilot who had flown halfway around the world with his boss.
It was no night to board a plane, but in the end he yielded, started
the engine, and took off. A Junkers D 1608. The fog swallowed
them up. Full throttle, 1250 r.p.m., 145 k.p.h. on the dial. A few
minutes in the air, a few minutes of the engine's roar, a factory
chimney appeared a few meters away like an invisible annihilating

giant. A deafening noise, a crash, and a deathly hush. Minutes before six o'clock, two men with their backs broken. They were dead the moment they hit the ground. Tomáš Baťa, industrialist, his heart punctured by one of his ribs.

The recently created cemetery on the hill beyond town covered a hundred acres of woodland. Spruce and pine, oak and beech. The mixture of needles and leaves crackled beneath the mourners' feet. Tomáš Baťa, the cemetery's own founder, was one of the first to be laid to rest in the newly consecrated ground.

On July 12, 1932, the cogs of the great machine stopped turning, but only for a fraction of a second, only for the space of a single breath. "The work we do is not for people who wish to be indispensable," the boss himself would have said. If he had come back a few days after his death, he would have been overjoyed. The company he had built stayed on course, as smoothly, as steadily as before. Not even his death could jeopardize it.

His seat was taken by his half-brother. Otherwise, nothing changed.

In November of 1932, Thomas took his family to sunnier shores.

The boat sailed from Marseilles. The *Monarch of Bermuda*. Opulent soirées, evening gowns, and dancing. A magician and a ventriloquist. The English everywhere. *How do you do?* Polished manners and specialities of the *chef de cuisine*. My mother's stomach billowed like dough in a kneading trough. The sails bulged in the strengthening wind and the waves grew bigger and fiercer. The sky clouded over and the horizon disappeared. Strings of rain created a visible screen, a veil growing ever closer. A bright curtain divided the dry from the drenched. Bewitching. The stern stayed dry for some seconds after the first raindrops hit the prow. Then the wall of rain progressed a few more meters and engulfed the entire ship. At the sight of this unprecedented phenomenon, the dough in the kneading trough collapsed, and Rachel totally forgot how sick she had been feeling.

In Madras, Rachel crumpled again. She spent a half-day throwing up; maybe it was because of the cholera and typhus pills. They reached Calcutta two weeks before Christmas. She spent three days in bed before she unpacked.

One evening, she was waiting in the dining room in the near-darkness when she heard Tom enter the house. He sat down with her, reached into his pocket, and tossed some scuffed coins onto the table.

"Is that the local currency?" she said.

"Yes. One *rupee* is about ten crowns."

"And is there a smaller unit?"

"Of course. There are sixteen *annas* to the *rupee*, four *pices* to the *anna* and three *pies* to the *pice*."

Her eyes popped out of her head. "What sort of math is that?"

"A *rupee* has sixteen *annas*, sixty-four *pices* or one hundred and ninety-two *pies*. Easy!"

"Crazy!"

"You'll get used to it. The Indians are proud of it."

"Of what?"

"The math. Population is calculated in *crores*. A population of three *crores* is thirty million people."

She did a mental calculation. "So one *crore* is ten million."

"Right. Didn't I say it was easy? One *crore* has one hundred *lakhs*, a hundred *crores* is one *arb* and a hundred *arbs* is one *kharb* —"

"Stop! I don't want to know."

He lay a soothing hand on her shoulder. "You're going to like it here. You'll see."

She didn't like India at all. She saw the grime, the crumbling walls of the houses, the refuse floating in slurry. It made her sick when she caught the stench of decay, or when dozens of half-hairless, mangy dogs and cats ran past her. She had fits at the sight of the crippled children in the dust of the streets or the wretched club-footed beggars with outstretched hands; an unbearable, naked vision of reality--the poverty, sickness, and dying. She was assailed by phobias: the dirt and disease. Traffic on the Ganges, the surface of the river with its steamboats, a street barber. People drying cow patties in the streets for fuel, primitive carts with massive wheels, spindly palms like upturned comets.

After seeing her first snake, she wanted to go home.

Mother India. A land of ancient culture, mysterious and inscrutable. Broad rivers, the yellow-grey water rolling on quietly, eternally. India. Thomas had tried to merge with the country and extract the very best from its hodgepodge of people, its cultures and religions. Rachel also tried to get a grasp on the place, to see its essence in everything. But she hated it at first.

India didn't change on my mother's account. It remained the same as it had been for thousands of years. But Rachel did change. She became reconciled. Through her obsession with ancient myths, with images of faith and the power of the word, she discovered for herself the poetry of the sub-continent, and let herself be carried away by its extremes, its many destinies. Ultimately, she fell in love with it, a love we shared. India: hot and implacable, sweet and distressing, sensuous and disapproving. I grew up in the embrace of its contradictions, among people who ignited in me a yearning for harmony with my own self. My India. I didn't try to understand it. I loved it.

My nurse—my *ayah*—was called Kavita. A squat woman of uncertain age with eyes like coals and a nose that ran the whole length of her face and whose hooked tip touched her full lips. She wore a blue sari, one single strip of material mysteriously wound, python-like, around both the upper and lower parts of her body. Dozens of shimmering bangles and chains jingled against each other in time with her movement. She moved like a cat, with an easy grace. As she walked, her voluptuous body flowed as though being poured from one vessel into another, changing shape and returning to its original form. She radiated an aura of peace and kindness. She became an integral part of our home and an autonomous member of our family. With me she spoke a peculiar mixture of English and Hindi that only I understood. My father laughed at our way of communicating, but my mother was irritated by it at first. Eventually, though, she got used to it as well, and stopped agitating about it, because I became touchingly devoted to Kavita and she adored me.

Rachel's sister Regina wrote that old Aunt Esther had died. Her will was a bandage for a bad conscience: she had left her apartment in Olomouc, her jewels, and her fat bank balance to Rachel.

Rachel struggled with the heat. She couldn't breathe, and was worried about me. Thomas didn't notice the heat. He came home late, worn out with fighting the authorities and the workmen on the building site. From time to time he made demands she found difficult to accommodate.

"We'll have to hire a cook."

"Why? I don't want a cook. I can do my own cooking."

"No you can't. We're in India. We have to have a cook to do the cooking and shopping. You can't go wandering the markets on your own."

"I can't stand that sort of social edict!"

"I agree, sweetheart. I can't think of anything more stupid."

"There you are then!"

"Just do me a favor and work it out—so I don't have to bother about it myself."

She seethed. "It's people like you, so serious and sensible, who thought up all this nonsense! Rules, taxes, religions, and even those neckties you strangle yourself with so casually!"

He laughed at her rebellion. He stood up and went to the door.

"Aha! So the audience is over, is it?" She grabbed a box of

matches and threw it at him. "I don't want another man in the house! I want a female cook!"

He poked his head back through the doorway, trying to keep a straight face, but the corners of his mouth were twitching and his eyes were full of mischief. "If you can manage that, my hat's off to you. Being a cook's a question of caste—and they're always male."

One Sunday, Tom got back from the site before lunch and announced that they'd have the afternoon to themselves. They spent it sitting in the garden. The scent of fresh coffee and the mango tree, the playpen under a handwoven mosquito net, noontime dreams in the shade of a banyan.

Suddenly, Rachel jumped up. "I've got something for you!" She was smiling broadly as she placed an enormous melon in front of him. The knife drove gently into the pulp, and the dark green skin oozed pink goo and a sour smell.

"Where've you been keeping it?"

"On the veranda."

"It's cooked. Or fermented more like." He delved into it with the spoon she offered and couldn't stop laughing. "Would you share some overdone goo with me?"

"No! But I'll hire you that cook."

Zam Singh brought another breath of the Indian spirit into the house with his countless bewitching perfumes: coriander, ginger, cardamom, turmeric, and chili. He was always smiling and he hummed continuously. He sounded like a double bass. A turban on his head and a moustache under his nose, his well-kept beard in braids that disappeared up into his hair like two baby snakes. He was friendly, affable, avoiding only the dog. For his part, Amon pursued Zam eagerly, his perpetually hungry snout never missed what was cooking.

Rachel barely noticed, but Tom was amused. "Zam, I hate to admit this, but that dog is fonder of you than me!"

In the middle of January 1934, the earth shook. Part of

neighboring Assam was transformed into a lunar landscape. The front pages of the papers were full of the tons of rubble and thousands of corpses, headlines that screamed for help. Photographs of Jamalpore, where no stone was left standing. The military laid dynamite and blew up the remains of ruined buildings. Clerks from demolished offices worked out in the open, and whoever felt able dug into their savings and gave for the homeless.

The factory in Konnagar, miraculously spared by the earthquake, kept going at full speed. Cracked ceilings were repaired while the work continued below. They had to increase their plimsoll production to compete with the Japanese, who had come to dominate the market. Baťa's Young Men put their hearts and souls into it, and finally surpassed even the Japanese with their dirt-cheap rubber shoes.

A celebration took place on the banks of the Hooghly, not far from the village of Nangi, surrounded by swamps and jungle. On October 28, 1934, the anniversary of the birth of Czechoslovakia, the foundation stone of a new factory was laid by Jan Bartoš, head of Baťa's Indian operations. In a few years a town would stand here. Thomas talked to the architect, Karfík. Hunched over heaps of building plans, they discussed it fervently. They examined every detail, sought solutions to the treacherous climate, and penciled in the final changes. They strolled through a town that did not yet exist. It was a dream on paper, realistically and carefully planned. Batanagar. Three years after the foundations were laid it would contain—besides the factory and houses—its own wharf, post office, telephone exchange, and church; a soccer field, tennis court, cricket pitch, and swimming pool. A cinema and theater were also being built, and plans were nearly finished for a school for the employees' children.

As time passed and my mother grew more accustomed to life in India, she asked Zam more and more to make Bengali meals.

Zam would flutter around the kitchen like a white bat. His kingdom was populated with all the best utensils, including a pulverizer handed down from generation to generation. I had admired the thing from my earliest childhood. Zam would clutch a smooth oval stone in one hand and run it back and forth across the surface of a larger pentagonal block spread with lentils or other such foods. Apart from *payesh*, Zam's version of rice pudding, I adored fish cooked in the Bengali manner. Any kind. There was nothing better than fresh fish braised in a mustard sauce thickened with poppy seeds and served with rice.

When my mother first allowed me to accompany Zam to the fish market, I was in raptures. I ran here and there in the stifling Babel of smells and chatter, peeking into baskets full of wonderfully pink prawns, crabs, catfish, and sardines. Dumbstruck, I followed the flashes of the sharp *boti*, with which the fishmongers cut up their wares. Zam offered to let me choose, to point out which fish I wanted, but that was a superhuman task. I couldn't decide, I pointed to the right and to the left and at yet another one. I wanted them all. In the end I picked a gold-colored fish. *Topshey.* The English call it mango fish, but I thought of it as a golden fish, and it was mine. I did not relish the prospect that my golden fish would be for dinner. When we got back, I wanted it to play with; I wanted to take it to bed with my teddy bear.

My mother got annoyed. "You can't take a dead fish to bed!"

"It's not dead, it's mine! I chose it!"

"Listen to me. I know you chose it, but that fish is not a pet. If you like, we'll get you an aquarium for your birthday and you can put another golden fish in that and look after it, all right?"

"And why can't we have *my* fish in the aquarium?"

"Because it's dead, and dead fish don't swim. They have to be eaten. As soon as possible!"

I scowled. My mother lost her patience. "If you can't be sensible, I won't let you go to the market next time!"

Then I lost *my* patience. "Don't care!"

I spent that evening crying in my bedroom while my parents ate their golden fish. I had fought in vain and now I was afraid my mother would never let me go back to the fish market. I crept into the dining room and watched them finish the meal. My father looked at me and set his knife aside. His sinewy forearm beckoned, poking out of his rolled-up sleeve.

"Do you want to taste the golden fish?" He sat me on his knee. He hardly ever lost his temper. I looked sideways at my mother, and she was smiling. That gave me courage.

"And when can I have my aquarium?"

They exchanged looks over my head and started laughing.

More than once, I was an eyewitness to flying saucers in our house. They would crash into the wall and descend like snowflakes to the floor when my mother got angry. Then it was better to stay out of sight and range, because at moments like that she lost all self-control. My dad could spot a domestic typhoon looming and make himself scarce in time, reappearing once calm was restored. He called these outbursts "Spring cleaning."

Rachel sometimes felt that despite all the love she had for Thomas, she hated him completely. But he was indulgent about her endless mistakes. Sometimes she wasted money and he would only laugh, and she was artlessly gullible and he would rib her for that, too. She believed in the goodness of man. He knew that idealism was impractical, though he was sympathetic about her illusions. She acknowledged that some of her reactions were contradictory to social convention, yet he remained amiable. He knew how to pacify her.

In public, he gave out all the right social signals. In private, he could shock her with his unexpected behavior and sarcastic remarks. She failed to understand how he could mercilessly mock prejudices and social norms while outwardly maintaining them. But he came off looking like a respectable, upright citizen, and she sometimes looked like a crazy fool.

Tom came back from work early one day and found the house deserted. He took off his jacket, went into the kitchen, and lifted the lid of the teapot. He raised an eyebrow and let out a sigh. He poured the remaining tea into a cup and looked briefly for the sugar, but mentally he had already abandoned the idea. He headed for the living room, loosened his tie, undid his top button, and sprawled out in an armchair with the *Times of India*. Having read it, he reached for the week-old paper from Zlín. In March 1936, a headline proclaimed: *Germany arms—France has qualms!*

Beneath the headline was a cartoon of an arrogant Nazi fully armed with the modern trappings of war, and a cowering Frenchman equipped for an Iron Age encounter. A shiver ran down his spine.

Suddenly Rachel was standing behind him. Immersed in the red-hot news, he hadn't heard her approach. She placed a hand on his shoulder, bent over him, and inhaled deeply. She loved that smell. His sweat. A mix of cedar and peppermint. And the tobacco that clung to his white shirts. He stretched out his right hand and touched her face above him. She took the long fingers between her palms and put them to her lips. She took another breath. A waft of nicotine between his middle and index fingers. He watched her for a moment, then tipped back his head and pulled her face towards him. He parted his lips as if ready to swallow her.

I stood in the doorway, staring at my parents as they kissed with all the passion of a pair of film stars. I dropped my tennis ball, forgotten in the intensity of the moment, and it rolled across the floor and was lost. My parents shot apart. At first they looked startled, then they burst out laughing.

"Don't you know how to knock?" said Mommy.

"Come here," Dad said, with the gesture that so typified him. Beckoning, giving his permission to approach. I sat on his knee. Dad put one arm around my shoulders, slapped his free thigh with the other, and nodded to Mommy that she could sit down too. He winked at me, but my mother was quicker than my father expected and sat right down on his hand. He howled and tried to pull his squashed fingers out. When he was in the mood, he could be very funny.

That evening, I watched the intruders I'd discovered in my room. When the light went out, they began their silent perambulations. When I turned the light back on, they froze on the spot. Colorful, almost transparent little bodies and goggling eyes, clinging to the wall.

"Mommy, there's a lizard hiding in here. Behind the furniture. And there's another one underneath the picture."

"That's good. Lizards are the guardians of your dreams. They clamber up the walls and catch moths and mosquitoes. And they drive away elves and ghosts. You have nothing to fear."

She was smiling. I never hurt them. Ever.

Years later, during my first year at boarding school, I thrashed Sid Hindley for snapping lizards' tails off. I had wanted to give him a good thumping because he was such a show-off, and his cruelty to the lizards was just the pretext I needed to start a fight. I tore the boy's shirt and his stiff collar came off in my hand. A few shirt buttons with bits of fabric still attached, blood trickling from his nose. It was a strange feeling. After that, he steered clear of me. And the lizards, too, I hoped.

As a small boy, I demanded bedtime stories. My mother, who was the daughter of a history teacher and herself passionate about history, adored myths and legends. She would always describe in detail what each of the gods looked like.

Stories of sun gods and goddesses fascinated me most. "Tell me the story of the Sun and Moon again, the one where the Sun is like a hummingbird and they run away together."

"All right. Or I can tell another one, the one the Aztecs used to tell. About how the Sun and Moon came into being and about

Nanahuatzin's great courage. How's that?"

"All right."

"It all began long, long ago, at the beginning of time, with a quarrel among the four brothers who were the most powerful gods of the Aztecs. In the end they became so mad at one another that instead of working together to create the Sun, they each tried to do it alone. But none succeeded. So they made up, and met with the other gods at the sacred place called Teotihuacán. The wisest of them, the Plumed Serpent, mounted the top of the pyramid and spoke. 'It is time to put an end to our quarrelling and create the Sun. Because all our attempts have failed, we must make a sacrifice. One of us must enter the sacred fire in order to be transformed into the new Sun. Which of you will make the sacrifice? Which of you will enter the fire?' Silence descended. No one said a word. Then one handsome youth, Tecusistecatl, rose and strode proudly forward. 'I will sacrifice myself for you all!' From somewhere in the back came a timid call. 'I also want to enter the fire and become the Sun!' Nanahuatzin, thin and ill-favored, eyes scanning the dust, stepped up before the gods. Tecusistecatl laughed mockingly. 'What an ugly Sun you would be!' The Plumed Serpent checked him. No one had the right to scorn such a sacrifice. The next day the sacred fire blazed up. Tecusistecatl ran toward it. At two paces from the fire he felt the terrible heat and stopped. He hid his eyes and burst into tears. 'Jump!' the gods cried. 'Jump!' When the Plumed Serpent saw Tecusistecatl quaking with fear, he looked towards Nanahuatzin. 'You jump, since this coward cannot.'' Without a moment's hesitation, Nanahuatzin ran, and his wretched frame disappeared in the flames. They all waited there with breath held. Nanahuatzin appeared in the sky, a golden sun with a glorious, bright face. When Tecusistecatl saw that, he too ran into the sacred fire. The gods were stunned. Another sun rose into the heavens. The Plumed Serpent flew into a rage. 'Tecusistecatl must not shine down on us like a sun! I will not have it!' That instant

he saw a hare scampering down the valley. He grabbed it by the
ears and hurled it at the sun that was Tecusistecatl. His golden
face changed into the pale Moon. The Plumed Serpent gave his
verdict. 'Nanahuatzin's Sun shall shine all day for us. And when he
goes to bed in the west, his place will be taken by the Moon, who
will cast his gentle light upon the world of night. In the morning,
the Sun, having had a good rest, will chase the Moon back into the
darkness where it belongs. And so it shall remain!' All the gods
agreed, and as they decreed, so it is to this day."

As ever, I was in raptures, but something puzzled me. I sat up and
grabbed my mother urgently by the hand. "But, Mommy, what
happened to the hare?"
　　"The hare? I expect he stayed on the Moon."
　　"I want to go and see!"
　　"All right, come on. But get your shoes."
　　We went out onto the veranda and craned our necks back to
look for Tecusistecatl's face.
　　"Two days ago it was full moon, and today the moon is already
beginning to shrink away. Can you see the hare?"
　　I was all aglow. "Yes, yes. I see him! Curled up in a ball asleep!"
Breathless, I clapped for joy.
　　"And you ought to be asleep as well, you know."
　　My dad appeared at the door to the veranda, strong arms
raising me up. "Come on, it's high time you were in bed."

The climate in Calcutta was made up of sunlight, water vapor,
and columns of white ants. Mildew found its way into every nook,
and the exterior wall of the kitchen looked like a mushroom farm.
Rachel was amazed to discover that the pins and needles in the
sewing kit she had inherited from Aunt Esther had turned rusty
in only a few months, and the thread had shredded. Clothing,
even of the stoutest material, disintegrated, and the carpets were

in tatters. "You should put your clothes in mothballs," she was advised. The crumbling books pained her the most. Frequently, after taking one off the shelf, she would find herself gathering it up from the floor, with just the binding left in her hand.

India does not obsess over immortality. On the contrary: every Hindu yearns to attain *moksha*, liberation from *samsara*, the endless chain of birth and death.

Late Afternoon

A stray dog ran across the immaculate garden at Mrs. Vanier's B&B. The snow crunched beneath his paws like the bits of Christmas cookies between my teeth. Mrs Vanier, touched her temples with her fingertips and blinked rapidly several times in succession. I felt a sense of pride that my story had so captivated her, and I wanted to give her time to get her breath back.

Her eyes shone feverishly. "So you're Daniel? Daniel Keppler?"

"Yes, I should have introduced myself."

She appeared astonished. "But your...your reservation was... in the name of Welsh."

"Yes, I expect it was. It was my son's wife, Frances, who did the booking. She's kept her maiden name. Women do that nowadays, you know. Times change, Mrs Vanier."

She was visibly shaken. She took a deep breath and said, "Please, call me Anna. I...I believe I knew your mother."

IV

Anna: How I Met My Sister

Before the war, I lived in Prague. My father died of tuberculosis when I was six, leaving my mother to manage our fabric shop on her own. She learned to survive on modest means. She used to say that it was easier to save a penny than earn one. Each evening she would sit and, with her circular needle, produce little mats and tablecloths from thin yarn, or make bobbin lace. It was only after I left school that the Germans arrived. I wanted to be a nurse, but by then it was too late. I used to help my mother in the shop and go to see my aunt—my father's sister—who was a dressmaker, to learn something from her. Aunt Elsa had always lived alone. She had nursed both her parents until the end, resisting all the offers of marriage, which must have been positively heroic when she was in the bloom of youth. She never did marry.

Now she plied her trade as a fifty-year-old spinster. She was different, and everyone knew it: a tiny wren with her chestnut hair in a bun. She didn't walk, but pottered noisily around on her spindly legs, babbling so fast that sometimes I could only guess what she meant. The blades of her scissors would scythe their way through yards of silk, satin, and georgette. Velvet, chiffon, crêpe-de-chine, in every permutation. She would go down on her knees next to her customers, a tape measure around her neck and forests of pins sticking out of the lapels of her orange dress. With pins in

55

her mouth, chalk in her right hand, and a T-square in her left, she would mark out the length of a skirt, chattering nonstop. "Turn a little this way, miss. Should we let it down a little, miss? Though I think we could leave it as it is, you've got such pretty ankles and life is so short." Through her clenched jaws she would gush torrents of ideas, and as soon as she stood back up, she would scribble them down on paper with bold strokes.

"Let's try the blouse on, gently, gently, watch the pins. So what do you think, miss? Mhm, mhm. No, the sleeve isn't quite right yet..." and rrrip, with a single tug, off came the loosely tacked sleeve. "And I think we'll reduce the collar a tiny bit..." and rrrip, the blouse lost its collar; "and let's move the pockets ever so slightly..." Rrrip, rrrip, and *miss* was standing there in front of the mirror in just her bra, the blouse in pieces.

I thought it was fun. I would sit in the workshop and trace and cut and tack. Before long I was capable of making almost anything unaided. With time, I began to invent my own patterns, original fabric designs, smart suits, and evening gowns; but none of my sketches ever came to anything, because in wartime people were concerned with matters other than fashion. Most of our customers brought us older garments that they wanted altered so they could get more wear out of them. I made my drawings and dreamed that I, too, would one day have impeccable suits and extravagant hats and buckskin gloves. I dreamed for as long as I could.

Then the shop was aryanized. They took the radio and the jewels and closed my aunt's business down. They confiscated her sewing machine. This was a bitter pill she could never swallow.

In late February 1943, the Jewish Community Center sent instructions for us to present ourselves at the Trade Fair Hall assembly point. That winter was harsh; Aunt Elsa called it a bitch of a winter. We set about packing the barest necessities to take with us to Theresienstadt. But what was a bare necessity? Food? Books? Was crockery more essential, or clothing? Twenty-five kilograms is lamentably little when you don't know what lies ahead. Mrs Maláč from next door rang the bell; she ran the general store on the ground floor and had brought my mother a bag of flour. We used it to bake a mountain of biscuits.

When we arrived at the assembly point, they confiscated my mother's wedding ring and watch. After that, we left it to the Germans—with their unfailing precision—to worry about the passage of time. Three layers of clothing, a coat, and ski boots, and a wool blanket cradled in our arms. A three-day wait squatting on our travelling bags, a drop of soup sloshed out of an urn into tin mugs; we tucked our spoons into our boots. We were beginning to have an idea of what things would be like at Theresienstadt.

My mind's craziest inventions were nothing compared to the truth. Arriving at the ghetto, I had the greatest shock of my life. Goose bumps, and my stomach like a lump of concrete. The harsh reality of the conditions. The first time I visited the latrines I wanted to die. Really. Never before, and probably never since, not even in Auschwitz, did I contemplate suicide with such intensity as then. The latrine. A pit, some crude planking, no walls, no door. Splinters, and my dignity in tatters. The horror of it. "I can't do it! I can't sit here and watch people passing by." I wanted to end it. If I'd had some poison handy I would have downed it without hesitation. But in the end I told myself that there was no hurry.

Two weeks later my mother died. They disinfected our rooms without telling the other shivering old women to keep the windows and doors open. Four died of poisoning. I last saw their bodies piled onto a cart pulled by people instead of horses; they used the same one for delivering bread in the morning and carrying off the dead in the evening.

Soon after that, I became acquainted with a young man who worked as head cook in one of the barracks. He offered me a job in the kitchens. What a prize! Like winning the jackpot. After weeks of starving, weeks of the perpetual cycle of ersatz coffee for breakfast, turnip soup and a few potatoes for lunch, and a chunk of bread for supper, the prospect of plenty opened up before me. I lugged out the great wooden vats of soup, then ladled it into the endless line of tin bowls on the endless queue.

"I'll keep my helping for you."

I looked up from my urn and there in front of me stood Aunt Elsa. Since my mother's death, Elsa's veins had run with venom. She refused to eat. She would say it was time for her to die too.

"Eat it, auntie. You must eat something."

Elsa squinted conspiratorially. "I've discovered that Míla Bauch has been transported to the East with her son and daughter."

That was bad news. Míla Bauch was my mother's sister, who had lived in Pilsen; we called her "our Pilsen auntie."

Elsa patted my shoulder and stared into the distance, into some lost world. She gave an embittered shake of her head. "They took my sewing machine," she told me, as if I didn't know. "They stole my sewing machine, the bastards."

I worked sixteen, sometimes eighteen hours a day. The work was a blessing because it left no time for thinking. When I wasn't working, I would escape from our damp little cell for some cultural relief. Those were unforgettable evenings.

To this day, I can feel the confusion, the faltering breath, and the streams of sweat. The excitement. I can still feel it. The confusion, faltering breath and sweat, the strange excitement. And there I saw him, in candlelight. I won't ever forget that.

A dark cellar, its pores blocked. Two windows below street level plugged with sacks of straw, black rags as curtains, so that not a note, not a sound would leak out. And music flowing through the gloom. Flickers of candlelight dancing across a legless piano propped on battered old crates from who knows where. A Beethoven sonata. *Appassionata.* His face bent low, slender fingers webbing the keys.

He looked at me. A smile, maybe more. I wanted to hope. His

hands steeled in rhythm, supple in legato. At the Prague Academy, a dazzling career had been forecast for him, worldwide success; he was to become the king of the world's concert halls. Gideon Klein. Now he was trying to redeem a handful of souls in the twilight of a stuffy cellar. Muffled applause for a star that would never rise. And who was I? A nobody. A tadpole, my cousin Hugo used to say. When Gideon spoke to me, I mumbled, I blurted clusters of consonants, all vowels ceased to exist. After that, I had to write him a letter. To crown it all, I included a poem.

You are an avalanche
enchanted in the keys
a misplaced diary
with all addressees.
The last hour
of colorless days
fingers black on white
on the wings of grace.

A brave attempt by the seamstress from Karlín.

He came to see me. Said nothing, shrewdly guessing that there wasn't much point. He took my face in his hands, examined me for a while, then kissed me. He turned without a word and left. I stood there rigid, motionless, like a big, blinking doll.

At the door of the stinking hole behind the kitchens he paused and looked back over his shoulder. "We're doing Brahms and Dvořák tonight. Will you come?"

I nodded awkwardly, as if someone had just whacked me hard on the head.

I really could have used someone to knock some sense into me. As I tell it now, I feel like the cheap author of a cheap romance. *Silly fiction*, my son, Michael, would call it when I finally told him. But I don't care. It was exactly as I say.

Of course we made love; a flawless composition in the hands of a maestro. For the first time, someone was really making love to me—though he wasn't *exactly* my first.

I had lost my virginity in Prague, to some boy who was neither good-looking nor clever. In fact there was nothing attractive about him at all. But he appeared to be madly in love with me: he brought me books I didn't intend to read, told me funny stories I didn't listen to; I think he simply wore me down. And my first time? There was nothing romantic about it—it was a lesson in sheer naturalism, raw and sticky. The whole thing ended when the Germans took us back into the thirteenth century and forbade all intercourse with Jews, and not only sexual. To make a long story short, the boy dumped me. I was deeply offended and sobbed one whole night away, yet I hadn't even liked him. It was just my wounded pride, my vanity. I got over it quickly.

And then came Theresienstadt, and Gideon Klein. Perfect fingering.

After three months of starvation, Aunt Elsa died of malnutrition and exhaustion. She had stubbornly refused all food, always pushing her meager rations towards me, and, for as long as she could still speak, forcing me to eat them right away. "I want to die. You must live." That's what she wanted, and, as usual, she got her way. I could do nothing to haul her out of her apathy, or to revive in her any taste for living, or make her eat even a mouthful of food. Toward the end, Elsa would stare vacantly ahead of her, unblinking, not a twitch in her facial muscles. She moved farther and farther from her old self, shrinking before my eyes until she disappeared.

In the winter of 1944, another transport arrived. Nothing out of the ordinary in the life of the ghetto, but for me...for me...it was exceptional. The frightened newcomers were huddled in their winter coats, looking helplessly around. Rachel stood out among them: a beautiful, elegant woman of around thirty with her raven hair cropped short. This modern style emphasized the delicacy of her facial features. She was wearing a pale blue coat with white fur trim around the neck and cuffs, and moved as if in a dream.

For me, that moment remains ever-present. Rachel walked with a supple grace that contained within it something so utterly sad that it gripped my throat. It was then that I realized how much I missed my mother. Rachel reminded me of her. With Aunt Elsa's death, the last bit of feminine warmth had left my life, but now my heart stirred. Rachel radiated something so feminine and maternal that it brought tears to my eyes. I don't know what got into me, there was no logical explanation for it, but I ran straight towards her, took her by the hand, and helped her with her heavy suitcase.

After that, we were always together. Sisters. I had chosen her.

V

Samsara

I have always been intrigued by the fact that cows in India are sacred. They roamed unmolested through the Indian towns and villages, sometimes with a bell around their necks and a jasmine topknot on their heads, or with their heads gaily painted. But mostly it was awful. Gaunt, filthy and sickly, they munched away on pounds of rotting waste, idly eating up slops, paper, or bits of fabric they found by the wayside. Drivers, rickshaw men, and pedestrians risked their necks to avoid the cows that lay sprawled in the middle of the road. The unfortunate who accidentally bumped into one must face the outrage of the crowd. Cows had power. They could bring traffic to a standstill, and people showed them respect. Yet scores of them died of starvation.

My mother would be brisk and impatient with Zam, who was as slow as a cow's digestive system with its four different stomachs – abomasum, reticulum, rumen, and omasum. By the time anything finally labored its way the length of Zam's grey cells, my mother's nerves would be jangling, but I had no problem at all with his sluggishness.

Zam would make dough out of water and dark, coarse wheat flour with a little bran. He would pinch off a bit of the dough, make it into a ball, and roll it out flat as a pancake. Then he would flip it from one hand to the other, and that regular slapping sound was music to my ears. A ritual: chapatti. Very, very thin, but as soon as it landed across the circular opening over the firebox it inflated; Zam's skilled hand instantly turned it over; and it was done. The Indians ate chapattis with everything. The used them to scoop up sauce, they stuffed them with vegetables, and they wiped their plates clean with them. The chapatti was not just their bread but their knife, fork, and spoon—a complete place setting in one.

My father would work until he dropped. Whenever things were going badly, he would stay on at the site until he felt he had them more or less under control. Sometimes he didn't come home for days on end. The Indians were mulish, but he didn't let it get to him. He had personal experience: no one was more obstinate than his own wife.

Thomas attempted to mollify his team: the good-hearted coolies weren't lazy—they merely refused to work with anything technical, or with any new tools that they hadn't tested themselves over the course of centuries.

The sorely tried Ruda Martinec had been leveling the same site for three days, and had nothing to show for it but deep furrows and gaping holes sixty yards across and twelve feet deep.

"Sorry, boss. I really don't know what to do. I've brought in some carts so they won't wear themselves out filling the holes, but they just beg me to let them carry the stuff on their heads. I tell them hell will freeze over before they're done, but they complain that shovels make their hands and arms ache. 'We don't know how to shovel soil,' they moan, 'just let us carry it in baskets on our heads!' Yesterday they demonstrated how useless they were at shoveling—and today they're on strike."

"Hell freezing over probably doesn't mean much to them."

"How on earth am I supposed to oversee such a primitive bunch? How can I make them do what I want?"

Thomas looked serious. "You do realize what the hitch is,

don't you?"

Ruda just shrugged and made a long face.

"If you treat them like idiots, they'll act like idiots." He set aside the roll of drawings, locked the office, and accompanied Martinec back to the worksite. He picked up a shovel. "Let's show them how it's done. If the white sahib can use a shovel, the brown coolie will follow suit."

Martinec grabbed a shovel and joined in. "You're taking a bit of a chance, aren't you, boss? Suppose they don't join in? I bet they could spend hours just watching us."

"Let's wait and see who gives up first."

"Hm. I bet we'll be fit to drop, and they'll still have the strength to stand there gaping."

The Indians stuck it out long enough for both sahibs to be collapsing with exhaustion, but not long enough for Thomas to give up. After two or three hours, the knot of onlookers had grown to quite a crowd, and some of them started fidgeting and fingering the wooden handles of the shovels. Then gradually, cautiously, they yielded to the monotonous rhythm. Spade in, scoop, and heave it into the cart. Again and again and again.

Ruda stood up and, with a slap on his boss's shoulder, acknowledged he had been right. They tottered on wobbly legs like old drunkards.

Thomas was invited to pay a visit to his own boss. When he arrived, Bartoš was pacing the office and waving his arms. The open space on the riverbank was visible outside his window: piles of bricks, bamboo scaffold poles, the ground looking as though a bomb had gone off. And people everywhere: an anthill on fast forward.

"We need a three-storey building and we need it now," said Bartoš. "The old warehouse is bursting at the seams. When can you start?"

"Just as soon as we complete the loading bays at the station and get the drains linked up. I figure two weeks."

"What? You want to start cementing during the rainy season?"

"Yes."

"Seriously?"

"Yes."

"Okay, you know what you're doing. And when are you going to start re-aligning the retaining wall? Is there any hope of speeding things up?" Bartoš waited for Thomas to answer. He had no time for deceit and false promises.

"Well, there could be, but I'd need more people from home."

"Don't you have enough?"

Thomas was exhausted. His neck spoke of a string of sleepless nights and his lungs complained of his forty cigarettes a day. Here was an opportunity not to be missed. He fought hard to concentrate and make his point so there could be no room for doubt.

"Martinec is busting his back, but he can't keep up with ordering all the materials. I deal with the suppliers myself, or he'd never get any sleep. Kielkowský spends every moment of the day and night on the plans, but doesn't have time to deal with budgets, so I do that myself too. Švarc is handling deliveries as they arrive and Zítek spends all his time doing the accounts. So there's no one to oversee the actual site."

"How many?"

"Two or three should be enough, but no new boys. I need men who know what they're doing, leaders who understand construction and can keep the workmen on their toes—this needs redoing, mix that mortar properly, get this plasterwork fixed." Worn out, he paused for breath. "I need men who can get these coolies to stop being so damn stubborn and carrying everything on their heads. Bricks, cement, mortar, all at a snail's pace. Otherwise we're going nowhere fast. They'd have to be people who can meet these folks' perpetual *tomorrow* with a loud *today*."

"I'll ask for two foremen. You'll have them here within eight weeks."

"Thanks. We'll leave the retaining wall till after the monsoons."

Weeks later, he stood knee-deep in muddy water, which was rising at a dizzy rate. Scaffolding strained to the limit, clay soil dissolved into a brown mush, and the endless patter of raindrops landing in puddles that never seemed to fill up.

"Where the hell are they?"

Ruda Martinec, his wild mop of hair now plastered down on his head like a custom-made helmet, bellowed through the banisters of rain. "Dunno. But if they don't get here soon, we'll be up shit's creek, boss!"

Thomas took two flamingo steps closer and surveyed the scene. "Get out now! I mean it."

"What about you?"

"Move, or we're both screwed!"

A landslide. Great holes were opening up like bomb craters and mighty molehills were taking shape. The ground was shifting from place to place like a fretful squirrel. This was grist to the mill of the doubters and the prophets of doom. Not one company was doing any building work for miles around, except those lunatics at Baťa's. Sinking foundations and laying concrete with the monsoon breathing down their necks—they'd have to be crazy, or suicidal.

But Thomas knew he was neither. And he knew what was needed to cope with this mess: more pumps. Many more. By the time a week had passed, he had evolved an efficient working method: a bank of pumps coped with the cloudbursts, and the mixer churned out concrete at a rate rapid enough to fill in the holes they dug before they disappeared under water. Going inch by inch, they poured the concrete into the crisscross of shuttering. The finished footings were capped with strips of reinforced concrete to deaden the shocks from earthquakes. The foundations were ready in six weeks.

One day, Ruda Martinec shouted theatrically to him over his

shoulder: "Your wife called, boss."

Thomas straightened up and stared, wondering what that meant. "Has something happened?"

"She asked the same thing. Said she hadn't heard from you for a week. She wanted to know if you're still alive."

He nodded. "Thanks, Ruda."

"You ought to go and see her. I can take care of things here."

"Thanks, Ruda."

Rachel was pouring herself a cup of tea. Her arm was bent, her fingers gripped the white handle, the pale brown liquid filled a china cup. Leaning against the doorframe, Tom watched the curve of her back.

"Did you send for me, Madam?"

Her startled cry bounced off the walls. She swung around and the teapot lid clinked. "You scared the hell out of me!"

His footsteps left visible traces of mud on this side of the doorway. "Scared?"

"I didn't recognize you." Her smile was strained with fright.

Layers of dust had turned his hair a strange grey color, half an inch of stubble betrayed his razor's weeklong absence, and his complexion was darkened by dirt and sun. The armpits of his shirt were millwheels of sweat.

"You look like a savage." She was overwhelmed by a medley of odors. Sweat, cement, tobacco, lime, mortar, rain.

He took the teacup from her hand and set it back down on the tray. The tablecloth behind her was a field of flowers and tropical fruit. He lifted her onto it. "Where is he?"

"Who? Daniel? In bed." Breathless, she tried to resist. "He isn't asleep yet. He's waiting for his story."

"Let him wait."

"Mo-mmyyyyy!"

"I don't think he's going to."

Tom's eyes widened and he let go of her dress. "Can you tell him something short?"

"Can you go and wash up?" She ran her hands down the dress to smooth away his grip marks.

He turned off the dining room lights, headed for the bathroom, and reached for the soap. He left the door ajar to catch the bedtime story.

"I'm going to tell you about the brave warrior of the Mixtecs who became their first ruler," Rachel began. "One day, he climbed a hill and cried out: 'Whosoever wishes to be lord of this land must defeat me in battle.' Everyone heard, but no one wanted to pit his strength against the warrior. As he came back down the hill, the rising Sun tickled his face. The warrior thought that the Sun was challenging him to a duel. So he took his bow and shot an arrow at the Sun.

"And the Sun? He didn't even notice as he continued on his way across the sky. Still the warrior watched carefully, right until the moment the Sun set. 'I've beaten the Sun!' he shouted into the silent landscape. 'I've beaten the Sun!' And so he became the first ruler of the Mixtecs. Ever since that time, the Mixtecs have called their rulers *He Who Beat The Sun*.

"But that was only a short story!" came Dan's voice.

"I'll tell you a longer one tomorrow."

"But the Sun didn't even fight with him!"

"No, it didn't."

"So how could it win, without a fight?"

"Sometimes you can win if the other guy doesn't put up a fight. And sometimes you can win by not fighting yourself. You let the other guy think he's won. Grown-ups sometimes say that *discretion is the better part of valor*. And the Sun had the discretion not to put up a fight. You can only do that when you are so strong that you don't have to prove you're better. Now go to sleep."

When she entered the bedroom, Tom was grinning. "So how

could he win, without a fight?"

"Stop it!"

"I'm not sure he understood your definition of a victory that isn't one and a fight without fighting. I certainly didn't."

"Well, he did."

"And here I'm always wondering who he gets his brains from."

He laughed and grabbed at her.

"You're roaring like a tiger; if Dan hears you he'll be afraid."

"Just as long as he doesn't come in here."

A monsoon swept across Batanagar. It was too much for the warehouse roof. The iron sheeting rolled up like wrapping paper, the roof fittings and mountings gave under the sheer weight of water. The wall of the factory collapsed, and the bamboo scaffolding on the filling station scattered all around the site like matchsticks. The skeleton frame of building 23 also had to be redone. Thomas's prospects for a decent night's sleep melted away in a rain-sodden haze.

My mother, Kavita, and I took refuge in Darjeeling for a few summer weeks to avoid the stifling heat and floods. But I looked forward to getting back to Calcutta; once the monsoon season passed, my father came to get us.

I sat in our Calcutta kitchen watching Zam's hands. He crushed cooked lentils, heated some oil in a frying pan, browned a spoonful of cumin seeds in it, and added a finely chopped onion. He waited until it turned golden-brown, then he tipped the mashed lentils into the pan and sprinkled the whole with a spoonful of turmeric, a pinch of salt, and some green chillies. In fifteen minutes it was done.

The Estates Division was given the task of refurbishing some of the larger shoe stores as quickly as possible. Yesterday was already too late. They carved India up into several unequal portions and disappeared for a couple of weeks. Thomas headed south, to Hyderabad and Madras.

He came home late one night, tired and hungry. He crept into the bedroom, sat on the bed, and watched Rachel sleeping, her breath filling his lungs, her dreams shifting stars and planets in his sky. He fell asleep next to her, still dressed.

In the morning he woke to an empty bed and found her in the bathroom. She was sitting on the bathtub, head in hands, breathing deeply.

"Rachel, darling, what's the matter?" He bent over her and looked at her closely. She was unusually pale. "I'll send for Doctor Seagal."

"He was here yesterday. I'm all right."

"All right? Did he say that?"

She gave him an enigmatic look. "I've got another construction worker for you in here."

He raised an eyebrow and let out a whistle. "I bet I'm the last to know."

"But you're hardly ever here."

"You could have written, like last time."

For my sixth birthday, they told me I would be having a little brother or a little sister. I wanted a brother. Girls in India counted for nothing. One day, Kavita had told my mother that when her cousin had a baby girl, her husband was so angry that he cut his wife's ear off. Clearly, girls were a punishment.

There were days when my mother was all out of sorts. One morning, I came straight to the dining table from bed, and she looked at me severely. "Go and brush your teeth and get dressed, now. You're not having breakfast in your pajamas!"

"Why do I have to brush my teeth in the morning when I haven't eaten anything all night?"

She glanced at my father, who went on intently stirring his coffee. That made her even more annoyed. "Daddy will explain."

"Do what Mommy says, Dan, I'll explain afterwards."

I huffed off towards the bathroom and listened to snatches of what they were saying.

"Darling, how am I supposed to explain why he has to brush his teeth in the morning when he hasn't eaten all night? Besides, I'm in a rush to get to work."

"I just haven't got the energy to argue with either of you, Tom."

"I know. But you look good!"

I could almost hear her rolling her eyes.

"He so takes after you, Rachel. Analyzing everything—and look out if something doesn't make sense. He can't stand rules for rules' sake."

"Don't be silly, Tom. Brushing your teeth in the morning isn't just some rule; it's basic hygiene!"

"There you are! Now that you've given me a decent case to make, I can go and explain it to him."

He knew how to make her laugh even if she meant to be serious. As I came back in, she was looking for something to throw at him. There was a bowl of oranges behind her. She reached for one, but my father was already at the door.

"I'll get you some knives, the kind they use in the circus. That'll be more fun," he said.

One day, Martinec came hurtling into Thomas's office, frantic. "There's cobras in the warehouse, boss. All in a heap."

"So, chase 'em out!"

"But...but how? The men are scared."

"Christ! A storm system at home and cobras at work."

A few minutes later, Tom showed up at the warehouse with a bunch of grinning natives at his heels. Each was armed with a stick and had a sack over his shoulder. "Okay, Ruda. These guys will show you how to get rid of a couple of snakes." He marched straight inside with a stick in his hand. Ruda Martinec was wracked with doubt.

"Are the bastards poisonous?"

Tom paused at the door and treated Martinec to a lukewarm smile. "Their bite is fatal," he responded dryly. "But people who die of a cobra bite are cleansed of their sins. They get buried whole, you know? Not cremated. It's a kind of liberation."

"Oh good. That makes me feel a lot better."

The baby was stillborn.

Kavita said that my mother had had a spell cast on her by that little witch, Savitri. I didn't really understand, but I knew something dreadful had happened. I remember my parents, their bodies wrapped up in pain, my mother's eyes blank pages, no stories to tell. I walked through the house, silent, invisible to everyone. I overheard Kavita telling Zam that the mistress had been possessed by demons. I was frightened, but I knew my father would do everything to drive the demons out.

Something inside Rachel had turned in a circle and flown away. Thomas tried to reach her.

"Rachel?"

She was disappearing at the speed of light, somewhere he couldn't go. He held her tight, but his arms felt empty, his voice fractured in his mouth. He kept saying her name. *Stay with me. His fingers gripping her loose flesh. You can't leave me like this. Do you hear?*

Slowly her eyes came back, her face unfolded as she recognized him, reappeared in the grip of his arms.

He was shaking, his lips against her face.

"Promise me you won't go insane!"

Through the crack in the door I watched the people in the house, Dr. Seagal and others I'd never seen before. Then they took something away in a small wooden box. I stayed with Kavita, who kept chanting her mantras, calling on her gods and good spirits, leaving me behind in a wake of broken shapes and sounds. After that, everything changed. My mother stopped telling me bedtime stories for the whole summer. My father would come home early and take me for walks or to the movies. There were lots of cinemas on Chauringi. I remember them all–and the cartoons, too. Mickey Mouse, Felix the Cat, Popeye the Sailorman, and my father next to me, laughing, as if we were two boys together.

Before I went to sleep, he would tell me me what he had been doing at work, and talk about the most beautiful buildings in the world.

"The Taj Mahal, a gem of Mogul architecture, a white marble mausoleum on the edge of the desert. The Taj Mahal is about the immortal love of a man for a woman. Rabindranath Tagore wrote that the Taj Mahal was a teardrop on the face of time. In 1631, when his beloved wife, the Persian princess Mumtaz Mahal, died in childbirth, Shah Jahan summoned the best of Asia's artists, craftsmen, and builders to Agra. It took them twenty-two years before they completed the spectacular shrine. Legend has it that Shah Jahan was so distressed by his wife's death that in just a few months his black beard and hair went completely white.

"The palace changes color with the seasons and even by the time of day: from pink at dawn to dazzling gold at night with the moonlight on it. The changing colors are said to reflect his wife's moods."

"Mommy also has pink moods sometimes."

"Yes, she does."

"Can we go and see it?"

"Would you like to?"

A year later, our shared dream came true.

On the way to Agra, we stopped at Benares. Pilgrims at the landings on the river of rituals. The sacred rite of bathing. A Hindu with the golden beads of a Brahmin around his neck: the highest caste. The goddess washes away all human sins. The Ganges. They say that once it flowed in Heaven.

Benares is older than Jerusalem, my father told me. A city that was already ancient when Rome was being built, the holiest place on the Ganges, center of the world. A microcosm. If you die in Benares, you merge with the universe.

Two paces from my mother sat a young man in the lotus position, almost naked, his dark skin and chest covered in black hairs. Profound meditation in the midst of the hubbub at the *ghats,* the woodpiles where dead bodies were burned so the ashes could be carried away by the river.

A knot of people squatting around a fire caught my attention. My mother and father were deeply engrossed in discussing something or other, and I had strayed away from them in the delirium wrought by the atmosphere of the place. Fire: the power of the element. Unknown gods. I crept nearer. On the pile of wood lay a charred body. The flames hadn't yet reached the dehydrated feet poking out from it. I stood transfixed, tried to turn back, but was unable to look away from the remains of the burning corpse.

Then I saw a legless man with a humped back whose arms served him as legs to carry him to his eternal liberation. The pilgrim had no trouble walking on his hands; in fact, he moved with such ease that it made me wonder why we needed legs at all.

"The body is a prison in which we sit out our punishment for past lives," the man said. "The Ganges is a goddess. The Ganges is pure. For eternity." As he immersed himself in the river, the legless Jaman Lal recalled his previous night's dream. His mother's soul had bent over him and told him: "Be happy, my boy, you don't have anything to worry about, so be happy."

I believed the Ganges had entered the legless body and taken charge of the man's soul.

Rain streamed down the ghats. We heard a cry: *The name of Ram is the truth. The name of Ram is the truth. The name of Ram is the truth.*

"Do you see that, Dan? They're burying a holy man."

74

"His body won't be burned?"

"No. They'll wrap it in cloth, weigh it down with stones, and throw it in the river. Only the bodies of holy men and children are without sin. So they don't have to be purified by fire."

"And if I died now, would you throw me in the river, too?"

Benares. Etched in my memory: hundreds of fires and stinging smoke in the river at night. A dark orange glow on the walls of temples, the purple sky above. The dead swathed in embroidered covers, and the living in colorful plaids, creatures of the night, of the demonic fire. Human bodies were torches in the chain of temples and recurring births and deaths, in the cycle of day and night, of months and years, in the boundless river of a human yearning for purification and eternal liberation. Salvation on the stone steps beside the sacred waters.

At Benares, our route left the banks of the Ganges and turned towards Agra. Others continued on upstream. The legless Jaman Lal carried the ashes of his late mother with him in a canvas bag to throw them in the river at Hardvar and add his name to the book of Hindu pilgrims. Up in the Himalayas, the goddess Ganges flowed down the hair of the dancing Siva. Burning garlands of flowers drifted down the river to unite the soul of the deceased with the souls of the grieving. There the legless pilgrim would have his head shaved and set off once more into the desert.

Rachel wrote to her sister, Regina:

If I hadn't fallen in love with India long before this, I would have been swept off my feet by it on the way to Agra. The discovery of a new world. Like when I started dancing lessons. I don't have much to compare it with, because I've never been anywhere else abroad, but the Orient enchants me. No one's in a hurry, no one makes plans, cows meander through the streets in a flood of sounds and colors like an endless carnival, one costume more imaginative than the next. Everything here is in color, even the

75

air. In the daytime it shimmers in the glinting golden sunlight. And the night—the night is blue. You bathe in a magical blue that turns reality into dreams and dreams into reality. In my unexplainable love for India, I can no longer see her faults; I do not suffer at the cruel sight of abject poverty, though it is all around. I've even gotten used to the dreadfully crippled beggars, crawling in the dust of the streets, the little children who never stop grabbing your sleeve until you give them something. The longer you stay in this country, the more ordinary all these absurd contradictions seem. Cashmere scarves and pearls and coral beads from the Indian Ocean. A myriad of human faces, languages, and gods.

The Rowlatt Act of 1919 had allowed imprisonment without trial for opposition to British rule. Oppression and revolt: Mohandas Karamchand Gandhi had taught passive non-violent resistance—a tiny man with hundreds of millions of people behind him. Under the weight of Gandhi's words the temples opened. "There is no god," he said. "If god were here, everyone would have access, for he resides in each of us." Gates that had been closed for centuries to lower-caste mortals now swung wide. Ancient prejudices had begun to drain away into the sewer of time.

In 1935, the British parliament approved a new constitution for India, but the Indians were unenthusiastic. Officials of the Indian National Congress condemned the new Act. A year later they contested the elections held under the new constitution. These officials won and took office in seven of the eleven provinces. The gentlemen of the Muslim League drew in their horns and Muhammad Ali Jinnah came up with a conciliatory offer of cooperation. The representatives of the Congress, intoxicated by their triumph and blinded by their own arrogance, sneered at his offer and thumbed their noses at the League. The gulf between the two sides grew too wide for even Gandhi to straddle.

By 1939, when the Viceroy announced that India was at war with Germany, these same ministers of the Indian Congress would be shocked and amazed, and would tender their resignation. No one had asked them what they thought.

My parents admired Gandhi, his non-violent struggle for the liberation of India.

Rachel had read the *Bhagavadgita*. She knew whole passages by heart. She had studied Buddhism, carried away by its simplicity and conciliatory nature. Unlike Hinduism, it did not seek to justify the caste system. She had taught Tom about the basic ideas and principles of non-violent resistance. *Ahimsa*. In Sanskrit, *sin* means *longing to kill*, and *ahimsa* is its opposite, *not longing to kill*. *Ahimsa* equals non-violence.

Tom had been interested. "So you favor non-violence? Unbelievable. If I weren't physically stronger than you, I'd have been dead ten times over."

As her eyes flashed his way, he recalled the shattered crockery from their last scene. *Ahimsa*. Self-preservation made him keep certain other thoughts to himself. *I've spent a fortune on cups and plates. China's pointless. Paper plates would be more practical.*

Though the subject of Indian independence was taboo with their British friends, my parents had been gripped by Gandhi's philosophy, his non-violent struggle for the liberation of India, his fight against the dumb arrogance of the British.

Now we stood outside the Taj Mahal. I looked at the black marble inscriptions and the grand gateway. I was burning with impatience to go inside, but my father was enchanted. "The gate is a symbol of the divide between the world of the senses and the world of the spirit. For Muslims it is the gateway to Paradise."

"What does it say here?"

"They're quotations from the Koran. See how the writing is

the same size wherever you stand? It's a trick by the masters of calligraphy. The perfect optical illusion."

Finally we went through the gateway. The symmetry of the Persian garden, the arrays of cypresses and fountains. The strip of water was a mirror in which the Taj Mahal was reflected. At first sight it seemed small and distant, but that was just another optical illusion, instantly dispersed only to be replaced yet again. The Taj Mahal began to grow, to inflate; with every step it grew in magnitude, with us at its feet. I felt as if I were looking at the greatest building in the world.

For the Muslims, four is a magic number, Dad used to tell us; every element of the structure is made up of four parts, or a multiple of four. Only the mosque is one, facing towards Mecca, its inside walls spangled with quotations from the holy books. I stood, head back, and admired the design of the dome, which kept changing as I turned slowly on the spot. Suddenly the image above me became a maelstrom, the ornamentation whizzed around my head, and before I realized what was happening I hit the ground. My father hauled me to my feet. "Silly boy! You can't go spinning like a top while looking upwards!"

The mosque had a twin, a guest house, but instead of quotations from the Koran it had white marble flowers on red sandstone. The centerpiece was the queen's tomb in an octagonal space. The echoes of ages. Shivers down my spine. For an instant, I saw the queen in the tangle of rays of light that shattered against the misty, milky glass. She was there—an ethereal being created by the play of the light.

Outside, everything looked different. Even more than the mosque, more than the tomb, the minarets seized my imagination. Four slender fingers reaching up to the sky, giving the giant wings. We waited until dusk, when the coming darkness would show us her ever-changing moods. In the evening she was white. Very white, like a bride; ancient love reflected in cold marble.

"What will you say if someone asks you what the Taj Mahal is?"

I had to think. My father asked some very strange questions. "The most beautiful dream that's real."

The construction of Batanagar proceeded at a dizzy rate once they sent my father a couple of top-notch men. Jirka Pešat and Vladimir Semotám.

"Here, Jirka. Do something about this mess. The bureaucrats will have a field day otherwise. They could ruin us—and our shoes."

Pešat hurled himself on the drawings and paperwork that had been shuffled here and there for several weeks and were crying out to be dealt with. Thomas leaned back against one heap and nodded.

Then he took Semotám on a tour of the site. They stopped by a group that was digging trenches and putting in the shutters. "What do you think you're doing?" Thomas said, leaning forward and blinking.

Ruda Martinec stood to attention, his gaze switching between Thomas and the tall, greying man who shuffled shyly behind him.

Thomas pointed to the shuttering. "Is this some sort of joke? Where are the plans?"

"No joke, this is the formwork for the foundations."

"Fine, but what are you using as a guide?"

"The fence, boss. The blueprints are no damn use, sorry to say."

Thomas smiled. "Let me introduce you. Vladimír Semotám, site foreman, reinforcement from Zlín. Ruda Martinec, site foreman in India, takes fences as guidelines. So next time you've got problems with the plans, Ruda, get Vladimír here to keep an eye on the men, and you go and talk it out with Kielkowský. From now on, I don't want to hear there isn't time."

"Sorry, boss, but it's no good talking to Kielkowský."

"It's perfectly possible to talk to anyone. Even Kielkowský."
Even my wife, crossed his mind. "Before you start pouring the
concrete, give me a shout. I'll come and check the dimensions.
Take Vladimír out for a drink this evening and while you're still
sober, piece together a basic vocabulary of building terms and
instructions. Vladimír doesn't know a word of Hindi, so you'll be
doing him a favor. Otherwise there's no point him being here."

That same evening Martinec and Semotám stitched together a
model Czech-Hindi dictionary of building terms and instructions:
"mix that mortar better," "add more cement," "more water,"
"it's all crooked," "take it apart." They tried to condense it to the
minimum, and theoretically it was perfect; but practically, even
the twenty closely-typed pages were a bit too crude as a reference
tool. The very next day Semotám could be seen roaming the site
with his nose in his notebook, flicking through it this way and that.

A few days after the arrival of the merciful reinforcements,
Thomas set off on his own rounds. He walked quickly but quietly,
trying to be as inconspicuous as possible, as was his habit whenever
he needed to check how things were really going. He stole towards
a group of coolies who weren't exactly overdoing it. Suddenly they
got to work. He was sure he hadn't been spotted yet, so he couldn't
understand the abrupt change.

One of the men gave a warning nod. "Watch it. Dammit-Sahib
coming!"

They were at it hammer and tongs by the time Semotám
came around the corner with his vocabulary list. His loose canvas
pants flapped around his thin legs, now and again he tripped, not
looking where he was going, and he kept scratching his head, as if
thinking hard about something.

Dammit-Sahib. Had Tom heard right? Where had they gotten
that from? Semotám tottered across to the knot of workmen and
pointed to a group of badly laid bricks. He obviously wanted to say
something, but he was floundering among the pages of his Czech-

Hindi dictionary, ruffling them backwards and forwards, trying to find what he needed.

"Dammit, where is it," he mumbled. "Dammit, I've seen it somewhere." The men were nudging each other.

"How do you say it, dammit. Ah, here it is!" Dammit-Sahib beamed triumphantly and delivered the relevant sentence from his notes. The coolies listened with smiles playing on their lips and began dismantling the bricks.

"So that's Dammit-Sahib," Tom chuckled as he made his way back to the office. "I wonder what those dawdlers call me."

When my mother was completely well again, she said it was time for me to learn to read. She gave me a book full of pictures and letters and taught me how the letters went together to make up words. I could write *DAN* and wanted to know how to write *RACHEL* and *TOM*. I practiced all day long. *Tom* was easy, but *Rachel* is tough for beginners. I had a lot of fun tracing around the letters with crayons and decorating them with the faces and bodies of people and animals, outlines of the temples we had seen, or the flowers and trees that grew everywhere around. My father would try to find the original letters or numbers hiding among my drawings. "Come on, let me see those darn doodles," he would say as he sat down to dinner.

Again and again my mother told me I had to study. "Knowledge is important," she would say.

Sluggish footsteps reached us from the hallway. "Knowledge is no guarantee of anything." A suntanned forearm in a rolled-up shirt appeared on the doorframe. My father stood there with a skeptical smile and a cigarette hanging from his lips. He was mumbling and his words traveled on whiskey fumes. "Far from it. People who overstress education create a false sense of security for themselves."

"What?" Rachel squinted uneasily at the corner of his

shirt poking out of his pants, and at his unbuttoned collar. Unconsciously she ran a hand down her own blouse to check that she was put together, and waited.

"Yes, a false sense of security. The security that comes from feeling superior to the uneducated. So the *educated* are proud of something that doesn't exist." He casually removed the cigarette from his lips and continued pontificating. "Knowing something for a fact, my son, does not mean you have learned anything. The depth of real human knowledge can't be measured by the quantity of known facts, can it, Mommy?"

She turned to me unhappily. "Go and get washed, Dan. Daddy's a bit overworked today."

I left overworked Daddy and scowling Mommy alone together. From the stairs I could hear her telling him that he was right as usual, but that he might consider keeping it to himself, if he didn't mind.

"Don't go confusing him, Tom. You don't have anything against him learning to read and write, do you?"

He agreed with her about that, and then her tone changed. "What happened? Are you all right?"

"Absolutely. We've just had a little party. We've handed over a brand new set of homes for the snakes. Baťa's Czechoslovak-Indian workforce now has roofs over their heads, though they occasionally have to share them with the denizens of the local jungle. Glorious! You can take a look around tomorrow."

Batanagar. Baťa's city on the banks of the Hoogli. The river was alive with passing barges, boats laden with rice, construction materials, jute. Corpses wrapped in cloths.

Thomas had planned the project with Karfík years ago: the railway would be brought through. The port would be here, the factory there, the administration block, the workmen's homes. Now the houses smelled of fresh paint and drying concrete. The pavement was covered in gravel and the occasional cobra.

Tom took Rachel around: little brick boxes with white trim in an orderly row. Living-dining room, kitchen and cook's quarters on the ground floor, three bedroom suites and a balcony upstairs. Bamboo fences. They looked like sugar cubes.

"We can move in. Take your pick."

Her eyes bulged. "Me? I...No! I don't want to."

"But everyone else is here. Even Bartoš. We're among the last few not to have moved in. Don't you like it? It's just like the house in Zlín."

"Just like? It's not like it at all! It's completely different! There's nothing to do here. Look at it! Look around you!"

He said nothing, thrust his hands in his pockets, and quietly counted to ten. He knew how this would end.

"What do the women do here when their men are at work? Embroidery? Knitting? I'm no good at embroidery, I don't want to do embroidery!"

He crossed from the window to the door and back. He fished his silver cigarette case out of his pocket and cautiously patted his other pockets. He located his lighter. He rolled it between his hands as if warming it.

"I couldn't stand it! There's someone to do the cooking, a nanny for the kids, and it's an hour to town by car, so what the hell do they do all day? What *can* they do?"

He clicked the cigarette case open, took out a cigarette, and snapped the case shut by reflex. He tapped the cigarette against the case and rolled it between his hands as well.

"Well, tell me!"

He turned his back on her. He ran his thumb across the little knurled wheel and the lighter flared. He brought it up towards his face, jammed the cigarette between his lips, and pushed the other end into the flame. He took a deep pull. The tobacco crackled and blazed orange.

"I don't want to move. Our house in town has character and—"

He removed his cigarette and exhaled the smoke. "Crumbling plaster, mold in the corners—" He had said whatever came to mind, hoping to defer the inevitable by a few seconds.

She dismissed his idle attempt with a wave of the hand. "It's not that bad, and it isn't even very expensive. We can afford it. If you don't want to pay for it, I've still got Aunt Esther's money. I can use that. Tom, I...I'm used to it there. Here it's so..."

He kept pulling on his cigarette, the cigarette case and lighter now back in his pockets. He gazed at her through the smokescreen behind which he was hiding like a bulletproof shield.

His silence infuriated her. "I don't want to! I like your job, I respect it, but we don't have to live at the factory because of it. You can see it from the window and it's just around the corner. I'd go mad here. We're not going to swap our banyan trees for this bush country with a factory. I don't want it!"

He looked at her as if he were watching a play. Like a consummate actress she clasped a hand to her bosom and sobbed.

"And Daniel! When he goes away to school, I'll... I'll die here!" She was about to collapse. Then she saw that he was laughing.

He put up his arms as if staring down the barrel of a gun. "Enough! Enough! Stop! Spare me the agony! My heart's bleeding!"

She put her fingers to her lips and tried to calm down. Her hand was itching to hit him. She couldn't stand his amused, indulgent expression.

"All right," he said. "We'll stay in town."

"You don't mind?"

How could he mind? She was still shifting her feet like a stubborn child. He couldn't refuse. It wasn't worth the fire and brimstone. "They'll point at us and call us anti-social, but what wouldn't I do for your peace of mind?" And for his own.

The next time he came in from the site, my father opened the mail and leafed through the month-old, September 1937 issue of *Svět*. He chortled with delight and began reading aloud a piece on the construction of the Zlín skyscraper:

> The seventy-seven meter tall administrative building will house a staff of two hundred. The skeleton went up in five months. One floor every ten days! It rises to sixteen stories all linked by four elevators: an elevator for visitors, a paternoster lift, and a service elevator; but the pièce de résistance is the office of the company head—an office in an elevator, with air-conditioning, a sink, pneumatic mail delivery, electric outlets, and a telephone. So the boss can pop up on any floor, behind anyone's back.

Dad smirked. How had they contrived to put a sink in the elevator?

They signed me up for an English school. I really didn't like the idea of boarding, but the fact that I was going to be in the same class as Sam McCormick put me at ease. His real name was Samuel, but everyone called him Sam. His dad was an officer in the British Army, who sometimes came with his wife, Betsy, to visit my parents. I preferred going to their house, because Sam's elder brother Rupert had a rifle and during the holidays he taught us how to fire it.

Mr. McCormick was a typical English gentleman. He would sit in the living room or on the terrace behind his newspaper, which gave him theoretical protection from the verbal onslaughts of his energetic wife. In his hand he would have a cigar the size of a stick of salami. He rarely spoke, just a word now and then, as if they were precious gems. One whole clause coming from him was as rare as rain in the desert.

On a couple of occasions he invited my father to his club. "So, did you have a good time with Mr. McCormick?" My mother would ask when my father got back. "I'd be intrigued to know whether he actually *speaks* at his gentlemen's club."

"Yes, when he orders the whiskey."

Betsy McCormick, on the other hand, had plenty to say for both of them. Mostly she went on about problems with the servants and the unbearable climate of Calcutta. Here and there she would skate onto the thin ice of how the boys should be brought up. Such a responsibility, such a burden to be borne by her shoulders alone, yes, just imagine, alone, with no help. Or did you think that that husband of hers, that waxwork with a cigar, ever got involved? He never lifted a finger, unless it was to light another cigar. Left everything to her. One day she would stuff some dynamite down his cigar, she giggled, and went babbling on.

I knew what my new school was like because we had been there once with the McCormicks to visit Rupert. Each boy had the full paraphernalia: uniform, textbooks, gym bag. We had gone for a walk around the grounds, looked into the classrooms and the boys' studies, ambled around the tennis courts and playing fields. It had all smacked of discipline and a rod of iron. I felt pangs in the pit of my stomach. The ritual of mealtimes made the greatest impression on me. The whole school gathered for lunch at once, pushing and squabbling, then sat down and instantly stopped talking. A graveyard silence descended, plates steamed, but no one touched his food. All you could hear was the sound of breathing. Then a man in a black gown and a funny hat appeared with a little flag in his hand. With all eyes turned towards him he slowly and solemnly raised the flag above his head like before a race. Then he lowered the flag. Now! And a symphony of knives and forks on plates broke out.

Before I went away to school, Mom taught me how to keep my things neat and clean. She insisted it was a matter of principle and she was uncompromising. It was interesting that she was less concerned about my messy desk, or the books and pencils scattered here and there, than about unfolded clothes or unpolished shoes, which drove her berserk. "Your room's a disaster," she would say. When, in my own defense, I pointed out that Dad didn't clean up after himself either, she blew her top. Over dinner that night she announced that it would do *neither of us* any harm to watch where we dropped things.

Dad's mouth muscles froze in mid-chomp. He looked as if he'd never heard such heresy. "I don't know about you, Daniel, but my things are *always* tidy," he said.

I assumed the same expression. "Mine too."

Mom exhaled with a hissing sound, stiffly laid aside her knife and fork, stabbed us through with her eyes, and marched out of the dining room. We winked conspiratorially at each other, but then couldn't resist going to check where she had gone.

My mother was unpredictable. She had run upstairs and into my room. She didn't need to look far. Just inside the door there was a pile of clothes; two drawers of the antique chest hung half-open exposing a jumble of socks and underwear; bits of modeling clay, a brand-new pencil case and two dog-eared exercise books graced the floor under the table, and some crutches and my book bag lay a little way off. The desk looked as if a bomb had hit it. But the real bomb was still only smoldering: she scooped the clothes up from the floor, flitted the length and breadth of the room, sometimes tripping, her arms full of dirty socks and underwear. She paused and crammed them into one of the half-open drawers, which she pulled all the way out; she swept everything off the desk into it, threw the pencil case and exercise books on top, and hurtled past us out of the room.

Red in the face, she propped the drawer on the window ledge, holding it level with one hand while she flung wide the shutter with her other hand.

I couldn't believe my eyes. My underwear, socks, shirts, pencils, and exercise books went whizzing out the window and floating down into the busy street below. "No...don't...not that..." I spluttered.

"Mess overboard," she snapped.

I watched, paralyzed, as passers-by looked up, bewildered to see what strange rain the gods had sent down on them, dodging each flying object, then nudging one another in amusement as they realized it was the contents of a boy's wardrobe. I felt Dad staring at me as I hurried downstairs to gather up my intimate possessions and school things just as the last ones landed. The utter shame! Before I had gathered everything up, another load descended.

As I stood in the hall with my bundle of clothes and broken pencils, it flashed through my mind that it must be Dad's turn next. I deposited my load on the shiny checkerboard of the tiled floor and sprang up the stairs two at a time.

My parents were having a debate through the closed bedroom door. Mom was pounding her fist on the oak and demanding to be let in. Dad had exploited the advantage of being second in line and barricaded himself in. From his refuge he was trying to make a deal.

"Promise me you won't throw my underwear in the street and I'll let you in."

"Open up!"

"You have to promise, or I'm afraid we'll be spending the night apart. And you wouldn't want that, would you?"

"Coward! Stop making threats and open that door!"

After some moments of uneven battle, Mom gave up and promised what he asked. He even made her swear she wouldn't get revenge. After they'd had it all out, Dad came to help me get my things together. He called it solidarity. I was grateful, though I would have liked to see him running around the street after his socks under the unpleasant gazes of inquisitive bystanders. The embarrassment of it!

Between December and March, a cold wind would blow down from the peaks of the Himalayas, briefly driving the heat from the streets of Calcutta and its clammy houses. In April, the wind would change direction and the hot air of the south would hold all India in thrall once more. Extreme temperatures, extreme drought. Then in the summer the long-awaited monsoon rains came, which lasted until September. If they didn't arrive, the place would be stricken by murderous heat and starvation. In late September and October, the wind would turn back again, bringing with it the threat of tropical cyclones.

News kept arriving from Europe. Munich. The area inside Czechoslovakia's borders was annexed on September 29, 1938. Two weeks later, the Wehrmacht occupied the Sudetenland.

"It can't be! What a con! They've sold us for a pocketful of lies like some lousy whore. That idiot Daladier. And Chamberlain. Aristocratic jerk!" That was one of the rare occasions when Dad was really angry.

Rachel put a hand on her forehead. "I can't believe it. Germany. The land of Beethoven, Goethe, Schiller. Heine!"

Tom gave a snide laugh. "And what about Nietzsche? I guess there were always more cretins than normal people among the Germans and we just never spotted it. They got pounded during the first war and now they're crawling back out of the woodwork and dusting off their epaulettes. They cheer on that bastard with the moustache and swallow all the bull he churns out as if it were the bible. But I say, once a Prussian, always a Prussian."

She stared at him. He never spoke like that. "But Tom, you've got German blood yourself!"

"That's what frightens me. Treitschke, Nietzsche, Hitler. Hear how they rhyme? The myth of the Übermensch who can do anything in the name of innate superiority! Isn't it insane?"

"But Nietzsche's indifference to the sufferings of others is a long way from wanting to harm anyone."

"Is that less depraved? The net result, my dear Rachel, the net result is the same."

Everyone considered my father an optimist because of his even temper, but it wasn't true. Rather, it was my mother who

89

held out for the good in everyone. He harboured no such illusions. After the events of 1938, my father had no doubt that the Germans were serious about racial purity, and that any Jew who got in their way was a potential corpse.

Dusk

Dusk crept in through the heavy air and gently falling snow as we sat together at Anna's table. My posture was strange, as still as if I were holding my breath.

Sudden voices and laughter in the corridor. Ellen and Nick were coming back in.

I glanced apologetically at Anna. "I'll be right back."

I caught up with them. Nicky hung on my neck and flooded me with an exalted report of the day's events. Ellen said nothing, just gave me that look. I tried to smile, my lips slow and stiff.

"Anna used to know... Rachel," I said.

She nodded and gently touched the creases above my eyes. "I'm having a nice evening with Nick. Will you come and clink glasses at midnight?"

After the events of '38, my father was convinced that the fate of Czechoslovakia was sealed. Ten years later, when Ghandi was assassinated in January 1948, he just sat there and said nothing. A month later we read in the papers that the Czech Communist Party had taken control, and my father, who hardly ever swore, said that now we were really fucked.

Back in Anna's sitting room, I studied the picture over the

mantelpiece, the young man in uniform whose eyes were like unshelled almonds. When Anna saw me looking, she smiled.

"That's Michael when he graduated from West Point. He was born right after the war, in '46."

She placed a scruffy leather-bound journal on the table.

"My husband was enraptured. I could never have imagined that a man who had lived through the war would display such unfeigned joy because of a baby. You know, I get lonely sometimes. He lives in New York with his wife and he doesn't get much time off, so we only see each other twice a year. As if he were living on another planet. They go to Mexico for Christmas and then fly back after New Year's Day and do a detour to come and see me. Nancy doesn't ski, so they never stay long, but I'm grateful even for the four days I can have them. They don't have children. Not that they can't, but Nancy has her career and still feels young. And children, well they're a burden, they say. Just between you and me, she isn't that young anymore, she'll be thirty-five next year. And children, a burden? That's just an excuse, they're too self-absorbed, too selfish and can't be bothered, that's what it is. But I don't say anything, it's their business, they can do without sermons from me.

"They keep inviting me to New York, but what would I do there? Imagine an old woman like me in that Babylon. My legs quake even at the idea of flying to Prague, yet once it was my home. But New York? I tell them, let's not talk about it, the papers say people shoot each other in the street in broad daylight. Of course they think I'm a funny old thing. They tell me not to watch so much television, there's more than just criminals and junkies in New York.

"When Michael was about to go to Vietnam, I went crazy. I was so afraid I'd never see him again. He always wanted to be like his father."

Lost in thought, Anna stroked the brown leather of the dilapidated journal, the jottings of her frontline soldier.

VI

The Witch Savitri

In December of 1938, Baťa launched a new kind of waterproof shoe on the Indian market. Shop windows displayed metal bowls of water with shoes bobbing in them. *In wet and dry.* They were an immediate hit; the Indians went wild over them. They cost fifteen *annas* a pair.

In the middle of January our dog, Amon, died. My father said he'd reached that age. I cried a lot; he'd been in the family since before I was born. I missed him terribly.

Then, in February of 1939, my mother's sister, Regina, wrote us a letter that changed our lives completely:

Erik, Lily, and little Irma have emigrated. They're in England now. Lily has some relatives there, but I don't know where they'll end up. Mother fell ill soon after; it's become clear she's actually been ill for some time. There's no hope. The doctors say she has a month left, maybe two. I've taken time off because it would be hard for Father to look after her. They talk about you all the time. I think life's playing games with us. Father finally seemed to have come around after his stroke last year, but everything has begun to slide back again. You'd hardly recognize them.

Thomas could hear the despair in his own voice, which was failing.

"Rachel, try to understand. We can't go back!"

"My mother is dying."

"I know. I know it's hard, but we can't go back now."

"I have to go back! I owe it to her."

"Rachel – "

"I haven't seen her since you and I met."

His throat tightened. "There's going to be a war. It's—suicide." He couldn't swallow. He was sticking a leg out to stop a train.

"I have to go home. If you won't come with me, I'm going alone!"

"You can't do that."

"I will!"

She shot out of her chair and slammed the door behind her.

Thomas remained sitting in the garden till dusk, stifled by the muggy heat, and listened to the evening ritual of the parched earth. Thousands of leaves in the tops of the banyan trees, like naked hearts with sharp tips, ready to defend their own vulnerability. The cicadas brought darkness. The clamor of night invaded his life.

I made my farewells. To India. To Kavita and her embraces, songs, and incantations. To the people with their countless stories and gods. A small pack on my back, I became a pilgrim against the flow of time.

I'd never been on an airplane before. It seemed incredible that the heap of metal would actually lift itself off the ground. It was against nature, against all logic. We rose into the sun, and the land below us looked like an enormous map, without frontiers or customs regulations, without watchtowers. I had turned into a giant and was striding with seven-league boots over deserts and mountains, and I saw rivers like thin threads, like tiny veins on the curved body of mother earth. One day I'll be a pilot, I vowed. Definitely. Behind us we left Calcutta and Batanagar, now the biggest shoe factory in India. It employed six thousand Indians and a handful of Czechoslovaks. My father was no longer one of them.

We landed in Vienna and switched to the train. On the evening of Sunday, March 12, I alighted at the station in the town of my birth—a town I didn't know. Zlín. Not even my parents recognized it. In six years it had grown by thousands of inhabitants and hundreds of houses and other buildings. The skyscraper as the modern city's landmark, the Tomáš Baťa Memorial in glass and concrete, schools and film studios. The uniformity of style; the parks and gardens.

Three days later, snow floated down incessantly onto the roofs of the little brick houses while armored cars, personnel carriers, and motorcycles streamed across the flimsy frontier of the Protectorate. The Legionnaires in front of Prague Castle were replaced by a battalion of Death's Heads, clad in black to render homage to Hitler. Winston Churchill sulked, but that was no help. Czechoslovakia became a ghost.

We were swimming against the tide. By then a lot of the Baťa management were already out of the country, yet we were coming home to Zlín. We moved into a vacant house near the woods. Hallway, living room, kitchen, and powder room on the ground floor; three bedrooms, dressing rooms, and bathroom upstairs. The house had a glazed veranda with a terrace, a cellar, a garage, and a little garden facing the woods. We collected our piano from the Wassermans—an ebony Petrof. Dad had bought it for Mom's birthday a week before their wedding.

My mother set off to Prague to visit Grandma. She phoned to say that we should come. My grandparents wanted to meet me.

In Prague, a new world opened before me. The handle of the door to the Vinohrady apartment was so high up I could barely reach it. An affable gentleman appeared, walking with a stick. He had a short but full greying beard and pince-nez on his aquiline nose. He gazed at Dad for a long time, his eyes like little balls of quicksilver. They had never seen each other before; now they stood face to face, gazing at each other as though a wordless dialogue passed between them. Seconds and minutes went by in awkward silence, and I waited throughout that eternity for someone to finally speak.

I slipped my hand into Dad's. He looked at me and winked.

"Come on, say hello to Grandpa, Daniel. Or has the cat got your tongue?"

The old man laughed. "Come in, you strangers from faraway, let's get to know each other at last." He shook my hand and put on an official expression.

I liked him. I had always wanted a grandfather like that. With a strange tightness in my throat, I crossed the threshold. High ceilings, stucco, and antique furniture, the place engulfed in Persian carpets, some even hanging on the walls, clocks ticking in every corner.

Grandma. Dwarfed by her goose-down quilt, she looked like a girl, tiny and feeble, a sickly child with the face of an old woman. The massive bed only magnified her fragility. Eyes full of pain, lost in a web of wrinkles, skin cracked like earth in the dry season. I gave her my hand. She grabbed it eagerly, held on, and tried to say something, but instead she burst into tears. Her slight hand, those bony fingers with their prominent, swollen knuckles hid a surprising strength. It was as if my hand were in a vice; she squeezed it as if she would never let go of me. It was unpleasant. I felt uncomfortable and wanted to get out of there. I looked around the shadowy room and breathed in a smell that suddenly made my stomach heave: a whiff of age and approaching death.

Mom freed me from Grandma's iron grasp and sent me to Grandpa. The old housemaid, Margit, was just serving supper. In the dining room, Dad and Grandpa were at a huge oval table

THE SOUND OF THE SUNDIAL

that could easily have sat twelve. They were obviously discussing something serious.

Grandpa saw how taken I was by the antique sideboard, made from the same wood as the table and chairs. "If only some of these pieces of furniture could speak, that would be something," he winked at me.

He tapped the tabletop. Walnut. He told me that two hundred years ago, a French count had it made as a wedding present for his betrothed. As the cabinetmaker was putting in the finishing touches and the wedding preparations began, life had taken up the cards and reshuffled them: the count's beloved didn't live to see her own wedding, and so the fate of this furniture changed course.

By the window, the dining room took an L-shaped turn, with the living room around the corner. I caught my breath: in an alcove on a raised platform stood a grand piano. Mom had once told me all about it; she said it was *sacred*. A Bösendorfer: a mahogany giant that had been handed down from generation to generation. To play or practice on such an instrument was a great honor. Angular lines, delicate mechanics, a wooden music stand, and two brass candle holders.

Dad left immediately on the Sunday, but I stayed for two weeks; an incredible fourteen days with Grandpa. I would sidle up the gloomy staircase and finger the elaborately wrought banisters with their wooden handrail, worn with the patina of dozens of years and hundreds of hands. I would run my own hand over the grain and imagine all those people who had touched it. The matriarchs of the past squeezed into corsets and crinolines that rustled at every step; worthy, top-hatted gentlemen; neatly pressed young ladies in dainty gloves.

Mom and her sister, Regi, looked after Grandma, helped by the ancient Margit, while Grandpa introduced me to Prague and bathed me in the wellspring of Jewish wisdom. The old professor of history was the best possible guide to Prague, with its undertone of servitude and its gloss of majesty. The city, in all its shame and glory, seemed to want me to find out its secrets, but somehow it still remained mysterious. Vyšehrad, Petřín, the gardens that were gradually coming to life; Prague Castle and the *orloj*—the astronomical clock on the Old Town Hall. The legend of Master Hanuš with his eyes gouged out through human folly. *Orloj* comes from the Latin *horologium*, Grandpa told me.

The Jewish cemetery. The Old-New Synagogue. In the gloom of its Gothic walls stood an old man with a yarmulke on his bald head. His lips released the colors of Hebrew words, he swayed to their rhythm, hunched into himself, a bundle of atoms making up a human frame beneath a prayer shawl, stooping over a book of psalms, putting on his leather phylacteries. For the first time in my life I heard Hebrew spoken, I saw the Torah and listened to stories from the time of Abraham and Sarah. I dropped off to sleep with an image of Moses in my head: the sea parting before him and the Jews leaving Egypt. I added a stone to the grave of Rabbi Löw, and in my dreams I searched the lost corners of Josefov for the *shem* so I could bring the Golem to life.

"Why do we put stones on the grave, and not flowers?" I asked.

"Because we come from inhospitable lands, from deserts and highlands where flowers are hard to find. The stone means the same as a flower: that you have stood by the grave of the deceased and thought of him."

Grandpa gave me a leather-bound copy of Hans Christian Andersen's fairy tales, full of eerie illustrations. A dog with huge eyes, shining like lanterns out of the yellowed paper, guarded some treasure. He looked a bit funny, and his furrowed brow reminded me of Amon.

And then a celebration: Passover. The Jewish holiday of spring, in memory of Moses and the Exodus. Passover comes from *pessah*, which means to pass by, leave out. *Yahweh* would go from house to house, and wherever he did not see a mark of blood, he struck down the firstborn son. He passed over the homes of the Israelites.

On the eve of the holiday there was a festive supper, the Seder. I ate matzos: *". . . in all your habitations shall ye eat unleavened bread."* The meal was served on blue-and-white Rosenthal china. During the evening the Haggadah was read, a retelling of the story of Moses, how he led his people out of their Egyptian bondage, wandered through the wilderness and crossed the Red Sea.

Grandpa told me how my mother used to be nervous before Seder, because, as the youngest, she had to recite the *Mah Nishtanah*—the so-called Four Questions. She would fidget during the reading of the Haggadah, and could never manage to sit through to the end. She would run around making faces at Regi and Erik.

He fell into a reverie and said that the last twenty years had been the first years of this free and beautiful Republic. Then he grew sad.

"And now it's over." He blew across his palm, as if blowing a kiss. "Puff, and it's gone."

He gave me a pocket watch—the first watch I ever had. A Remontoir patent, big Roman numerals and a tiny winder, with a second hand, too. I opened the back. Sparkling and perfect. An interplay of delicate wheels, minuscule teeth that interlocked and spun the web of time. Fifteen jewels and grandpa's monogram in gold.

Meeting my Prague grandfather marked me profoundly, indelibly. I left there with a sense of having discovered another god. Years later I understood that I had discovered something more: primordial matter. Roots that belonged to me, and someone who had parted the ground cover and showed me how deep they went.

I never saw him again.

Grandma died on the first Sunday in May, and I left Prague with a number of picture books, all of them about history.

A few days after she died, I was poking around on a pale green, miserable plate of stewed kohlrabi, picking out minute slivers of meat and pushing the rest to one side. I couldn't stomach it. No matter how it was cooked, my taste buds could never come to terms with it or its insipid color. I fidgeted on my chair as if I had worms, wondering how to dispose of the stuff. To draw attention away from my ever-fuller plate, I decided to make a momentous declaration, and with all the earnestness at my command I announced to my parents that I was going to devote the rest of my life to studying history.

Dad stopped chewing and raised an eyebrow.

"Oh? And why?"

"Because history teaches us how to live. History is life's teacher."

I paused for effect, so that what I said next would hit home. "*Historia magistra vitae*," I parroted Grandpa's beautiful, ringing Latin words that sprang from the depths of human cognition.

Mom smiled admiringly and nodded, but Dad refused to be dazzled.

"History teaches us that we're unteachable," he mumbled with his mouth full, indolently sticking his fork in a piece of kohlrabi.

It was all very confusing.

For my eighth birthday I got the most beautiful present ever. The tiny ball of fluff tottered around the kitchen, its paws flopping away in every direction and its bewildered eyes blinking helplessly at me. I cradled it in my arms and shrieked with glee.

"Come to me, little one. I wonder what your name is."

"It still hasn't got one. But it ought to start with B. Mom thinks it should be called Benaiah."

"Good. And I'll call it Benny."

My parents smiled at my rapid-fire decision. The puppy was a German shepherd. Dad said he could become sharp as mustard if I trained him right.

"He's the most gorgeous puppy I've ever seen!"

We became inseparable. Wherever I happened to be, there too was Benny. For the first time in my life someone belonged to me, was mine and mine alone, depended on me, and I was seized with fits of boundless care and anxiety for him.

Dad would take the puppy's head in his hands and say: "Benny my boy, your master's going to make a real sissy out of you."

That really got to me, so one day I took Benny away to be trained right. I stuck out my chest and requested Mr Šaler turn him into a *real* dog for me. "Come back in a couple of months' time," he said, "when he's six months old."

July 22, 1939—Zlín
Thomas was summoned by his boss, Mr Hlavnička. He sat in an armchair behind mountains of paper.

"I've got an overseas project for you, since you were looking for one. But it's a bit out of the way."

"Where?"

"Argentina."

"Argentina, eh? Okay."

"Okay? Great. Let me know what you need. And Thomas?" Hlavnička's tone was urgent. "Set off as soon as you can."

Thomas attempted a smile and disappeared out the door.

In the evening, the entire sky over Zlín darkened. Summer storms rampaged through the streets of the town like an evil omen. Hailstones the size of eggs came crashing down on greenhouses, windows, storefronts, leaving a havoc of crystal in their wake.

Rachel was still loath to believe the dreadful news seeping in from Germany like mildew through old walls. The furrows on my father's brow deepened by the day; my mother's willful blindness made him despair.

"You still don't get it, do you? You want to stay and see German thoroughness in practice? Here is Hitler's solution to the Jewish problem: they'll strip you of your rights, kick you out into the street, steal every last cent of your money, and finally stand you up against a wall!"

"Are you afraid of *people*?"

"Yes, I am," said Dad.

"Goethe said you can only be afraid of people if you don't know them."

"Well, I prefer the saying: The better I know people, the more I love dogs."

He clicked his fingers and whistled. Benny came running and lay his head in my father's lap.

My mother laughed tersely. "Sharks are everywhere, not just in the sea, Tom."

It was hard for him to fight her denial when people all around were afflicted by blindness. They couldn't or wouldn't see that the young Czechoslovak Republic had disappeared through the trapdoor of history and nothing would ever be the same.

August 22, 1939—Zlín
"Rachel! Our permits have arrived. There are just a few formalities left, but they've promised to sort them out quickly."

"My father's got pneumonia."

In her reddened eyes he could read a thought that scared him.

"But Rachel, we have to go!"

"So take Dan and I'll follow later."

"Don't you get it? I can't leave you here!"

August 24, 1939—Prague
Rachel's father, Otto Weinstein, had missed his footing. He didn't remember much, but his stick might have slipped. He had fallen

over and broken his leg at the top, and then caught pneumonia. His funeral was only two days later. Both of his daughters saw him off on his final journey.

August 31, 1939—Zlín
Thomas sat on his packed suitcases and checked off items on the list of things he must not leave without.

"What's this, Rachel?"

"A present for Regi. I'm saying goodbye to her tomorrow."

"But we'll only have half an hour between trains."

"I have to say goodbye to her."

"There won't be time!"

"I tell you, I'm not going to leave without saying goodbye. Do you understand?"

She was shouting desperately. Her voice was a dagger, a garden of fear.

Her fragility pained him. He walked over and clasped her in his arms. His hands shook as he inhaled the smell of her tears.

I checked my own suitcase and kept asking things, a stream of questions in no logical order, anything that flashed into my mind. Dad pulled answers to every bit of nonsense from his deep well of knowledge, tossing some new item into his hand luggage every now and then. That evening he was smiling. He looked relieved of some huge burden.

At ten-thirty he chased me to my room.

"For the fifth time, go to bed, Dan. I don't want to have to say it again. I *will not* say it again."

With all the excitement I couldn't get to sleep. Argentina, Argentina, Argentina, I repeated it over and over again like a magic spell. When I fell asleep at last, I was transported back to India.

We went away to the mountains in June. It was cooler in

Darjeeling in the summer, and that was a welcome relief from the sweltering humidity of Calcutta. The humble cottages of the hill folk, farms like little matchboxes clinging to hillsides, and the modest Nepalese who raised cattle and grew tea. During the summer season, the climate of Darjeeling became an oasis in the desert for the wealthy. The journey there was endless and exhausting. Our black Chevrolet chugged bravely up the hills, bumping along the rough roads, with the steering wheel sweating under the burden of my father's hands. Over the last few miles the road twisted and turned like a serpent and we had to make frequent stops while my mother threw up. All those hairpins were more than her poor stomach could take.

Darjeeling. Tennis courts, cafés, cinemas, horse racing and beautiful swarthy maidens in woven wraps. We lived with Mrs. Tenduf-la from Tibet at the Hotel Windermere, set in a fabulous garden. In the half-light of daybreak, a dense mist would cover the valley, gradually lifting to reveal the panorama of mountains floating above the clouds. Shreds of mist reflected the purple of the sun, Kanchenjunga reared up to heaven among them, and finally there was Mount Everest, like a crystal spike. Indians believed that long, long ago the mountains were flying elephants. Solid as rocks, indomitable and unyielding. The king of the gods, thousand-eyed Indra, grew angry at their obstinacy and punished them cruelly, cutting off their wings.

After a two-day rest in the Darjeeling mountains, Thomas would go back to stifling Calcutta. One day, the wall facing the garden at the back of the house started to bulge, and two days later half the plaster came crashing down. It took him all of Sunday to clear up the mess, a seemingly endless mountain of debris, and during the week he sent three of the workmen to re-render it.

As he gazed at the fresh plaster, smooth and level, with no pits and no bubbles, he had an idea.

He pulled together a plumb line, a spirit level, and an outsized protractor and T-square. He slipped his folding rule and hammer into his pocket. He screwed two planks together at a right angle, and after careful measurement, stuck a needle from Rachel's sewing basket into just the right spot to serve as a gnomon. He waited until the stroke of midday, and then ran up and down beside the wall with his primitive goniometric instrument and the plumb line in his hand. The wall was nearly perfect. It faced south, with just the slightest deflection eastwards. He laughed for joy to discover that the wall's azimuth was a mere ten degrees.

He drew out the whole device on a large sheet of paper, scribbling formulas onto it and checking everything against his astronomy reference books and tables. Then from a piece of stiff cardboard he cut out a right-angled set-square to serve as a template for anchoring the polos. He put a steel rod in the vice and bent it to the required angle according to his template. Then he hammered the shorter end of the angled rod flat and went outside. There wasn't a cloud in the sky. He propped a ladder against the new plaster and scrambled up, weighed down with rulers and T-squares, taking care not to lose his balance. He transferred his calculations to the wall, measuring and re-measuring to make doubly sure of everything, then descended to collect the steel rod, whose flat end he nailed to the wall. He surrounded it with bricks, waited for them to dry, then painted it with a few flicks of his brush. He was careful not to overdo the paint and to spread it out evenly; he didn't want it trickling down. Having finished the job, he surveyed the large ochre rectangle and its projecting steel rod with a critical eye.

That Tuesday, he called a metalworking shop and explained to the amused foreman what he needed. "Can you do it by Friday?"

"Yes, I can," the foreman assured him.

Tom spent the following Sunday keeping a close eye on the time. He ran outside every hour on the hour, dashed up the ladder again, and traced the shadow of the rod on the wall. At sundown he flopped into the grass, dog-tired and triumphant.

In India the dark doesn't arrive gradually, it falls in an instant, a second, maybe two. It spills out over the scorching land as if at the wave of a magic wand. The inky blue of a Bengal night is a great illusionist.

Three months later, my father came back to Darjeeling to get us. He told us he had renovated a number of major stores in Maharashtra, and on his travels, he had met up with an English archaeologist, who had told him with great excitement about one of the most wonderful experiences of his career—a discovery: rock temples carved into grey cliffs. Ajanta. Sacred Buddhist caves in the wooded gorge in front of the waterfalls on the River Waghora, granite cliffs, monasteries, and temples. Bats and snakes in the dusts of time, like guardians of sacred mysteries. Frescoes of the Buddha and all his past lives.

"Can you imagine it?" Dad asked us. "The dim half-light of passageways, internal courtyards, narrow corridors, unexpected galleries, dark wells, and silence. Stairways worn smooth over the ages by the passage of thousands of bare feet."

My mother closed her eyes and laid her head back.

"I want to see them. I must see those frescoes. Promise me."

We were on the way back to Calcutta. Forests of chestnut and magnolia on the lower slopes of the Himalayas. Darjeeling and tea. Then we crossed the Tropic of Cancer, where the landscape became truly tropical. Bengal. Masses of water in vast riverbeds. Palm groves alternating with tall reed beds and stands of fern. Mangroves in the delta. Hovels in the villages, bamboo shacks roofed with straw, their walls of compacted clay. And finally Calcutta. A seaport. Malaria, cholera, tuberculosis.

It was dark before we reached home. Zam had dinner ready, but apart from the ever-ravenous Amon, none of us felt like eating. I fell asleep with my head full of images. Rock temples and portraits of the Buddha, the damp smell of dark corners in caves that hadn't seen the sunlight for millennia.

In the morning, I was running my spoon round the edge of my bowl of porridge and watching Mom. Two narrow slits for eyes and her head as heavy as the world itself. It slipped lower and lower until she had to prop it up with her hand.

"Mommy, didn't you sleep?"

She blinked.

"Yes, darling? What was that?"

Dad put down his paper.

"Madame, you look as if you haven't slept a wink all night."

He always called her *madame* when he wanted to tease her. He turned to me and asked the time. I looked at the wall clock. It said 1:30.

"The clock stopped," I said.

"Rachel, do *you* know what time it is?" my father said.

She shook her head and dropped her chin into her hand.

"Come with me then."

It sounded like an invitation to go for a ride in a new car. I leapt off my chair.

"You come too, Rachel. Come on, wake up!"

She hauled herself to her feet and followed us outside. A few yards from the house he ordered us to turn around and look back.

There was a sundial on the newly plastered façade. Our house had a face, its mouth wide open as it mirrored the motion of the sun, shafts of golden ochre spreading from the middle of the half-circle, tracing time. And standing out from the wall were three shapes in beaten brass: our signs of the zodiac. Cancer for me at the hyperbola of the summer solstice, Mom's Aries at the equator of the spring equinox, and Dad's Capricorn at the upper hyperbola. Winter solstice.

I was silent with wonder.

"Get up, Dan. We have a long journey ahead of us. I've made you some tea."

India vanished. I was back in Bohemia, and Argentina was calling. Half asleep, I shuffled into the bathroom. Argentina. Argentina. I brushed my teeth and mumbled along. Argentina. Argentina. I liked the sound of it.

"Rachel, darling, get up, please!"

Dad went back to the kitchen and turned on the radio. He poured himself a cup of white coffee.

"Oh God, oh my God!"

My mother came rushing into the kitchen. He had never yelled like that before.

"What's the matter? Tom!"

My father pointed stiffly at the radio.

"What happened?" she asked. "Have you scalded yourself?"

His eyes were wild like a trapped animal. Unrecognizable.

"Hitler invaded Poland!"

We went nowhere. At that instant, Dad's work permit became a worthless scrap of paper. The frontiers were hermetically sealed and we were trapped. But Dad didn't give up. He said he would move heaven and earth to get us out of the country, away from the clutches of that maniac.

Initially, nothing about our lives changed. Delicate gossamer fluttered around us, the air laced with apple cider. A vee-formation of migrating birds in the sky.

I started year two at the Masaryk Experimental Primary School. The first day coming home I caught a butterfly. A yellow brimstone. A little nothing. In India I'd seen butterflies four inches across. *Graphium Agamemnon*—the tailed jay. Mottled like a salamander. Gigantic wings, yellow spots on black velvet. In the darkness of rainforests shot through by flashes of sunlight, it can vanish from view. You wouldn't know it was there.

At the 1930 census, my parents had given their nationality as Czechoslovak. In the "Religion" column they had entered *none*. He was the son of a German and his Czech Catholic wife; she was the daughter of a Czech Jew and a German Jewess.

Thomas's father and his sister Hilda had declared German nationality and had now automatically become citizens of the Reich.

There were demonstrations in Prague. The Germans shut down the universities and started locking up students. Some they executed.

When winter struck, the first I ever experienced in Zlín, it was absolutely freezing. Even the Dřevnice River froze over. Dad gave me some skates and in a few days I could nearly match him for skill. I bullied him into getting me an ice hockey stick so I could go out and play with the other guys. But unlike Venda and Míra Zajíc and Jakub Novotný, I had to be in before dusk. They had to show up for dinner, but afterwards they went back on the ice. I envied them.

Only one time I got lucky. Mom wanted to go to the movies. They were showing a Czech comedy, fittingly titled *Life's a Bitch*. My parents dressed up, gave me some unnecessary advice about what to do if the house caught fire or a stranger came to the door, then assured me they'd back right after the film. At seven-thirty the door closed behind them, and I jubilantly put on my anorak and tossed my skates over my shoulder. At the door I remembered that the boys carried paraffin lamps with them, so I went down to the cellar and grabbed an extremely dusty one.

When I reached the river, the boys cheered. There were only three of them and they were glad to see me because it meant we could have a game. Two against two. I put the paraffin lamp down on the frozen water and Venda got his matches out. The smooth surface of the ice reflected the yellow flickering of the lamp like a mirror, and the snow fell into the silence of our frozen, infantile souls. A snowflake landed on the lamp-glass with a hiss, changing into a droplet of water and trickling down until it vanished. The light from the paraffin lamps made a kaleidoscope, so different from the candles reflected on the river at Benares. Water reflects exactly what it sees, but ice is not the same: it multiplies light, refracts it, plays with it. I was spellbound. The world shattered, chaotic yet transparent. I took one glove off to touch—it was so cold. As though it wanted to trap me, draw me in, it breathed out chill and grabbed my fingertips like suckers.

The furrows from our skates cut through the light. I was in a trance. I skated right and left, but I didn't play well. At that moment the play of light fascinated me more than anything else.

"Daniel?! Daniel!"

It was Mom's voice, trembling with cold or rage. "What are you doing there? Why aren't you at home?"

Why aren't you at the movies? was my first thought, but unlike her, I choked the question back. Dad was standing on the bank next to her, watching the scene as if from a distance.

The showing had begun at eight fifteen with a newsreel. *Reichsprotektor* Neurath's speech affected the audience like a flu virus. Just a couple of people started coughing at first, but then the infection spread like wildfire, jumping from row to row, rising like a wave and flooding the whole cinema until everyone was coughing so loudly that not a word of the muscular rhetoric of the *Reichsprotektor* could be heard. The terrified duty sergeant had commanded silence. When the afflicted failed to obey, he had the lights turned up and the show stopped. The flu-stricken audience were given a stern warning. "Ladies and gentlemen, there must be complete silence! Otherwise I'll have to clear the cinema."

Silence had descended. The sick calmed down and after a short interval the film restarted. The opening sequence of *Life's a Bitch* appeared on screen and the coughing fit was not repeated, but ten minutes into the movie, three Gestapo and an SA officer burst in. They stopped the projection, called up police and gendarme reinforcements, and booted the paying audience out of the cinema.

So my parents had headed for home, and on arrival, found to their surprise that their only child was neither at his desk nor in bed. They had rushed out into the dark to see if they could find their lost son, and now they were standing on the bank and Mom was wringing her hands.

I did not know where to hide. I wanted to burrow into the ground, disappear under the ice.

I slunk to the bank. A delicate situation. I was embarrassed in front of my friends, and at the same time I knew I had violated the trust of my trusting mother. Not that my father didn't trust me, but he had no illusions about anyone or anything. With Mom it was bad. First she would get angry, then she would appeal to my better side. She turned it into a matter of principle and honor, then really tugged at my finer feelings; I had disappointed her and saddened her.

I shrunk to the size of a wretched little beetle, melted under her omniscient gaze, and turned into the kind of pathetic blabbermouth that blurts out everything he knows and much that he doesn't. I was a rotten liar and an even worse man of honor. In the end, she pronounced the verdict:

"No more skating till the ice melts."

For a moment there was silence. Then Dad spoke up for the first time that evening, and declared that never in his life had he heard anything more fiendish. He laughed. "Clever woman, your mom!"

He'd always refrained from comment and silently let it be understood that they sang from the same hymn book. They were as one, bulletproof and unrelenting.

But it turned out this was the one time he intervened in my mother's disciplinary methods. He couldn't seem to help himself;

he slyly translated my mother's injunction: "You're not allowed to go on the river while it's covered with ice, Dan. Once the ice melts, then you can go skating again."

She swore that wasn't at all what she'd meant. The ice had to melt, then freeze again, and then I could go skating again. Was that clear?

Dad stuck out his lower lip and the corners of his mouth drooped. "In other words, when pigs fly."

I was hysterical. "But that means I might not get to skate at all this winter!"

"Exactly," she snapped and went into the house.

My eyes were on Dad. He winked at me.

"I'll try and bring her around tomorrow, but no promises."

I embraced him and poured out my thanks.

He did bring her around. She commuted the sentence to one week; seven days, seven nights of indescribable torment. Every day I watched the ice on the river and begged it to hold on, but by the time my sentence expired, the river was awash with gigantic chunks of ice.

Annoying, but still better than nothing. The boys and I got hold of sticks and poked at the pieces; soaking wet and freezing, we dared each other to cross the river without getting our shoes wet. We jumped from one chunk of ice to the next right across to the far bank. I was just balancing on a lump when Mom appeared again out of the blue. I could never figure out how she managed to catch me when I was up to something, but I knew I was in for it this time. I would be totally grounded, and would probably have to do some unpleasant chore as well.

"Now you've had it," she said.

I jumped onto another chunk of ice floating close to the bank, rammed my stick into the water, and waved dashingly at her so the guys wouldn't think I was a Mama's boy. What came next only took a second.

My stick snapped. The ice was rocking and slippery. Mom's eyes stared wildly, her mouth gaping. The implacable weight of my own body. A short flight, freefall. A loud plop, and I went down under the icy water. Pins and needles, a pain like knives, shards of glass.

I have no idea how I got out of the water or how they got me home. Lost memories started flowing back with the warmth of a bath, Mom's hands, her soothing voice, but then I blacked out again. Dad was there, hazily, carrying me to bed in his strong arms. He was saying something to Mom in a blunt tone.

Still in a fever, I returned to the sultry streets of Calcutta. Everything was dark, as black as Savitri's eyes.

At the height of that hot summer in India, I fell in love for the first time.

I can't remember why, but I had gotten up earlier than usual, and saw my nanny, Kavita, standing by a window that looked onto the street, her arms akimbo as if trying to arrest the avalanche of fat that billowed over her hips. When she saw me she cried: "Come and see! Just look at that guttersnipe of the Shivors! Trash!"

Kavita and Zam shared a blatant contempt for anyone of a lower caste, the scrounging riffraff that roamed the streets of Calcutta.

Through the sleep in my eyes I squinted down. A little girl astride a scrawny mule, tangled cords of hair like a nest of vipers, grubby face and wild, sullen eyes. The ragamuffin, wrapped in scraps of sackcloth, struggled to move the bones beneath her. Stick in hand, she held it like a sword, slammed it down with all her force; behind the one-eyed mule rattled a two-wheeled cart loaded with twigs, all in a jumble, ready to fall into the road. Kavita extended her arm, her index finger outstretched.

"Look at her! That witch. It used to be the old man, but he's

on his last legs, fizzling out in that hovel of theirs, can't even sit up in bed so he sends that little demon. What a fate. Bad karma."
I stood on tiptoe and exhaled throatily.
"What—what's her name?"
"Savitri."
Savitri. Fate. Bare feet, rough, blackened skin on her heels; she jabbed them into the flanks of the barely crawling bag of bones. Savitri, I repeated to myself. Savitri. The dull clatter of wooden wheels on the roadway. Ah, Savitri, my poor Savitri. The sound of her name and of her stick landing on the beast's moth-eaten coat cut into my infant soul like the cruel bit in the mouth of a foundering animal. Her face contracted with exertion and malevolence, her mouth in a grimace, inhuman and crazed.
I gazed at her. Savitri. She might have been my age, perhaps a little more, but it was as if she had lived long before me. She was older by several lifetimes from all the suffering Fate had etched into her features. I felt dizzy from an avalanche of love and revulsion. It made me squeamish just to look at her, but I couldn't pull my eyes away. I wanted to run and hide. I wanted to run to her and take the reins and stick to drive back Fate. But I stood there, feet frozen to the tiled floor, hands fused onto the windowledge, and I couldn't get my breath.
She was like Kali. Red eyes and dark skin, features angular and drawn. Bloody Kali: I had seen a picture of her, hair fluttering free, teeth like fangs, making a terrible clamor as she rode a lion into battle to stop the demon Raktabidja. Adorned with the severed heads, limbs, and entrails of all who had crossed her path, the enraged goddess only calmed down when her husband, Siva himself, fell on his knees before her. At that moment, Kali embraced her husband, cast off her terrifying form, and was transmuted into Gauri, the beautiful, all-embracing mother.
Savitri was cursed. I wanted to fall on my knees before her, I wanted to call her, stop her; there was so much I wanted to do.

114

But I couldn't move or let out a sound. Compassion and terror filled my mouth, bitter and everlasting. I tried to banish her from my dreams, but every morning when I rose, I shuffled to the window and looked down onto the street, waiting for Savitri, the witch. I have never forgotten her.

After two weeks of these dawn awakenings, I left for boarding school. I didn't mind my English school, though I did miss Mom. I thought of Dad too, but I didn't miss him half as much. Probably because he was hardly ever home.

Three months later, I became ill with malaria. My parents came to take me back to Calcutta. Mom cried her eyes out and the doctors stuffed me with quinine. A hemosporid protozoon was tearing my red corpuscles and liver apart. My very first morning back in Calcutta, I rallied a little and waited in a fever by the window. Savitri didn't show.

She never came again. But all my life she pursued me during attacks of malaria. I would see her, on a mangy mule harnessed to a rickety cart, her eyes bloodshot like Kali's. She returned again and again as I was wracked with tremors. The fever took Savitri's form. My delusions bore her name. I would repeat it like a prayer and my helpless mother had no idea who I was summoning. Savitri. She still runs in my blood.

The grim march of Time was not deterred by my boyish hijinks on the ice.

My grandmother, Stella Weinstein, died, and my mother and Aunt Regina divided up her jewelry box between them. Rachel and Regi took some of her things from their parents' house; some they gave to friends and relations, some my mother brought home.

Three months later they were told to surrender all their valuables to the prudent care of the Reich. They were summoned to the Gestapo office in Prague-Střešovice. After being kept waiting for hours they were led inside. A young, handsome Gestapo officer politely said the Third Reich would like to buy the family's two houses in Vinohrady and some land in Jevany. He placed before them a piece of paper on which it said that they were selling the land and houses voluntarily for one million crowns. He wanted them to sign.

"We can't sign. It's all co-owned by our brother, who's abroad. We don't have the authority."

The Gestapo officer calmly explained that it didn't matter, that he wasn't concerned about such details; it wasn't until he started bellowing that he'd have them locked up that they finally understood. They signed "voluntarily."

Regina accompanied Rachel to the station, and as they stood at the ticket office, Rachel suddenly burst out laughing.

"Regina, show me that paper." Regi blinked quizzically at her sister, then rummaged in her handbag and withdrew the document, rubber-stamped and signed by the representative of the Reich. Rachel couldn't stop laughing.

"We sold our house for this scrap of paper! What a bargain! This calls for a drink!"

By the time they headed for the platform, their feet were leaden with wine, and their heads light with freedom from the weight of family property.

My father communicated diligently with Uncle Erik to try and get us to England or America. Permits to emigrate had to be approved by the Gestapo; they were not given to everyone.

It took a whole year for his efforts to bear fruit, but Dad managed to get the affidavit to enable us to go to America. After the gratis transfer of the Weinsteins' property into the claws of the Third Reich, the Gestapo whacked a great big rubber stamp on their exit.

There was one small snag: the consulates of most countries in warring Europe were closed at the time and it was a mammoth task to get transit visas for the countries we had to travel through in order to sail for the New World. To make matters worse, an emigration passport was valid for a limited time only: twelve months. This was a Gordian knot, and finally it was our undoing. By the time we secured our transit visas, the exit permit had expired. This meant starting the whole agony over again. Time was dwindling, and the war was consuming money, days, countries, people.

One day, I watched my father come home from work, sit down in an armchair in the living room, and hide behind his newspaper. I was beavering away at my math homework but my head was swirling with other thoughts.

"Dad, why are the Jews the enemies of mankind?"

The newspaper he held in front of his face slid slowly downwards, like a stage curtain dropping. His wide-open eyes appeared.

"Who told you that?"

"It said so on a leaflet at Schindlers'. It was in their shop window."

"Come here."

His expression was terribly grave, the delicate wrinkles between his eyebrows turned into deep furrows. He rubbed the corners of his eyes with the thumb and forefinger of his right hand.

"The Jews are not the enemy of mankind, Danny. The greatest enemy is men's ignorance and fear. Fear of difference, fear of other cultures, of the things they don't know. Soon the symbols of those other cultures become symbols for their own fear. The Sikh's turban, the Red Indian's headdress, the Muslim headscarf, anything that isn't part of the world they know. The greatest enemy of people is their own stupidity. Do you understand?"

When Spring was supposed to be coming, but was too timid to show its face, we were sitting at dinner and the house was filled with the aroma of onion soup. There were blows on the front door.

The clinking of knives and forks on plates fell silent. Dad set down his silverware.

"Who's there?"

"*Gestapo! Aufmachen!*"

Dad turned the key in the lock. The door flew open and three men marched in.

"Thomas Keppler?"

He nodded. One of the men was wearing leather. He looked at Mom and then at me, but he was speaking forcefully to Dad, who replied in calm tones.

I stared at the other two, who were in uniform with caps on their heads. The skull and crossbones eyed me like a toad. It was spine-chilling. I didn't understand much German, but I knew the presence of these men boded no good. Mom gestured to me to remain seated. She stayed put herself, but kept a close watch on Dad and the man in leather, who kept raising his voice as if he were talking to someone with defective hearing. The other two scoured the house, poking in every nook and cranny and turning everything upside down. When it looked as if they had finished their "work," the man without a uniform barked a sentence that even I could understand: "*Mitkommen!*"

Dad nodded and asked one more thing. The Gestapo officer looked at Mom and indicated that she should leave us. I didn't understand, but Mom jumped up and ran upstairs. Each tread groaned ominously beneath her as if to express its displeasure. I grew one with my chair, shrivelling up, and if things had gone on much longer I would have dissolved in my own fear. But Dad was looking at me, his eyes full of determination, that quiet strength. I straightened my spine as he poured his iron into my veins.

Mom was back in an instant. I saw her hands trembling as she passed Dad a sweater and some underwear. He gave her a smile of encouragement and left the house.

I was beside myself. Anxiety hung around my neck like a dead mouse. I watched at the window, quaking behind the curtain as the car disappeared in the grey darkness.

The next morning, Mom phoned Olomouc. She spoke to Grandpa Rudolf and fought to push back her tears. What was she to do?

She travelled to the prison regularly, taking food and clean clothes to my father. Afterward, I would hear the key in the lock and the scuffing of shoes on the mat as she came in and took off her coat.

"When's Daddy coming home?"

"Soon. They'll let him out soon."

She flopped absently down on a chair and set a bundle of his dirty things on the table. I rested my hands on the wooden tabletop and tried to say something sensible, but the words stuck in my throat like a fishbone. A pile of crumpled washing. Pieces of Dad's clothing.

Once, I couldn't tear my gaze from a dirty patch of fabric. "Blood! Blood!" A hysterical scream burst from my throat. "That's his blood! They've been beating him!"

She was on her feet in a second, and swiped the blood-stained clothes from the table. She grabbed me by the hands. "Calm down, Danny! Please calm down! It isn't his blood."

"It *is* his blood!" I was shrieking like someone possessed.

She shook me hard.

"Listen to me! Daddy works there—and they have to, they work as... Danny, look at me and listen! They, they work—they do butchering there, you know, cutting up meat and skinning animals. They have to do all kinds of jobs. He *has* to work! That's why there's blood on his clothes. But it isn't *his* blood! Do you hear? It isn't *his* blood! Calm down!"

I believed her. She never lied to me. It sounded strange, but it was believable. I wanted to believe her.

I believed her until I saw him again.

In India he had given donations in support of the government-in-exile, just like most of Baťa's men in Batanagar. They'd collected almost half a million. The Germans had gotten hold of a list, and they suspected he was in the resistance, but couldn't prove anything.

After four weeks they let him out.

He went back to work. When I asked him what he did there, he told me he squatted over a drawing-board making lines on paper. He didn't try to pretend he enjoyed it. Designs for a future town square, or bus station, or sports arena. It was all going nowhere. He would go to Gahura's workshop at Zlín town hall, a meeting place for artists and architects during the war, and there he became friends with one particular architect, Mr. Lorenc, who would sometimes come over for coffee. Lorenc wore glasses with round frames and a well-cut suit. Thin lips and low-set ears. He looked grave, but he was often fun.

I stopped going to school. No entry for Jews, and I was half-Jewish.

Not even with the apocalypse that followed did I ever forget Mrs. Novotný telling me that my friend, Jakub, wasn't home. It was odd: I felt sure I'd spotted him at the window. When the same thing happened again the next day, it dawned on me that Jakub just wasn't home for *me*.

In late September, 1941, my mother opened an issue of *Zlín* and read aloud:

> From this Friday it will be possible to implement in full those orders by which Jews are now banned from cinemas, theatres, coffee-houses, parks and other places. Henceforth, Jews throughout the Reich will be visibly marked. On their coats they will wear a yellow star, the so-called Star of David. This measure is not only of moral and ideological significance, but also practical, in that in many cases it will cut down the illicit trading in which Jews continue to engage.

History had turned in a half-circle. Dad said we were hurtling back into the Middle Ages—when they wore yellow armbands instead of stars.

Two pages later, there was a report on how the solution of the Jewish problem was proceeding abroad:

> In Warsaw, the Jews have been concentrated in a single quarter. Roughly half a million live there, all together. There is no obstacle to a similar solution being adopted in this country. Plainly, what has been done so far, such as the ban on entering swimming pools, taking the front car of the tram, or shopping between certain hours, has not been sufficient. Jews are circumventing these orders, working the black market, spreading whispered propaganda and provoking the Czech people.

The streets of the Czech towns were blazing with yellow stars.

> The average Czech can scarcely believe his eyes, now that he can see who all the Jews among us are and were. The papers carry photographs of the powerful Jews who controlled public life during the erstwhile Republic. There was hardly a single editorial office without its Jew, and names such as Fuchs, Lustig, Bloch, Stránský, Kisch, and others are the disturbing evidence. Jews contribute the lion's share to all the trouble-making, whereas the Czech man-in-the-street is merely a witness. Jews used to sit on the boards of banks and businesses, they threatened to take over the theater, and had the greatest influence in cinema. Of all there once was, the only thing left to them now are the radio broadcasts from London...

My father stood up and took the paper from her hand.

The fact that I couldn't go to school didn't mean my education was neglected. Mom took it upon herself to teach me. I had a timetable, subject after subject, six periods a day. I fought it, but I have to admit she was good. I loved history. She told me, often at the expense of geography or science, about the great battles of history, about good and bad rulers, about those great guys who changed the world. Spartacus. Caesar and Cleopatra. Alfred the Great, and Napoleon. She asked Dad to give me some math exercises. I practiced the piano an hour every day, and in the evenings I read. I was only too willing to bury myself in books. I gorged on anything that was made up of letters.

I had also reached the age when I could read the papers out loud to myself with interest.

October 29, 1941 - No treats for the Jew
From now on shopkeepers are forbidden to sell Jews any fruit, cheese, sweets, fish, poultry or meat. To prevent this order being bypassed, Aryans are forbidden to make gifts of any such provisions to a Jew.

November 5, 1941 - Now it's the Jew-lovers' turn
The Jew has disappeared, but Jew-lovers remain. There is no point in waiting for them to dwindle away; they should follow swiftly the fate of the Jews they care so much about.

Beneath this, there were two cartoons that stick in my memory. In the first, Jews were pictured with brooms in their hands, stars on their lapels, hooked noses taking up most of their faces, and bulging eyes. They had bloated features with the expression of insatiable money-grubbers and framed by jug ears. In the second picture they were departing, hunched, with bundles over their shoulders. *As they came, so shall they go*, the caption mocked.

Mom played the piano more than ever before. I think it was her consolation. Around the house she wore simple, button-down sleeveless dresses over colorful blouses. She did the housework, cleaned, cooked, washed, and ironed. And tormented me with my lessons. By the time Dad was due home from work she would be sitting with a book, neat and tidy and dressed as if to go out for a walk. Or playing the piano. I often begged her to play one particular piece, though it took me ages to remember who the composer was. It was just a short piece, four minutes long, like the babbling of a brook. *Play me that babbling,* I used to say.

"That babbling, Dan, is Tchaikovsky's *Troika*. And it's not babbling, it's sleigh bells. Listen."

It's snowing. I can see snow and white horses—a troika racing across the plain, hooves scrunching into a frosty quilt. Drawing a sleigh. It is empty, just a white-faced driver sitting on the box. Branches bending under the weight of the snow. The horses tearing across the landscape, then racing even faster and making the bells on their collar jingle, tinkling and merry, but also melancholy.

As she played, my mother kept her eyes closed. She had jumped into the white sleigh and was riding on and on, away from reality, into a white paradise.

I have never stopped looking for the tracks of that sleigh.

In April 1942 the newspapers reported on further measures to be taken against the Jewish element:

> By a government order of 20 April, those with Jewish blood will lose their posts. Anyone who is part Jewish or is married to a Jewess or to a half-Jew will be dismissed. Public employees may enter into matrimony only with persons who are not Jewish or part-Jewish.

Rachel looked at Tom. "They're going to fire you because of me."

A month later, a reward was offered: ten million crowns for the capture of the vile criminal responsible for assassinating acting Reichsprotektor SS Obergruppenführer and General of Police, model husband and loving father, Reinhard Heydrich. Two days later the reward was raised to twenty million and a state of emergency was declared.

I'd finished celebrating my eleventh birthday and was gazing into the darkness. The stars were disappearing, vanishing from sight, heading for the unknown. All that remained were empty houses and empty rooms. And no one dared ask where they would wind up. It was all done by order of the authorities, so most onlookers were not particularly concerned.

In March 1943, my aunt Regina Weinstein and a thousand others boarded the train to Theresienstadt.

At the end of the year the architect, Mr. Lorenc, also disappeared—even without a star. He had lain low for a while, but in the end they sniffed him out, or someone turned him in. I think they executed him for involvement with the resistance.

On the evening of January 21, 1944 an official of the Jewish community appeared at our door. *Jüdische Kulturgemeinde*: sign here. He disappeared into the cold darkness like an evil warning.

My mother set the paper on the table.

"They want me."

My father picked up the document and ran his eyes over it.

"One thing at least: I'll see Regi again," she said.

"Then we're all going."

"Tom, please! Don't make it worse than it is."

A sleepless night. Thomas lay beside her, enveloped in darkness. Her eyes were streaming like a river, and the current of her tears tore him away. He wanted to stop the stream from dividing them. He cried out to her, but the other bank was already too far.

"I should have taken you away, I should—maybe I still can—"

"No."

"But I—"

"No!"

"Then what—what will I do?"

His voice knocked against his clenched teeth. For the first time in his life he was asking. The first time in his life he was helpless.

"Look after him."

It was coming closer, attacking the dearest thing he had. He pressed himself to her and breathed in his own tears.

"I can't do it. I can't let you go!"

Her hair was darkness in the desert. That night it melted away under his hands.

Grandpa Rudolf came from Olomouc the day before my mother left, and we saw her to the station.

She told me we would see each other again soon. "And look after your father, won't you?"

She was so beautiful. I loved her with a love of pure ownership, blind and thoughtless. I took her for granted. Like air. Like bread.

As she was leaving, she told me that the rays of the sun were the messengers of the sun god, and that we would send each other signs by them.

"When you see the sun, when you feel its rays on your face, you will know they are my hands. I am close by. The moon will tell you stories to send you to sleep."

I clung to her one last time, breathing in her familiar scent.

"Remember, you can never lose someone you truly love."

She got on the train, and Dad went with her. Grandpa and I stayed behind.

Prostějov Interchange Station. It was as far as Thomas was permitted to go. She gave him her hand through the window. He caught it convulsively and gazed up into the face above him. The whistle blew, an electric shock. He turned his head towards the engine, saw the dispatcher pull the signal disc from under his arm and cast a practiced glance over the closed carriages, then at his wristwatch. The oval disc with a red bull's eye cut through the air as the dispatcher swung it upwards.

It was January. Trickles of sweat ran down his back. His face muscles were taut as strings, his expression wild, a faithful dog, running up and down beside a fence that was too high. He was still convinced there was a point where it could be jumped.

She smiled.

"Soon it will be over. You'll see. I'll be back before long."

He tried to nod. The train pulled slowly away and her slender fingers slipped from his hands. She waved.

He stood motionless long after the last carriage had disappeared from sight.

When my father returned, I didn't recognize him. He had changed, like a tree that lost all its leaves at once.

I spent hours staring into the sun, trying to catch a glimpse of her. When I turned away, the world would disappear. It took time for the vague outlines of things to emerge again, a world where her essence was missing—scattered into the sunlight.That first night without her I had a dream. We were wandering together through an unfamiliar landscape, in deep snow, in a dense forest. Wolves howled around us. We ran, stumbling over the roots of trees that caught at our legs like the tentacles of an octopus. I kept running for a long time, maybe hours, before I realized I was alone.

I recalled my Prague grandfather. The gold casket with the Torah, the gloom of the synagogue in which lived the invisible God.

I prayed. "Oh God, you created this world, you created man. Please keep her safe."

Where was Theresienstadt and what was Mom doing there? We had always done everything together. Now I only had my father, who was trying hard, but I knew he was terribly sad. I was sad, too.

VII

Anna: Hidden Notes

I arranged for Rachel to move into the Theresienstadt house where I was living. The others protested because we were already crammed into a few square meters without an ounce of privacy. I told them she was my sister.

But Rachel was looking for her real sister. I threw myself into the search, and after two days discovered that Regina Weinstein had left on the last transport to the East. They had missed each other by a few weeks. Maybe that was why Rachel didn't resist my excessive attention. I had found an older sister in her.

When she came to our attic for the first time, the tiny airless hole we were so proud of, she stood and looked around in silence. Then she spoke. "*The Trial*. This is—Kafka. He knew it all." She turned her head. "So accurate. These houses, the squalid loft spaces, everything. The condemned who had no idea what crimes they committed. The man was a genius—as if he knew it first hand."

I thought she was raving. I had no idea what she was talking about. What trial? What Kafka? I'd never heard the name in my life. I couldn't make sense of any of it.

When the camp's ghetto officials learned that Rachel had been in the Red Cross, they assigned her to do nursing work in the

127

home for the old and infirm. The *Siechenheim*. Hell with the fires gone out. The sick lay like mangy animals in an unheated, stinking room, amid troops of lice and bed bugs, in their own excrement. They got no medicine.

Rachel raged impotently. "For God's sake, how can I keep them clean without warm water and fresh linen?"

They died by the score. Their sheets were their shrouds. The cellar was a morgue. They were stacked in piles, like bread to be kept from going stale; like logs for the fire. She got terribly exhausted.

"Dozens of them, dying under my hands, Annie. Abandoned and broken down, so terribly alone. And I—I can do nothing to help them!"

She sat with her head in her hands. I passed her a lump of bread, but she couldn't touch it. Her hands just drooped into her lap.

I was afraid for her. I made her ask for a transfer, and in the end they took pity on her. Egon Redlich, the Jew who was in charge of young people in the camp, offered her work in the home for girls, the *Mädchenheim*—or just the *Heim* in Theresienstadt jargon. She was happy. The work gave her back the will to live.

Rachel and the head of the girls' block, Růžena Engländer, got along well, but there was no love lost between her and Egon Redlich. He was almost fanatical in his Zionism, and insisted on applying the strictest religious standards to young people. Rachel saw all upbringings as split between good and bad, and she thought Redlich was pretentious.

"How ridiculous he is, with his: 'You're right, but basically you're wrong.' By which he means that only what *he* thinks is right. And his censorship of *Videm*! He says, 'Yes, yes, I have to admit the literary value of the magazine is considerable, but I've searched in vain for any Jewish spirit.' Can you believe it, Annie? Boys of fifteen, surrounded by all these horrors, publish their own

THE SOUND OF THE SUNDIAL

magazine. They write poems and articles so mature and deeply felt that they knock you out, and he—he whines on about a lack of Jewish spirit! Every one of these boys has more spirit than all those sour-faced old fossils on the Council of Elders put together. No *Jewish* spirit maybe, but *human* spirit for sure."

The German authorities had saddled the Council of Elders with organizing things in the ghetto, including the dreaded transports to the East. They had frequent conferences, and Rachel got firsthand reports from Walter Löwinger, whom she'd known in Prague when he was studying law with her brother. The Council of Elders as a body always got her worked up.

"Are they just? Are they wise? Each one goes against the other, and when one person issues an order, the next one cancels it. And d'you know what they discussed today? Whether it's better to try serious or minor cases. *Who is guilty and who blameless?* And above all: their everlasting *who is pure and who impure?* What goes on inside their thick skulls? Walter Löwinger tells me dreadful stories: none of them cares for anything beyond his own grandeur. Arrogant, blind old men."

In the middle of all this, my world was Gideon. Zest and energy—he had to be involved, threw himself into everything head-first. He performed solos, played in quartets and trios, accompanied choirs for oratorios. He collaborated with Rafael Schächter on Verdi's *Requiem*. He played constantly, drawing me into a tonal world no less beautiful than the man himself. And he composed. He wrote a *Sonata for Piano* and said it was for me. His enthusiasm was catching, his discoveries exciting. He even admired Leoš Janáček, but no matter how I tried I couldn't join him in that. For a total musical ignoramus like me, Janáček was too much.

Gideon conjured up a *Trio for Violin, Viola, and Cello*, and nine days after finishing it, he left on the transport. "Your hair is cast in bronze," he said to me.

I tried to forget by escaping into the past. I told Rachel all about my mother and my aunt Elsa. Sometimes she told me about her brother, Erik, and her sister, Regina. She rarely spoke of her parents.

Rachel's mother, Stella Weinstein, seemed not to have understood any of her children very well, but her youngest was the biggest problem. Erik was polite and sophisticated, and though he could be aggressive and noisy, he moved with a natural elegance. Even as a child he bore himself like a lord, with grace and distinction. His father, Otto Weinstein claimed he could already see the future lawyer in the three-year-old whelp. Poor Regi, on the other hand, had a limp, and all her movements seemed disjointed and sort of wrong.

Rachel was most in her element when she was running. She had scarcely learned to stand upright on her tiny gangly legs when she skipped over walking and went right to a funny little hop. In a couple of days she was running around and she never stopped. She went off to school at a trot and came home at a gallop. When the family went for walks, Rachel and the dog ran on ahead, then back to the group, then way out in front again. For every hundred yards the others covered, Rachel ran five times as far. She couldn't understand why she wasn't allowed to wear boys' clothes or why she shouldn't climb trees.

Otto Weinstein taught at a high school, which in those days meant something. His authority was recognized, and he knew how to maintain discipline. When Rachel was little there was only one thing she feared: that her father would "put her name down."

It was rare for Otto Weinstein to be cross with his youngest daughter. Only when she got too out of hand would he assume his schoolmasterly expression and raise a forefinger. "If you don't get a grip on yourself, *I'll put your name down!*"

The emphasis he placed on the phrase *put your name down* filled her with awe. Rachel pictured something immeasurably terrible, something inconceivable for her five-year-old brain couldn't grasp. It was the worst punishment she could imagine. There was no way she could allow her father to put her name down. As soon as she heard those magic words, she stopped fooling around and was on her best behavior for the rest of the day.

So when Rachel's mother told her she had "put her name down" to start school, she had a fit of hysterics.

Her brother, Erik, went to college because he was bright, and the only boy in the family—a potential breadwinner. He chose Law, and their father paid for his studies without blinking. It was a matter of course. Regi was a girl, and under normal circumstances she wouldn't have had a chance for college. But an exception was made because part of her left foot was missing; when she was twelve, she had had her toes and a piece of her instep amputated. Her father was convinced that with such a handicap, Regi had little hope of a decent husband, and was relieved to note that she was a diligent and gifted pupil. He decided it would be best for the poor little cripple if she had a proper education to help her find fulfillment in something other than marriage and children. He selected a teacher training college for her. Regina relished the prospect.

But that left the youngest, Rachel. Daddy's pet; his spoiled little darling. She was clever, and she could play the piano, and dance, and draw. Whatever she turned to, she excelled at it. And her father doted on her like Narcissus on his reflection. How could he refuse her anything? How could he not pay for his little Princess to go to college, his gifted little girl, when both her brother and sister were there? That wouldn't be fair. Moreover, she had chosen to study her father's subject: history. He couldn't resist her.

Otto decided to send her to university in Olomouc, where his own aging sister lived. She had heart trouble, and had openly complained of loneliness and failing health in her recent letters. He killed two birds with one stone: Rachel could be a student and at the same time she could be company for Aunt Esther.

Her mother had protested, wringing her hands and berating him. "Otto, you'll be throwing good money away and doing the girl a disservice as well! What young man is going to court such an intellectual girl? Already her attitude is unacceptable. She's developing into a free thinker."

Rachel at university? It wasn't natural. It was audacious and all too emancipated. Rachel's education, her broad reading and intellectual interests reduced her value as a potential wife. "No woman should be too clever," her mother used to say. "And if she is, it shouldn't be visible. Least of all to her husband."

Mrs. Weinstein had grown up in the German tradition: *Kinder—Küche—Kirche.* She baked bread for the Sabbath and lit candles, drawing the smoke towards her with her hands, inhaling it with her eyes closed, her head beneath her shawl. She was obsessed with twin ideals of cleanliness, the German and the Jewish. She was always busy, the embodiment of practicality, but enclosed in her own little world, or at least consigned to it. She could knit, sew, crochet, and embroider. It made her sad that neither of her daughters showed any interest in handwork. She wore plain but elegant dresses, retaining an outward modesty though her vanity flared up when she saw the latest fashions in the Rosenbaum salon. She played the harmonium and the piano. *The Book of Psalms* in Hebrew and German lay on her bedside table, but only God knows if she ever really prayed. Once a year she travelled to her native Vienna to see her relatives.

Rachel's mother had been fourteen when she left school. Times had been different back then. She had continued to study music privately, and waited for a husband. She had been young and beautiful, and had enchanted the educated Otto Weinstein. They could be seen side by side in yellowing photographs. He, thin and shortsighted, looking gravely into the camera, horn pince-nez on his nose, hooked by a gold chain to the second button of his waistcoat. And she, smiling mischievously, wearing an airy dress, a black ribbon fastened with an inlaid clasp around her neck. All her life she had relied upon her feminine charm, the only weapon available in those days to a woman of her position.

But she remained quiet, and to all appearances, submissive.

"Remember, Rachel, any man can be managed with a little diplomacy. No scenes, no dramatics. That won't get you anywhere. An irritable wife is a disaster. They don't like it, and it doesn't work on them. Go gently, gently; appear to acquiesce in everything: 'Yes, Papa, you're right. You know best, Papa.' And then do it your way. That's feminine diplomacy."

Rachel had squirmed. What diplomacy? Deception, she'd call it! But she had been astonished when she saw her mother's theory put into practice. Her father was no fool, yet it worked on him just as her mother claimed it would. Strategy and tactical maneuvers handled with a bravura from which many a politician could learn a thing or two. But Rachel never did.

Her mother spoke German, and had never learnt Czech properly. She associated only with the German-speaking Jews who lived in Prague and thought themselves a cut above the rest. It was different with Rachel's father. He spoke Czech to the children, and Rachel and Regi went to Czech theaters and read Czech books. Their governess taught them French and English; everything French was in vogue at the time.

Erik enjoyed himself and sometimes forgot where he was. He was too frivolous for Otto's taste, and their mother worried that he might turn into a coffeehouse Jew. He travelled to Vienna regularly: glorious Vienna, vivacious and full of dancing; Vienna, degenerate and antisemitic.

Stella Weinstein worried too much about her children. The older she got, the more she had suffered from insomnia and bouts of coughing. Year after year, Otto had sent her off somewhere to take the waters and restore her strength: Carlsbad, Marienbad, or

Baden-Baden.

Stella had invested a great deal of effort trying to tame her willful youngest daughter and smooth her path towards adulthood. It was all in vain. Only a miracle would bring Rachel a perfect husband.

Rachel had wanted a miracle. She had insisted on it.

The girls from the Mädchenheim worked most of the day. In the spring they moved to the fields, where from time to time they managed to steal something. Sweet corn, potatoes, beetroot that they would stuff inside their bras and smuggle past the random checkpoints erected by the female SS guards. When they got back from the fields, Rachel would chase the girls to the cold-water troughs in the washroom, insisting they keep themselves and their rooms clean and neat.

"Even a garbage dump can be kept tidy!"

At six in the evening, after working all day, she sat them down to study. Languages, history, and geography; they wrote essays and drew on cardboard with stumps of coal from the stove. It was often difficult to spark anything worthwhile in those weary heads, and teaching was strictly forbidden. No pencils, paper, or books. One of the girls kept watch for three or four hours on end so that if an inspector came around, the others had time to pretend to be doing housework or some other physical task. Spring cleaning always pleased the Germans.

Rachel struggled against the sense of hopelessness to which the girls were prone. The daily sight of the barrow piled with corpses, the departures of their friends and relatives to the East, the deaths of loved ones were her constant concern. She would analyze the girls' drawings, and sometimes bring them to show me. "Look, Annie, this is how my girls see the world. They're in an age of grace."

The Council of Elders had decided that great attention should be devoted to how the young were raised in Theresienstadt. "They are our future," the Council declared, and, at the expense of the elderly, they increased the food rations for children and adolescents—and themselves.

Rachel invited the more interesting residents to pass on some of their knowledge to the girls. Gideon talked about music, Gustav Schorsch about Chekhov's plays and the anarchist movement. Ungar Hermann attempted to explain the theory of relativity. And then came Karel Poláček, the novelist, who talked about Russian Realism and how he had written *Men Offside*.

Poláček left Rachel feeling uncomfortable. "He seemed so turned in on himself, wounded and broken. No spark in his eye, no vitality. Such a sorry sight."

I understood that Aunt Elsa was not the only one who wrote off her life once in the ghetto. Poláček was already over fifty when they hauled him off to Theresienstadt. Two years later, he would clamber resignedly into the cattle wagon, indifferent to his fate. Final destination: Auschwitz. Nothing could move him any more.

Lethargy was a sure route to the Theresienstadt crematorium, and Rachel fought it with all her strength. She dusted off her treasure chest of stories, myths, and fairy tales, and shared them with the rest of us.

She cherished her memories. When I first asked about Tom she smiled. "He has wolf's eyes," she said. "Steel-grey irises with dark blue rims. They change color depending on what he is looking at, from deep blue to pale grey to light green. They devour the world." She said from time to time she had detected a flash of perversion and brutality in those eyes; those were the moments when he would pounce on her as if she were his prey. She saw the suppressed animal in him—naked instincts beneath a smooth, civilized veneer—and she wanted it to bubble up to the surface. She would provoke him. He was obsessed with work, and that aroused her; and though he was habitually clean-shaven and courteous, she also liked it when he didn't shave.

Or when he let her shave him. He would lean back, his head sunk into her stomach. She would rinse the brush, dry her hands and wipe the razor. She knew every feature of his face: his cheeks with their sharp cheekbones and shallow depressions; the muscles connecting the ends of his jaw bone to his ears—always slightly prominent when he was concentrating; the pale scar on his chin, fine as a needle; and the miniature dimple on his left temple, souvenir of an encounter with a coal-scuttle. In the gleam of the razorblade she would see his long eyelashes, quivering like a butterfly, and she could sense his vulnerability.

When she thought about what attracted her to Thomas, she recalled his loosened tie and rolled-up sleeves; the intense, focused gaze sparking silver and blue; and his hands. She would close her eyes and see them touching her. To her, his hands were the perfect synonym for sex.

She remembered the moment when it had first dawned on her. Spring had been in the air and snowdrop-sellers in the streets. Sunday after Sunday he had travelled to Olomouc to see her, and after a few months of secret dating, she had gotten on a train and gone to him. She had wanted to surprise him.

They showed her into the makeshift office he had set up in one of the partly-built houses on Zálešná, in the middle of the construction site. "Wait for him here, he'll be along any moment." She snuggled into an armchair, half hidden behind heaps of papers and boxes.

He had come into the room deep in thought, wearing a white poplin shirt with rolled-up sleeves, dark blue suspenders, and a tie of the same color. The grey jacket of his suit was slung over his shoulder. He hung it up and strolled casually across to the table. He raised his chin and half-turned his head as he loosened his tie and sat down. He put his feet on the table, pulled out his cigarettes and lighter, but didn't light up. He clasped his hands behind his head.

There was something in that gesture that was stored in her memory, something exciting. In that moment, she had wanted him. His hands were an aphrodisiac.

It was only then that he noticed he was not alone. He stood up. "Rachel?"

"Touch me."

She had softened under his hands like a rag doll. When he touched her, she became devoid of form—her eyes, fingers, tongue, even her name. He ran his electric hands through her hair. He held her, and she felt how she had entered his blood.

Then there was a knock at the door. He let go of her and straightened his tie; he had to go. "Sorry," he said.

She had left there with the imprint of his fingers on her skin.

Sleep within the walls of Theresienstadt was an unfathomable well. Sometimes I woke limpid and childishly free of care, but mostly it felt as wearisome as the long day's work. Only rarely did I drop into such a deep sleep that even the zealous gnawing of the fleas and bedbugs could not wake me. In the morning I would examine the afflicted parts of my body, swollen with revulsion and bites.

One day, Rachel made a great bust. She was passing the room of her "girls," as she called them, when she heard a suspicious whooping coming from inside. She stopped and silently turned the handle to look in. The girls were in their underwear, fluttering around the tiny space between the bunks, jumping from one to the other, yelling and yodeling in excitement. Matchbox in hand, they were leaping into the stale air as though catching invisible fireflies. They seemed to be enraptured, but Rachel couldn't make sense of it. She flung the door wide and marched into the middle of the romping vortex. The girls, petrified, froze where they stood and then quickly got out of range of their tutor.

Rachel reached out to the nearest girl and took her matchbox. Cautiously she held it to her ear and shook it, then was about to open it.

"For goodness's sake, please don't open it!" The girl was red in the face, sweaty, stammering. "It's, ehm—it's, there's – inside – "

"What are you going on about?" Rachel said.

"It's full of—I've got—"

"What?"

"It's—fleas."

"Fleas?"

She demanded an explanation, and the girls let the story out piecemeal, in hard-won, unkempt scraps of sentences.

It was a game. The object was to catch as many fleas as possible in a matchbox. This was not at all easy, because the little beasts, when physically fit, could easily jump half a meter. You had to be a skilled hunter to catch them. It took practice and a natural talent to capture a flea in mid-jump. First prize was a lump of bread.

Rachel had the whole of the girls' block disinfected, and flea-hunting was over for the next few weeks.

In the adult huts, there was no such fun, least of all in those housing the old and infirm. In addition to fleas, they were teeming with body lice. Typhus.

Rachel was carried away by the culture of Theresienstadt. She used to play the legless piano in the cellar of the *Heim*, unless Gideon was already there. She knew that his life was in that ancient cripple with no pedals; he spent all his spare time at it. Music was his oxygen, the most precious gift.

She exhausted herself lecturing on the Phoenicians, the Greeks, and the Persians. She gave one or two lectures every week, usually in the library, the *Ghettobücherei,* preparing each one with great care.

"Svarog was the greatest of all the old Slavic gods. His name comes from the Sanskrit for heaven—*svarga*. He had two sons,

Dazhbog, the god of the sun, and Svarozhich, the god of fire."

She would smile, squinting into the faces of shadows, offering manna to her wretched audience. An emaciated old man with thinning white fluff for hair, his eyes veiled by cataracts and his hands and face covered by liver marks, put one hand behind his ear and adjusted it like a sail to the wind so he could hear her better. Insatiable for her stories, the listeners held out their spoons, savoring every moment they could reach out and touch the divine by seeing the majesty of these gods and goddesses.

She showed them the shapes of the world from the beginning of time.

"The doors of perception are open. What was hidden has come to light. I see myself in a thousand swirling colors. I am where the sun sets beyond the mountains. I am in this body. I am a star rising above the clouds, hanging by a thread from an ocean moon. I see myself as I cross through eternity, walking among gods, flying above mirages like a shuttle through the loom of time. All is one. Flowers grow, snakes crawl, and wisdom slumbers in the palm of a hand.

"Thus spoke Osiris," said Rachel, "the Egyptian god of death and rebirth, the revealer of mysteries, the lord of light and dark. So it is written in *The Book of the Dead.*"

Rachel was held in high esteem: her knowledge, her strong opinions, her charm, and her sense of humor. Dozens of admirers danced attendance on her, but nobody worthy of special mention. Not because they weren't sufficiently intelligent, artistic, or personable, but simply because she treated them all with nothing more than cursory politeness.

Except for one: Gustav Schorsch.

He was tall, with a high forehead and baleful eyes. For a while he had been the caregiver in the boys' home, so he could understand her concern for the wellbeing of her girls. But his real life had played out on stage: before the war, he had been assistant director at the National Theater.

She spent a lot of time with him, fascinated by his pigheadedness. She used to call it zeal, but I say he was pigheaded, driven by his own compulsion, a successor to the Prague avant-garde. At the camp he experimented with theater, directed performances, and gave poetry recitations. He was everywhere—concerts, plays, lectures—and met Rachel at one of them. She discussed his plays with him enthusiastically, and sat through the rehearsals where the actors congregated after work. She quietly noted the determination with which Gustav fussed over every detail, every trifle; he used to say that Rachel came to his rehearsals so that she could tear him to shreds afterwards.

Schorsch rarely laughed. He couldn't stand half-truths and illusions, either in the theater or in life. He chose difficult works and employed the least sensible methods. From his actors, he demanded performances that would pass muster on any professional stage. He would never allow the ghetto conditions to affect quality. He would explain things over and over and over again, and if that didn't help, he would act them out himself. Stanislavsky's *My Life in Art* was his Bible; he would quote whole passages in uncontrollable fits.

"These aren't rehearsals," Rachel would say, "they're seminars."

He had a phenomenal memory and was obsessed. When he had an insight he would come in to our block, even at four-thirty in the morning. He had to tell us, had to get it out of his system. He gave no thought to the time or to the danger of being caught in the streets of the ghetto at night. I think he was crazy.

Gogol's *Marriage*, that cruel satire of the archetypes of stupidity and egoism, was refined to perfection through his artistry. His production was wondrous: a set built from old rags, cardboard boxes, umbrellas, sacks, crates, and planks. The planks were the world. The costumes were made of sheets that also served as shrouds for the dead. This was Schorsch's peculiar conception, one he had wanted to mount onstage before the war, but instead was realized in Theresienstadt.

His production was brutal: his distortions reached grotesque dimensions; it was shocking and repellent.

It was the last dream of Gustav Schorsch to be fulfilled.

Rachel was wonderful, and in spite of our age difference, we really were like sisters. There was only one area in which we found no common ground: she had little understanding for my faith, and I couldn't understand her lack of it.

When she was small she had loved the holy days—Rosh Hashanah, the New Year, and Yom Kippur, the Day of Atonement; the synagogue; and the Chief Rabbi who carried the Torah. In those days she had still been allowed to touch the scrolls, and though it had left her unmoved, it was the only moment when she was permitted to come down from the balcony where the women were set apart.

She could never stay long on the balcony anyway. In her neatly ironed little dress, she would steal down to the synagogue courtyard where she could run around whooping. "Play quietly!" the synagogue warden would reprove the boisterous youngsters, and sometimes he reported them to their parents. She used to walk home with her clothes a mess, her mother scolding her on the way for disgracing the family.

At Yom Kippur she used to sit at the table with Regi, making sweet-smelling hedgehogs by sticking cloves into apples that had been given out to the fasting women so they could smell them and fend off their hunger.

But the older she grew, the more rebellious she became. She couldn't understand why women were relegated to the synagogue balcony. It really annoyed her and she thought God was unjust. She took it personally.

She described how, the day before her thirteenth birthday, she was curled up in an armchair sobbing in self-disgust over her first period; she couldn't imagine ever learning to live with it. Her stomach heaved and she saw her body as a vessel full of filth. Religion had an apt expression for it: *Impure.* A woman who menstruates is *impure.* This thought intensified her nausea, her repulsion. She wanted to die.

From that time on she felt that if there was a God, it had to be a stupid male. Women were assigned to an enclosure as if they were sheep; no man would even touch a menstruating woman. *Pure, impure.* That was not written by an invisible God, but by some man who couldn't stand the sight of blood. Of that she was absolutely sure.

The first time Tom made love to her in the middle of her period, she felt strange. She told him it was proscribed by the Jewish faith: a man may not sleep with a woman who is menstruating.

"Why?"

"Because she's unclean. It's a serious offense to sleep with her. A sin. Even if it happens by accident, he must make a sacrifice to cleanse himself."

He shrugged. "I just have to wash up."

She had thumped on his chest till it echoed, and burst out laughing. "You're such a heathen!"

In February, Gustav Schorsch gave us an official invitation to Verdi's *Requiem.* I went as the girls' chaperone, though I had seen the performance several times.

Gideon was still there to play the piano accompaniment under the direction of his relentless conductor, Rafael Schächter: purity of rhythm, perfect dynamics. "Raf's a fanatic," Gideon used to say, "he puts all he's got into it. Every note resonates with his love."

Rachel dressed in her best: a blue fitted costume with lapels and velvet buttons, and a light grey fur tippet instead of a collar.

If Schorsch hadn't been head over heels in love with her before, he would have to be now. I asked her if she thought he loved her, because I didn't dare ask how she felt. She gave a brief shrug and answered in one sentence: "He's not Tom."

Theresienstadt Town Hall. Unfinished walls, feeble light bulbs, and the light of hope. Gideon Klein at the piano in the corner, his fingers on the black and yellowed keys. Rafael Schächter's hands transformed into flying doves as he conducted. The singing of the chorus: divine music, soothing and stirring the senses to distraction. *Requiem aeternam dona eis, Domine.* The choir, neatly lined up, ordinary people in ordinary clothes with yellow stars on their lapels. Sixty stars in a row melded into one as they sang the *Requiem*—the Mass for the Dead.

How many months had Schächter worked, exulted, cursed, and ranted, how many nights had he tossed to the nightmare beat of his baton? All those voices had passed through his hands— singer after singer, men and women who came and went to the rhythm of the transports bound for the East. With each new arrival, he summoned his strength to begin again. He proved to everyone that he could do it, despite everything. This was the third time in Theresienstadt that his *Requiem* had risen from the dead. The scar-like furrows on Schächter's face were proliferating, marking the passage of time, the paths he had sought and taken. He directed the performance from memory, with subtle, evocative gestures.

Rachel looked around the hall, her eyes roaming from face to face, and smiled as if in a trance. *Dies irae, dies illa* thundered over their heads, dark and chilling. *Day of Judgement, Day of Wrath.* The flower of Christian faith in the recriminating voices of Jews. There was power in it, and pride, untold hardship and fervent prayer. Jews singing a *Requiem*. For themselves? Or for others? Tears glinted on her eyelashes and landed on her grey fur cape like snowflakes landing on ice. The image of this absurd world was drowned by her weeping.

The applause went on forever, but it was long after the performance ended before her calm was restored. Gustav sat at her feet and spoke soothingly to her. He put one hand on her knee and searched in his pocket with the other.

Between sobs she apologized to him. "I have never witnessed anything so--"

"Here, take my handkerchief."

"Thank you. Thank you so much." She told him the performance was a victory of mind over matter.

Sometimes Rachel received packages. She had told Tom they couldn't weigh more than half a kilo because the contents would be hand-checked by the overseers, who would steal anything they wanted. So Tom sent old cigar boxes into which he'd built false bottoms. Neat little cubes of roux, butter caramels, honey, smoked meat baked inside homemade bread, zwieback, sometimes even a few squares of chocolate. Everything was made from recipes with the smallest volume and the highest calorie count that were the most likely to keep.

And then there was food for the soul: a Berlioz score he had transcribed and encoded with everything Rachel meant to him. Little dots squeezed into the limits of five narrow lines, the key signature and rhythmic instructions reproduced in his tiny engineer's lettering as though following a template. *Andante. Allegretto. Forte. Pianissimo.* He interwove them with messages like: *Infernum Romam deliquit.* Hell has left Rome. Under the last row of scattered music notes was a message for her alone: *Causa mea vivendi.* My reason for living. Then nothing more.

After a while, he changed his method of sending secret messages, scrapping the false bottoms and instead pushing little rolls of paper inside of onions. We only discovered the first one after we'd cut the onion into thin slices. It took us two hours to fit the jigsaw together and find the mystery text: *The Allies have landed in Normandy.*

She sent short messages home on official postcards. Thirty words in German as permitted by Nazi benevolence—and still they were checked thoroughly. Rachel wrote the real message between the lines in invisible ink. Tom had given her a little bottle of wine vinegar and some instructions as she was leaving: vinegar can't be seen, and you can use lemon juice as well, or sulfuric acid diluted with water and sugar. But vinegar is best. So she dipped her quill in vinegar and wrote.

When a card reached him from Theresienstadt, he warmed it over the stove, until the brownish capitals began to appear.

MY DEAREST! YOU HAVE NO IDEA THE EFFECT THE DIVINE BERLIOZ HAD! I CAN'T FIND THE WORDS! THANK YOU, A THOUSAND KISSES. I KISS YOU BOTH. HUG DANNY FOR ME. THERE ARE SO MANY INTERESTING PEOPLE HERE, THEY DON'T GIVE UP EVEN IN THIS SURREAL WORLD, SO MANY AMAZING ENCOUNTERS THAT IF IT WEREN'T FOR THE CONSTANT FEAR OF BEING TRANSPORTED TO THE EAST, IT MIGHT EVEN BE POSSIBLE TO LIVE HERE. PLEASE SEND SOME MORE NOTEBOOKS, COUGH DROPS, AND THE LAST ACT OF JIRÁSEK'S "LANTERN." I AM QUITE WELL. DON'T WORRY ABOUT ME. I AM WITH YOU ALWAYS. RACHEL.

Rachel told me she had first been to Zlín at the end of her first year in Olomouc University, leaving the safety of her Aunt Esther's apartment to visit her classmate, Edita Wasserman, for a week. It was almost a miracle that her father had consented; she suspected that in the end it wasn't the flood of requests from Aunt Esther that made her parents yield, but the fact that she was going to the Wassermans'—a Jewish household.

They had lived on the square in the centre of Zlín and had

received Rachel kindly. Compared to her native Prague or even Olomouc, the whole of Zlín had seemed little more than a large village dominated by a factory. But with Edita she was never bored, and eventually she came to perceive a sort of poetry in the small town's rustic atmosphere.

The day before their planned return to Prague, Edita had dragged Rachel on a hilly walk around the back of Zlín as far as Kudlov. On the way home, a fierce wind started and the town grew dark. They had quickened their pace, passing the church just as the clock struck half past two. The first heavy drops of rain hit the ground with the last few dozen yards to run, and they started along Dlouhá Street, but before they reached the Cross, enormous hail stones came pelting down on them and, already soaked, they burst through the nearest door.

The Turns' bakery smelled of fresh bread and roasted coffee. It was a single-storey corner house with a shingle roof and a chimney in the middle. A sign on the left half of the door said *Bakery*, on the right, *Grocery*. The living room next to the bakery had been home to the legendary early-evening discussion groups of the townswomen of Zlín.

"Come on in, Miss Edita, sit down, you and your friend, till the worst of it passes."

As they sipped their coffee, the doors flew open again, and another soaking wet customer dashed in: a young man with a roll of drawings in his hand, trying to protect them from the rain. He gave a perfunctory nod in the direction of the ladies, and passed a fleeting glance over their summer dresses, which the rain had transformed into transparent nothings that clung superbly to their bodies. He struck up a conversation with the proprietor.

Rachel and Edita whispered and giggled self-consciously in the corner, trying to attract his attention. From time to time he glanced their way, a direct and penetrating glance, with eyes like steel.

After half an hour the hail stopped, but rain still drummed on the windows. The man politely requested something waterproof, and with his carefully wrapped plans under his arm, said goodbye.

He disappeared into the sheets of rain.

That rain of July 3, 1926 flooded several parts of Zlín. Water from the Kudlov and Březnice brooks had surged down the streets and filled the cellars. The Dřevnice had burst its banks and flooded houses and gardens, washing fences and sheds away. It destroyed a bridge, and left behind it uprooted trees, damaged walls, and impassable roads.

Rachel had extended her stay.

Edita opened her wardrobe. "Here, I'll lend you some jodpurs. These'll fit you."

"How will we get out of the house?"

Everyone was trying to help wherever they could, but Mrs. Wasserman had said she couldn't allow the genteel visitor from Prague to risk injury by dragging sandbags around or performing other backbreaking feats best left to strong men. She didn't like the idea of being held to account for that.

"We'll have to use the back door. Let's go!"

Edita and Rachel had headed for the Dřevnice, and an hour later they were pushing a wheelbarrow with two sandbags towards the river. Turbid water, noisy and ruthless, dragged tree trunks, junk, and parts of the bridge it had brought down as easily as blowing at a pile of feathers. A horrendous scene. Mud deposits, eroded banks, animal bodies. A little dog paddled in the dirty flow, howling faintly, fighting for its life.

The remains of the bridge had formed a dam. More timbers were getting caught in it, and branches, dirt, and bits of furniture had slowed down the water which was spreading around it, looking for another path, pouring across the surrounding area, inundating houses and their little gardens. It flooded cellars and rose through ground floors. The broken beams of the wrecked bridge got wedged in tight, creating another dam; a yard upstream, a few desperate men were trying to check the flow of water with sandbags.

A builder stood with a group of firemen and volunteers. He was debating with a man in a black plastic raincoat, who had brought with him a small wooden case out of which he took some intriguing equipment. As they talked, he assembled an explosive charge with a dexterous and practiced hand, as if he could do it in the dark, even in his sleep. Their words were carried away by the noise of the water and the ceaseless rain. The group moved over towards the barricade of beams in the river.

A disheveled woman came running up to the black-coated man with the explosives in his hand. Screaming, she flung herself on his neck, then turned to the builder.

"Please don't let him do it. We've got three children!"

The man with the explosives said, "Go home, Jarka, please! Nothing's going to happen to me."

A tussle. Dozens of witnesses. The woman turned again to the startled builder. She spoke vehemently, strands of hair sticking to her forehead. "I beg you, sir, don't make him go out there. Send someone who's got no family!"

Her husband tried to shout her down. "I told you, go home! Now!"

The builder took him by the shoulder; he didn't like scenes and he had no time to lose. "Give it to me and tell me what to do."

Rachel and Edita were straining to hear. They caught fragments of sentences amid the roar of the water. They watched the excited gestures, but the skirmish was soon over. The builder took the explosive charge in his hand and gestured toward the dam. The man in the black raincoat removed his watch, pointed to the buckle on the builder's belt, mimed checking his clothing as though with a detector. There could be no metal.

Armed with the dynamite and his terse instructions, the builder stepped into the river. He battled against the surging water and the slippery surface, balancing on mud-caked beams and tree trunks. He could see the black raincoat shouting something to him, but he couldn't hear a word. He set the charge and made his way back, the hero of the day. They'd be writing about him in the local papers.

Someone held out a hand to help him with the last, slippery, awkward step, but the ground crumbled under his feet, and like a ragdoll, his body slid under the water and disappeared.

Beneath the surface, he scraped against something. A sharp-edged rock. His shirt hooked on a granite projection. He jerked his arm but could not free himself. He was running out of breath. He tugged with all his strength and his shirt came free. When they dragged him out, his left sleeve was ripped along its entire length.

By the time the man in the black raincoat pressed the button, the builder—Thomas Keppler—was lying on the riverbank, losing consciousness and a lot of blood. The explosion freed the blockage. Beams and splinters flew through the air, an avalanche of water went crashing downstream. Thomas's clothes hung off of him, his face and body were covered with bruises, and he spewed up the filth he had swallowed. His left forearm was slashed from wrist to elbow. He moved it, groaned loudly, and passed out.

Rachel, who was standing four paces from him, thrust through the crowd. "Let me get to him, someone find me a belt! Or some suspenders, or a piece of string. Hurry!"

She stripped off her riding jacket and tried to tear a sleeve off her own shirt. The man in the raincoat gave her somebody's suspenders, then grabbed her sleeve and with one wrench pulled it off. She tied the suspenders tight on Thomas's arm above the wound, then drew the two jagged edges of his skin together and bandaged them with her sleeve.

In a black-and-white dream, Thomas was aware only of the pain and the dark eyes above him. Fingers touched him, deft and icy. Strands of black hair escaped from under her riding cap and coiled up like grass snakes. He was cold. He heard voices as if from a distance.

The man in the raincoat never took his eyes off the girl, who was dripping wet. "Are you a doctor?"

"I've taken some Red Cross courses. We have to get him to the hospital. It's a deep wound and it needs cleaning."

Thomas wanted to say something. He lifted his head and opened his mouth. He felt like he was freezing, and the eyes above him radiated the only warmth. Words would not come. All sound faded away, and the picture slowly followed.

Those who were there at the time said it was the worst flood in fifty years.

In February came heavy frost, and with it the annual ball.

A week beforehand, Aunt Esther was already on edge. It would be a difficult, thankless task to chaperone Rachel and Edita. To make things worse, none of her evening dresses fit, which meant an unplanned expenditure. That made her even edgier.

This year as every year, she lectured her niece on the principles that no decent woman should ever violate, which every year Rachel violated with gusto. "That's the last time I'll take you," Aunt Esther would threaten. "I'll write to your mother." But Rachel knew the old lady loathed writing letters, and anyway it was a whole year until the next ball. That would be plenty of time for her aunt to forget her threats.

Aunt Esther had come to live in Olomouc upon marrying a local man two generations older than her. He had an established bookbinding firm and a spacious apartment looking out onto the spireless Church of St. Maurice. They had had a two-year marriage without children, and by twenty-four, Esther was a widow. She had never remarried. Rachel didn't know whether that was because she had been so deeply in love with her husband, or because she equated marriage with hell.

They arrived at The National House. Ball gowns and jewels, the scent of talc and eau-de-cologne. Music, and the body language of the dance. The critical gazes of elderly matrons, and the smiles of young men and women in the dazzling glow of crystal chandeliers. Rachel in her yellow organdy dress, like a ray of sunshine.

They went out to the foyer and stood in front of the mirror. Rachel needed to cool down. She was sorry Thomas hadn't come, but she tried not to think about it. A robust male figure smiled at her in the mirror.

Edita looked the grinning young man up and down, took Rachel by the hand, and dragged her back to the table. "Aunt Esther is having a fit wondering where you've gone." They sat down decorously next to the old lady and sized up the available men in whispers. "Your last partner looked like a wrung-out sock, Edita."

"May I?"

Through narrowed eyes, Aunt Esther made a careful assessment of the enquirer and nodded. Edita took the proffered arm. They were playing a waltz. The young man's name was Willy Sonnenschein. Three years later he and Edita married and moved to Ostrava.

When Gideon left, he said, "They can't kill music," and walked off towards the train. I curled up in the empty attic, once full of Gideon's handprints, and water lilies, and magic. Rachel kept the orphaned piano warm. I begged her to play Beethoven's *Pathétique*. Or the *Appassionata*. Or Gershwin's *Rhapsody in Blue*. She nodded. I let the music flow over me and erected a shield against the present from my fragments of memory.

A tall figure emerged out of the hazy gloom, the soles of his shoes tapping out hesitant steps. Rachel's fingers died on the ribs of the piano and the music evaporated. He stopped and smiled apologetically, shoulders hunched as if he had lead in his pockets.

Rachel quivered. "Gustav?"

A scrap of paper hung from his clenched fist like a white flag. The room was filled with his question, short as a stab. "Tomorrow?"

His head sunk down between his shoulders. He slipped to the floor and hid his face in her lap. He was fleeing from the summons, hoping to buy a brief moment before they hunted him down and ground him like a grain of salt.

"*I sowed millet on the headland, and will not live to mow it...*" Rachel sang.

"My friend Jiří wrote that," Gustav said. "Jiří Orten."

She bent over him, a wave breaking over a solitary rock.

I got up and left them alone to count the time that was already not theirs. I don't know what happened between them that night. She never spoke of it, and I never asked.

Dawn gazed aloof at the ants teeming around the drawn-up cattle trucks. Uniformed men, smoking, watched them with indifference.

Gustav rolled some papers tightly, and pushed them into the pocket of his woolen coat. Rachel held out her hand.

He didn't touch it, just shook his head. "I'm not going to say good bye—" His voice was bitter as black coffee. "—because I believe I will meet you again—"

She nodded. She knew he hadn't finished. He had to say everything.

"—in another life." His eyes were migrating birds. "In another world."

He turned and left. Rachel saw him straighten his shoulders under the black raglan, a movement that embodied both defiance and acceptance, the strength to bear anything. He climbed into the train without a glance at the remnants of his past life.

In October, I too received a narrow strip of paper with my name and number and tomorrow's date. *Einberufung. Freitag, 27.10.1944, um 12 Uhr bis längstens 18 Uhr nachm.*

Rachel helped me pack.

Even those who had so far held positions of privilege were leaving on the autumn transports. The Germans had abolished the children's and young people's homes, and the caretakers were travelling East with the young ones, so that they could, as SS Rahm put it, "take good care of their wards at their destination." He accompanied this statement with the rusty, creaking guffaw of a smoker.

Rachel was not included in any of the transports. She would stay at Theresienstadt with the few remaining children.

It was difficult to say goodbye, but I was happy for her. Or was I? I don't know. I don't really know what I know. I desperately wanted her to stay with me. I was afraid and I thought that she would make me stronger.

The future snapped its wolfish teeth. Theresienstadt we knew, but no one had any idea what the East held for us. Something inside told me it was not going to be like winning the lottery.

Late Evening

Outside, the snow swirled in horn-shaped vortexes. A car hooted in the distance. The squishy sound of tires driving through slush faded away at the end of the street.

I shook my head. I had never heard before how my parents met. I'd never actually asked. It had not occurred to me: they seemed to have known each other since the beginning of time.

"Do you speak German?" Anna asked.

I made a face. "Huh-uh, not much. We used to speak Czech at home. If our parents didn't want us to understand, they spoke German. I learned a bit during the war, while I was still at school. But I did as well at German as a sunflower in shade. Unlike English or Hindi, I couldn't get my tongue around it."

My son, Scott, entered the darkening room.

"Am I intruding?"

It was obvious why he'd come.

"No, it's all right. Tell Nick I'll be right there. Our hostess will excuse me."

I had always loved my children unconditionally. All three of them. Only every now and then I had an intense desire to beat the daylights out of them. I was nowhere near as patient as my own father. I often had an itchy hand and in my mind, at least, I

154

was very creative in the invention of physical and psychological punishments.

In reality, I confined myself to harmless, quiet, verbal rebukes, to which they reacted like deaf mutes. Once they reached puberty, I changed from being *Dad* to some anonymous pronoun. "What did *he* say?" They would look at one another. "Who? You mean *him*?...Oh nothing."

I never felt like telling them anything about my parents; they hadn't known either of them anyway. Sometimes one of the kids would ask a question, but I would put them off with an empty answer like: "That was a long time ago." Or I would change the subject.

My grandson, Nicky, on the other hand, could really get me talking. He opened me like a book, and all the stories from my childhood came pouring out.

When I came back to Anna, she looked at me, concerned. "You said you've had malaria."

"Yes, my liver's a mess and sometimes, just once in a while, it gives me hell. *That's Savitri coming back,* I tell myself. *Fate.*"

VIII

The World Walks on its Hands

Ever since my mother left, I felt anxious, as if I were in danger.

In my room in Zlín, there was a picture from the ceiling of the tomb of Rameses VI: the nocturnal peregrination of the sun god. A dark blue sky merged into a black river down which floated the serpent-shaped sun barge. And on it sat the sublime Ra, the ruler of gods and men in his nocturnal form, a man with the head of a ram. The Egyptians believed that by night, the sun god traversed the underworld, meeting thousands of the dead, powerful deities, demons and the damned, all condemned to torment without end.

My mother had told me that in the morning, Ra was a child or a scarab, at midday he was a man with a falcon's head and the sun's disk for a crown. He sailed his sun barge across the sky from East to West and aged with the aging day, and by sunset he was an old man with a double crown, like the one worn by the rulers of Egypt. At dusk he entered the darkness of the underworld.

I could find no consolation when I looked into my father's eyes, which remained somehow shuttered. He stared at me without seeing, focused on some point outside this world, which had lost all order and sense. His eyes seemed to be living a life of their own, independent of what he was doing or who he was looking at. They roamed the darkness like the sun god roamed the underworld.

His muscular arms were the only thing that gave me some comfort: their grip, the dense hairs on his forearms, the warmth of his hands, his nicotine-stained fingers. When I felt his hand on my shoulder, got a whiff of tobacco, I knew I was safe.

Then Mother's Day arrived: gorgeous spring weather, the promise of better times to come, and Zlín woke from its winter slumber.

Something in me snapped.

Only one year ago, Dad and I had walked through the meadow picking flowers for her. We had brought a whole armload of them home. She had laughed happily, clasped me to her, given me a kiss. Then I had rotated the piano stool up as far as it could go and played her *Für Elise*, which I'd been practicing in secret.

I shot outside and furiously grabbed a bunch of meadow flowers, squeezing their slender stems like lizards' tails, strangling them. I couldn't stop myself. Grasshoppers jumped aside in fright, their little green bodies flicking through the air. The slope I was standing on ran crazily downwards. My head spun with noise and my knees gave out.

I lay in the grass and my heart tried to jump out of my ribcage, to break out of its prison so it could fly after her. I looked up into the sun and saw her face above me. A smile. Eyes. My pulse gradually slowed; little white clouds were floating westwards, envelopes in which I could send her my wishes. "Can you hear me, Mommy?"

When Dad saw the haphazard bouquet in a vase on the dining table, he looked perplexed. He was about to say something, but couldn't get it out. He gulped and seemed to shrink down as he took two steps towards me. He ran his fingers through my hair.

In the evening he sat in the garden, submerged in the darkness and his memories. He started when I appeared in the door in my pajamas. "What's going on? Why aren't you asleep?"

"I can't sleep. Can't you sleep either, Daddy?"

"Here, take this. We don't want you getting cold." He tossed his sweater across my shoulders. "No, I can't sleep either."

I told him I was missing Mom. "You miss her, too, don't you?"

He nodded. "Yes, I miss her a great deal."

"I was thinking that our lives are the same."

"Whose? Ours? Where did you get that from?"

"Well, you told me yourself that you were thirteen when you lost your mom. And I'm thirteen and I've lost Mommy."

A shiver ran down Thomas's back; something heavy and ice cold was sitting on his neck and pressing him to the ground. He bent his head beneath the weight of it and closed his eyes. He straightened up with an effort and forced himself to look at the world again. When he spoke, it sounded like a prayer.

"The difference is that my mom died. But Rachel—Rachel's alive, even if she's not here. You have not lost your mom because your mom's alive. And she's *definitely* coming back."

At the start of June, the lilac blossomed. A familiar melody floated through the air, and with it the scent of magnolias and pansies and wild thyme.

Saturday, June 17, 1944. Pavel Tigrid from the Czechoslovak Service of the BBC announced: "Reports have reached London that the German authorities have ordered the imminent murder of three thousand Czech Jews in the gas chambers of Birkenau concentration camp."

Dad's eyes were wild, jabbing at the radio as if it were a target.

"The Council of State requests that all Czechoslovaks at home try to help their Jewish fellow citizens by any means available, to save them from death at the hands of the German assassins."

That same day we went to Olomouc. I didn't speak for the entire journey, unable to summon up the courage to put a single question into words. But my head was bursting with question marks, wriggling like a knot of venomous snakes. *Are we going to see Grandpa Rudolf? Or to see Daddy's friend from school? Or just for fun?*

Dad never did anything just for fun.

Trips in India contained none of this foreboding. I loved them. The Sundarban. The swampy forest of the Ganges delta. A sea of crocodiles—the slender-snouted Ganges crocodile is called the *gavial*. Tall ferns and interlaced lianas, the smell of eucalyptus and drops of dew. The rustling of the tropics in strange waves: a mysterious silence, and, a few steps later, the roar of cicadas, grasshoppers, and frogs.

On the way to Konarak we meet a flood of people, colorful turbans with suitcases, packages, sacks, and baskets on top. Dancing in the streets, women in saris with little bundles of future life in shawls on their backs. The babies peep out and squint in surprise at the world. An old man who can barely move, bent double under the weight of the bar he carries across his shoulder, with a load at each end like the pans of a scale. We're approaching Konarak. The beaches at Puri, villages big and small. A man's bare feet rush past us, and he holds a gigantic shock of straw that conceals his gaunt body down to his chest. He looks headless. The road runs with the coastline, a boat bobs on the sea, its sail a patchwork of a hundred pieces, inflated by the arrogant wind.

We are standing with our heads tipped back. Dad's eyes are sparkling and Mom is smiling. Konarak in Uris. Its conical towers represent the mystical Mount Meru. The thirteenth-century Hindu temple is the grand chariot of Suryi the sun god on twenty-four stone wheels. Erotic statues in naughty poses and the sun, shining into each hall by turn until it reaches the sun god and endows him with life-giving energy.

The Temple of the Sun. Thousands of pilgrims from all over India gather here every year for the Feast of the Chariot. Rath yatra. And we are leaving. I nod off on the back seat, the drone of the engine my lullaby, Dad's hands on the wheel. He always knows where he's going.

159

"Wake up, Dan. We have to get off here."

Olomouc. The train pulled into the station and the passengers thrust towards the exit. I came to my senses and staggered out into the maelstrom of the city. Dad walked as if he had gone this way a thousand times before, like a robot, like a blind man in an apartment whose every detail he knows intimately, all its shapes and edges, corners and crannies, shortcuts and detours.

We rang the bell at one of the large detached houses on Letná. I was captivated by the house: a wooden trellis on the south-facing wall with straggling green stems bearing purple flowers the size of your hand. A nebula of scent and buzzing. Bumble bees, flies, butterflies. Dozens of butterfly wings in the space of two square meters: ordinary whites and brimstones, swallowtails and peacocks, a red admiral.

The maid came to the door. She spoke in German. She led us through the spacious hallway with its spiral staircase into the reception room and disappeared.

A world of luxury. Pieces of antique furniture, glass cases with hunting weapons along the walls and bookcases packed with the leather bindings of the world's classics. A shiny harp by the French window.

A beautiful woman entered. She threw herself on Dad and let herself be hugged. Then she came to me. We looked each other over very openly. She had ash blonde hair and translucent blue eyes, and although she was smiling, she gave off a strange coldness. She gave me her hand and stroked my cheek. Her white fingers turned my hand cold. A winter queen. The maid served coffee in fine china cups and left.

They sat opposite each other and seemed reluctant to speak. Dad cleared his throat and broke the tense silence.

"I need help."

She seemed not to have heard him. "Oscar hasn't written for three months," she said. "I pray for him and hope he hasn't been captured. I've heard what the Russians have been doing to prisoners-of-war. I can't sleep because of it."

"I'm sorry. And I've heard what the Germans are doing to Jews."

She smiled nonchalantly. Little wrinkles formed at the corners of her mouth.

"We're in the same boat, Thomas. Desperate people torn from their nearest and dearest by the war."

"And yet there's a world of difference between us."

The wrinkles disappeared. She removed a hair from the sleeve of her blue blouse with her manicured fingers. She raised an eyebrow. "It looks as if we're on opposite sides of the front once more."

He smiled. "But we're still brother and sister."

Her expression suddenly altered. It held an unexpected warmth, and the smile she gave him was genuine. Tender. "Come on then, tell me what a little sister can do for her big brother."

This was the first time I had met Aunt Hilda. I would not see her again until a year later, and then under even more trying circumstances.

We left Olomouc in the afternoon. We passed City Hall, where the astronomical clock has been measuring time for five centuries. "Legend has it that it was constructed by Anton Pohl from Saxony," my father explained, "but what you see is its late nineteenth century neo-Gothic makeover."

On the way home he was in higher spirits. He even told me how Aunt Hilda used to steal sweets when she was little. She had a real sweet tooth. Even if she was full to bursting, she always had room for more goodies, as if she had a special compartment for them in her stomach. She had once confessed that she had stolen a truffle. Thomas had said sternly, "Stole? Where?"

"In the corridor of the Sokol sports center."

The local confectioner, a Mr Dejmal, rented a workshop on

the Sokol premises and used the corridor to let his wares dry. Little truffles dipped in chocolate, coconut rings, Vienna creams, all laid out within easy reach. She simply couldn't resist.

She had to promise Thomas never to do it again. At the time he was at boarding school and had begun to play tennis. He learned how to string rackets so he could make some extra pocket money. He would take Hilda to her singing lessons, and whenever the choirmaster, Mr Pivoňka, praised her, he would take her to the bakery. There, the big brother in him would buy her a truffle.

When we reached Zlín, we made some mashed potatoes and had them with the bit of smoked ham that Hilda had wrapped for us to take home. Later that evening, Dad phoned her. They spoke German, so I didn't get much of it, though I did catch the word 'Prag' several times.

Two days later, he left me and went to Prague, to the Central Office for Regulating the Jewish Question in Bohemia and Moravia.

The SS officer treated him very politely. "That's not in question, Mr Keppler. The Jewish partners of mixed marriages are not included in transports to the East. They fall into the category of prisoners who will not leave the territory of the Protectorate. That is what has been decreed. I assure you, you have no cause for concern."

Thomas nodded hesitantly.

The officer crossed the room and stopped next to a portrait of the Führer.

"For your peace of mind, I will send you special notification. Your wife will not leave Theresienstadt."

All the way back home, those few sentences went around and around in his head to the rhythm of the wheels on the rails. "... Jewish partners...mixed marriages...Protectorate...your wife... category of prisoners..."

A prisoner! So Rachel was a prisoner. Terrible word. The noise of the train was deafening. Prisoner. Rachel. Prisoner. Rachel.

The world had gone mad. Everything was upside down. What was striking was how quickly some people had learned to walk on their hands and pretend it was normal.

In the late summer, an official summons arrived. Conscription. He was told to report to the Zlín Sokol building. A rubber stamp with the imperial eagle.

Somewhere I found an old atlas with a double-page spread of the sky at night. The stars. Flickering lights in the darkness. I taught myself to recognize them. The Moon was a mute confessor who knew my secrets and innermost wishes. I had millions of plans and yearnings, but they were invariably conflated into one wish: I wanted it to be the end. The end of the war meant Mom would return home. Each time I learned a new constellation, I sent her a message by it. I used to talk to her. Or whine, like wolves and dogs howling when the Moon is full. I wanted to be good. But I would confess to her that I hadn't washed. That always used to make her mad. "Your neck's as black as a huntsman's boots," she would shout. I might confess that I hadn't practiced my piano, or made my bed, and I would promise I'd do better. "If only you were here." I tried hard for her sake, and I spent my nights learning to read the stars.

I often felt I could actually hear her voice as if it was coming from inside me. It was a mysterious genie, and I only had to close my eyes and let it out. Stories she had told me retold themselves, stories I thought were long forgotten. Often I would find myself back in India. Endless varieties of rice. The island of Sagar and devotional bathing in the sacred waters of the Ganges. The fluid wisdom of the Hindus. A call blown into a shell was the summons to evening prayers.

Long ago, I had sat huddled in a sheet and told Mom about will-o'-the-wisps and wood nymphs. I could see them. They would jump around beneath the banyan tree, dancing and wiggling. They would wrap their secrets in leaves and send them to the pixies that lived in the roots of the tree. Dad heard me and pronounced me old enough to know there were no fairies and nymphs.

That annoyed Mom. She dragged him out of my room. I could hear her hissing at him. "Don't go spoiling it for him. Kids can see fairies, elves, and nymphs because they believe in them. They live with them, talk to them. When they grow a bit older, adults start drumming it into them that they don't exist. And they go on about it for so long that the poor kids end up believing them."

My dad threw up his hands and made a face.

She took a quick breath to stop him from interrupting. "But how can we be so sure that such things don't exist just because we've lost the ability to see them? Is it that they don't exist just because we can't see them any more?"

"We don't live in a fairytale, Rachel. Even Daniel will grow up one day. You'd better get used to the idea."

Dad was a realist. And that drove her crazy.

Living with my mother was like lying on a bed of roses. Hundreds, thousands of thorns. Scratches and pricks. When she started throwing things, my father knew it was time to make himself scarce, but he felt as if he were walking barefoot on the shattered pieces. When she was in a rage, screaming, banging pots and pans, he withdrew. On nights like that she could do whatever she liked, she could turn somersaults, but he couldn't bring himself to make love to her. He became a block of ice, with eyes like glass.

He once told me jokingly that my mother had never understood Newton's law of action and reaction. That intrigued him.

Mom was an eternal child and Dad was a grown up. I was somewhere in the middle. Inside I sensed that Dad, and even I, were somehow more practical. And more careful. If he wasn't around, I would keep an eye on her myself. So she wouldn't leave her groceries behind, so she wouldn't leave the front door unlocked, so she wouldn't lose her keys.

I loved and admired her unreservedly, but in character I was more like my father. Sometimes she said that I was just like him, but that wasn't quite true. A couple of times she and I clashed openly, and she mowed me down, blew me away like a tornado.

Dad never argued with her. That confused her and infuriated her even more. She was not of this world, and in her eyes we men were tight-lipped sphinxes.

Thomas prowled around the house all night. Sometimes he felt he was asleep. But it wasn't sleep, more a drifting into a strange coma-like state. At moments like that she would come to him, she would lean over him just as she did when they made love.

He was lost in the darkness of her hair. She was leaning against the trunk of a fig tree with her legs slightly apart. The neighbors were having a celebration, but she bent her head back, her eyes half-closed.

"Do it to me."

The tip of his tongue roamed her little cells, her taste buds.

"How can you tell it's honey and grapes?"

She laughed in peals of warm colors. "I can tell tobacco. And chocolate."

He kneeled on the hard earth, both hands under her gathered skirt, rolled up to her waist. "Here you taste of yogurt and lemon." He breathed into her. His tongue danced under her skirt, in the folds of her flesh. Laughter frisked on the other side of the fence, sitar strings moaned beneath practiced hands, palms like a raging rain.

The days without Rachel were like dead children. Thomas was assailed by images and nightmares, and by the thought of what the future held. He was afraid to hope. He was afraid to sleep. He would wake himself shouting, the empty pillow next to his head. Cold. He sank his sweaty face into it and called out her name as if in a dream. He never knew if the tears were real or if he dreamed them, too.

Rachel, I've had that dream again. I'm going back to our beach and looking for the prints of your bare feet in the sand. I have to hurry to find you before the sea swallows them up. The waves come rolling in one after another and your footprints disappear. I look back. How can I find the wind in your hair? I leave my own footprints behind for you to find, an abandoned trail in the sand. One rush of salt water and my prints will also disappear. There's nothing. Just the sea that carries everything away. I wake with the taste of salt on my tongue.

In the morning he would cough with his smokers' hack, thick and husky. The seared cilia in his lungs squirmed. In his chest cavity, bits of phlegm detached from the mucous membrane and gravitated up to his throat in clots, passing with his first cigarette.

Conscription in German is *Sichtung*. My shepherd, Benny, and I went to the Sokol center with Dad. German officers were waiting. There were bursts of machine gun fire and rockets exploding. The outdoor training area had been transformed into the chaos of battle. Some dogs fled, others crept between their masters' legs, one was literally shit-scared. My Benny wasn't frightened. He barked furiously and quivered with excitement, all set to hurl himself into the fury of war. He waited for my command. Razor sharp, totally obedient. Dad stood a little way off, disguised as an imperturbable gentleman. Only his eyes darted here and there.

When Dad's business was finished, I left with a sense of pride, the taste of victory on my palate. I had seen those lily-livered specimens who lost it at the first shot, and I realized what a wonderful dog I had. On the way home I sang Benny's praises. Dad said nothing. He didn't seem the least bit proud of Benny's success.

A few days later Grandpa came to visit from Olomouc. I looked forward to seeing him: he was such a great storyteller. In the evening we sat round the woodstove and talked and talked, trying to outdo each other with our stories. I told him how Zam's uncle Jasbir had taught me to fix fishing nets. I had been his apprentice, a novice among those fishermen. Grandpa knew plenty about fish, but only the ones you find in rivers. As a boy he used to catch crayfish. They would lie hidden under stones close to the bank, concealed among the roots of trees, backing away and defending themselves. They knew how to move when the going got tough.

Dad listened in silence. He picked up the poker and opened the stove door. He poked at the embers and added some more wood. He stared briefly into the fire, then closed the door on the roaring flames. The fire crackled and Grandpa Rudolf and I giggled together as if there were no war raging outside.

The next day an official letter arrived. We waited anxiously for Dad to come in. His hands shook as he tore open the envelope. It was an order: draft papers. We were to take Benny to Zlín station and place him at the disposal of the Wehrmacht.

Bewildered, I looked from Dad to Grandpa, straight into their two tense faces, but their eyes avoided me. Finally Dad explained that Benny had been selected for military duty. He had simply been drafted, like a soldier to the front. I finally understood what that combat parade of the dogs of Zlín had meant. *Sichtung*. Into the German army.

A week later Grandpa and I took Benny to the station. I tried explaining everything to my dog, but I don't know whether he understood. I didn't understand it myself. We hovered around on the same platform where I had waved goodbye to Mom eight months before, and waited for the train to Otrokovice. It arrived on time. Benny seemed to be the only dog selected. A soldier in the uniform of the Wehrmacht got out of the middle carriage, looked around, and headed straight toward us. He was holding a muzzle and a leather collar and leash. He spoke to Grandpa first, exchanging a few sentences in German, then indicated that I should remove Benny's collar and fit the new tackle on him. Grandpa helped me, and after we had given Benny his German muzzle, he handed the soldier the leash and said something to him. I stroked Benny and ordered him to go with the soldier. He didn't budge or even take his eyes off me. The soldier tried to force him, but then indicated by a nod of his head that I should accompany him to the train. I climbed into the carriage and ordered Benny to sit. I hugged him.

"Good dog. Stay, Benny, stay."

He stayed put. He was quivering, his ears pricked up. I could hear his breath, that faint, rhythmical whimper he always gave out as he waited tensely for me to call *Here, boy!* He hung onto me with his eyes, spoke to me with his entire being. He didn't believe for a minute that I would let him leave my side.

As the train pulled away, a smudgy bitterness trickled down my face. I remembered how Mom had left, saying we would meet again soon. I was six months older now, and I knew that Benny was never coming back.

IX

Anna: Find Your Own God

Snow was in the air. The filtering shed. A great barn of a place, the assembly point for those awaiting a train into the unknown. Late in the evening, Rachel slipped out through the barracks gate and spent the last night with me and thousands of other outcasts, lying on our packed bags. The transport, marked *Ev*, was also to remove the members of the last autonomous Jewish administration, the Council of Elders or *Altestenrat*. They knew too much.

I don't think anyone slept that night. Time dragged and the air turned foul with fear of the future. My sole consolation was the prospect of seeing Gideon. I felt sure of finding him again.

With the autumn daybreak came barbaric shouts of *Schnell! Schnell!* Rachel helped the cowering shadows into the train cars. For cattle, the floors would be strewn with straw; for us, that would be a wasteful luxury.

I spotted Karel Švenk, rib-tickling star of the music halls of Prague in the years before the war. He had no luggage except an oblong bundle that looked like a wad of papers: a book containing years of memories, bearing the fingerprints of generations past. He trudged up and down beside the platform with it, and each time he was out of sight of the SS he held it above his head like a monstrance and showed it to the people crammed inside the trucks. *Ivanhoe.* Sir Walter Scott. A tale from the times of King Richard The Lion Heart. What did he mean by it? Ivanhoe and

Robin Hood undaunted. I leafed through my memory and recalled one of the heroines, a Jewish girl, Rebecca. She had been tried and convicted as a witch at a Preceptory of the Knights Templar, only for "divine judgment" to prove her innocent. Why, on a journey into the unknown, had Karel taken nothing but this one book? The smile on his face intimated that he would need no luggage where he was going. I don't know whether I felt admiration or aversion for him. Probably both.

A final embrace beside the last cattle car. I pressed her hand one more time. Rachel. The air trembled with a question that neither of us dared put into words. They sealed us in. We were a gang of dangerous criminals. Wild animals.

Rachel started away from the loading bay. Head down, steps faltering, tired and sorrowful. A piercing voice battered against the outside of the sealed trucks.

"Where d'you think you're going? Not keen on leaving us, eh?" The SS officer grabbed Rachel and dragged her off to the commanding officer. "She tried to run."

They wouldn't listen to what she was saying; it was as if they couldn't understand German. They were blind and they were deaf. Without a word, the commanding officer made the decision with a single motion of his head, and the young SS officer ripped off the seal of the truck. Rachel was suddenly in my arms.

Two days and two nights, sixty people crammed into a cattle car. One bucket of drinking water and one bucket for waste. There is nothing more pitiful than performing one's bodily functions in public: the obliteration of any difference between a person and a suckling pig. An indescribable stench as the omnipresent guide on a journey to who knows where. The train grumbled monotonously. When on earth would we get there? And where were we going, anyway? Stray shadows in the dark of night and the squeal of brakes.

At last! The siding at Auschwitz-Birkenau. Blinding lights,

insane shouting, and the furious barking of dogs. An avalanche broke loose as we, half-dead, fell out of the trucks. The actually dead remained lying inside.

Schnell! Jüdische Schweine!

What were those floodlights for? Were they making a film? It was a horror, but no one was filming it. Terse, endlessly repeated questions from a tall SS man: Age? Well or sick? A marketplace for the trash of human life. These to the left, those to the right. Novices on the dance floor, trying to get the steps right. May I? To the right, to the left. Right. Left. Uniforms in jackboots shining like razor blades, beating time. *Schneller! Schneller!*

I clung to Rachel like a leech. A child was torn from its mother, a wife from her husband. Terror in every eye, arms outstretched, desperate cries. Pleading. Mothers with babies, the old and infirm who had miraculously survived the journey stood just yards from us, segregated by the ravings of a superior race. With kicks and blows they lined us up in fives and led us off to the huts.

Those left over were loaded onto a truck. We could hear the crying of babies and the groaning of the sick slowly fading away.

Another raw autumn dawn, and a reality worse than any nightmare.

Barbs, barbs, current, current, barbs, current, wire, wire, barbs, wire, and current. And beyond, people, people, people. Auschwitz: a horizon of barbed wire. Black smoke, a grey future, and death in white crystals.

Another ritual of welcome. Stripped naked, showered, heads shaved. Ice-cold water, the stench of sulfur, and blunt scissors. A rotund Polish woman tattooed a number on my left forearm, doing her job like clockwork, with the dexterity of an artist. Blood spurted. "Done. Next!"

Branded with a short red-hot needle, like cattle.

After the initial festivities, we were driven out to the parade ground in the linen rags and wooden clogs we'd been issued. I ran a hand over the short stubble on my head; it tickled my palm like moss. I glanced at Rachel to get an idea of how I looked. She knew what I meant and found it funny. "Thank your lucky stars they didn't scalp us," she said. I couldn't laugh.

She thought for a moment and shrugged. "I don't suppose they've read Karel May."

"We look like tramps."

She shook her head. "No! We look like holy men. Tibetan lamas. They also have shaved heads and simple clothes, plain fare and meditation. This way we're closer to enlightenment."

Slowly I began to register the strange smell in the air. The stench of the cattle truck had been replaced by another, and it was everywhere.

Rachel's features froze. Her eyes fixed on a cloud. The acrid reek of burnt human flesh. She knew that clinging smell, smoke with a whiff of bodily fluids. The burning pyres on the ghats, the ritual on the bank of the sacred waters, the end of one link in the chain of life.

A shiver ran like smoke down my spine. Thick fumes rose up to the sky from the chimneys nearby. That was the direction in which they had taken the old and infirm. That was where they had taken the children. I grabbed her hand and held her tight. I wanted to cry out, I wanted to shout, but I could only manage a croaking whisper: "It can't be true! Rachel, tell me it isn't true!"

She closed her eyes and said nothing. I don't know how long they left us standing there. Five hours, six? I was past caring. The last shards of reason were gone from my life.

They herded us into our huts. Dinner. Like ravenous beasts we bolted down our pieces of bread with their aftertaste of burnt hair and bones. And turnip sludge. I had never eaten anything so revolting.

"Their chef isn't up to much," said Rachel.

I couldn't find the humor. My taste buds convulsed at the

unimaginable chemical composition. "I'd rather die than pour this down my throat."

Then three-storey bunks like cages, the cold, the smell of chlorinated lime, and bodies, and latrines. Bedbugs. We climbed onto the top bunk, tossed blankets over ourselves, and huddled close to one another. It was very gloomy, and after dark the only light came from naked bulbs like tiny, timid fireflies in the middle of a swamp. The bunks were so low that you couldn't sit up on them.

My head was full of smoke. It dawned on me where all of the autumn transports had ended up and I felt sick. I couldn't believe that the greater part of the Jewish cultural elite had literally gone up in smoke.

Rachel told me then that myths were memories of the life we wanted to live.

"Daniel was obsessed with sun gods," she said, "all those tales about how the sun and the heavenly bodies came into being."

He used to snuggle down in the double bed and plead for a bedtime story. He would lay his head on her lap and she would begin. Tom would come in and sprawl out across the foot of the bed. His grey eyes were a mirror. Like a cat, he would yield to the stroking of her voice.

"Once long ago, at the beginning of time, the Sun fell in love with a beautiful weaver. She lived with her grandfather in a cottage surrounded by a garden full of flowers and tobacco bushes. The Sun was so deeply in love that he wanted to be noticed, so every day he brought a deer to the cottage as a gift for his beloved. But her grandfather was not keen on their liaison. He turned the Sun into a hummingbird. Then the lovesick hummingbird would fly into the garden and gaze sadly at his darling. Her grandfather still wasn't satisfied. One day, he grabbed a bow and arrow and

shot the hummingbird down. The girl's heart broke. In the night, she carried the injured bird to her room and treated it. She nursed it until the Sun was well again and had reverted to human form. Then the girl changed into the Moon and the two lovers escaped.

"As they were speeding down the river in a canoe, Chak, the rain god, spotted them and sent wind and rain down on them. Sun and Moon ran and ran, each time barely eluding Chak's snares. Desperate, Sun changed into a crab and Moon into a turtle, but it didn't help: in the end, Moon perished.

"Sun, a forsaken youth, gathered up his beloved's bodily remains and placed them for safekeeping in the cavities of thirteen trees. After thirteen days and thirteen nights, twelve of the trees opened up and snakes and scorpions came crawling out from their depths. In the thirteenth, there was Moon, alive again.

"I think he's asleep," Rachel said.

They tiptoed out onto the veranda. The Moon was golden orange against the blue-black sky.

"And how did it end?"

"Moon remained in the hollow of the thirteenth tree. A deer came and made a womb in her with its hoof. Then Sun made love to his wife for the first time."

"I'm glad for him!"

"One legend adds that the Moon was unfaithful to the Sun. He punished her by blinding her in one eye, which is why the Moon shines more weakly than the Sun.

"It's a good thing the boy went off to sleep. Would you have told him that part as well?"

"No, I'd spare him that for now."

"You didn't spare me."

She smiled. "You can take it."

"I can take you!"

That night they made love like Sun and Moon. Her legs floated in a throng of seahorses and kelp. There were no bounds,

*no frontiers they could not cross together. All beliefs and illusions
fell by the wayside.*

*He was never lost for words when the subject was anything
practical, or work, or politics, or nonsense. His meaning was
crystal clear whenever he wanted to make fun of something,
when he wanted to be caustic, when he was indulging in self-
mockery. But when it came to emotions, he couldn't find a single
useful word. Words and phrases were empty molds, clusters of
letters, a jumble of scribblings that lacked all meaning. At these
times he said nothing.*

*He wanted to share everything with her. Making love was
the one way he could express himself in the purest terms, without
inhibitions. He was aroused by her arousal. The desire in her eyes
was dizzying, a flash of immortality. He erased all the taboos
that could distance them from one another. And she put herself
at his mercy, her body coming to meet him halfway. She wanted
him to find her, to lose himself in her.*

*She felt him to the tips of her fingers, her nerves exquisite
with longing.*

And then the awakening. The first morning in the camp and
the first beating. It didn't come from the SS. The first blows and
kicks came from an unexpected quarter—other women prisoners,
who already had several months of hell behind them. Women in
authority. The existing occupants of the camp hurled themselves
at us like the Furies, with frenzied eyes, arms like winter-bare tree
limbs, bones tearing at skin. They must have sensed the breath of
home emanating from us, as though we were reviving an appetite
they had already lost. How long would it be before we were like
them?

The first kick came from the head of our block, an ugly,
repulsive woman. She was so ill-featured that her sadism didn't
even surprise me. She prowled around us in polished jackboots

with a stick in her hand, puffed up like a turkeycock, gushing with her own crudity. "Anyone who refuses to obey will go up in smoke!" She pointed her stick upwards.

It left me feeling faint. Rachel held me up. "Annie! Get a grip." She looked up at the smudges that were veiling the sun, half-closed her eyes. She never mentioned it, but I knew she was thinking of her sister, Regi. She couldn't bring herself to talk about it.

Auschwitz was another planet; a different galaxy, without life, without humanity. Terrible hunger and acute cold. Human dignity was on its knees, and pride was beheaded like Mary Stuart. Every bedbug and louse had a better chance of survival than we did. The base of the chimney in our hut provided no warmth. It was November, but at Auschwitz there was no heat.

The Germans claimed to have tuned their unique methods of erasing us to perfection, and had applied it on a massive scale, an efficient obliterator of millions of Mother Nature's blots and misprints. They said it had taken superhuman effort to work with this vile material; had demanded great courage and sacrifice on the part of stalwart individuals. Only the crème de la crème could have achieved it. The Supermen. They had hailed it as a brilliant twentieth-century invention. But a few days after our arrival, they suddenly abandoned it. The chimneys stopped belching smoke and the ovens of Auschwitz fell silent.

Still, they continued with other tried and tested methods, like phenol injections to the heart for those labeled incurable, lest they consume to no purpose the bread of their magnanimous providers.

They would lead the rest of us outside the camp, where we shifted a huge pile of rocks from one place to another, then back again the following day. The high point of the day was the tasty turnip soup, enlivened with maggots. *Arbeit macht frei.* Labor makes us free. There was a cruel truth in that: in work we could forget our other troubles, the chronic hunger, the pain, the proximity of death. Though we didn't really have time to think about death. Fighting to stay alive cost too much energy, and we had important problems to deal with: where to find a scarf for the winter, how to get an extra bowl of soup, how to dodge beatings, how to avoid dropping with exhaustion, how to rid ourselves of lice.

Work was by no means the worst thing. Far worse was the mortifying routine in the huts, the idiotic bedmaking rules applied to our pallets, the acme of perfect tidiness for the Germans. Rachel called them "fits of methodical madness." There would be a sharp and piercing light, a sudden earthquake in every corner of the camp, frenzied activity crammed into two minutes. *Bettenbau.* Bed-making. Shaking out blankets, clouds of dust and lice. The occupants of the lower bunks diving between the legs of those who slept on top, the latter balancing on the side frames, trying not to fall. A highwire act. Hopping and stumbling, swearing in every language, an agony of tension. One bunk amounted to a thin mattress filled with wood shavings, two blankets, one horsehair pillow, and two to three occupants. That was not counting the fleas, lice, and bedbugs. If they were counted, occupancy would rise to hundreds.

Bettenbau was a reverential activity, a German symbol of discipline. It had precise rules, iron laws. No deviation could be countenanced.

Step 1: "plumping up" the mildewed mattress, for which there were two hand holes cut into the cover for ease of manipulation;

Step 2: insertion of one of the blankets under the mattress, known as "tucking in";

Step 3: shaping the pillow into a perfect cube at the head end, but careful, it *must not protrude* beyond the frame;

Step 4: spreading the second blanket over the bed, followed by "smoothing out."

The required result: a smooth, taut, right-angled prism with a symmetrical chimney at one end. Precision geometry: clipped edges, sharp angles, parallel lines and perpendiculars.

After two minutes' effort, the ordinary bed-makers cleared the scene and made way for a pair of experts. *Bettenachzieher*—bed overseers. Their task was an important one: to check the beds and make sure that everything was level.

Zosja and Blange. Their equipment was a piece of string as long as the hut. They stretched it out and held it over the beds. "It's crooked." *Scheisse!* Blange was patient. "Redo it!" And again. Blange pointed. "Two more inches to the left." They put their shoulders against the bunks and pushed them a couple of centimeters closer to the wall. With utter pedantry, they lined the pallets up along the entire length of the hut. Not even the slightest irregularity would be tolerated.

Bettenbau was the limit. German madness. An expression of symmetrical imbecility, and the local substitute for traditional bourgeois culture. Anyone who couldn't make a bed properly was open to public opprobrium.

I lay on Zolka's bunk with my legs apart, propped back on my elbows so that I could see her boots. Solid, leather boots. Good for sleet, frost, and snowdrifts. A promise. A hope of survival. Admiringly, I gazed at them over Zolka's head, which was sunk in my lap. She was making slurping sounds. I tried not to think of my own performance, which still lay ahead. Zolka's ever-wet crotch with its stench of urine and fish. Those boots were more than just hope. Those boots were a symbol. A solid leather guarantee of life.

When the head of our block had first ordered me to go to her, I hadn't understood those hungry eyes of someone whose *glans clitoridis* was straining at the leash. She gave me some bread. "Come and see me. I need you to tidy up for me." She had her own quarters in a poky room next to the entrance, no more than two strides front to back, two strides side to side. Luxury for the elect. The first time she just looked at me like a professional portrait painter. What did she see in me? A frail vessel for the slop from the local kitchen. Skin and bones yearning for a bite more to eat. The next day she gave me an apple. Her eager hands stroked my hair, and her lips simpered in sibilant Polish: "My dear girl, my sweetest darling."

Finally it dawned. Oh God! Before I knew what was happening, her sweaty hand was groping between my thighs and her cracked lips were scratching my shoulder. Rooted to the floor of her hutch, two strides front to back, two strides side to side, I didn't dare move. Now her breath and scaly tongue were in my crotch, and I was panicking at the horrendous prospect of having to reciprocate.

I felt I would spew my guts into that insatiable fish can.

One day Inge collapsed, exhausted, and dropped her rock on my foot, cutting it open. "Go to sick bay," said the wooden puppet in black. Blood streamed unchecked from my ankle and the spots behind my eyelids leaped around in multicolored droves.

Krankenhaus. Anything but that! Besides the sick, the hospital block housed those guinea pigs made to suffer Mengele's experiments—this man who had once taken the Hippocratic oath. With my heart jumping, I hobbled across the camp, squelching on the muddy pathways next to the huts. But one of the other doctors just bandaged my instep and told me to stay off my feet for a few days. I was glad to escape from that hell.

The next day, thanks to my injured foot, I sat beside the pile of rocks and helped by passing them to the other women. Rachel was bending down to pick up her next load when the young SS officer came over. I gestured to her to watch out. She got the message, chose a large rock and staggered off towards the other pile with it. The SS man bent down, picked up a smaller stone that sat neatly in the palm of his hand, and followed her. Nervously I awaited the sequel. Was he going to kick her? He was toying with the stone like a ball. Would he throw it at her? They did that sort of thing frequently and for no obvious reason, just for the fun of it. They were quite up to beating someone to death for nothing at all. The SS man was getting near. Rachel didn't see him behind her as she struggled toward the pile of rocks. Only two more steps. Suddenly, he shot ahead of her and blocked her path. He shook his head. He took the rock from her and put his own stone in her hand. *"Trag nicht so große Steine."* Don't carry such large stones. He nodded to show he meant it. "Pick smaller ones."

Rachel glanced my way. The world of Auschwitz was inscrutable, a place where anything was possible. We became phantoms. And no one outside knew what was going on.

I had to keep asking questions—sometimes reams of them. "That they want to kill us, I understand. But why do they have to humiliate us like this first? Why do they do it?"

At first, Rachel tried to find answers. "Because it is easier to administer the *coup de grace* to someone who no longer even looks human than to beat to death a proud human being who knows his worth. They're giving themselves an alibi with which to salve their own consciences."

But gradually she realized that these answers offered no solutions. Being an intellectual and in Auschwitz was a lethal combination, and she sought ways to break free. One evening, when we were all in our bunks, I just couldn't slow the avalanche of questions crushing me down. "What lies ahead? How can we survive? Will we even survive? How can anyone survive this?"

I was whispering into the darkness, my eyes wide open, my hand trapped between Rachel's fingers.

She gave it a gentle squeeze. Her voice was like the rustling of leaves. "You must stop."

"Stop what? Stop asking questions?"

"Stop thinking."

Thoughts were an acid that ate you away from the inside.

"Stop thinking. That's the only way you will find what you call

God."

I couldn't believe my ears. She had never had a kind word for my God. But it was worth it to keep believing. My faith helped me to survive. For me it was a source of strength, a rock on which to repose, a consolation. Rachel's conviction that there was no God was merely reinforced by the horror all around us.

"But I am looking for him," I told her. "Even here I'm looking."

"Auschwitz is the proof, Annie dear, that there *is* no God."

That is perhaps why she had such a hard time coming to terms with reality. Her inability to make sense of the world that surrounded us threatened to drive her mad.

Shortly after we arrived at the camp, she spat out: "Man isn't a phoenix, Annie. The dead won't rise from their ashes here, unless that damn God of yours pops up at last and performs a miracle!"

She shouted and flailed her arms, hurling all her rage and self-pity at me. I kept my distance. I kept as far away as possible from all the others, too. I had never been so alone. She did the same. For the first time, we were shocked into isolation, each on her own.

I looked for a way through the darkness, without company, without light, without a map. Utter despair comes when one is totally alone. For two days we didn't speak. For two days we slept next to each other and exchanged not one word. I couldn't understand what was going on inside her, nor did I try to find out. I had enough trouble coping with myself.

After those two unbearably long days, she put her arms around me in the night and whispered: "Sorry, Annie. I'm so sorry. I don't know why your God gets up my nose the way he does. Maybe— maybe it's just envy." She radiated warmth. "Find him," she said. "I know you will. I have faith in you. Find him, for me too. I can't."

Time dragged on, a fugitive in tatters. Weeks were like years. I would stare into the dark at her lying next to me. Eyes fixed on one spot, unblinking, not a muscle twitching, as if she were dead. She wasn't even in the room. She was floating somewhere far away, where the sea meets the sky, where blue melds with blue, where the sea finally drinks up all tears and the sky vanishes.

It was dark. In the dark, the sea starts in the sand at your feet and ends nowhere. Maybe she had found Him.

"Rachel? Have *you* found God?"

She smiled. Her eyes didn't move. "I've found silence. Total, deep silence. It's...like a drug. I'm not afraid any more. Of anything. Not even of death. I'm not clinging to life."

"Rachel!"

"No, I don't want to die. I'm not giving up. But suddenly it's different. It's not that I don't care what happens, but whatever does come, I'll cope. I know I'll cope."

Rachel, who insisted that there was no God, became my evidence that there *is* one. I believe that she really found Him. It had nothing to do with any formal religion or deity. It had nothing to do with the holy men she mocked so mercilessly as impotent drones. It had nothing to do with holy books. It was her own God. A drug. Like the space between two words, there was nothing to hold on to, nothing at all. She had banished thought and settled herself in blessed silence.

Work at the camp took up the whole day, from morning to night, and every day was the same. Only Sunday was different. We made the best of the time off to wash ourselves thoroughly, to pick the lice and fleas from the folds of our clothes, to sing quietly, and to flex our memories. We thought back to the times when we had lived as people.

Rachel told me of the strange day at the height of the Indian summer when Aunt Esther had betrayal her and Tom.

Her mother and father had appeared out of the blue, standing in the door of the Olomouc apartment. They had come the moment they found out, as soon as they received Aunt Esther's letter with the alarming news that little Miss Rachel was consorting with a *goy*. They had wasted no time trying to bring their wayward daughter under control. There was quite a scene. How they had shouted at each other! Actually, her father had shouted most. Her mother had been silent, but finally had joined in.

"Out of the question," her father had said. "You must finish college, and anyway—he's a *goy*. You must forget him."

She hadn't expected that it would strike such a dusty chord in Otto. But being a Jew carried an obligation, and he heard the voices of his grandfather and great uncle, an ancient biblical injunction. Consorting with one of a different faith was a betrayal. No Daughter of Israel may be married to a non-Jew, for it is written: *Thou shalt not give thy daughters to a son of theirs.*

She might have expected it.

Nightfall had filled the streets of the city with a fine drizzle and the first breath of autumn. She had shot out the door of the apartment. The twilit corridor was darker than usual and the stairs steep and hazardous. Her head buzzed. As if from inside a beehive, she had heard her mother imploring: "Rachel, come back!" At the front door she had been assailed by her father's ferocious bass. "She may not come back!" It had sounded like the chanting of the night watch.

She had run amid the droplets of rain that splattered against her flaming face. Only the steady rocking of the carriages restored her calm. She closed her eyes, her boiling blood cooled. What had she actually told them? "You haven't even met him! Just because he isn't a Jew! How stupid!" That's what she'd said. She was a stranger to herself. Her father had nearly had a seizure and her mother had almost passed out. Aunt Esther had fluttered about like an injured cock-sparrow, trying to patch things up in her squeaky voice, but no one had paid her any attention.

Father wouldn't yield an inch. He had stuttered with rage. "If you refuse to obey me, stay out of my sight!"

Mother had tried to intervene, but too late. Rachel, as short-fused and stubborn as her father, fired the last shot.

"I am not a *sheep*! I cannot obey you when you're so obviously petty-minded!" She'd said *that* to her father! *Petty-minded.* Tears burned her eyes. The world had changed into a murky river.

It was dark, and as she alighted from the carriage, the church clock was striking eleven. She ran all the way from the station, as if in a dream, towards the door of the little brick house. That door was her way out. She leaned against it and breathed deeply. The dim light behind the blinds glimmered like hope. She bunched her sweating hand into a fist and hammered.

"Rachel! What is it?" His grimace of surprise, his unbuttoned shirt.

She flung her arms around his neck and broke into sobs. He drew her inside, gave her a handkerchief, and stroked her disheveled hair. After she calmed down, he sat her in an armchair. Slowly, he did up his shirt.

"Tell me about it?"

She struggled to repeat snatches of the scene with her parents, disjointed and interspersed with bouts of sobbing. He listened attentively. Then he stood up and went into the kitchen. He returned with a pot of tea, some cookies, and an encouraging smile. The water flowed into the cups amid clouds of steam; he steadied the teapot lid with two fingers.

"We'll figure it out somehow."

She was frightened. "What do you mean, figure it out? Are you going to leave me?"

"What? Why should I leave you?"

"Because this can't be figured out! Daddy's thrown me out! He's done with me!"

He took a sip of tea, raised a quizzical eyebrow, and leaned forward. "Let's try talking to him."

"You don't understand! He won't give in, ever! It's simple— you're a *goy*!"

He tried to understand. He rubbed his eyes and poured more tea. "Let's sleep on it, okay? We'll think of something."

He led her upstairs to the bedroom and gave her a shirt to sleep in. For himself he made up a bed on the living room sofa.

He awoke to the sound of tiptoeing along the wall, stairs groaning under bare feet. He tried to think.

"What is it? Can't you sleep?"

She didn't reply. Her shirt glowed in the dark, white poplin and buttons opening one by one. He didn't have the strength to stop her. Fingers slipping, tongues searching, one body fusing into the other, hardening into iron. He traced the muscles of her calves and arms, the folds in her skin; he molded her to receive him, placed a hand on her inner thigh and opened her like a book. He hovered on the threshold and gravity did the rest. He yielded hungrily, tasted the irresistible pain of it, opened his mouth to share it with her. Scratches ran like red hair down his back.

He lay next to her and his thoughts ran ahead. She had brought him to his knees. No, it was more than that. Night slipped away, his world upended. He knew what he had set in motion: he knew she would want more, she would want to devour him, and he was deep in it. He wanted to be devoured.

They saw each other every weekend.

No one would marry them without parental consent because she was still under twenty-one. Otto had dug his heels in and written his daughter off; her mother would send money in secret to Aunt Esther. The chief thing was for young Rachel to finish college. Rachel was touched. She wrote her mother a letter, but received no reply.

On April 9, 1928, a week after her twenty-first birthday, they were married. Because of her studies, the honeymoon to Paris was postponed until further notice, and while Thomas's father and sister gradually accepted the situation for what it was, Rachel's parents were obdurate. The wedding had erected a high dam between them, and even her brother Erik fell silent for a few months. Only her mother continued silently contributing to Rachel's education with liberal sums; she went on sending them for the next ten years.

"I told you that this would stick in his craw."

Rachel carried it around inside her like a stone. All the more did she cling to Regina. All the more did she love Tom. She wanted to leave university, but he disagreed. "That's not up for discussion," he said. "You will stay on to the end."

"Not up for discussion? So I've escaped one dictatorship to fall into the clutches of another!"

But she attended her lectures and carried on living with Aunt Esther. She would spend Sundays in Zlín. Thomas bought an electric washing machine and vacuum cleaner: every household should benefit from the advances in modern technology that liberated women from daily drudgery. Aunt Esther grew to like Thomas, and did her best to bring the fractured family back together.

Rachel guessed that he had been thoroughly schooled in sexual practices. How many women had been touched by his hands with their intimations of eternity? They wreathed her like ivy. He knew so many ways to get to her.

But he was no picnic. He could be distant and distracted, even cold. He was obstinate and singleminded where his work was concerned. She couldn't stand it when he spoke of accountability, duties. He would bring it up constantly. She hated the word *responsibility*. How boring he could be! She felt like screaming herself hoarse, shaking sense into him, trying to bring him back to her. She tried to chip away at the rock of his seclusion in which he evidently delighted. She would accuse him of not loving her.

And then she would be ashamed. How could she be so wrong? How could she fail to see all that lay concealed beneath his rigid façade? It didn't make sense, but even behind his iron mask he could be despairing and lost. She found the sketches that lay under a pile of tracings and construction plans, a few cursory charcoal strokes, and yet Rachel looked real in them. He had tried to capture her fragrance, her breath, the way she spoke. Why had he never shown them to her?

She gradually unveiled his secrets and longings, and little by little he opened up to her, let her come closer. She gloried in her successes. At last! She would think the dam was breached. But in a few days the intoxication would pass and she would run into the impregnable citadel again.

He would stammer: "I'm sorry, Rachel. I...I've never been... an open book."

And he would close up, a master of caution, like a turtle or a snail. When he did finally emerge ever so slightly, just two fingers' width, she would rush to him euphorically, impetuously. She flung herself at him—and he withdrew again, startled, into his solid shell. Then she consigned him to all the devils in hell. She was suffocating on caution and discipline! He was an emotional jellyfish. She wanted to fly, carefree and unfettered, on the wild ride of life's carousel.

She asked herself: could they live together when they were like fire and ice? There were breakdowns in communication, two-way misunderstandings. Incompatibility. Her intensity and his reticence. She struggled against it, strove to overcome it. He tried not to see it. But when she was upset, her voice rose, she raved, she smashed things. She swamped him with her ardor and her temper. He never shouted. It was when he spoke slowly and quietly, so that she could barely hear him, that she knew things were bad. His voice betrayed him. He could be abrupt and severe. He was fond of the expression, "Let's say no more about it," and then not even the most ingenious coaxing would break him. She could drown in the ocean of his stubborn silence.

The biggest fight had come at the moment she graduated.

She had clutched her diploma and contemplated her future: she wanted to go into teaching. He was against it, stuck on the notion that no married woman should go out to work. And at the Baťa shoe company it was a matter of principle that married women were not hired, since everyone knew that a good worker could not be a good housewife and mother at the same time. *Man* was synonymous with *provider,* Baťa would say, and every man employed at his factory earned enough in wages and profit-sharing to provide for himself and his family.

Thomas Keppler, despite his sneering comments on social prejudices, stood his ground when it came to Rachel.

"Out of the question," he declared.

At the time, she was slicing an onion into rings with a large knife and streaming eyes. She roared at him like a caged puma. "So it was all right for me to study, but not to work? That's what I call progressive thinking! It makes no sense! Why the hell did you make me finish my degree? To *cook* better for you? History—my field was *history*, not homemaking!"

She tossed the sliced onion into a pan, put the knife away, and reached for a wooden spoon. He watched her closely: her perfect profile, concentrated expression, and pursed lips, the blue veins pulsating at her temples. He felt a tickling sensation in his tongue. *Whatever you say now will be used against you.*

"Let's forget it. It's pointless."

"What's pointless? Discussing things with you? Or living with you? Don't you have an ounce of common sense? I'll tell you what's *not* pointless to me! Teaching! I—I *will* teach!"

She flung her arms around, smashing her fist on the counter and even on her chest.

He knew she was stubborn, but this was going too far. Hands in pockets, he stared at her. "Over my dead body," he said quietly. It sounded like a threat.

He was standing perilously close and could almost see smoke

coming out of her nostrils. Her eyes radiated menace.

She looked around, her right hand flying towards the wooden chopping block. She grabbed a handle, and steel flashed from the blade of a meat cleaver.

"You asked for it!"

She walked towards him. There was something crazed about her movements. He stood his ground, watching her, his Adam's apple jumping like a piston as he swallowed.

His uncle Karl had told him once that if he was ever approached by a wild animal—a bear or a wolf—he mustn't move, mustn't show fear. The worst thing you could do at such a moment was to make a run for it.

This was the moment. He was a rock.

The impact broke her down. Once she reached him, she collapsed. Between sobs she kept repeating that she would kill him unless he gave her one solid reason why she couldn't teach. She was clutching the cleaver the whole time.

He spoke tenderly. "There is no solid reason, Rachel. You'll have to kill me."

She spared his life. And in the end, he let her teach.

Rachel lacked physical courage, so she called herself a coward; but she had incredible moral fiber. In that I was her opposite. Once, a Polish woman from the adjacent hut saw me standing by the vat of turnip slurry, came over to me, and punched me on the nose. I staggered, heard the crunching sound echo inside my head. I saw red, caught my breath, and lunged. There was a crack, a sound of rage. I gave her such a blow to the jaw that she fell. I just stood there, staring in amazement. I'd put everything into that blow. Anger and humiliation, the longing to break free, to defend myself, not to let them get to me. I put all the last dregs of my human dignity into that blow. When she picked herself up, she beat me brutally, jumping up and down on me until I just lay there. It had to end like that because physically she was far stronger than I, but I didn't care.

I spat out a molar. Even with the taste of blood in my throat I was overwhelmed by a wave of pride. I'd done it! I'd held my head high.

Rachel wasn't capable of that. Rachel, who at home would have fits of rage, slam doors, throw dishes, could never stand up physically to an aggressor. They paralyzed her. She couldn't return a blow. She couldn't find dignity in her own self-defense. Several times I saw her with her lips drawn in rage, but she never lashed out. She tried with the last remnants of her strength not to lose her faith in man.

Crazy rumors began circulating in the camp, false alarms claiming that the war would be over by Christmas, that Polish partisans were about to liberate the camp, and other fairytales. Some would have made you laugh.

It was then that the idea of death came to me, tempting and seductive. I toyed with it, tried to drive it away with the solid stick of faith. All it would take was a few steps; just one fleeting touch. the lightest touch with my frozen finger-ends...like malevolent wood-nymphs...and the warmth for a fraction of a second. To touch the electric wire. Every day someone did it.

I confessed to Rachel that I was thinking about it.

She shook her head. "It's highly questionable," she said. "Seneca might have approved—the Stoics advocated suicide. They used it to prove their independence of externals. But the Hindus, for example, believe that if you kill yourself, your karma will remain out of equilibrium. It will come back to you in a later life. And your own God is none too keen on it either. So take your pick."

"Thanks a lot!"

One day, we spent hours standing for muster until the protagonist of that day's story was brought in. We had driven nails into a wooden rostrum with endless blows of the hammer, expectation in our weary eyes. In came a fine figure of a man in black, wearing a cape. The condemned. He wasn't a Jew but a political prisoner. His name ran from one to another in Chinese whispers: *Tadeusz Tomczak.* Polish blood, young and proud.

Camp Commandant Kramer obviously relished his role. Red, puffy cheeks, with a scar down one side of a face that exuded brutality. A tub of lard in uniform. Chortling, he approached the prisoner and made great play of asking him if he had a final wish.

"I'd like to play a trumpet."

"Trumpet? Okay! Why not!" He was enjoying himself. He had a sense of humor. An execution with a cultural interlude? It was a lark, a farce. He sent for the instrument and ordered a piano as well, to make a real show of it.

And we stood there, mute and translucent in the open-air auditorium. The woman who sat at the piano was scarcely in control of herself, her muscles twitched unnaturally and her eyelids danced up and down in a chaotic rhythm. The SS officers were having a good time watching.

"All right, play something!"

The man at the center of the execution site put the trumpet to his bloodless face, his ossified lips. His throat pinched, no breath came, the cold instrument remained lifeless. A deathly hush fell. Then suddenly, a note: intimate, ardent, transparent. Tadeusz Tomczak played. His lips, clamped to the piece of dead metal, breathed life into it one last time. He caressed the instrument, which sang and sighed with melancholy. Schumann's *Träumerei.* The audience mellowed: those in prison uniforms and the clutch of SS men didn't know which way to look, how to hide their embarrassment.

Kramer, a big hulk with no inhibitions, turned his back, sheepish at the thought of being taken for a crybaby. He waited for the last note to die away, then he said a few earnest words. Never in his life had he heard anything so magnificent, he said. He pointed at Tomczak. "The camp needs this man."

The execution ended, and we left the parade ground, overcome. That same day, Kramer reported to Berlin that he had commuted Tomczak's sentence to life in prison.

Rachel's stories were the one treasure no one could take from her. They were the tie that bound her to life, to the past, hauling her out of her apathy and giving her back her true self. They reminded her that her brain was still working, that she wasn't an animal. Her stories were her liberation. We basked in the glow of her myths and legends, and for a while we were also free.

We tried to program our dreams, an absurd, childish effort that—like a stubborn case of constipation—ended with spleen and disillusion in the morning. But once, Rachel really startled me with a nightmare. Stretched out on her bunk, she stared up at the kick-marked ceiling. The night swayed to the regular breathing and groaning, the pale light over the door grew and grew, the gouges in the ceiling came out like stars. The bunks disappeared and the space overhead dissolved into a summer sky.

It is night. Hundreds of lights—fires and candles. A stream of water. Sticky air and the squawking of night birds. Two figures in a crowd, hand in hand. Music in the colors and shapes of Indian ornaments. A ceremony, a dedication ritual. They weave in and out among the smells and undulating bodies, their fingers making a wicker bridge. The heat is swimming with a sea of people, heads like scattered poppy seeds. Their breath dwindles above the surface.

They thrust their way to the podium. A rhythm binds the crowd of captives, slaves to their senses. A woman is on the stage, her beguiling and bitter voice forming syllables like magic spells. Deft fingers of drummers, swirling dancers, bellies bared, graceful movements from their flowing hips. Rachel half-closes

*her eyes. The rhythm cracks its whip. Rachel and Tom. Magnetic
poles. They almost touch. She raises one hand as if to stroke him,
but his face is under a spell, trapped under invisible glass. Her
touch is a thought. The music rises in a spiral.*

*Tom and Rachel, in a room with brass candlesticks, bursts of
waxen flickering. The sounds have changed to outer space, flying
above the laws of gravity, a black hole with magical power. His
breath is rocking in the chains of her clasped arms, scratches
from her hard nails like the wrinkles of wise old men. Drops of
sweat weave their way through the hair on his chest, and her
lips gather them up like pearls. "Don't stop. Promise me you'll
never stop. Promise." Her body is like a Gothic arch. Her burning
palms brand his skin. "I'll never stop." He flows into her like a
river. "I'll never stop loving you."*

*The last wisp of music wafts in through the open window,
higher and higher, the curtain billows and flaps around the candle
like laundry on a line until the moment of climax. Suddenly the
flame catches the hem of the curtain, scrambles up to the ceiling.
The fire jumps onto the tapestries lining the wall and flashes
around the room like a lightning ball. In an instant everything is
ablaze, everything is turning to ashes.*

Rachel screamed and screamed. I sat her up on the bunk and bent
over her, but the desperate sound woke the others. She clung to me
and wept in convulsions. She needed to wash the memory away.

Roll call again. More hours of standing in the freezing cold;
German arithmetic, counting us this way and that way, around
and around. Rachel didn't fidget, she didn't hop up and down or
flap her arms to keep warm like the others. She didn't squander her
energy. She took the ice cold air in through her nose and breathed
it out through her mouth onto her chest. She focused solely on
breathing, on the warmth that spread out to the rest of her body
from the pump that was her heart. She thought of nothing else,

her head as vacant as an abandoned parade ground. Even after hours of standing in the freezing cold, her hands were warm.

I tried it, but it did not work. It was a trick that defied all my attempts to learn it. Instead, I endeavored to fill my mind with thoughts of something pleasant, with a tune in my ears to distract my attention. But my arms and legs remained numb with the cold, my fingers like icicles, and my feet frozen.

After roll call they led us out through the camp gate. From the terrace we could hear a band playing: marches and those trite, folksy German tunes, one much like the next, performed by women, all fractured and jangling, utterly deranged. It was pleasant to be out of earshot.

Eventually we stopped, rolled up our sleeves, and spat on our hands. We shifted turf, moved sand by wheelbarrow, did those important jobs on which it would have been a shame to waste costly machinery. Men in well-fitting uniforms were hanging around nearby and smoking. Made-to-order; you can always tell. Next to their jet-black boots, dogs lolled, handsome German shepherds, trained to kill. During our last break, they were fed, while our lips dribbled with saliva and envy, our tongues pleaded—just one bit, one tiny morsel.

Rachel stared at one of them: he looked a bit like Benny. But Benny had a white spot on his right leg, it couln't be him. We were quite close. The dog lay within an arm's length, immobile as a statue, just his eyes blinking like neon lights. She whispered, and the waves set up by her quiet voice made him prick up his ears. He moved towards her, head on one side as if asking a question, the skin on his forehead crumpled in concentration. "You look a bit like someone I know. You remind me of Benny," she told him. He crept even closer, let himself be stroked.

Without warning, the smoking uniforms turned around. Stunned looks; a cocktail of rage and amazement. One of them drew his revolver. Rachel closed her eyes. "You!" He roared. "Get down there!" The dog ran obediently down the slope to where his master had pointed.

A gunshot shattered the fragile air and made our tense faces jump. A trickle of blood, and the life drained from his felled body. One last tremor, an audible exhalation from deep within, like the last puff in a stove before it goes out. The SS officer ran to the spot where his dog lay. He bent over it like a mother and wept copious tears into the shaggy coat. In the intensity of his grief, he forgot completely about Rachel.

The sun was setting and we watched a group of men lining up in fives. They were returning from work. The camp band by the gate played a snappy tune, with the drum setting the pace. Specters in rags, pain sloshing around in battered shoes, walking as if with a ball and chain, one foot in the grave. They looked ancient, a throng of desiccated, hunchbacked old men no more than thirty or forty years old. It was so peculiar to see these sorry, shaven-headed men shuffling past us with the resignation of slaves. Shadows of slaves. There was something so shameful, so abnormal and pathetic in the picture, that I almost cried.

Rachel said that one of them reminded her of her father. It took her back five years.

The rotund Margit filled the entire doorway. Her parents' housekeeper had always been plump, fuller-figured, but now she was bursting at the seams with lard. She had a slight stoop and her spine was working overtime. "Well, bless my soul, if it isn't Miss Rachel!" All excited, she fussed as they came in. "We haven't seen you in ages! Ten, eleven years, isn't it?" Rachel entered the apartment, which reverberated with memories. Whispers in the walls, her unease at embarking on the path of life, traces of smells and footsteps. Her father's soothing bass and velvet eyes, the dimples in her mother's cheeks when she laughed.

With the silent step of thieves and cats she approached her father's study. The old man was sitting at the window, his right hand leaning on his stick. With his shaking left hand he took out his pocket watch. His eyes turned from the puddle in the yard and were briefly reflected on the watch face. "Margit, who is it?"

From the door, Rachel scanned the bent, shrunken figure, the graying hair and dried up hands, and tried to discern her father. The wall of time crumbled against her retina.

"It's me, Daddy."

Gold in his palm and a trembling in his arm; with an unsteady motion he slipped the watch back in his pocket, tortoiseshell spectacles perched on his nose, their misted lenses turning towards the voice. Those eyes said everything: in the face of his lost child, he read the years that had passed. He tried to talk over the noise of unspoken words.

"Rachel! Rachel. I expect...we must have aged a bit, eh?" Then he raised a shaking hand, his index finger pointing upwards in admonition. "But I wonder if we've also grown wiser..."

The gentle gust of his familiar irony made the corners of her mouth twitch. Those words had travelled far; and when whispered, they had summoned the question she would repeat a thousand times in her bitter dreams. "Have you...forgiven me?"

A shadow passed across his forehead. "That was easy. But how could I—" Hunched in on himself, he rubbed the nape of his neck and dropped his head. The gesture resounded with extinction. The currents of the present had short-circuited as they made contact with the past. He was utterly in the dark. "—how could I forgive myself?"

She took two steps to cross the breach of ten years and took the wrinkled hand in her own as a sacrament. He was an old man, supporting himself on the flimsy crutch of introspection.

He shook his head. "So obstinate—"

She nodded and smiled. "I know. It runs in the family."

He laughed through his tears at the chasm that had vanished.

From time to time, the supermen would let us in on the world of their unique culture. They herded us inside an improvised big top. Then we waited for the ringmaster, who declaimed his bombastic: "Step right up! Step right up! Never before have you seen the likes of what you are about to see today!"

Theater in Hell. A cage separated the tamers in their starched uniforms from the wild beasts. The ragged crowd pressed forward, eyes full of tension and hunger for the heavenly sight. The all-female orchestra, dressed in a comical variety of fashions, was tuning up. They struck up a foxtrot, half-baked and grotesque, and, in the center of the arena, midgets from a Hungarian circus troupe hopped around ludicrously, wiggling as if their life depended on it. Skirts flapped over their stumpy legs, gaudy colors whirling crazily, and the conductor waved her imaginary baton as if hoping to impose some order on the pathetically scraping strings. Legs in the air, then a somersault and a backward flip onto stubby arms. Next a juggler, colored balls flying through the air in front of him and behind his back, grinned awkwardly at his audience. Tongue-in-cheek applause and the SS laughed hysterically. Mengele licked his chops in anticipation of his next batch of guinea pigs; small but tough—something to sink his teeth into.

"My God, Rachel. Is this real, or are we dreaming?"

The atmosphere was like Dante's *Inferno*, stifling and insane. Bows wrestled with strings, the percussion section escalated the pandemonium. Curveting dwarves, agile and supple, played the comb and paper, the jam jars, the mess tins. They swallowed swords and flaming torches as their wiggling and giggling flew over the heads and haggard bodies of the prisoners, staring like petrified skeletons, their hunger forgotten. Who was the madman in all of this? The painted dwarf smirked, his bent fangs like daggers to the soul, his bracelets of fool's gold burning like false suns, jangling and merging into a single chain of heavy iron.

It was an absurd one-act farce, like a *tableau vivant* straight out of Hieronymus Bosch. Life was a fairground knick knack.

Midnight

Anna was crying. Her tears flowed from the circus arena of the Reich to the snow-capped mountains of Colorado. Memories are a glacier that will never melt. Outside it was dark and the grey spots of snowflakes clung to the windowpanes. They slithered down to the wooden frame like transparent lizards.

She rolled up her left sleeve and showed me her forearm. Not a trace of a tattoo. "I had it removed. I wanted to blot out the past. Judaic law forbids tattooing. When they did it to me, it broke my spirit. It was like spitting in my face.

"In my life I have tried not to look back. Tried to forget. And I still haven't succeeded. Those terrible events have stayed locked up inside. They creep up on me and I don't see them coming. They catch me by the hair and toss me back into the sewers. It makes me feel so sick, but there is no stopping it, whatever I do. Each time I have to relive it all, go through all the suffering yet again. Back into the cesspit. I have to drink from the bitter cup as an antidote; to accept the fact that everything I have been through is part of my life. I will take it with me to my grave."

The phone rang. Anna brightened. "That'll be Michael." She hurried into the next room.

I inspected the photograph on the mantelpiece again. Anna had told me, "When Michael left for Vietnam, my husband staggered. His fear was like a curse. He knew what lay ahead of the boy. He trembled for him, though he was seeing himself, his own war wounds. With each letter from Michael he opened his own box of sand and rubble. Does it ever heal?

"As if dragged down by an undertow, Pete would read the news from Vietnam and between the lines he heard the pounding of guns. He set off after the voices and shrieking. He saw pieces of human bodies on every dinner plate, whether it was steak or rice. His soul dissolved in the gusts of sudden change. Apathy interspersed with bursts of activity, mindless gaping at the television, then conversations about nothing. Splitting headaches. His shoulder like concrete, a steel pin in the bone, his arm a tangle of wires and bolts. And waves of daily hallucinations, induced by a combination of pills.

"Then he sailed out to the sea of madness. In mid-ocean, Michael and his pals came to visit, arriving on motorcycles, their long hair like horses' tails. But Pete saw broken bones, entrails spewing, calling him, reaching out with the stumps of their arms. The ranks of the dead, bodies in wet sand, lined up like matchsticks. The meaning of words escaped him, his eyes like blank pages.

"One day Pete was gone. The doctor certified cardiac arrest. *He may have overdosed, Mrs Vanier*, he told me. Perhaps it's for the best."

Midnight struck.

I shot up the stairs two at a time. Ellen was sitting with a book on her lap, two tall goblets shining on the coffee table in front of her. When I came in she stood up, her skirt crackling with static. She went to get a bottle of champagne and handed it to me without a word. I pushed hard at the cork with my thumb, my hands sweat-soaked. The cork protested, resisted, but I overcame it by brute force; with a shout it shot over my head. The liquid started bubbling out of the bottle; Ellen pushed the glasses towards me. Then she handed me one. She was staring into my eyes as if looking for something.

"Happy New Year, Daniel."

As our glasses touched, the bubbles twinkled and that clink, pure and translucent, lightened up the whole room.

"Happy New Year, Ellen."

The wine tickled my tongue.

"Do you want to talk about it?"

"No, I can't. I have to go back again."

I found Anna by the hearth. The room smelled of the fire she had just lit.

After my own father, died, I went through his things. On one piece of rough, yellowing paper, part of a flour bag, there was some writing.

Suttee
I saw her on the banks of the Ganges
in the last of the sacred ashes.
I saw her on the pyre
as she cursed all the gods.
I saw with her sari
falling in little grey flakes
into my dream before she was consumed.

It was his handwriting. I don't know when he wrote it, though I have an idea. When I came back to Calcutta from my boarding school, Mom had described how they'd stopped at a village near Vishnupur, and had run into a flood of people who had come in throngs to watch.

Suttee: the burial of a widow with her late husband. Burning alive. The goddess Sati was Shiva's wife, and she was said to have jumped into the flames because her father had insulted Shiva.

Suttee's name had become synonymous with a woman of virtue, a woman who sacrificed herself. In the Middle Ages, upper-class Indian women performed *suttee*; with their husbands gone, they were so badly off that it was the best way out of misery.

Seeing it must have shaken my parents. The memory of it had lived on in Tom, returning in dreams like a poisoned arrow.

Memories do that. They come back as dreams, betraying and denying themselves, making a mockery of everything. In sleep, the brain changes into a confused telephone operator who plugs incoming calls into the wrong sockets and links up people who have nothing to do with one another. Chaos ensues, a tangled web that not even the best interpreter can unravel.

He had to do something to while away those long, sleepless nights. I imagined how it had come to him, a memory surfacing out of the darkness.

The jostling throngs, all crammed together, thousands of necks craning. Mourners accompany the deceased on his final journey. First his next of kin, then anyone who knew the family, or knew people who knew them. Then anyone who happened to have heard, and anyone who was in the area.

It's daytime, the midday sun blazes. The desolate widow, a young woman, semiconscious, who almost seems to be drugged with opium, ignites her late husband's pyre. She watches the fire flicker around his body, gather strength, and finally seize on the corpse. The woman leans on the shoulder of her father, who gives her arm an encouraging squeeze, for strength and as if to cajole her, mesmerize her. Thousands of flames reflect in the eyes of the crowd and there is one movement, a leap, she is flying over the blazing torch. The fire snatches at her young body, the crowd draws breath with a hiss. She takes a last breath, then she rises once more on the pyre, fire in her eyes, fire which drinks her in to the last drop. The young widow's father glows with pride. She's done it! His daughter has done it. She has dutifully observed the sacred tradition. Suttee.

Watching, Rachel is like a pillar of salt, Thomas's breaths are labored. He is overcome by a raging impulse to smash through the crowd of onlookers and drag the girl from the flames. But it is too late; they are too far away and rooted to the spot. A few dozen yards beyond the wall of the crowd a woman is dying, and they are watching. He ought to—but it's too late. Too late.

He turns to his wife. "Rachel, come away now." She nods her agreement and he looks back one last time at the figure of the woman on the fire.

"Rachel?" He reaches for her hand. "Rachel? Where...?" He looks around, confused, thrusts his way nervously through the forest of bodies. His calls turn into a desperate wail, growing louder and louder. The fire burns and the noisy crowd swallows up his futile cries, his wild eyes scan the air above their heads and out of one corner he glimpses the blazing pyre. He gulps and turns away in compassion. But he has to come back, he has to look once more into those eyes. He knows those eyes. They are her eyes. He has found her at last. "Rachel!"

She is standing on the pyre. Her weeping eyes strike at his heart. The fire in her dilated pupils, a world in flames, her face convulsed with pain.

He cannot recognize his own voice, breaking up in frantic cadences on the brink of insanity. "Rachel!"

Tom looked up at the bedroom ceiling. It was night, yet he could feel the glare of the midday sun, the fire, he could see those eyes. His loneliness on salty ropes scrambled down his temples, hanging memories, dreams, scraps of reality above his head, mixing them, shuffling them, leading him on.

Among Dad's things I found the Eversharp fountain pen Mom

once bought him for his birthday, with its transparent reservoir and gold nib. With it a pile of old, crumbling letters, First World War postcards sent from the front by Grandpa Rudolf, and others sent to him by his nearest and dearest when he was at Bozen and Branzoll. With breath held I excavated them, read snatches of the lives of my ancestors separated by thousands of miles and thousands of days. One of the letters, yellow as gall, shook me to the core. It was to Rudolf from his beloved sister-in-law, Fanny, in Vienna.

Vienna, 12.4.1916
Dear Rudolf, I have told you umpteen times already, and Karl has also written three times to tell you, that your Marie is now a great deal better, having gone to meet her Maker.

My grandfather had been stranded at the front somewhere, and I was shocked at the tone in which some great aunt of mine was reporting to him that his wife had died. One "tactful" sentence written with every possible calligraphic curlicue on paper that still, half a century later, reeked of eau de cologne and snobbery. Or was this just her bleak sense of humor?

Then I hit on something that looked like pages torn from a diary: my father's jottings.

Rachel! You are a mute accusation. I am afraid you might not come back. I'm afraid you will not acquit me. I hate my own fear. I look at those few sketches I made of you when we were together. My aloneness is testament to my guilt. I think of you and can smell death.

Thoughts of his own death hadn't frightened him, but the idea that she might die scared him to death. He couldn't come to terms with it. He battled with it every single night, and these thoughts were the knife with which he excised his feelings. Fear and pain. Midnight brought the living water. Then came the resurrection of morning. Newborn fear and fresh, lush pain.

It's like that feeling when an elevator stops midway, a confined space that becomes a cell, an airtight prison from which there is no escape. The elevator is suspended between floors. A few cubic feet of air and then...

His life was a house without windows.

Apart from Uncle Erik and his family, I had no relatives. Erik never came back from England. We sometimes exchanged a few polite words by mail, but that did no more than mask the burden of all those unwritten questions and all the things that had happened. They lay between us like the Atlantic Ocean, and no one was willing to make the voyage across. I finally stopped bothering.

X

Incurable

I had finished *The Three Musketeers* and couldn't get it out of my mind. I scoured the house for something to eat and something different to read. The bookshelves in the living room and study sagged beneath the weight of words. Books in Czech and German, and some in English that my parents had bought in India. I regularly cruised their spines, pulling out one and another, blowing the dust off them, sneezing into their pages and flicking through them, or stopping to really look. My choice was governed by a constellation of random considerations, from the color of the jacket to the title to a few sentences from the introduction or wherever I happened to open it. I ignored the shelves with the German classics because my German wasn't really up to it. But once, by total chance, I took out a bulky tome stuck between Goethe and Heine and my first thought was that it was probably in the wrong place. The *Kama Sutra*. Clearly, I had uncovered a thematic or linguistic mistake on the part of one of my parents. Or had it been deliberate? Anyway, I took it to bed with me and spent all night reading it—and many evenings afterward—my eyes the size of ostrich eggs. The illustrations impressed themselves on my brain. They stayed there even after I closed that miraculous book. So three-dimensional, so detailed and colorful, like watching a film.

Grandpa Otto had said that I would find all knowledge and all wisdom in books. He was right about that! The *Kama Sutra* contained everything I needed to know: a hell of a lesson. Night after night I had visions of lovers in the most amazing positions; my favorite sequences in the book came back time and again, and I would regularly wake up with damp pajama bottoms. By the morning the wet parts went stiff, as if they'd been starched. After a week of studying oriental wisdom, I started wondering what to do with my pajamas, which were turning into armor plating.

In more of a fog than ever, I continued on with school and my piano lessons.

Despite my heritage and the official ban, my old teacher, Mrs. Jírů, went on teaching me. She was stinting with her praise and hardly ever smiled. She looked like Božena Němcová, but with a few more wrinkles and even sadder eyes. As I played, I would squint at her out of the corner of my eye. She looked miles away. She didn't seem to be listening or even to know that I was there in the room. I hammered away at the keys, amazed at how good I was.

Her voice startled me out of my reverie. "Rhythm, Daniel, rhythm! What's the hurry?" I slowed down and stared hard at the score to prove I was concentrating. After a short while I stole another glance. She was standing by the window and looking at a lady outside, who was attacking a pile of leaves with a birch broom and a string of oaths. "She can't be listening now," I thought. Mozart went sailing away under my fingers. Then Mrs. Jírů stirred. Her bony hand shot upwards. "C sharp, Daniel, that's C sharp there, not C," she hissed, puckering her lips.

I walked home afterward, sat down to dinner, and watched Dad poking at his potato stew. He looked up and stared at me quizzically, as if inspecting something he'd never seen before.

"I've given you a change of pajamas."

My heart skipped a beat, as if he had just set a bucket of vomit down in front of me and asked if it was mine.

"Put them in the wash from time to time."

A smile danced across his face.

"It's nothing to worry about. It happens to us guys. Especially reading certain books."

His gentle smile drove all my fears and embarrassment away. I was profoundly grateful that he hadn't started moralizing.

He shrugged and looked dubious. "I just hope that's not too much for you."

When my father first received official notification that they wanted to send me to Theresienstadt by April, he broke out in a cold sweat. There must be a mistake! Mixed-race children weren't put in camps until the age of fourteen and I wouldn't be fourteen until June! What the hell had happened to that famous German precision?

Not that it really mattered. April or June. With the opening of a second front, the perfectionist Germans were getting short of breath.

The next day after leaving work, Thomas headed for the hospital. There wasn't a soul in the corridors of the surgical wing as he knocked on Dr Bartošík's office door. It was opened by a nurse who couldn't grasp that he'd only come to see his friend and that there was nothing wrong with him.

"He's in surgery. If you insist on seeing him today, you'll have to wait."

"Of course. I'll wait."

Thomas had first met Jarda Bartošík in Mrs Roubalová's lodging house in Prague, where he had spent four years in a single room. Královské Vinohrady. Glorious times. In those days they'd mostly spent their evenings together. Jarda would slog away at anatomy until it gave him a headache, and Thomas practiced his technical drawing until he was crosseyed. Then they would hit the cabarets. And it had been Jarda who, with his East Moravian enthusiasm, had convinced him that the town of shoemakers that he came from—Zlín—had a bright future.

"As soon as I graduate, I'm going back there."

Thomas had laughed at him.

"You're studying medicine here at Charles University in Prague just to end up working for some shoemaker in the sticks?"

After they got their degrees they had gone their separate ways, but it wasn't long before they ran into each other again, in Zlín. Bartošík had bowed deeply before him.

"So, it's come to my notice that your Olomouc Excellency has deigned to take up employment with some shoemaker in the sticks. Tell me I'm wrong, you old rogue!"

Now it was dark outside by the time Jarda joined him in the office for a cup of tea. Thomas gave a barely perceptible nod and desperately laid out his case.

"For God's sake, pull yourself together! What do you want from me?" the doctor said, lighting a cigarette. His head sank into his shoulders, but his chin still jutted out, and he puffed nervously away. His gaze returned to the familiar face of his friend. This was just how all his patients looked at him: eyes fixed on his face, wanting to be told he would cure them, save them. They trusted him unconditionally, not interested in the details, the risks, the possible consequences. They needed words of consolation and understanding, they came for encouragement and a positive prognosis. They wanted hope. They wanted to be told they were going to live. They didn't want much. *You are our salvation, Doctor Bartošík. Our last hope.* He had taken up the scalpel, and with it responsibility for the lives of others. They surrendered their bodies to him, their failed organs, their tumors. The burden of knife-edge decisions kept him awake at night, dancing on his duvet, sometimes until daybreak.

Distractedly he stubbed out his cigarette.

The guy just kept staring at him; he licked his dry lips and tried to straighten his back. He glanced out the window and his gaze swam in the rain-drenched street. Then he looked back to his helpless friend, shrugged apologetically, and heaved a deep sigh. It sounded like a curt laugh.

He shook his head. Thomas's strange, half-dreamy, half-despairing look would imprint itself on his memory.

He scratched his balding head and started gnawing at his nails. He imagined his own wife and children. He tried not to think what would happen if they knew what he was about to do. He prowled around the room, thinking aloud.

"Typhus. It'll be typhus. The hospital's full of it. I'll come and see you the day after tomorrow. Meanwhile get hold of a coffin."

Before Thomas could open his mouth, Bartošík pushed him out the door. "Go on, get out of here, before I change my mind."

Dad came home that night and took me down to the cellar. He said it was our only chance: he'd told Mom that he would do anything to stop me having to go to the camps.

His experience in the building trade was invaluable. In half a day we had drilled a hole through the cellar wall to the boiler room, bricked part of the opening back in, and left a hole at ground level measuring about forty times seventy centimeters. Then we made a lattice of the same size, mounted some bricks onto it that were split in half lengthwise, plastered over them and set it in like a little door. We spent all night reconstructing the laundry, where I would live. Two little ventilator windows opened into the shaft that let in a tiny amount of air and light. From the back of the house, all you could see was an iron vent cut into the ground and a hole beneath it. There was a similar window into the boiler room. Whenever there was a coal delivery, the vent cover was removed, the window opened, and the coal tipped out of the barrow, down through the vent, straight into the boiler room.

The next day, Dad painted the boiler room walls black, so that our anti-Nazi bolt hole wasn't visible. Once he was done, I had to admit that even I would have had a problem finding the secret entrance. I got a mattress, two blankets, and some books, and I dusted off the creaky old paraffin lamp that had once gone skating with me.

"You have to keep the place nice and messy. If anyone comes down, stand the mattress up against the wall on top of the blankets and hide behind it. Don't even stick your nose out until I come down. If you're reading, take the book with you. Leave the lamp on the ground, but unlit. There can't be anything else. I'll bring you everything you need. Food, clean clothes, water to wash in, a chamber pot. And I'll leave the door to the kitchen open so I can hear you. We need a signal! This is what I'll do: one knock, a pause, then three quick knocks in a row. You can only use the lamp in the daytime. Never at night."

After years of Mom's badgering about being tidy, cleaning my shoes, putting things away, folding my clothes, it was fun to hear Dad telling me to be untidy.

He found a tin of ground pepper and stood it next to the jars of jam.

"If they come, this will confuse the dogs. Are you going to remember everything? Tomorrow we'll do a trial run."

Finally I helped him reorganize the kitchen furniture so the bench seat was closest to the cellar door. My clothes all went into Mom's wardrobe. We threw everything else into boxes and carried them down to the basement. My old room couldn't have looked barer if it tried. The bed with no bedding, the desk and bookshelves empty. I had ceased to exist.

A black hearse drew up in front of the garage on a raw morning in November. Thomas went out and approached the car and its driver. A flustered Mrs Liška from next door ran out to ask who had died. He looked at her without a word. She noticed that he was all in black and crossed herself in consternation. "Oh God, Mr

Keppler, surely not your –"

He turned his careworn face towards her and nodded. "It was typhus," he said.

She started weeping hysterically. "Merciful heaven, how dreadful!"

Obviously, the Nazis came to do a house search. "Where's your son? You were supposed to report to Holešov with him a week ago."

"He's dead. He died on November sixth." He showed them the death certificate. "It was typhus," he repeated.

The Gestapo officer studied the paper closely, turning it this way and that, then nodded to his two underlings. "Search the place!"

Tom stood in the kitchen watching the officer, the same one who had hauled him off to prison three years before. Not daring to breathe, he listened to the noises coming from around the house.

"You must take me for a real idiot. You don't seriously think I'd be hiding him here?"

"I'll take that certificate with me."

Tom swallowed hard and waited. The Gestapo officer was subjecting the rubber stamp and signature to another close scrutiny. "I'm going to check this out."

"By all means. Do you want the urn as well?"

The leather-coated puppet's eyes blazed. "And how is your wife, Mr Keppler?"

Tom froze. Before he came to his senses, the man was gushing on: "*Ja, ja*, I'm sure she's well." He guffawed, the laughter dripping out of him.

Tom felt faint. The man's chortling was an iron boot to the stomach. Finally the door closed behind them. He tottered over to the table and sank heavily onto a chair.

From that moment, I rotted away in the cellar and read and read. The *Kama Sutra*. Karl May—his books with a unique patina from the damp-ridden walls of his cell. He used to write in prison and I was reading him in a prison cell buried beneath a regular house of brick, the isolation on my walls turned to mildew. The flickering light of a candle. Or did he have a paraffin lamp like me? *The Three Musketeers* again, and Jules Verne. I traveled the high seas and Africa with the fifteen-year-old captain, I discovered Stevenson's *Treasure Island*; at night I could hear the tap-tapping of Long John Silver's peg leg, coming out of the darkness, his parrot squawking "pieces of eight!" along with a thousand other characters, all promenading through my head.

I was a castaway. Robinson Crusoe. I turned the pages a hundred times over, and they shone in the dark like fireflies. I inhabited Crusoe's skin and waited for my ship to come. I thought about what I was going to be and beefed up my German vocabulary. I drew a piano keyboard to practice fingering, but playing without sound soon bored me. I kept a diary. In it I scrawled pictures of my dreams, and images from the books I'd read. A Red Indian with a pipe, a still life with an inkwell and lute, a horse at water. I wrote down snatches of stories, fountains of the brilliant and stupid ideas that streamed through my head. Each day I wrote the day of the week in illuminated capitals. I read about the heroes of old. The myth of Atrahasis. The Epic of Gilgamesh.

"The sea grew calm, pacific, the storms and inundations eased...it turned into mud."

I wrote down all the ideas, sensations, and confusions that seemed important to this thirteen-year-old, pubertal prisoner. I confided every last thing to that paper, thoughts of my mother in the back of my mind. "When you come back to me, I'll read you my life. Those days without your warmth and your smile. Days as dark as night."

In Canada, I threw it away. Mom was gone and the journal no longer made sense. Years later, I wanted to kick myself for being such an idiot.

A few days after I was buried, the doorbell rang. It must have been late evening. Afterward, Dad came down to the cellar acting odd. It turned out he had learned that Mom had been transported to the east, to somewhere in Poland. He kept shaking his head and saying it was ridiculous. A week before, he had had a card from her in Theresienstadt. He was convinced they must be wrong. He kept on repeating it: they had to be wrong. He was sure there was some mistake.

The next day, November 20, 1944, around eleven in the morning, the sirens went off. I jammed my cap on with the earflaps down so no one would recognize me, waited ten minutes, and ran behind the house, across the meadow, and towards the forest. I crept hunchbacked through the long grass. A few yards from the first spruces, a swarm of twenty planes appeared above me, then more and more, in groups of twenty. They flew over Zlín with a tremendous din, and then silence reigned again. I hid in the hollow trunk of an ancient oak that Mom and I had discovered on one of our last forays. After about half an hour there was a dull rumbling in the distance, the kind we would hear from time to time, that Dad would say was the Allies bombing Bratislava or Vienna. This time it came more from the direction of Brno.

Quiet returned. I came out of my hiding place and headed a little way back into the meadow. I squatted down in the yellowing grass and watched the cobwebbed sky. The bits of fluff took on the shapes of the bodies and faces of people, or animals, some more like cars, houses, or planes. One cloud looked like Amon. Perhaps it was Amon. Then I remembered Benny nipping my big toe when he was still a puppy. I wondered where he was. I thought of Mom.

We were driving along the Great Trunk Road in India, and my parents' friends the McCormicks were behind us. Mom was smiling at me and pointing out the window. Packs of wild monkeys jumped into the nearest tree and screamed at the passing cars, as if swearing at them. Herds of grey cows and black goats. A nimble mongoose dashed across the road and disappeared in a ditch. We stopped at a village. A toothy old man with a pipe steered us in and out among the weavers and the makers of baskets or jacaranda-wood sandals. Goldsmiths primitively drawing threads of gold. Sellers of sugar-cane. All sitting in their little shops the size of a European wardrobe and smoking hookahs.

We were heading for a certain small, quiet town. Buddhist monasteries, prayer wheels and flags. Bodhgaya. Ancient ruins, the temple of Mahabodhi and the sacred tree beneath which the Buddha would meditate. The scene of his enlightenment.

Mom told me that the Buddha was once a prince. His name was Siddhartha. He gave up all his privileges and wealth in order to find absolute Truth. Exhausted from fasting, he sat down under this tree and meditated for seven weeks. He realized that enlightenment hadn't come to him through asceticism because he had wanted it too much. As soon as he gave up yearning for enlightenment, it came to him.

Beneath the tower of the temple sat the Buddha himself. Erect, all in gold, with a swastika on his breast. As Mother explained that the swastika symbol stood for the cycle of life, Betsy McCormick inspected the statue. I heard my mother's voice as I gazed into the Buddha's half-closed eyes. His tender, feminine face, his thumb and forefinger pressed together in a gesture of meditation, he rose out of a lotus blossom.

The peace was shattered by Betsy McCormick's shrill voice:
"Why does the Buddha guy always sit on that artichoke?"

Mom gave me such a funny look that I could barely stifle a giggle. Then she explained to the woman that it wasn't an artichoke, but a lotus flower, which grew in bogs and marshes, rising above all mire and decay.

215

Mom's image dispersed. I saw two ears in the grass. They took two hops towards me and stopped. A hare stood there staring at me in surprise. I was an unexpected guest. He twitched his nose in a funny way, pricked up his ears, and disappeared through the green field with nothing but the white flash of his scut. The growl of engines returned. I took my cap off, shaded my eyes with my hand, and watched the sky. Fourteen planes appeared from the south. They were flying low, skimming the treetops. I had never seen planes so low; seven to one side, seven to the other, in close formation like wild geese, forging across the cloud cover of tattered grey in the southeast. The planes looked suspicious. I quickly picked myself up, jammed my cap on, and edged back towards the forest.

Thomas's meeting at the city hall was over, and before he could finish writing up his notes and packing up his drawings, there was a shrill whistling sound—a strange, high-pitched tone that grew louder and reverberated so close that he thought the falling bombs were coming straight at him.

A quickening of his pulse and a dizzy sensation. Not exactly fear, but nervous tension so powerful that he could hear the blood pounding in his temples. His head was like a balloon about to burst. Several bombs landed, eight tremendous explosions that merged into a single peal of thunder. He looked out the window and saw nothing but an impenetrable fog, smelled nothing but the stench of cordite and sulfur, heard nothing but a loud hissing, like a railway engine letting off steam. At that moment, one dilatory member of the office staff ran past him, taking the stairs four at a time to hide in the shelter beneath the building. He was overcome with dread. Daniel! What would become of him if Thomas got buried here? What if...

He dashed towards the stairs, but felt he was barely crawling along. His brain whirled. Everything unfolded like a slow-motion film, his own movements, the shaking of the windowpanes, the never-ending stairway down. Two flights struck him as such a great descent. How long did it take him? Twenty seconds? Before he reached the basement he had aged twenty years.

His terror was borne on the wings of American planes. The people in the basement cleaved to the walls, some crying out, others cursing or weeping. Tom peeped under his cuff at his watch. At that moment, a bomb hit the electric main or the power station. The lights failed and they were left in darkness, awaiting disaster, the end of the world. Then Thomas's brain started working: in his bag, besides pencils and drafting paper, there was a flashlight. He rifled around and flicked it on. Light in the darkness, terror-stricken faces along the walls. For three more minutes they were in suspended animation as the explosions went on, the deafening echo of destruction. Three minutes that lasted an eternity.

When he finally ran up into the street, he couldn't see a thing: dust, like India in the dry season. With every puff of wind the unmade roads would turn impenetrable and the people on them became grey shadows swathed in fine powder. There was dust as far as he could see. He ran for ten minutes through the fog until gradually it thinned out and the sun reappeared in a cloudless sky. He headed for the hollow oak in the woods. He heard himself saying to Daniel just a few days before: "Wait there until I come. We can go back home after dark."

He ran up to the scorched stump. A few yards further—a huge hole in the ground, a bomb crater and blackened, uprooted trees. His feet turned to lead. Oh Dan! He ran crazily here and there among the burning trees and bits of branches, looking closely at the charred remains of their oak tree and circling the crater again and again. Dan!

Coming to his senses, he set off along the paths they both knew so well, crisscrossing the whole forest. It began to grow dark and dew fell. He came back to the oak. The trees next to the crater had been reduced to ashes. Once more he scrutinized every inch of ground for several yards around it. He looked for a sign, a hint. Any sign. Any hint. Nothing.

Bending over the torso of their hiding place, he tried to reassemble his scattered thoughts. It was dark when he switched on his flashlight for the second time that day, and headed out of the forest. He returned home, brittle with cold and exhaustion, as dawn was about to break.

He stood outside the front door in the half-light, looking for keys in his briefcase. He felt a pencil and some crayons, his folding rule and cigarettes, but no keys. He got out his flashlight and tipped the contents out onto the steps. Damn! He left everything lying where it was, followed the wall back to the kitchen window and broke one of the panes. He reached for the key hanging on the frame and opened the window. He didn't even register that he had cut his arm. He hopped up onto the ledge and hauled himself through, listening for any sounds in the house. Nothing. The silence of night. He ran down the stairs, through the laundry and boiler room, and scoured the whole house again, and again, but found no one. He went back to the cellar. He collapsed on the floor, propped against the wall, crumpled and lost. He couldn't feel the cold wall, couldn't feel his frozen hands, couldn't feel the trickles of icy sweat running down his back and forehead. He couldn't feel a single thing.

I crept out of my homemade Nazi-proof hiding place, where I had spent several gloomy hours, and found Dad lying there on the floor. He wasn't moving and there was dried blood on his arm. I was afraid he was dead. When I saw he was still breathing, I tried to sit him up. He opened his eyes and looked at me as if he didn't know who I was, as if he was seeing me for the first time.

"Dan?"

"I was so scared, Daddy."

"Dan!"

He hugged me so hard that I could barely breathe. As we talked later about what had happened, we kept stopping to laugh. But it was a strange sort of laughter; a mixture of stress and relief, tinged with hysteria.

I had reached the tree only after the first bombs landed. Our old oak was in flames, burning bushes and trees, the pounding and rumbling at my heels. I was terribly scared. I spotted some people in the distance, so I ran deeper into the forest. I thought of hiding in the feeder on the other side of the spring. It wasn't far. I burrowed deep into the soggy hay and waited for darkness to fall.

"It took me a long time to get back home because I lost my way," I said. "I crawled towards the house, but there wasn't a soul in sight. I searched and couldn't find you anywhere. I felt awful and wanted to cry. I didn't know what to do. I thought something might have happened to you, that you might be lying hurt somewhere and need help, that I ought to go out and try to find you. Then I thought you might be looking for me, so I stayed. I stayed hidden here in the cellar all night and hoped you'd come back."

"But why—why did you crawl into your hole?" my father asked.

"I heard a bang, breaking glass. I thought it was a burglar, or some stranger, because you would have come in the door."

"I would, but I've lost my key," he said.

"Lost your key? But I didn't even lock up."

"What?"

"I left the door unlocked!"

Dad clapped his hand to his forehead and had another good chuckle. "And I didn't even notice. I was so far gone, I didn't even try the handle. I must have a screw loose."

The Allies dropped almost three hundred bombs on Zlín with great accuracy. Dozens of houses destroyed, the community center, cinema, stadium, and several factory buildings damaged. It took the fire brigade a week to extinguish a blaze at the central warehouse, but it collapsed anyway. My father lent a hand in the cleanup and designed a new type of steel formwork for renovating the damaged buildings. He was still struggling with it in mid-January.

In March of 1945 the mailman brought an envelope with a Hamburg postmark.

Herr Keppler,
Your wife has asked me to let you know about her whereabouts in the labor camp in Hamburg. You can reply to my address. I'll gladly pass it on to her.

Thomas supported himself on the table and slowly sat down. Hot waves alternated with ice in his blood. The crumpled shred of a burlap bag fell out of the folded letter, and his iron-stiff fingers grabbed at it.

Dearest Tom,
After the trials of Auschwitz, the work in Hamburg is a liberation. My thoughts are with you always. Write and tell me you're both all right. I hope we shall see each other soon.

He gripped the scrap of burlap, his face twisted. Wild sounds ruptured his throat. His forehead touched the table, his eyes flowing, and her tiny writing smudged.

XI

Anna: Beneath a White Star

I was cleaning Zolka's cubbyhole when a pockmarked SS-man came in. He glanced around the room and asked where the block manager was. I said she would be here any minute. He sat down on the chair, crossed his legs and nodded me back to work. Arms folded, he watched me from the heights of his superiority. When Zolka came back, he sent her away. "Take this message," he ordered her after hastily scribbling something down. She dropped her gaze and withdrew. The whole business looked like a game that I didn't understand.

He stood, staring at my skirt. "Pull it up."

I couldn't move. He drew his pistol and pointed it at me.

"Let's go!"

My fingers felt like wood as I tried to lift the tattered ends of my dress. He returned his pistol to his belt.

"Turn around."

He pressed me up against the table, his breath on the back of my neck, dense and heavy. With a jerk he undid his belt and latched onto me, his metal buttons piercing my back, my belly sunk into Zolka's sweater that I had folded a moment ago, my hand gripping the edge of the desk. He was vicious, and his anger grew when he couldn't get inside. With all his might he rammed in. I felt a piercing and let out a weak yelp.

"*Ruhe!*" he grunted in my ear. He was panting. I tried not to think about it. He held me tight, digging his nails into my rear and thrusting brutally. It hurt and I felt sick, but I also realized that this position had one big advantage. I didn't have to look at the bastard. When he finished, I heard his belt and buckle snap back into place, then his footsteps and the squeak of the door. I sank to the ground, the imprint of Zolka's sweater tattooed on my belly.

Zolka came back and tried to console me, but the last thing I needed was her sympathy. She may actually have cared for me though, because she got me assigned to another unit, far away from the pig. It was almost touching, but ultimately it was irrelevant. One week later, we left Auschwitz.

With Christmas around the corner, and a freezing drizzle penetrating the putrid morning air, we went through the "selection" process. They claimed that those picked would be sent to work in Germany. It was hard to believe anything of the kind, but at such moments you will believe anything.

There was Mengele, in riding breeches and immaculately polished boots, with a whip in his hand. How can evil look so magnetic? We proceeded naked past him and another SS doctor, who asked me what I did. I said I was a seamstress, but he plainly didn't believe me, with my hands of a retired quarryman. I couldn't believe it myself. I tried to salvage the situation. "I've also been a laundress," I gibbered. "Yes, seamstress and laundress."

He was tickled. "That's like being a goldsmith and a butcher!"

With a wave of his hand he sent me to join those pronounced fit for work. I prayed fervently for Rachel. She wasn't looking good; she had coughed a lot in the night and had dark bags under her eyes. The SS doctor was unhesitating. "You'll be staying."

I began to shake. *This can't be true. They can't split us up.*

One woman in the queue collapsed. In the commotion that ensued, Rachel had the presence of mind to run behind the backs of the SS men and rejoin the queue. My heart was in my mouth.

I couldn't even pray. She was looking at me. I'm not sure if I knew what I was doing, but I started pinching both my cheeks as if trying to come out of a dream. Rachel understood. Before she reached the SS doctor, she looked like a blushing high schooler at the blackboard. I held my breath. Yes. Yes! In a few seconds she was standing next to me.

It was a miracle. We were leaving Auschwitz together.

For the journey they gave us half a loaf of bread each and a smidgen of margarine. To our surprise, this time our cattle cars had wooden bench seats and we were not sealed in. The soldiers who accompanied us sometimes offered us a drink.

Rachel dreamed of the aroma of tea. Boiling water and tea leaves, swirling, turning gradually golden, brown, black. The English had taught the Indians how to grow tea. They tossed a handful of Darjeeling into a pot with the gravity of ritual. Hundreds of kinds of tea and thousands of ways to make it.

Afternoon tea. The glinting and clinking of silver spoons, the hot sides of china teacups and the exchange of pleasantries. Gossip. At one of the last afternoon teas at the home of the jolly and eternally loquacious Betsy McCormick, Rachel had met Claire Bennet, a middle aged but remarkably sprightly lady, a member of the Campaign for the Eradication of Tuberculosis. Lady Claire had a gift of eloquence that could captivate any audience.

"We started with collections India-wide, rattling our charm along with our collecting tins under the noses of the rich. We approached artists, shopkeepers, and businessmen, but also office workers and ordinary folk. We held charity performances and Children's Days. Health and Hygiene Days.

"And the money rolls in. We've already got a few million rupees and some devilish good plans. The designs for first aid stations, clinics, and hospitals in the worst-affected regions are all ready. Yes, yes, save your applause—none of this means a thing until we've followed it through to the end. We underestimated the need for education in rural areas. There is no great fanfare. The people we are doing it for have never heard of us, which is disappointing. We need reinforcements. People to go around the villages and explain to the locals what we can do for them. And above all, what they can do for themselves."

Rachel always responded to appeals to help others, and Claire Bennet stoked her enthusiasm. Her mind was made up in an instant. Once Daniel went off to boarding school, she would have time on her hands.

Claire Bennet tilted her head and half-closed her eyes in sheer delight. "This calls for a sherry, my dear. I can call you 'my dear', can't I? Welcome to the Saints of Sanitation! I shall write to Marchioness Linlithgow. The viceroy's wife is our committee chairwoman."

In those days, Tom was so tied up on the site that he didn't have much time to resist the notion. He confined himself to a few verbal warnings, then let it pass. Work at the site was proceeding at a murderous pace and he was glad not to have to worry about other things. Daniel was away at school, he barely saw Rachel, so he could concentrate on the job in hand.

One afternoon, he was listening to Ruda Martinec's suggestions, head propped in his hands on the tabletop.

"You know, boss, I'd rather leave steamrolling the main road for now and get on with digging the access road. And realigning the dam could also wait—I know you won't agree entirely, but now the water level's gone down and..."

Honza Samek came running in, out of breath and excited.

"Boss, your wife..." The words snagged on the dry surface of his mouth.

"What's the matter with her?"

"She hurt herself when..."

"Well? Where is she?"

"At Dr Seagal's. He says it's not serious."

Tom exchanged glances with Ruda and ran out to his car.

Rachel had been gallivanting through the villages and outermost hamlets around Calcutta. Ravi, her young driver, in a white shirt and with a smile on his lips, would pick her up early and bring her back after dark. Once she took something into her head, she got stuck and wouldn't let go.

That day had been steaming hot. She might have spent too long in the sun, or perhaps she had drunk too much or hadn't had a decent night's sleep. She hadn't felt quite herself since morning, but she had been unwilling to cancel the trip.

Worn out, with beads of sweat on her brow, she had been about to leave the village, to put it behind her after doing what she could. She patted the head of a little girl with a kitten in her arms, and went down the dusty track towards the car, with her interpreter and a gaggle of children at her heels. Ravi went to open the car door, observing her unsteady gait with concern. Suddenly she got dizzy and ended up in the dust of the street, one arm twisted awkwardly beneath the full weight of her body with a crunching sound. They picked her up, dusted her off, and started gesturing wildly. Ravi pushed her into the car and took off at full speed. By the time they reached Calcutta, her left wrist was twice as thick as her right.

Tom ran up the stairs and knocked at the door to Dr Seagal's consulting rooms. The doctor offered him his hand, sat him down in an armchair in the cozy waiting room, and poured him a whisky. The ice cubes clinked. Then he ran his middle finger up his nose and pushed back his spectacles.

"Your wife, Mr Keppler, has had a fall and fractured one of her left carpals. I've put her in a splint until the swelling goes down. In a couple of days we'll replace it with plaster."

Thomas took a swig of the golden liquid. He sensed the doctor's stare.

"She probably fainted from exhaustion." Seagal paused for a

moment, as if not knowing how to go on. "The idea they've got, I agree, is unquestionably a noble one, especially in the present instance. Yes, education and public health work is all, how shall I put it, it's something I can't disapprove of, but as far as your wife is concerned—can I be frank? This isn't a job for European women. It's—forgive the expression—it's foolhardy. She's wearing herself out and the villages are riddled with lots of diseases that white people aren't commonly exposed to. There's a lot of risk in it. She could catch something. We know from experience that the natives can live with these diseases—often for many years, but for us they can be fatal. Do you understand? It's my belief that your wife is taking far too many risks with her own health."

Tom looked at the last bits of ice floating in his glass, then at the doctor. "Have you spoken to her about it?"

"Yes, but I'm afraid she doesn't take me seriously. You ought to talk to her yourself."

Tom nodded and rose to go. The doctor opened the door between the waiting room and the clinic. Next to the cupboard containing drugs and dressings stood a plump nurse with disinfectant and a bandage in her hands. Rachel was sitting in one corner with her wrist wrapped. Tom stared at her.

"Would you excuse us for a moment?"

Seagal and the nurse backed out of the room, closing the padded door behind them. Rachel watched him as he cautiously approached. There was fatigue in his steps and the burden of recent apprehension.

When he reached her, he said, "You just can't help yourself, can you?"

She did not utter a sound.

With a barely perceptible nod, as if settling some idea in his mind, he turned his back on her and crossed to the window. Penetrating her thoughts was like solving a crossword. He gazed into the chaos and confusion of the street below. His mind was buzzing.

"You frightened the life out of me."

"I'm sorry."

He turned back to face her. "I ought to put a stop to it. I ought to forbid it." He thrust his hands in his pockets and took a deep breath. "But would it help? You wouldn't even notice, would you? Would you stop doing it?"

"I... Tom...I can't. I can't give up now. I *don't want* to give up."

"Are you trying to save the world? Oh, Rachel, why do you have to be so stubborn?"

"Because... because that's me. The person I've become, thanks to you. Because you have supported me. It's you who have shown me how to live."

"*Me?* I've shown *you?* Did *I* give you this prescription?" He stopped short. He couldn't stand scenes, and here was one in the making. He switched to persuasion. "You know what the doctor said. You're taking chances with your own health. And do you know what others will say? What they'll be thinking if I let you continue?"

"Who cares! I mean, do you really care what other people think about you? What they might say about us?" She smiled mysteriously. "Have you ever cared?"

It was never going to be easy. He had known that much when he married her. He had known that his was going to be pretty far removed from the standard model of a well-ordered marriage. And she was right: he couldn't care less what other people thought. He was afraid for her, but he couldn't forbid her anything. He didn't want to fight with her. All he desired was her happiness. She stood before him with her Mona Lisa smile, eyes half-closed and expectant. His mouth twitched at the corners.

"Oh, to hell with it! Fine. May I drive you home now, Madame?"

We got off the train at Hamburg, on the Dessauer Ufer. No

shouting, no pushing, no barking dogs. It was a dream. A five-star hotel. They put us up in a grain warehouse overlooking the water: showers and latrines; we each had our own bunk; and a herring for dinner. Sheer luxury! Except for the cold.

The Germans who took charge of us stared at our tattoos and insisted that they had never even heard of Auschwitz. We were issued unbleached linen overalls and men's handkerchiefs for our heads. And we got a speech: "You are a women's labor unit from the Protectorate of Bohemia and Moravia, which is under the watch of the Third Reich. By your honest endeavor and hard work, you will be promoting the good name of your country."

How very inspiring!

We were given spades. Lined up in fives, we marched to our factory through the city streets. It was a shock. Hamburg looked like Tokyo after an earthquake. We stacked bricks, cleared rubble, chipped the mortar off more bricks from bombed-out buildings so they could be reused. Our introductory fish feast was followed by a fast. In the morning they gave us some hot dishwater instead of tea, and in the evening a bit of bread and two mouthfuls of soup. After a day's hard work it was like a drop of water on a red-hot stove. Then the cold and the air raids. Life amid falling bombs, in the ruins of the city, until they moved us to the concentration camp at Neugraben, where we went back to sleeping like sardines. At five in the morning, a special train would take us to the factory, where the overseers treated us well. When the SS officer went off duty, one or other of the locals would give us a little bread or cake. In the evening it was back to our moldy pallets, three to a bunk: Rachel on one side of me, Renée on the other.

Beautiful Renée. We got to know her on the train journey from Auschwitz. She was a bit younger than me, and considering that she had spent a year longer in Auschwitz, she looked remarkably good. There was an air about her, a mixture of the lightness of youth and a kind of desperate heaviness that sprang from deep within her. Over two nights, she spilled out snatches of her story like pebbles.

At Theresienstadt she had enchanted someone in a position of influence. He wasn't that young, but she had slept with him and he had saved her from being transported away. He had also retrieved her little brother, Walter. He had not succeeded in saving her elderly parents—her ailing mother and her father who had been maimed in the Great War. "I didn't want to abandon them," Renée said, and we believed her. But her father had insisted, she should stay and look after Walter. They said goodbye to her, two desiccated figures, graying and pale, each giving support to the other. The frail old gentleman held his wife by the arm, both lost within their winter coats, shuffling step by step towards the train, a little bundle of food over his shoulder. They struggled into the railcar and were swallowed up by the darkness within.

Renée was very frank about everything. Her mother's last words to her had been: "Do anything, child, anything at all to stay alive." Seventeen-year-old Renée never forgot those words. She exploited her extraordinary allure; not even exhaustion and a lack of sleep could obliterate the unique beauty of her features.

When her protector at Theresienstadt suddenly died, she found herself back on the transport register. But at Auschwitz she had again been one of the privileged. The transport on which she had arrived in September 1943 was exceptional. The Germans set up a family camp for them. They were allowed to keep all their hair. Renée had grown up in Teschen, she could speak German and French and could get by in Polish. The warder, Erika Drechsler, pointed her whip at her: "You'll be my interpreter and secretary!" Thus Renée joined the camp elite.

The SS couldn't bear the sight of dirt, they were terrified of catching something and everyone around them had to be as clean as a new pin. Renée got to wash everyday, they gave her real food and she gave everything she could lay her hands on to Walter.

The hut they put her in had flush toilets, and she wore a prison uniform: the luxury of it! She was hardworking and brisk, with a fine sense of order. And the camp commandant, Marie Mandel, liked her. Renée ended up cleaning for her, too.

A young SS officer used to visit Mandel's office. Every day he would present his report and every day he would gaze at Renée, this Jewish girl who didn't look like one: blonde and blue-eyed, sturdy and well built. He brought her little gifts. He was good looking and treated the prisoners as well as conditions permitted. He couldn't have been more than twenty. SS *Rottenführer* Viktor Pestek.

Six months after coming to the camp, Renée overheard a phone conversation from Berlin. If they had known she was behind the door, they would have shot her instantly. Marie Mandel was speaking, and an officer, Hessler, stood next to her. They were given an order: the prisoners in the family camp who had arrived by the September transport were to be subject to *special treatment*. That word, *Sonderbehandlung*, was repeated several times in succession. Hessler suggested to Berlin that at least the physically fit men and women could be kept aside. "We need them for work in the camp," he insisted, only to be officially reprimanded for his pains. The original order must be carried out.

Renée warned the prisoners, but they didn't believe her. She was desperate. How could she save Walter? She slept with Pestek, but he didn't have the clout.

On March 7, all prisoners who had arrived in September were put into quarantine. They were told that the men, women, and even children would be sent to the labor camp at Heidelberg. Only the old and infirm would stay at Auschwitz.

For the first time in the history of Auschwitz-Birkenau, the SS guarded the other cellblocks in the camp.

In the evening some trucks drew up and the quarantined were corralled quietly onboard, and transported by night to the blocks with chimneys reaching up to the sky. They were herded inside. The first batch of naked men, women, and children stood and waited. Crystals landed on the grate. *Cyclone B.* The *Sonderkommando*, prisoners whose job it was to cremate the corpses, waited outside until it was over.

At that moment, the shower area turned into a concert hall. A deep male voice rose from within, singing. At first he was the only one, but others gradually joined in. More and more and more, men, women, children. Eight-year-old Walter held hands with a woman he didn't even know, and he sang. The walls of the windowless concert hall shook with the mighty chorus, the stream of voices escaped like a vapor and spilled out everywhere. *Where is my home, where is my home?* The notes of the Czech anthem rose in a flood. *Water murmurs among the meadows, pinewoods sigh among the cliffs. Orchards are radiant with spring blossom.* The voices mingled with the sounds of stifled coughing and rasping, then grew faint and died away in shrivelled throats. *An earthly paradise to behold.* The choir fell silent: the last drops of music, the last breath of gas.

The concert hall was enfolded in a deathly silence.

Walter. He had been there alone, utterly alone, had slipped his hand into that of a stranger so as not to be lost in the end. Renée tried to live with this, but she could never forgive herself. Never. "I should have been there. I should have been with him."

Afterward, the *Sonderkommando* came to see Pestek: a sixteen-year-old girl had survived the gassing, unconscious beneath a pile of corpses that had formed a hermetic cell round her, blocking the gas. Pestek had never known that to happen. "Bring her here!" When they lay the girl's body down in front of him, he shuffled uncertainly, then he gathered her up in his arms and carried her to Mengele's unit.

He explained what had happened, scratching his chin, twisting the buttons on his uniform. Mengele listened with interest. He rose from his desk, reaching for an ampule and syringe. The needle passed through the girl's smooth skin and she opened her eyes. For a few seconds she took nothing in, just blinked heavily. Then she looked around the room and at the man leaning over her. Josef Mengele. She propped herself up, her eyes on him. She exhaled and smiled. A disarming smile. She was still a child, and yet she kept her eyes on him all the time. *You are beautiful,* she said. Mengele, surprised, saw himself in her golden-brown irises. He smiled back and took her hand.

"What shall we do with her now, *Herr Doktor?*"

Pestek's question jolted Mengele back to reality. He let go of the tiny hand. "Come with me," he said. They left the consulting room and stood in silence. Mengele thought: an eyewitness had survived. That wouldn't do. Maybe if she were older they could reason with her. But this was still a child. No. At last he spoke.

"Shoot her. Now."

Pestek clicked his heels. He led the girl away and a few seconds later pulled the trigger.

The *Lagerführerin*, Marie Mandel, aptly nicknamed "the beast," was the commandant of the female half of the camp. She rarely performed acts of brutality herself. She had people to do her butchery for her, dozens of henchmen ready to jump at her every bidding. She left most things to the Drechsler woman. Erika Drechsler was the very embodiment of discipline and blind obedience. She made no secret of the fact that she was in love with the *Führer*.

Every morning she stood in front of her mirror, delighting in the sight of herself as each time she confirmed that she was a consummate specimen of the German race. Like her boss: athletic of build, blond hair, sharp features. If only her eyes were blue. Her dark brown irises simply didn't suit her. She adjusted her collar, tugged the jacket of her gray uniform into place. She looked back at herself, her pupils dilated with concentration. Head erect, her heels clicked sharply, her right arm shot up. Not a muscle moved in her stern face. *Heil Hitler!* She dropped her arm but remained at attention. Then a second more of concentration and again her stiff right arm zoomed into the air. *Heil Hitler!* After ten minutes of exercises like this, she rewarded herself with a smile and left.

They brought her a message to look in on Mandel, the camp commandant. Mandel appeared tired and insecure: not her usual self. She had issued a gassing order and passed it now to Drechsler. As she did so, her face wore an expression of something like desperation.

"Do we have the right?"

Must be suffering from mental fatigue, flashed through Drechsler's mind. *Or she's not the woman I thought.*

Erika Drechsler was resolute. "*Ja,* of course we do. The right of a superior race. It's our duty."

Mandel herself had once told her that a pure race does whatever it has to. It makes no apologies, never looks back, never searches its conscience. Whatever it does, it does for the good of the world at large.

Mandel nodded and waved her back out. That day she stayed inside her office. She went through some old letters, checked the entries in her records and re-read some notes in her diary. A photo slipped out from the cover. It was of her, as she was just a few years ago before the war, on her first vacation in Italy. They had saved up two years to go there. She was sitting in a basketwork rocking chair, a broad smile on her face, in a fashionable swimsuit with alarmingly skimpy legs. She could feel the hot air, the burning sand between her toes, could hear the regular pounding of waves. She had teased the man behind the camera with her tanned body, chestnut hair, and bewitching eyes. She looked at the photo, let out a hiss and shook her head. How could she have enjoyed it with one of *them*? An inferior breed. When the times changed she had quickly broken it off.

The SS men and women had their work cut out to cope with the hordes. The pressure on the crematoria was tremendous. Chimneys and nerves alike were suffering from overload. Those charged with supervision were given plenty of booze to take the edge off their scruples. Thick skins obtained for the price of a bottle of spirits. Some complied out of cowardice, others out of malice, yet others out of greed.

Renée told us she knew that Viktor Pestek had just about had enough. Since the age of seventeen he'd been engaged in killing, or, more precisely, murdering. They hadn't sent him to the front, but put him instead on "cleansing" operations. He had sustained a gunshot wound at Minsk, and ever since had been classed as an invalid, unfit for frontline action, and they had dispatched him to Auschwitz. He had hated it here from the start, but to crown it all he was now in love. He would meet in secret with his beautiful Jewess, and had thought hard of ways to get her out of the camp before she went to the gas chamber. He could run away with her, but he didn't know anyone who would hide them. But there were certain Jews at the camp who could arrange matters. He told Renée that he was going to aid in the flight of one prisoner who had links to the resistance, and as soon as he took care of that, he would come back to the camp to collect her.

The next day was the last time she saw him. During evening roll call the sirens went off: a search was on for an escaped prisoner. Pestek had taken the day off, so no one was looking for him yet.

They were kept standing on the parade ground for sixteen hours. Renée was rigid with fear. A week later she learned that the escape had been successful. By then he must have been in Bohemia.

She didn't know whether she was truly in love with Viktor. He was her chance of freedom, and she believed he was serious. She would meet him, talk to him, make love with him. Unlike the fat geezer at Theresienstadt, Viktor didn't give her the creeps. She was sure he loved her. Now all she had to do was await his return. She tried to concentrate on her work and follow the orders of Drechsler and Mandel.

Marie Mandel was tall and slim, elegant and well-groomed. Delicate white hands, a gray uniform and blue, blue eyes. The uniform suited her, with its military cap in the shape of a little boat, sitting on her golden braids. She had teeth like crystal and legs in silk stockings—the very flower of racial purity. She was sophisticated and a music lover: hearing Alma Rosé, under whose fingers a piece of wood changed into a magic violin, Marie had quivered with emotion. Alma Rosé, the niece of Gustav Mahler, had just played Schubert's *Ave Maria*. Marie Mandel had given her a box of hazelnuts and started using her proper name.

Marie patrolled the camp with the stride of the Third Reich, not a hair out of place; nothing could escape her notice, not a mouse could slip past her. The latest consignment had just been tipped out of the cattle trucks and lined up. They were on tenterhooks, shifting their feet and waiting. They didn't know what for, but they were waiting. Time was gasping for air and about to run out. Aryan Polish women with a blot on their political record were expecting special treatment, calming their children, trying to settle them, stop them running around. "Where are you going? Don't go anywhere, stay here!"

A little girl with golden hair toddled about, unaware that she was lost. She lurched over to Marie's polished boots, shining like an expensive toy, and smiled up at those blue eyes. Marie Mandel stopped. They gazed at one another, the world watched, and one woman called the child's name. No one heard her. The day ended and the night passed.

Renée recognized the footfall of the camp boss, resolute and uncompromising. But now she was confused. She could hear her voice, yes, it was Marie, but the footsteps were fragmentary and irregular. Then a child toddled in, dragging someone by the hand:

Marie Mandel. She mumbled the morning orders: "Go to Canada and get me some clothes for her. All pink!"

Renée headed for Canada, the storehouse for the belongings of those who had been gassed. A few privileged prisoners sorted the luggage of all who had entered the Auschwitz soap and comb works.

Clothes for Marie Mandel's little girl? Self-assured, the seasoned Canadian took her inside and pointed. "Children's section. Take your pick."

Renée's feet felt like worn tires. Her eyes roamed the shelves piled high with children's clothing—a cascade of caps, tiny gloves, woollen mittens with an embroidered sun. Rows of little shoes lined up like soldiers on parade, arranged according to size. Little coats, sweaters, shirts on hangers, a neat garden of pretty flowers, a yellow star on every breast, falling like dust from the sky. Renée already knew why smoke rose from the chimneys, she knew full well where whole trainloads disappeared to, she knew, but here she was on the verge of suffocating. In every garment she saw Walter. A mass of children's things, irresistible and demented. A teddy bear sat dumbly in the corner, the sole witness.

She staggered back out with an armful of pink rags.

Marie Mandel: native of Upper Austria. Warder at Ravensbrück. One day she would wind up on the gallows for crimes against humanity, Renée thought. Marie Mandel: Madonna and Child. She walked about the camp with the dolled-up baby in her arms. Her usually spotless uniform was stained with chocolate, the little blonde rascal pulled her hair, wriggled around on her lap, kicked at her firm legs with her baby shoes, one sole catching her stocking and putting a run in it. And Marie Mandel was *laughing*! "Isn't she a treasure?" The little girl couldn't talk yet, she just cuddled her with her chocolaty fingers, then planted a sloppy kiss on that unblemished cheek.

For a week Marie Mandel paraded among the huts with her

baby girl, a picture straight out of a family album. Mother and child: a double image of perfection in the eyes of the gaunt and starving.

And then Kramer arrived. He entered without knocking and the door slammed behind him. Voices, excited, curt and smooth as steel. He didn't need this, emphatically not! He left again, red in the face and exhausted. He didn't even close the door behind him.

Marie Mandel stood in the middle of the room, her face muscles numb. "Send Erika Drechsler to me!"

Drechsler arrived and made her perfect salute. Mandel gave her a whispered order, staring blankly. A face without lips. There was a cold waft of death. "Take the child away."

Drechsler hesitated. "Where?" Her boss's gesture was eloquent enough, but she had to make sure. Mandel began shouting, aiming her anger at Drechsler, at all *überleute*. "Get on with it! Didn't you hear my order? *Move!*"

Drechsler took the baby away, all golden curls and ringlets. Marie Mandel's mouth twitched. That evening she poured herself a stiff one, full to the brim. Outside her window the fog smelled of weeping. Her eyes filled with smoke and the hands of children.

She summoned Renée. "My cape!" She put it on and went outside, her skin all gooseflesh in the dark, black night; she waded through the stench of flesh and her own thoughts, looking for something. She walked on through the dark and at the end there was music. Soothing, calming. A city of oblivion. In the music block she made them play on for her, took refuge in *Madame Butterfly*, escaped from herself as long as the music lasted. Then she went back out into the black night.

That night Viktor Pestek came back for Renée and was waiting not far from the camp. He sent a message to the insiders: "I'm in Mexico." But as day broke, so did one link in the chain, and he was betrayed. They brought him to the death block. Interrogations, torture for days and nights, weeks on end. Pestek knew he would die. And he knew he must say nothing.

Auschwitz hosted the court martial, which pronounced judgement: the death penalty for aiding prisoners and desertion. The twenty-year-old SS officer was shot.

Renée shed not one tear.

Not one, until she retold it to Rachel and me in Hamburg, and unburdened herself of her life behind barbed wire. Then she hid her face in her hands and wept. For her parents, for little Walter, for Viktor Pestek. For herself? In the morning her eyes were all puffy and red, and the first wrinkles had formed around her mouth.

The start of 1945 wrung the remnants of life from us with bitter frost. Hands froze to shovels, droplets of sweat turned into pearls. On the way back from work we would pass civilians in the streets, and their looks betrayed their disdain. It was like getting a splinter down behind your nail. We could read in their eyes what we were: the scum of humanity, the vilest of criminals and murderesses.

Rachel marched by my side, her lashes weighed down with snowflakes and her breath billowing in the stream of her words:

"Summer in India was lava-hot, the air thick with vapor and the smell of sweat. In India even the walls sweated. The sea breeze burned and the very sea itself was hot. You could be doing nothing and still be dying of the heat, squelching in your own juice. You came out of the shower, but didn't dry yourself off because even the towel was scorching, though soggy as a sponge. Everything was damp, soaked through. I couldn't breathe. I hung in the air like washing on a line and couldn't get dry. Sticky, gooey, musty.

"How I longed then for the chilling touch of snowflakes. I dreamed of them drifting down out of a gray sky and making my cheeks cold. I dreamed about the crazy flower patterns dry-etched onto windowpanes by the frost. How crazy can you get! But you see? One of my crazy dreams came true, in the most insane way possible."

It was my feet that fared the worst. I had a massive chilblain, my heels were split open, I shed torrents of tears as I put my shoes on. Rachel said I was like a little sea fairy.

At the station we unloaded trucks of bricks. Past us went trains full of turnips, cabbage, and *ossies*. That's what we called the Ukrainians, who wore white belts marked "OS." Sometimes they helped us steal a cabbage, which we had to crawl after on all fours like cats. You got shot for stealing. One day, we were standing in a knot, each with our poached cabbage, when an SS officer showed up. He had been watching the scene unfold through his telescope. He wanted to know whose idea it was. He was after the organizer. "If none of you comes forward, I'll shoot you all!"

Rachel stepped forward.

The SS officer looked her up and down. "So it was you, was it?"

She shrugged. "I can't imagine that it matters. One head's as good as another."

As she spoke, she looked meaningfully at her head of cabbage. A perfect bit of slapstick, but nobody laughed. She was taking an awful chance. The officer just stood and looked at her. That stare spoke of the meeting of two worlds, two galaxies, usually separated by the Milky Way of German superiority. But now his eyes briefly spurned the insanity of the Third Reich. He did an about-face and marched off. He let us keep both Rachel and the cabbage.

A few days after our cabbage triumph, the SS commanding officer pointed at me during rollcall. "*Komm her!*"

I gulped and stepped forward. He wasn't much older than I.

"Choose three others to come with you. You're being sent on a different job."

He pointed to the waiting truck. At Auschwitz, trucks took people to the gas chamber. My tongue turned to lead.

He looked at me, puzzled, then after a brief pause he bellowed: "*Was ist das?*"

I stuttered. I looked towards Rachel and she nodded. She came and stood next to me and pointed at Renée and Irma. Under armed guard we climbed onto the truck, which ran on wood gas. After a few miles it stopped outside some building. It might have been anything: a factory, a warehouse, a prison. A soldier led us into a room that made our hearts miss a beat. The room was lined all around with shelves, five or six one above the other, and they were full of bread. Never in my wildest dreams had I imagined such quantities, such acres of bread. Then I realized: we would be working on ration supplies.

We started carrying the loaves out to the truck, exactly ten at a time. With each batch we had to pass a pimply woman who checked each ten off, then went back to picking her teeth.

There was a glint in Rachel's eyes.

"Did you notice, Annie? That cow's not counting them!"

I could tell she had something up her sleeve, but I wasn't sure what.

"Suppose I slip up and get twelve loaves in a batch instead of ten?"

"What? Rachel, don't!"

She didn't need my approval. Transfixed, I waited to see what would happen. Nothing did. It worked. After two more trips she did it again.

She became a thief. The Rachel who had enjoined her "girls" to honesty in all circumstances, the Rachel who couldn't take so much as a crust from her fellow prisoners, this same Rachel was suddenly a great thief. It made me uneasy. "How are you going to get them into the hut?"

"Never mind that. The more bread we can steal from the Germans, the more the people back at the camp will get."

Ironclad logic. I struggled briefly with my conscience, then I did a run as well. It was a strange feeling. As I passed the warehousewoman, my heart was pounding so loud that she must have heard it. Rachel let Renée and Irma in on it. They joined in enthusiastically and before long we were a well-oiled team.

On the way back, we began puzzling how to get the spare loaves into the block. Down our blouses? Too visible. Under our skirts? Too difficult to walk. But as protection against the cold we had short coats. Yes, that was it. Coats.

Back at the camp, we transferred the bread to the food-store, which was ruled by the strict and punctilious Rita. When she reported the number of loaves delivered to the soldier, he mockingly suggested she couldn't count.

"I doubt they could have multiplied en route!"

She would have the same argument with the soldier day after day. Meanwhile, we would take turns running across to our block with loaves stuffed in our coat sleeves before coming back to continue unloading. After a week, when the conflict between Rita and the soldier was reaching the boiling point, Rachel announced that Rita would have to be told. But she wasn't Jewish; she was a political prisoner and German. We had to convince her of the noble impulse behind our actions, in which she saw nothing but petty crime. I don't know how Rachel finally did it, but Rita kept her mouth shut and with German exactitude shared out the stolen excess bread among the prisoners.

In late February, the pounding grew nearer. The Germans stopped being aggressive, stopped shouting, as their arrogance and high-handedness melted away with the last of the snow.

We grew accustomed to larger rations and daily air raids. The bombing was terrifying, but I noted that the sound of planes restored Rachel's spirits. The deafening explosions were divine music. "Can you hear it?" As if she were listening to Chopin or Tchaikovsky. During night raids she would run out in front of the block and, head thrown back, scan the sky. "Things are going to change," she would say.

Besides food, we brought coal, tools, and weapons into the

camp. We stole wherever they sent us: flour, sugar, even some clothing. The coal we used to heat the hut had also been knocked off from somewhere. We were forever refining our methods.

We also took dirty clothes to the laundry and picked up clean ones. Rachel patted her holdall like a horse's rump and placed one hand on her throat, her fingers on her arteries. "India has castes for everything. Even for laundering.

"The point where the Hoogly River bends is where the washerfolk live. They constitute a caste. Mountains of washing like fortifications. They don't have washboards. They soak the clothes in concrete tubs, bashing the dirt out against flat stones, then they steam them over primitive iron boilers. They soap them again and dash them against a stone. Thousands of shirts, sheets, and petticoats; lines stretched between crossed, split-wood trestles. The washing blows in the wind. Laundering is a man's job. Muscles and sweat."

When we carried our wash to the laundry, the German woman we handed it to would always slip us something. Some cake, a slice of bread, a piece of salami.

Around that time, Rachel's health started failing. She was up coughing half the night. In the laundry, we had to leave her sitting on a chair and haul the bags of clean linen onto the truck ourselves.

She stared ahead of her, letting her eyes close. She saw the play of sunlight and shade on the sheets billowing in the wind, projecting the past onto a screen washed out by the rays of the midday sun. She felt someone touch her lightly on the shoulder. When she looked up, a twelve-year-old boy was standing over her, offering her an apple.

"Dan?"

The boy looked surprised. "I'm Rolf," he said.

Tears flooded her eyes. She grabbed him by the hand and told him she had a boy just like him. Rolf shook off her grip and ran to his mother standing in the doorway.

"Do you want to send a letter?"

Rachel thought she must be dreaming. In a clumsy hand, she scribbled down the address and a message on a scrap of burlap.

In April, they herded us out for an extraordinary roll call: the camp was to be abandoned, effective immediately. Only the infirm and some nursing staff would be staying.

In twenty minutes we were marching five abreast towards the camp gate and out through it. Once more we boarded a train to be taken further and further away, no one knew where.

The train's brakes squealed. From the station at Bergen-Zelle they led us up a hill to a concentration camp cleverly tucked away in the forest. If they were systematic in trying to destroy us at Auschwitz, here they left us to die haphazardly. There were piles of corpses wherever you looked. Naked bodies, one on top of another, like a heap of manure. They were decaying, rotting, stinking. A fearful sight.

Rachel's eyelids quivered. "Apocalypse," she said.

Everything was different. No one counted us, no one shouted at us. They didn't force us to work, but they didn't feed us either. Just half a mug of muddy soup once a day. Bergen-Belsen was the final human garbage dump. Spring sunlight reflected in the gaping eyes of corpses. This was where they hauled off the detritus from the other concentration camps, which they were hastily closing down before fleeing in chaos ahead of the advancing Allies.

Not one drop of water for a week. Just a gulp of soup. It was intolerable. Even the cruellest starvation is nothing compared to thirst. Hunger debilitates, the knees give, the head spins. But thirst! Thirst can drive you mad.

An American plane flew over, so low that it must have seen us. They *must* have seen us! No one had any idea what a bird's-eye view of a tree-shrouded concentration camp would reveal. The camp commandant followed the plane through his telescope, and after it disappeared, he ordered all corpses, or what was left of them, to be buried. Everything but the stench.

Rachel brought a woman to meet me; she looked even worse than we did. They were holding hands. "Annie, this is Edita Wasserman. Actually Sonnenschein these days."

"Anna Adler. Pleased to meet you."

Edita Wasserman, the mischievous girl from Zlín, thanks to whom Rachel had met Thomas. Here was a wreck of an old woman, yet they'd been at university together. Edita was leaning on Rachel as she attempted a smile. My heart nearly stopped beating.

And then it finally came: Liberation.

I developed a splitting headache that day, and I felt like smashing it against something hard just for the relief. I was seeing little stars. No. It was one white star on armor plating. A tank was rolling into the camp. White star. It forged the way for more of them, star after star.

Everything was falling. Fences, wires. Half dead, I watched the tanks' tracks as they set the dust swirling. Suddenly it was here. The end. We were paralyzed. We were wrecks. Shades of the people we had once been.

As a little girl I had a parakeet. Freddy. His cage stood in the kitchen, close to the window, which my mother often left open. For years I trembled in fear it would fly away, and I would be careful to keep the cage door shut. So many times I went back five floors up to check that I hadn't forgotten! Then one day, after about three years, I came in from school and my heart stopped. The cage door was wide open, *and* the kitchen window. I had forgotten! As the wave of horror subsided, I discovered that Freddy was sitting there on his perch, just so. He clung to his cage for security and had no inclination to leave it. Door and window wide open—and he preferred to remain behind bars. A fear of taking wing? Or could he have forgotten that he had wings at all? I hugged and kissed him, and told him: "Oh Freddy, you are the silliest little parakeet in the world!"

That day they liberated us, I apologized to Freddy in my mind. I was just the same—afraid to leave my cage, paralyzed by fear of the future, that tomorrow there would be no one to tell me what to do.

I didn't know what to do. I could not rejoice. I felt terrible.

Suddenly I felt hands gripping my skin-clad bones and checking me over desperately. My mangled frame, a ruin that only remotely resembled a person.

"*Oh, my God. Oh, my God.*" He was a young soldier, his face chalk white, shaking, in utter confusion. "*Oh, my God, my God,*" he kept repeating again and again, as if this were all he knew how to say. "*My God. Oh, my God.*" He seemed incapable of pulling himself together. His prominent Adam's apple jumped up and down in the middle of his throat like a grasshopper.

At last he said: "You remind me of...you look like...my sister!" He stared at me and wept.

With my rough, dirt-encrusted fingers I wiped the tears from his face. I felt so terribly sorry for him.

A voice came over the loudspeaker, like a dream.

"You are free!"

Mobile water tanks, soap, a towel. Torrents of water, between our fingers, in our mouths, over our bodies.

The next day, that young British soldier—Collin Wadham was his name—drove us to Bergen. He commandeered a beautiful house, big enough for twenty happy people. I entered a forgotten world. In the living room with its fairy-tale conservatory, my headache briefly eased. Crystal chandeliers and brass doorknobs. A grand piano stood in the corner, a spell cast in ebony. Rachel approached it hesitantly, creeping along by the wall as if afraid it might dissolve before her eyes. Reverentially, she lifted the lid and just gazed at the keyboard. It was a long time before she summoned up the courage to touch the keys.

She screwed the stool up to her height, sat down, and half-closed her bluish eyelids. She sank into Handel's *Water Music*, touches of a butterfly on the black and white ivories. The notes burst and vanished. The piano had barely hit its stride when Rachel suddenly clenched her fist. Calluses and scars: her puffy, stiff, cracked fingers had tripped over one another, clumsy and wretched. Her nails were ragged slivers like mica. She began to weep into her ruined hands.

We got rid of our prison uniforms, and prepared a feast for ourselves and the British soldiers. What a sight we must have been! Bodies hunched over an exquisite spread, zero distance between plates and mouths, slurping, gobbling like pigs at a trough.

Rachel sat up straight and attempted to convey a spoonful of soup to her lips. It wasn't easy. And the temptation to slip a bit of everything into our pockets for later! It would make you laugh—and cry. I don't know whether we felt worse because of the good food or because of the humiliation. Suddenly we realized how badly we had been mutilated.

The tide coming from the radio was like balm, a stream of reports on the total collapse of the Third Reich. But I was collapsing with exhaustion and malnutrition, my entire body ached, and my head! The pain intensified until one morning I woke with a sense of having sprouted gigantic antlers in the night. Then came the stomach convulsions, and fever. Endless tripping between bed and toilet, day and night. Everything happening around me as if in a dream. I was one of the thousands infected. An epidemic of typhus.

Rachel came to the infirmary with me. First a circus tent, then a German hospital. Marble, showers, vast windows. Skulls and crossbones everywhere. Not on the caps of the SS, but on doors, walls, every pillar. Warning notices: Beware of infection.

I told Rachel to register for the buses that the Czechoslovak government had sent to retrieve the inmates of concentration camps. She shouldn't wait for me.

"Ridiculous!" she said. "I'm going to stay here until you pull through."

Her once-raven hair was slowly growing back.

"Your hair's like pepper and salt."

Before Dawn

"Liberation," Anna said. "Even after all this time, my recollection has not faltered, not even under the impact of other people's memories and the conventional clichés about the sheer joy and euphoria. Freedom."

I stole a glimpse under my shirt cuff at the face of the watch that used to be my father's. It was five to four. Time drags in the depth of night.

"But I felt fear. For several years I had dreamed of what it would be like. The flood of happiness, elation, ecstasy that would engulf me. Nothing of the kind came. Just tiredness. Exhaustion. Dejection. An oppressive feeling of fear and blame."

I couldn't believe my ears. "Blame? Why blame?"

"It's the brain. It starts thinking again. It returns to its normal channels and begins judging, assessing things. You look back: the horror of it! That we could have let it happen. That no one resisted. I should have died instead. Everyone is to blame, for our lack of courage. Better to see nothing, hear nothing, do nothing."

Anna closed her eyes. Her lips disappeared, leaving just a thin, painful thread. "Yes, blame. How can it be that *I* survived? At whose expense? But I try not to think about it, so as to keep the past at bay. In forty-five years, I have never spoken to anyone about this. Not even my husband. I wanted to escape from it. Yet you see, I've forgotten *nothing*! It dances before my eyes in vivid colors like some surrealist film, hot as a fresh brand."

She smiled. "But in the end, I can still see a human face—Rachel and all her stories. Then I know they never broke me."

Anna seemed to rifle through her memories as if through a trunk containing someone else's things.

"Everyone's writing about the Holocaust and the numbers of people tortured and murdered. But the average person who never experienced it is more affected when the neighbor's dog dies than by hearing how Hitler sent millions of people to their death.

"Stalin said that the death of a hundred people is a disaster, but a million people murdered—that's just a statistic. It sounds awful, but there's something to it. Numbers as colossal as six million are beyond comprehension. On the other hand, the mutt barking next door every day is real. One day it's there, the next day it's gone, dead and buried. A change you can't fail to notice, unlike the disappearance of six million anonymous people. It's so hard to see through the number to all the different fates, the different faces, their longings, hopes, disappointments, and deaths."

I needed a break. This night was too long, and the memories too raw. I had never wanted to know about people's experiences in the concentration camps. I was afraid. I would shut my eyes to it. I think my father knew a lot about it, but he never mentioned it.

One thread at a time, Anna had laid bare my mother's life, her youth, shreds and snatches that I didn't know. I had so feared those images of horror and suffering, but as the hidden pages of her life were opened before me, I felt her near. I lapped up every sentence. Anna had swamped me with facts, feelings, details. Each new fact was like a blow to the solar plexus, yet the more I knew, the closer to my mother I seemed to be.

Anna rubbed her eyes again and shrugged.

It is incredible how many times a person can summon up the strength to start again.

XII

Ways to Die

The Red Army liberated Zlín. At last I could crawl out of my fetid basement retreat. I discovered that I had outgrown all of my clothes, and there was nothing in the shops. I wore my dad's things, in which I looked like a scarecrow. He did manage to get me some pants, but they seemed to be made of a cloth woven from nettles. By comparison, sandpaper was like silk.

On May 7 a telegram arrived from Aunt Hilda. Grandpa Rudolf had had his customary nightcap, gone to bed, and never woken up. He was seventy-five.

We took the afternoon train to Olomouc. Dad in the black suit he used to wear when he went to a concert, which he called his funereals. He didn't say much, but when he had to say something, his voice sounded like a desiccated violin. I badly wanted to cry, but I contained myself until I saw Aunt Hilda's red eyes, and how her face looked like it had been hit by a hurricane.

We had dinner, then Hilda rose and said she was going to lie down. But right then, an ominous envelope arrived. The maid who brought it in remained at the dining room door in the pose of a runner waiting for the starting pistol. The idea of flight was embossed on her forehead in the shape of a deep furrow above her nose. The Grim Reaper wasn't satisfied yet.

The envelope revealed a terse message, and Hilda swallowed

it like a spoonful of cyanide. Oberleutnant Oskar Binder, a "brave soldier of the Wehrmacht" and Aunt Hilda's husband, had fallen in the fight for the better future of the Third Reich. White as chalk, Hilda thrust the scrap of paper towards Dad. He scanned it and looked up at her silently, as if he wanted to offer support or consolation, but he couldn't find the words. As if he wanted to embrace her, but couldn't move.

"It's late," she said. "I'm going to bed."

He seemed shocked by her hollow voice, her sightless eyes. "Hilda..."

She checked him with a wave of the hand and gave a wan smile. "It's all right, Thomas. I'll be all right. I want to be alone. Good night."

That night I couldn't sleep. I tossed in my strange bed in that strange house and thought of death: of Grandpa Rudolf, who had died in his sleep, Uncle Oskar, whom I had never seen and who had breathed his last on blood-soaked earth, riddled with cold and lead, beneath birches glowing pink in the setting sun. I recalled my Prague grandmother's protracted death, wracked by sickness and wheezily begging an invisible God to take her to Him. I remembered Grandpa Otto, who was the first to tell me the honest truth when he said that Grandma did not have long to live. I had asked him what he would do after she was gone, and he said he would soon follow her. And he did.

I wondered how many faces death had, and why it sometimes came in sleep, unobserved and silent like a fleeting kiss, and at other times with clangor and pain, squeezing its victim like a slice of lemon. The thought of death is no good when you are trying to get to sleep. The next morning it left a tickle in my throat.

Dawn came with the scent of forsythia and daffodils. It was a glorious day. I gazed out the window onto a garden hemmed in completely by arbor vitae and other conifers. A ladybird landed on the window ledge, but before I could count its spots, it spread its wings and flew off into the sky.

Dad and I sat at breakfast in our funeral suits, separated by the table and a hundred light years. But that day the funeral did not take place.

Hysterical screaming came from the bedroom above. I dropped my spoon into the saucer. A mouthful of bread and butter stuck in my throat. I was afraid the maid had gone mad. The clamor sounded like an air raid siren and it catapulted Dad out of his chair, which overturned abruptly and hit the parquet floor with a dull thud. He flew up the stairs four at a time, shouting something, but my meager German wasn't up to it.

Two days later, I stood in the gloom of a Catholic church for the first time, with its cold walls and its thundering organ. The statues and pictures of saints scared the wits out of me. I tried not to look at them, but by some magical power they drew me inexorably to them. Jesus Christ. Jesus at a table surrounded by the twelve Apostles, Jesus in the arms of the Virgin Mary. Jesus on the Cross. A tortured face, blood streaming down his bony chest, hands and feet impaled, the thorns of his crown sunk into the white flesh of his brow, and blood and blood and blood, streaming from every wound, like the blood of Aunt Hilda, who had slashed her wrists because she no longer wanted to live.

Mozart's *Requiem* floated down from the apex of the nave. *Kyrie eleison. Christe eleison.* Lord have mercy. The cold made me shudder. I was a speck of dust in a sea of sadness. The priest intoned Latin psalms in a mumble. *De profundis clamavi ad Te Domine; Domine exaudi vocem meam!*

I looked up at Dad. He was carved in stone, his eyes glued to the coffin in front of the altar. The man lying in it would be buried in consecrated earth, but his daughter's remains would end up by the cemetery wall, among the other suicides. Father and daughter, anguish and memories, anguish and fear.

I touched Dad gently. The statue came to life. He looked at me in surprise, seemed to gather his thoughts and return to earth. He gripped my fingers and gazed long into my eyes. I had a sense that he was seeing someone else.

The Church of St. Wenceslas. I did try to see God there—Grandpa Rudolf's God. I hoped to unearth more of my roots, more of the mysterious ties that bound me to the man in the coffin, and to the woman whose corpse would not be allowed to pass the church threshold. But I don't think I succeeded. The grief that enfolded me was too acute to allow clarity of vision. And no god could have liberated me.

We left for Prague about three weeks after the Germans capitulated. Timetables meant nothing. Chaos reigned and trains were hopelessly crammed. In Prague we rang the doorbell of little old Mrs Roubal, the apartment where Dad had lived twenty years earlier. Her antique furniture was gloomy.

Our cheerless present became entangled with my memories and dreams of India.

Zam, our Indian cook, had a great uncle, Jasbir Singh. He had been a diver, a shell-fisher. As old as the sea, he knew everything about it. Zam and Jasbir were very close, they spoke together in a resonant language no one else understood. Jasbir knew how to catch a fish in an old rag. He would laugh through his rough grey beard, toothless as a child.

He taught me how to make nets and catch whole shoals of fish in them. He taught me the underwater rules: how to delay exhaling, how to move without expending energy, how to love the salt of the sea. He took me far out in the ocean, so far that the shore disappeared from sight, leaving us surrounded by nothing but the waves. We jumped into the water and spread our nets out. Light blue, gaudy yellow, party-colored fish brushed against my legs, tumbled in the sway of the salty currents, their mouths full of a soundless song. A school of dark blue Koranic angels,

*lightly streaked with white. Jasbir's head like a Medusa, the
gray snakelets of his hair and beard endlessly intertwining like
restless lovers.*

*Suddenly he waved at me, urgently, uneconomically. "Look,
look, over there!"*

*I focused on the colossus circling gracefully under our boat's
keel. Bent snout, wrinkled skin, pocketed eyes. A hundred-year-
old turtle, winged and weightless, defying the passage of time, its
grave gaze fixed on the future, its wisdom shielded in the safety
of a carapace. The pale olive shell concealed a body as white as
milk. With slow strokes she flapped her wings and disappeared
into the dark sea like a bird of prey, an eagle in the wide sky of
the ocean.*

*In my excitement I forgot that my head was under the water
and tried to follow the white turtle into the deep. I surfaced with
great difficulty, having swallowed so much water that I still had
that burning sensation in my throat and entrails the next day.*

*A white turtle. I still dream about her, and sometimes I
imagine that at the hour of my death she will come for me. I
would like that.*

Years later, I had a dream of returning to the spot where I had
once seen the white turtle. I dived down. I spread my net and
waited for little fish to swim into it. I looked up toward the surface:
the sea was ruffled and the net above my head leaped with the
reflection of the sun's rays. I saw seahorses, pink, yellow, pale blue,
entwined like lovers. I saw hundreds of little fish, all gaily colored
like the circus. I saw starfish, eels, and water snakes. Suddenly I
was looking through the thick mesh at a shoal of frightened little
fish, caught in a trap. They whirled about in a confused huddle,
changing direction, looking for a way out. The net turned into a
prison, a tangle of barbed wire, and on the other side I could see
the face of Rachel. She was looking at me, trying to say something.

I woke from my childhood dream to a desolate adulthood. I was cold and wanted to cry.

In Prague, Dad would go to the Office of Repatriation and forage for information about concentration camp prisoners. He scoured the Red Cross lists for the names of those who had survived and those who had perished. The officials in charge assured him that they were only a fraction of the total.

Together we would go to Wilson Station, day after day, looking for Mom. There was no schedule. Trains kept arriving and some of them disgorged the strangest beings, in whom you could barely recognize people. The sight was so terrible that I used to have diarrhea as we left the Vinohrady apartment. They were all skin and bone, half-dead as they stumbled onto the platform, looking for someone. Their eyes were dry wells. My teeth tingled and I could feel every bone in my body. I searched those gaunt, sick faces for my mother. My mother was the most beautiful woman. I was so afraid she would not come, and equally afraid to see her among them.

My father would stand next to me, so still and silent that sometimes I wasn't sure he was breathing. Now and again he would remember I was there and give my shoulder a squeeze, his smile as sad as the human wrecks passing through our lives.

XIII

Anna: Hugo's Eyes

I eventually made my way back to Prague. That was where I belonged. Without Prague, I just blew in the wind. They disgorged us at Wilson Station and I plodded off to Karlín, where Mom and I used to live. Our neighbor, Mrs Maláč, took charge of me. She told me that some German had made himself at home in our apartment, and before the end of the war he had vanished along with a bundle of stolen items. She took me in, fed me, and fussed over me like a child. I was grateful not to be left alone in that empty, ravaged place.

I tried to lead a normal life, but it didn't work. It was hard to walk in the park, to eat with a knife and fork; I persisted in boarding the rear coaches of streetcars and sneaking something away at every mealtime. It took unbelievable effort to convert back from animal to human. After two weeks, I perked up a bit and despite all of Mrs Maláč's protests, I set off for Zlín. I did not even tell her what I had planned next. I was determined to find Gideon.

The trains still weren't running by any timetable, but rather according to the weather. They were jammed with people returning home, or with the disconsolate looking for someone lost. I squeezed in among those cramped bodies like so often before, but this time it was different. This time it was voluntary. We traveled with our belongings, masters of our own destiny.

It took me a full two days to reach Zlín, where I made straight for the Baťa works. The lady in personnel surveyed me with an eye sharpened by experience, and kindly informed me that Mr Keppler was out of town. I also got her to tell me that he was in Prague, but she either wouldn't or couldn't tell me when he'd be back, nor could she tell me whether he was there on private or company business. In fact she couldn't tell me a damn thing.

"Could you at least let me have his Zlín address, please?"

She scratched her cheek, swept her serpent eyes over me once more, and turned to her younger, bespectacled colleague, who so far had said nothing. "Ruženka, find Mr Keppler's address for the young lady."

Ruženka left her desk and reached up to a shelf with its neat rank of box files. She took out a folder and started flicking through the list of employees. She ran her finger unhurriedly down the names beginning with K until she stopped at one of them, and in her neat, rounded handwriting wrote the address out on a piece of paper, which she handed to me without a word. Maybe she was incapable of speech. I thanked her politely and made my exit.

On the way back to Prague I worked out in my mind all the things I would write to Thomas Keppler and how I would set about looking for Gideon. I let my imagination wander, and dreamed longingly of the moment when we would meet. Battered, hungry, and exhausted, I left the train and looked forward to the soothing atmosphere of Mrs Maláč's apartment. A surprised voice stopped me at the end of the platform. "Annie? Is that you, Annie?"

Bedřich Weiss. Every inch the jazzman. *In the Mood.* The Weiss Jazz Quintet of Theresienstadt and the unforgettable voice of his clarinet. Glen Miller, Duke Ellington, Irving Berlin. *The music of inferior races.* That's what the supermen of Germany called jazz. When the Dutch pianist Martin Roman turned up at Theresienstadt, he and Weiss would create their own compositions and play the best-known hits. My ears suddenly filled with Gershwin's *I Got Rhythm*, their signature tune. Gideon had loved jazz and Weiss's irrepressible music-making. They had been friends. Both had disappeared with the autumn transports to Auschwitz.

Neatly suited and clean-shaven, he was altered beyond recognition, but he was still painfully thin, a physical wreck, with furrows like scars around his mouth.

I flung myself at him. "Heaven must have sent you to me!"

Lost souls, we embraced amid a rush of people and a flood of sensations and memories.

"Where—where's Gideon?"

The question spread through the air like toxic gas. Bedřich seemed unable to breathe. He seemed not to have heard. He pushed his spectacles back with his forefinger, avoided my eyes, and shifted awkwardly.

I began to cry. "Tell me!"

They'd had no news of each other for a long time. Then they met on the transport from Auschwitz when they were being transferred to Silesia, somewhere near Katowice, to become galley-slaves. After three months' hard labor in the coalmines, the front line moved closer. In late January the SS grew agitated and the work ended.

Things changed. The weak and infirm were shot, the rest waited to be evacuated. Evacuation: how human that sounds! But this evacuation meant the death march. They drove them through the snow with no food and no rest.

Gideon had grown weak and his shoes were no good.

"I wanted to give him mine," said Weiss, "but he wouldn't hear of it. You know how stubborn he could be. He got frostbite in his feet. He couldn't take the murderous pace, but he fought on. After two days, they shot him."

I sent a letter to Thomas Keppler and took a train to Pilsen. I was hoping to seek out my relatives, the ones who might still be alive, who might have come back. I had to make the attempt. It was the only way of focusing on something else, and putting behind me, for a moment at least, the anguish that seized me as I thought about Gideon—and about Rachel.

We used to go to see our "Pilsen Auntie," as we called my mother's sister, during the long summer holidays. She was a buxom, kindly lady with her ginger hair done in a bun. Like my mother, she was a widow. Uncle Max had died in the final months of the Great War, just before the birth of his daughter, Klara, my cousin, with whom I got along as well as my mother did with my Auntie Mila. Cousin Klara was a little imp, though you'd never have guessed it. Three years older than I, she had long auburn hair and forget-me-not eyes, and an audacious mouth hidden behind her permanent grin. The things she would say out of parental earshot always had me giggling; I knew they were not things any nice little girl should be saying.

Her brother, my cousin Hugo, was a handsome guy who thought of us girls as furniture. They lived near the synagogue, in a house with a lively bar at street level and some even livelier tenants on the floor above. Mr and Mrs. Fousek. We waited expectantly for their regular squabbles as the high point of our summer days.

We would be sitting at dinner when barking voices and slamming doors came from upstairs. Auntie Míla would raise her voice to drown out the scene being played out above, but Klara had sharp ears and would grin maliciously. After their fifteen-minute fight, Mr Fousek sounded the retreat, then came puffing down the stairs and went straight into the bar. You couldn't even count the names he called his wife, and he would go past muttering to himself all the things he hadn't dared say to her desiccated face.

Klara would spring up from the table, press one ear to the front door, and make faces as she imitated Fousek: "... old hag... why I had to go an' marry her... how dare she, the cow... do I *need* this?"

"Klara! Come and sit down! Do you hear?"

Klara reluctantly detached herself from the door. "He's always the one that runs away. Why doesn't he kick the old bag out?"

"Klara!"

"Sorry. She's not an old bag, more a wicked witch. And he's not a stupid ass but a bag of shit. Instead of giving her a good spanking, he runs away to the bar. There he gets totally drunk and is glad to have a reason for doing it."

"Klara! That's enough!"

Auntie nearly had a fit, but Klara winked at me conspiratorially.

"They say he's stingy. So maybe he deserves the old cow."

Sometimes Aunt Míla sent Klara out of the room. "Who *does* the girl take after, Irene, tell me that?" she would ask my mother. "Not even the Švanda woman at Patočka's bar is so foul-mouthed!"

And my mom would try to cheer her up. "Let her be, Míla. At least she'll be able to look after herself."

Someone else was living in their apartment now. I rang the neighbors' bell.

"Excuse me, do you know anything about the Bauchs?"

The bald, elderly man with eyes that ran away in opposite directions nodded ruefully. "Things went badly for them, miss, badly. The young gentleman came back from the concentration camp and he was in a terrible way. He told us his sister and mother had gone to the gas chamber. At that Auswich place or somewhere. He got back here himself, see, but much good it did him. Last week they took him to hospital. Bad, he was. Very bad."

I turned away and walked straight to the hospital, cutting a wedge through the May breeze and pursued by the intoxicating smells and sounds of Spring. Buzzing, twittering, pink and white petals falling from the trees and flying through the air. As I crossed the square everything went dim, a small dark grey cloud blocked the sun's way, and drops of rain landed on people's heads. At the far side of the square I looked back at St Bartholomew's Cathedral, Gothic in the gloom, and above it saw a flawless arch, triumphant with color. I had never seen such a perfect rainbow. It was a good omen. I dashed through the hospital entrance.

It took me a long time to find him. I explained, I begged, I ran from one doctor to another. "He's my last living relative!"

Finally, they let me in to see him.

"Hugo! Hugo, it's me, Annie."

He sat on a chair, motionless and expressionless. They had said he might not recognize me, but I didn't believe them. I put my arms around him, spoke to him, cried, shouted, shook him. But he was like a chess piece, unseeing and unhearing. Just a dilapidated frame that bore no relationship to Hugo's once lively and charming figure.

I came staggering back out of the hospital, pursued by those eyes: fixed, desolate, vacant. I tried not to see them. I hobbled along Prague Street until I found myself back at the square. It opened out before me like a cold embrace, the cathedral spire straining up towards God, and beyond it fluffy white clouds projected up there as if onto a blue screen. The rainbow was gone.

I imagined giggling Klara and my plump auntie, hand in hand, going inside and down the stairs together. They took off their clothes and hung them on a hook set into the wall. They put their shoes neatly under a little bench, right beneath the coat hanger, so they could find them later. They went deeper inside, along a cold corridor and through a solid door, an undulating crowd carrying them on and on. The door closed. The showers above their heads were desert blooms. The light went out. They were holding hands when they turned into flakes of ash.

The bustle of the city faded into the distance, the double arches of the brewery gate merged into one, and Butchers' Row flashed by like the wind. Above the whole scene, Hugo's empty eyes stared down, and then there were hundreds of dead eyes that sent me spinning into the sky.

I crashed to the pavement.

When I came to, I saw those eyes again, but this time they weren't Hugo's. Horror gave way to surprise as the eyes above me radiated life and light. When I shifted my position, the face they belonged to blazed with delight, but before I could say anything, they vanished once more into darkness.

The next time I came to, I was in the hospital. Doctors and nurses flitted past like dragonflies. One of them took my pulse, a young doctor who smiled when he noticed me staring into the corridor through the half-open door, where I had glimpsed the eyes that had been pursuing me.

"Do you know him? He's the one who brought you in."

"When will I..."

He gave me some water and shook his head. "You'll be staying here for a while."

Total collapse, he explained.

The fairy-tale prince hiding in the half-light of the hospital corridor came to see me every day, brought me fruit and bars of chocolate, comforted me and spoke to me in soothing tones. I only understood every tenth word he said, but he was composed and patient, waiting until I squeezed out one whole sentence in English, full of schoolgirl mistakes. He hung on every word of nonsense I uttered and smiled his understanding, and I basked in his smile and let myself be carried away by the voice of my rescuer, my guardian angel.

After two weeks, they discharged me, and he came with me to Prague, where Mrs Maláč welcomed me back.

"So you're back, my dear. And with no less than an American soldier."

Despite the white noise in my head and the hiccups of language, we got along wonderfully together. Or maybe because of them. He held me firmly and pulled me, little by little, back into the world of the living.

I was an overflowing sewer, a garbage pail, a mess of human blood and terrible shame at having survived. I had not killed anyone, but I bore the guilt of all the things that had been allowed to happen. I was ashamed for all those who had pretended not to see, for those who had been persuaded that ignorance exonerated them. I was a doormat, and my rescuer bent down to me and raised me up over all those trampled dreams to be human again. He acted as if I were a woman; more than that—I was a princess.

When they discharged me from the hospital, I noticed that he was never still, that even while sitting he would tap his feet and drum his fingers on the table. He was the embodiment of impatience: how much it must have cost him to sit for hours beside my hospital bed and hold me calmly by the hand. I admired him all the more for it. He was happy and tender, and he literally met my every wish. In his embrace I was reborn. I could not avoid falling in love with him.

I shut the door to the old world behind me: our ruined continent, the dead faces of my loved ones. I wanted to be out of sight of those accursed shores as soon as I possibly could.

Dawn

Anna smiled as she leafed through the brown leather journal that had belonged to her husband. "Let me read you what he wrote about how we met," she said.

Today I saw a rainbow above the city. In the afternoon, I fell asleep in the park and then went for a walk through Pilsen's downtown. A few paces ahead of me there was this thin girl, just a skinny little thing, hobbling along. She had a comical hairdo – very short, golden-brown. She had a pronounced limp in her left leg. Suddenly she staggered and dropped like a stone. Before I could pick her up, she came to briefly. Her features were drawn, tired and unhappy, but when she opened her eyes, I found her beautiful. She was so light! I held her in my arms and had no sense of carrying anything at all. When I lay her on a table at the hospital, I spotted the number on her forearm. Little bluish marks under her skin. Rough hands. Nails edged like a slice of bread without the crust.

God, how could You have permitted this?

"Pete came back home, married me, and we both tried to live again. He had several operations performed on his shoulder. The joint loose, damaged blood vessels and nerves, a stiffness in the arm, and unbearable pain. They tried to reset the bone fragments, wiring him up and screwing him together like a chunk of wood. They did manage to patch up his shoulder blade, but the shoulder itself went from bad to worse. Finally, they drove a steel rod into the bone; it used to squeak in the socket. Osteomalacia and necrosis of the capitellum, they said. What they meant was that they thought the joint had simply atrophied.

"It ended in lingering arthritis and tons of painkillers. He tried to live with it, he really did."

Anna shifted in her chair and smoothed her skirt. She immersed herself in the past and I swam there with her, trying to fit everything together.

"That letter you sent to Dad," I said. "It never arrived."

She nodded. "Ruženka in personnel. The dumb girl. She must have given me the wrong address."

"Or it got swallowed up in the aftermath of the war. I don't think it would have helped Dad anyway.

"Do you know the legend of Shemkhazai?" I asked her. "It's an old Jewish myth that my mother told me once:

"Shortly after Creation, the angels noticed the beauty of young women. Blinded by their craving for love, they paid no heed to the warnings of God Himself, but descended from their heavenly heights and married the daughters of men. The angel Shemkhazai desired a girl called Ishtar, who was the most beautiful of all. He burned with a love for her such as no man had ever known, and he did everything he could to ensure Ishtar's happiness. But Ishtar was more and more troubled, and Shemkhazai tried to discover what lay so heavy upon her. 'I will do whatsoever you wish,' he said, 'only tell me what I must do for you to be happy.' Ishtar was reluctant, but in the end she revealed her secret wish to him: 'Just as you angels desired to know life on earth, so I, Ishtar, a human, would like to know God. Tell me His name, that I might address Him.' Shemkhazai implored her to ask for anything else instead. 'The name of God has been concealed from all mortals for eternity.' Ishtar shook her head. So the desperate Shemkhazai revealed the name of God to her and she raised up her arms to heaven and uttered the name. At that instant she floated up to heaven: God had rewarded her fervent love of Him by turning her into a star. You can imagine Shemkhazai's distress: Ishtar was in heaven and he was left on earth. He was like a lost soul, and he spent his sleepless nights gazing up at the stars. Meanwhile, down on earth, the first children of the angels and their earthly wives began to be born; but instead of perfect beings, they grew into ravaging giants. Humans were afraid of them, and even the angels themselves were defenseless. Chaos reigned. Some angels joined the side of the giants and did evil instead of good. Wars broke out and people began murdering each other. Shemkhazai was stricken with horror at the devastation brought to earth by the angels, which made his grief even harder to bear. Life without Ishtar was sheer torment. Shemkhazai's pain grew and grew like a tree, and he cried so much that not even God could bear to see such pain. He took pity on the angel and brought him back up to heaven, where he was closer to his beloved Ishtar. Shemkhazai suspended himself head-down so he might never lose sight of the destruction into which the angels had cast mankind. Thus he witnessed God's punishment—the great flood which swept all evil away. To this day, Shemkhazai hangs head-down from the heights of heaven. His repentance endures."

Anna looked at me and I knew that she understood: unutterable pain and never-ending guilt.

Someone knocked at the door. When he entered, I had a shock: I saw Tom. But it was only my son, Scott.

"Sorry, Dad. We're back. Happy New Year!"

"You too. Are you going to bed?"

"Not worth it now. We'll sleep on the plane."

The door squeaked and he vanished into the corridor.

I let out a deep breath. "He's so very like him. Even in character."

"Your father?"

"Yes. He must have looked a lot like that when he and Mom met. The older Scott grows, the more I see Tom in him. He's got my father's eyes."

Anna said that Alice looked like Rachel, but that's an illusion. It's her hair, black, dense, and rebellious; otherwise Alice looks more like Ellen's side.

"No, Rachel lurks somewhere in Ross. He's just as untameable and inscrutable as she used to be."

"But he's the spitting image of you," said Anna.

We exchanged looks and started laughing. We were like a pair of Weird Sisters.

XIV

Anna: We Are Stories

There was no euphoria at the Liberation. Just fatigue and fear—a strike force of mordant apprehension about the future. Still, I survived the typhus epidemic, and six weeks later, Rachel and I waited together to be put on buses bound for home.

Rachel's coughing fits had started up again. For several days her throat was inflamed. During our time in the concentration camp I had grown used to the fact that disease was a force to be reckoned with, and for many of us, there was no defense.

But this was Rachel.

When she coughed, I had visions of a quarry, a huge explosive charge and chunks of flying rock. My anxiety was overwhelming. I couldn't stomach the notion that something might happen to her. "You ought to see a doctor, Rachel."

She shook her head. "I don't want to. I want to go home."

"But you should..."

"I want to go home."

I gave up because I had seen this before. There weren't many occasions when she set her mind against something, but whenever she did, no power on earth could move her.

It turned out we didn't go by bus, but by train. It was a freight train with one passenger car hitched on at the end, full of straggling souls being drawn back to their Bohemian home. We sat on wooden benches, and the sound of the wheels lulled some of us to sleep. Others were shunned by sleep, or shunned sleep themselves in order to escape their dreams.

"Say something, Rachel. Tell us a story."

She sat huddled in one corner of the train and coughed at intervals, pressing a crumpled rag to her mouth. I was deeply shocked to notice, for the first time, clots of blood. Her lungs were rutted, red-veined bellows, full of holes and the shreds of mucous membrane she was coughing up. I rushed over to her and tore the handkerchief from her hand. I stared at the gobbets of dried blood.

"For God's sake, Rachel! Why wouldn't you see a doctor? How long have you had it? We must get you to the hospital!"

"Shhh."

She took the handkerchief back and looked steadily at me.

"I want to go home."

She gave a faint smile. Her thick voice floated through the silent carriage to the accompaniment of the strange metallic ring and rhythm of the wheels.

She coughed again and wiped the blood from her lips.

We are stories. We are myths and fairy tales. We are poetry. Our lives are books, covered with the handwriting of our joy, our grief, our successes and defeats. We are pages written by people and events that befell us. We cherish the manuscripts of those who have bewitched us with the beauty of their bodies and souls, those who have endowed us with light and knowledge. Manuscripts of the beloved.

But our books also conceal within them pages that are blacker than ink. Pages imprinted with pain and wounds. Pages scribbled over thoughtlessly, ravaged by the people and events that burst onto our lives like a deluge, like a plague. Pages dark with the dried blood of suffering and impotence. Barbed wire pages without human faces. We are books bursting with awful things we never meant to write. Cruel myths and ballads. We may try to erase them, tear them out. We may try to burn them. But if we throw them into the flames, we torch ourselves.

At that moment the train stopped in the middle of the countryside. No station anywhere.

XV

How Many More Times Must I Lose You?

To this day, I get a strange feeling when I find myself at a train station. The word *station* alone triggers memories; it is like a death-knell. *Wilson Station.* I have a perfect image of its appearance in 1945, down to the last detail. I knew it like my own house.

We were standing at Wilson Station again, in the second half of May, when a train arrived from Germany. A hunched old lady with thinning white hair came tottering towards us. Her gait was like a waddling duck, her legs oddly twisted. She seized Dad by the hand, gave a terrible, toothless smile. Her complexion was greenish-grey, there were dark blotches on her face, the yellowed whites of her eyes were bloodshot. She couldn't have weighed more than fifty-six pounds.

"Thomas!"

Dad caught her and tried to hold her up. In horror he stared at this human wreck, desperately seeking any familiar feature in the dried-up face, the emaciated form. His hands were shaking and he had no words.

"Thomas! It's me!"

His lips parted, but not a sound came. His eyelids flickered, his face like chalk.

"It's me..."

271

She faltered and started coughing. Dad supported her tightly, covering her mouth with a handkerchief, into which she coughed up whole dollops of congealed blood.

"Don't you recognize me?"

He fought to retain his self-control.

"It's me, Edita! Edita Wasserman!"

"My God, Edita! Where..."

"Auschwitz. Bergen-Belsen."

He clasped the woman, whom he must once have known well, to his chest.

"Is Rachel back?" she asked.

"What?"

"She must be in one of those trains. She was there."

"You're quite certain?"

A violent bout of coughing bent her double. Tom stared into her eyes and clutched her fleshless arms. His lips moved inaudibly.

We took her to the hospital. Dad explained to me that Edita had been my mother's classmate, and I thought it was odd that such an old woman could be the same age as Mom.

That night I opened the window wide. The frame creaked quietly and the pane shook. A star-spangled sky. I remembered the Jantar-Mantar at Jaipur: strange stone and marble structures in a vast open space, tracing the position of the sun, moon, and stars, a planetarium of huge dimensions like some futuristic city. Instruments showed the position of the signs of the zodiac. The Samratjantra sundial measures time accurately to within two seconds.

The stars twinkled above the rooftops. One of them winked and flared, quivering in all the colors of the rainbow. I half-closed my eyes and saw her hands. I let myself be caressed by the thought of her.

After that meeting with Edita Wasserman, we went to the station every day. Dad asked Mrs Roubal if we could stay a little longer, and he began shaving again. Some weeks passed. He visited Edita in the hospital several times and pried the details out of her.

Where exactly, when precisely, were those buses and trains going, how did people board them, what route did they take, why hadn't they all arrived by bus, why hadn't they taken the same train?

"I got a spot on a bus because a woman had a heart attack at the sheer joy of going home," Edita said. "I only came from Pilsen by train."

He asked thousands of questions and got thousands of unsatisfactory, vague answers. He trembled with dread and impotence.

He told me he had to go away, just for a couple of days. He deposited me with Mrs Roubal and set off for Germany. He was gone almost a month and I suffered torments at the possibility that he might not come back. When he showed up in the doorway, he was alone and distraught. He had managed to find out which train she should have, could have, might have taken. But how could he be certain she had been on it?

We said farewell to Prague and old Mrs Roubal, and headed home to Zlín. Our shared despair peaked. We each endured it in our own way. I stopped practicing my piano. He doubled his daily consumption of cigarettes.

One evening, Tom poured himself a glass of wine and went out into the garden. He inhaled a dose of nicotine, twisting his lighter in his fingers. He ran his finger over the date etched into the silver. *25.12.1932.* She had given it to him for his thirtieth birthday.

The half-moon shared his wine with him.

A noise came out of the darkness. A rustling. The sound nailed him to the wall of the house. He heard her footsteps, and when he turned toward them, he saw her coming closer, running gracefully over the meadow. His heart jumped to his throat. Then a black cat ran across the overgrown flower-beds and disappeared in the shrubbery.

He stared out over the neglected garden toward the empty meadow. He leaned against the wall and stamped his cigarette out, his palms full of tears and cold sweat. A bitter taste rose to his mouth. He ran to the bathroom, threw up his dinner, washed his face, and went to lie down.

The arms of the night were sore. He would have the most senseless dreams, and when he woke in the morning, he would remember them as if they were real. Rachel. A beautiful dream, changed into a nightmare.

Once she had told him: "Don't be afraid of the dark. Darkness uncovers the real aspect of things, the secrets hidden in daytime. Dreams are messages from your soul."

He could not bear those messages, but neither could he rid himself of them. Rachel was not only his wife. They were joined by a bond stronger than friendship, stronger than lust, stronger than love. It was something ineffable. Destiny. She had drawn him into her life; she had become his life. Living without her was like breathing without oxygen. It was futile.

Perhaps he could end it. There were moments when his head swirled with all the ingenious and certain means of killing himself. Some had slashed their wrists: Petronius, Seneca, Hilda. Virginia Woolf had walked into a cold river, her pockets weighed down with stones. Mayakovsky had put a bullet in his head. There so many ways to end it, and there was only one reason not to: every time he looked at me, he saw her. My eyes were like my mother's. That was why my father could not take his life.

The prospect of Rachel's return vanished on the wings of migrating birds. We found Aunt Regina's name in the lists of the dead. Auschwitz.

Barely six months after the war ended, when Beneš signed the decrees nationalizing industry, banks, and insurance houses,

Dad declared that our dear President was off his rocker and that there were no choices between the scum on the far Left and the scum on the far Right. From April 1945 onward, the Communists held the Ministry of the Interior in their lefty paws, and a year later they won forty percent of the vote in the general election. Dad voted for the Social Democrats, who managed barely fourteen percent. Around that time, Nosek was filling the security services with not only partisans and ex-resistance people, but also some of the vermin who had so recently hitched their horses loyally to the Nazi wagon and were now streaming into the open embrace of the Communist Party of Czechoslovakia.

The removal of the German element from the country became the main item on the agenda. Tom found the papers full of strident calls:

In Ostrava and Olomouc, any Germans still at large must carry conspicuous markings!

No woman who has married a German shall be deemed Czech!

We must set about Czechicizing our names. How many good Czechs do we know called Mühler, Forst or Schmidt? A Mühler can become a Mlynář. Name-change applications should be addressed to the provincial National Committee.

Mlynář. He broke out in a hot sweat. It was a good thing Keppler couldn't be translated into Czech.

Cleanse the Republic of Germans! The Government of the Czechoslovak Republic has adopted an Act whereby the public and private property of Germans, traitors, and collaborators will be placed under national administration.

Thomas was glad his father hadn't lived to see it. He couldn't imagine the broken old man being shunted out of the country with his little bundle of possessions.

Probate was short and sweet. The house in which he had grown up, in which his mother had died still maintining her Czech patriotism, was confiscated. Likewise the villa in which his sister had slashed her wrists: in 1930, Rudolf Keppler and Hildegarde Binder had registered as Germans, so that was the end of that.

Lukáš Hoffmann, a seasoned lawyer and old friend, waved his arms around in front of Tom. He didn't mince words.

"You're not interested? That's crazy! The Nazis took everything belonging to the Weinsteins. All right! You don't want to claim it back. Okay! But why let this new bunch walk off with what is rightfully the Kepplers'? You're not a commie, are you—taking from the rich and giving to the poor? You're losing your grip!"

"I've already lost far more than that."

"But what about your son? He's got a claim to the Weinstein property, and just as much to the Kepplers'! You can't want to deprive him of his inheritance!"

"Compared to what else he's lost, the riches of the Weinsteins and Kepplers are nothing. All the money in the world is—*nothing*."

Lukáš Hoffmann wearily removed his glasses, took out his handkerchief and began to clean the lenses.

"I don't know what to say."

"Nothing. Don't say anything."

He didn't care. These were insignificant details. Everything had already been taken from him.

On May 2, 1946 the first anniversary of the liberation of Zlín by the Red Army was celebrated with a "spontaneous yet pious commemoration of heroes."

The atmosphere in Comenius Park was far from a seemly act of remembrance. A memorial to the fallen had been designed by Vincenc Makovský, but at its unveiling the public administrators sprawled in their seats like a bunch of bystanders in a bar, their mouths full of pithy platitudes and cigarette smoke. The platform was dominated by Communist agitators. The outraged Sokol members could only stand there muttering, choked with dismay at the breast-beating of the Red fraternity. Some of them left halfway through the speeches.

Dad said it was all a farce. Barefaced Bolshevik propaganda. He had been working on the designs for some three-storey houses to be built at Obeciny. Modern flats with balconies. Red brick, as befitted the city of Baťa, the first ones to be completed by December 1947. But Dad wouldn't be there to see them.

In March, 1947, Comrade Ambassador Valerian Alexandrovich Zorin paid a "friendly" visit to the now nationalized Baťa company to address its comrade-employees.

Shortly after that, I ran home from school in the spring rain and found Dad leaning over his atlas.

"Are we going somewhere?"

With a strange smile on his face—I had almost forgotten that he smiled—he told me that there are places in the world where you can drive for days without meeting another living soul. I knew he didn't mean India.

I looked at the open map. "Don't you like it here any more?"

"I think it's time for a change of scene. For a bit of excitement."

Excitement. It didn't sound like him. Those days were long gone.

"We would just leave everything here and never come back?"

"Well, we can stay there a while and then we'll see. Here everything's sort of...These are strange times, you know."

I could hear the rain playing on the iron gutters. It was suddenly clear to me: he had simply stopped believing that Mom would come back.

"When are we leaving?"

"As soon as possible. Before it's too late."

His eyes were hungry, like a hawk circling over a glacial lake. "Though really, it's already too late..."

"Do you think we should have left before now?" I said.

He looked at Mom's piano, that strange smile again. A barren tree.

"Ten years ago."

Rain streamed down his cheeks. I had never seen him cry before. The thought of her had carved him up like a cutter's diamond. I was sorry I had asked, so I put my arms around him to show that I understood.

I think I did understand.

Rachel, I must leave this town where I first set eyes on you. Here there is neverending winter, and hordes of people pass me in the streets without a word, their destinies written in their faces, their eyes. I see you in every one of them. I rush to meet you at the far end of a deserted street. The freezing rain turns grey in my hair. I must get away. I never want to lose you again.

XVI

New Day—New Year

Anna cut me another slice of sponge cake. Next to it stood the Sabbath candles.

In the end, Dad and I didn't leave until the autumn. I still remember that awful hot summer, like a bad omen. The Marshall Plan passed us by. The Czechoslovakian cabinet unanimously approved its adoption, but old Comrade Stalin would have none of it. Dad said it was no different from when they sold us down the river at Munich. The crippling heat dried up the last remnants of the harvest and our hope.

We settled in Toronto. He wanted to live in a city which bore absolutely no resemblance to the places we had lived previously.

Shortly after he found a job and started working, one of his colleagues came to see us. Desmond Gibbons, Canadian-born with pride in his Irish ancestry. Over dinner we talked easily, but then he turned to work matters.

"They say you speak perfect German. That's quite handy, because we need..."

Uncharacteristically, Dad interrupted him. "I do not speak German," he said.

"But they told me that you grew up German, that you spoke German at home as a child." Desmond's voice had risen unnaturally. He must have sensed that something was wrong, but

279

couldn't quite fathom what.

Dad refilled our glasses with red wine and smiled a colorless smile.

"I grew up *Czech*." His voice was apologetic, but resolute. "I did speak German once, but I've lost it. *All of it*."

I think I understood why he didn't want to speak German, but I was certain he hadn't forgotten one word.

Five years later he died. Heart attack! Ridiculous. I was studying law in New Hampshire, and I came straight home, but by then it was all over.

Dad was the easy-going type. At work they said nothing ever ruffled him. He always knew what to do. A cool head, detached, never lost his temper, never shouted. Heart attack. I couldn't believe it.

The doctors told me his heart was in shreds. Both valves leaking like sieves.

Heart? Drowning in a bottle of Scotch, I kept whispering a single sentence, around and around like a coffee-grinder. "It can't be. It can't be."

I looked up and saw him standing there, with a sad smile and eyes like stolen emeralds. "It's true," he said. "I've had no heart for a very long time."

I came to in the morning, wrapped around a table leg, my ear cut by a piece of glass. I remembered every word he had told me in my drunken delirium. "I've had no heart for a very long time."

It was true. My father was a zombie.

Now I know that it *is* possible to die and yet continue to exist. My father's soul had lived outside his body—it had dwelt with the spirits. No one else could tell the difference, but I could. I had always wondered whether there was, somewhere in the world, a magic spell or a drug that could restore the soul to the body. A place where the gods went, where they could breathe life back into an empty shell.

THE SOUND OF THE SUNDIAL

One time, out of the blue, I had said, "Let's go to Mexico, Dad."
We were having dinner and finishing off a fish soup made from
the pieces he used to buy at the Toronto docks. He went there a
lot—to watch the ships come and go, to hear the crashing of pallets
containing exotic wares, to see the hulls full of freshly caught fish,
the sailors' hands, strong and ruthless, struggling with the white-
painted cables, to hear the eternal screaming of gulls. He would
walk up and down for hours on end, cigarette in hand, his gaze
hanging on the far horizon as if he were searching for someone,
waiting for someone.

"Why Mexico?"

I didn't know what to say. Damn. I couldn't tell him, *Well,
Dad, I think it's where you might find your soul.*

I began babbling something about wanting to see the pyramids
outside Mexico City—the one called, what is it...

"Teotihuacan?"

"That's the one. You know I always enjoyed reading about the
Mayans."

"Teotihuacan? But that was the Aztecs."

I had to laugh. He really was like no one else. Obviously, the
Aztecs. I could have saved myself the trouble. After dinner he said
he was sorry, but he wouldn't go to Mexico. "But you go on your
own. If you need money, that's not a problem."

Later, I realized that he could never be free. There were only
two ways open to him: the empty shell or madness. Dark voices,
hallucinations. Nightmares bore him back to the city of spirits,
to the rubble of bombed-out Hamburg, to abandoned Bergen-
Belsen, Kurzbach and Zelle; in his mind, he haunted the places
where she might have been, looking for traces of her that trickled
under his feet in streams of summer rain, dissolving all grime and
hope.

I had been witness to the entire painful process of his dying,
the gradual amputation of his soul, from the early stages of

insomnia and his fear of nightmares, to his melancholy apathy, to the final phase of mechanical survival. At the end, he had played the roles of perfect employee and loving father like a robot.

When he died, I couldn't cry. I was overcome by a strange sensation. I was sorry he was dead, dreadfully sorry, and yet somewhere inside I felt relief, even joy. If death brought him liberation, I was glad for him. I only mourned because I felt sorry for myself.

I stayed on alone in another wonderful foreign country. I wasn't even twenty. Shortly after that I met Ellen, who had everything that I was lacking. Her mother treated me as one of her own children and fussed over me unreservedly. Her father would take me fishing, and during our hours of shared silence, I was reminded of my Dad. Thanks to them, I began to feel at home in Canada.

India remained a memory of childhood dreams; Czechoslovakia a bitter reality I could not forget.

Anna shifted in her seat and pushed a wayward strand of grey hair back with the others. She shook her head.

"You can never forget the land of your birth. Any more than your mother. For better or worse, she's still your mother. We all have only one."

"I envy you your memories of your homeland—at least they are a mix of the good and the bad, and the good eventually wins," I said. "My memories of that country are as heavy as lead. Clenched teeth and fists. It's a kind of inner war I'm always waging with the place, even though it's probably futile."

The candle guttered. Anna got up, took another one, and lit it from the first, pressing it down into the dying mound of wax.

"But you're embittered, and that will get you nowhere. Try to accept it. Don't pass such a cruel inheritance on to your children. Rachel would be upset if you did."

I rubbed my eyes and stared a while at the undulating candle flame. I got up from the table, stretched, and went out onto the balcony. The moon sat on a carpet of snow, rocking the night to sleep.

Anna came out to join me.

"There was no station anywhere in sight," she said quietly. "God knows why that train stopped in the middle of the fields, by a meadow in full bloom. After we stood there for about an hour, some of us jumped off the train and wandered around in the meadow, picking flowers and weaving daisy chains, frolicking like children. Intoxicated with spring and freedom. Such sad fairies.

"Rachel came lurching off the train, lit up with fever. Roses in her cheeks, her eyes full of spirit. She held out her face to the sun and broke into a weak laugh with all the breath she had left. We laughed with her, but her laughter gave way to a hacking cough, and she stumbled off through the long grass. I called after her. *Rachel, don't go too far.* She smiled and waved back. *I'll stay here.*

"I lost sight of her. I settled down in the grass and began creating the most beautiful bouquet of my life. I was home.

"The engine whistled. The driver let off several hoots. We scrambled back into the carriage and in ten minutes we were off. I looked around the rows of seats and sprang up. *Rachel? Rachel! Where's Rachel?*

"Rachel wasn't there. I put my weight against the door and leaned out. Several pairs of arms held me tight to keep me from jumping off. I struggled on the steps and cried out for all I was worth, shouting myself hoarse. *Rachel! Rachel!* Desperate and crazed. *Let me go! Rachel!* I kept screaming until my voice gave out for good.

"I've heard that call for years, again and again. *Rachel.* How many times have I seen that last wave of her hand? *I'll stay here,* she said. *I'll stay here.*"

I looked out. On the canvas of the mountains I saw a meadow in bloom and her frail body, hair spilled on the ground, eyes wide open. A bed of smells and colors, cornflowers and oxeye daisies. Plantains, that ancient cure for all wounds. A stand of grass building an archway from the world, the sun falling on the sound of crickets and grasshoppers. I saw a goddess. She had heard someone's laughter and the echo of her heart. *Dan? Tom?* But the grey-white clouds in the sky were deserted mosques and minarets.

I'll find you. In the mahogany darkness deep inside rock temples, on frescoes once warm with the touch of human bodies. You open the sky and we cross centuries, filled with pages of events and memories, verses of people and places that held the keys to who we are. Our sole possession is our faith in the people we have loved. I will find you in the sunlight of a vanished world, so that you can offer my ashes to the river, carrying them in your bare hands.

I could not bear it. I wept for the small boy that remained within me. I shook with cold. But somewhere deep inside, there was a spark. The doubts and questions buried beneath the sediment of years dissipated and washed the bitter taste of wormwood away. We went back into the house and poured out the last of the lukewarm tea.

I have found peace with Ellen. I never wanted fireworks, no all-absorbing, searing love until death and beyond. I have a great family, a wonderful wife and children. In Canada, I am at home; I look back and see years of happiness. Only, until now it was mired in this mystery, this sense of loss I've been carrying since my childhood. It has been a constant pain, sometimes buried, almost forgotten, and at other times, for no obvious reason, resurfacing. Like the residual pain from an amputated limb, or a piece of shrapnel in the body. No one could remove it. With the passage of time it had fused with my flesh and become part of me, but I always knew it was there. I cannot count the times I have replayed this unfinished sonata.

Now I held the missing part of the score. This woman in front of me had handed it to me, page by page, untangling the loops of question marks. She had put on rubber gloves and a white coat, taken up a scalpel, and opened my old wound. With no anesthesia she delved into the living flesh, looking for that bit of rusty metal. The new pain was excruciating, but she extracted the fragment and closed the wound once and for all, freeing me from decades of conjecture and empty hopes.

"Demons always face you head-on," my mother had once told me. "They won't let you past them, because they have no back."

I had circled around my demon and seen its back, and now it was gone.

I glanced outside again to catch first light.

Sometimes I conjure the animal radiance of India and yearn for it: the little witch Savitri. The Ganges. The Taj Mahal. The eye of the white turtle. A beautiful dream, but real.

I don't think Ellen would love India.

I'm going home to Toronto. But my next journey will take me back across the ocean. I will be flying east, counter to the Earth's rotation, to the continent of my birth. There I will become a blind pilgrim, striding through an alien land, and slowly, step by step, I will remember the familiar voices, the rustling of heavy ears of corn, the rocking of a cradle.

I will set off along a railway track, carried by an endless chain of sleepers. I will find that meadow. I know I will. I'll lie down in the grass and let myself be lulled by the pulse of my native soil. We will make peace.

My family waited in the two rental cars while I said good-bye. Alice came running in. "Dad, we're all ready now."

"I'll be right with you."

Anna looked at me imploringly. "Would you send me a photo of Rachel? Anything will do."

I nodded and took from her the little package of Christmas cookies she had made up. "I am so glad to have met you."

"Good-bye, Daniel. And good luck."

She gave me her hand and stared at me searchingly.

"Did you ever hold it against him?"

"Sorry?"

"Your father. For failing to prevent it."

She startled me. Did I hold it against him?

"No. It didn't even cross my mind. I have never blamed him."

"That's good."

In the doorway, a thought like a stab made me turn back.

"Did she?"

Anna winked and gave me an unforgettable smile.

"Tom was her sundial."

I left Colorado and the past behind. Next to me on the plane sat Nicky with his face glued to the window, discovering the world.

"Not even birds can fly this high, can they, Grandpa?"

The stewardess came around with fruit juice and champagne; she walked down the gangway with unshakeable assurance. "Is everything all right?"

"Yes," I said. "Absolutely."

Silver wings carried us toward the future. The whole family sank into the embrace of sleep, into sweet unconsciousness following a long, exhausting night. Only little Nicky stayed awake with me and showered me with vitally important questions, of which he had an endless supply. I fished around for answers in my greying catalogue. Then he looked up at me, tipped his head to one side, and narrowed his eyes into slits. "Your eyes are different, Grandpa," he whispered. "You don't look the way you used to."

My chin began to quiver.

"Do you want me to tell you a story, Grandpa?" The wistful tale about the little mole sent us both to sleep.

I was woken by the heat of the monsoon and the violent rain. I fought to regain my sleep, but it was hopeless. I disentangled myself from the mosquito net and headed for the bathroom. The water I splashed onto my sweating face evaporated at once. I started back to bed, my bare footfalls slapping stickily on the tiles, but with one foot on the mattress I had second thoughts. I wanted to see if they were asleep.

As I entered their bedroom, a wind picked up and raked the curtains across the window. They were sleeping beneath the thin net veil in the midst of a white desert, a stream of raven hair, his arm framing the curve of her hip. I stopped on the threshold, breathing in their dreams. The next gust of wind woke him. He raised his head and looked at me. Slowly he removed his hand from her thigh and put one finger to his lips—a gesture of quiet. She moved as if sensing that someone was watching, her breath chanting through the rain and darkness. Wind whisked the curtain and my father smiled at me.

I went back to my bed and thought about the wind.

The plane was about to land. The Fasten Seatbelts sign came on. This city has grown on me. I could see the silhouette of the CN Tower and Skydome in colors saturated by the breath of winter.

Pinkish smudges on the horizon announced dusk. The pressure inside the plane changed, the engine noise rose. My ears popped gently; I heard the faint clunk of the landing wheels. Beneath me I felt solid ground. Beside me, my grandson woke up.

I closed my eyes and saw Anna's wrinkled face. *Tom was her sundial*, she said.

I smiled. And Rachel was the sun.

Obituary of Hana Andronikova

Antonín Bajaja

First published in the Spring-Summer 2012 issue of ZVUK Zlínského kraje ("Voice of the Zlín Region"), the culture and society newspaper of Hana's home town.

In 2003, I was asked by Jiří Severin, co-founder of the *Zlínský kraj* regional publishing house, and the František Bartoš Regional Library in Zlín to assist with editing a children's book, *Fairy Tales from Moravia*. Several names [of contributors] came to me at once: Květa Legátová, Eva Eliášová, František Pavlíček, Ludvík Vaculík, Antonín Přidal, Ivan Binar, Jiří Stránský and others.

Then one day, outside City Hall in Zlín, I happened to run into Hana Andronikova. We retired for a chat to the café inside the Pavel Jungmann bookshop, where we had a couple of glasses of wine. Her debut novel *Zvuk slunečních hodin* (*The Sound of the Sundial*) had been out for a year and had enjoyed considerable success, and in the meantime she had also had a collection of stories published. I was interested to know what she was planning next. "A book about native North Americans," she revealed. I said that I thought that there was a close kinship between the legends of the Indians and the fairy-tale genre, and we spent a while discussing this. She finally promised to send me something for "my" anthology, possibly about water sprites.

But we didn't spend the entire time talking about writing and literature. We found we had some common ground among the people of Zlín. For instance, she surprised me with the revelation that her grandmother's name was Hilda Turnová. I asked if she was related to the family that owned the famous bakery on the corner of Dlouhá Street, which my grandmother from the hotel Balkán regularly patronized and where she enjoyed a good gossip. Hana nodded, adding that in a few years' time her Grandma Turnová would *certainly*, as she asserted emphatically, live to see a hundred. "*Certainly* because she was," I joked, "one of my father's patients," to which I added a compliment intended to be encouraging: "But mostly I expect it's because she's as fit as a fiddle, and you take after her."

"Maybe," she said, and shrugged.

A few weeks later, she sent me the fairy tale *Jak vyšplouchnout Suchopára* ("How Arid 'Arry Came to Grief") and thereafter we would meet from time to time both in Zlín and in Prague, where she lived. At every meeting, I reminded her about the Indian legends she had promised. "They're still in my head," she assured me, but by then she was working on another book to be called *Blues*. Then came a long gap in our meetings because she was doing a lot of travelling. Her Grandma Turnová did eventually die – at the age of 102; Hana herself lived only to 44.

Towards the end, our communications had been long distance. My last was when I sent a text message to congratulate her on *Nebe nemá dno* (*Heaven Has No Ground*): she had been unable to collect in person the prize that the book had won. She replied by e-mail: "[...] I apologize again for the long silence occasioned by a somersault in my health; I want to say that your support has always meant a great deal to me [...] Kind regards and a hug, I look forward to having that glass of wine together at last :-) Hana." Ahead of her lay an operation. And hope.

We can read the customary facts about her scattered around the Internet: Hana Andronikova, Czech writer. Born September 9, 1967 in Zlín. She attended the local grammar school, later taking a degree in English and Czech at the Faculty of Arts of Charles University in Prague. After graduation she went into business, turning to literature full time in 1999. Her first work, *The Sound of the Sundial* [2001], won the Magnesia Litera "Discovery of the Year" prize in 2002. That same year she published the short story collection *Srdce na udici* (*Heart on a Hook*). In 2008 she was planning a new novel with the working title *Blues*, but eventually published *Heaven Has No Ground* in 2010. In 2011 this book earned her the Magnesia Litera Readers' Prize. Additionally, she published a number of short prose pieces in various anthologies, as well as the experimental plays *Tanec přes plot* (*Dancing*

Over the Fence, 2008) and *Pakosti a drabanti* (*Saboteurs and Guards*, 2010), reworked as Šašci, špioni *a prezidenti* (*Clowns, Spies, and Presidents*, 2010). These dramatic works were all done in collaboration with the [Archa Theater] director Jana Svobodová, and all deal with—and involve the participation of—asylum-seekers. On December 20, 2011 she succumbed to cancer.

I have to add that she was slim of build and quite frail. But those who knew her also knew how much grit and pluck she had. This is confirmed by her autobiographical novel *Heaven Has No Ground*, written in an untraditionally provocative style: in the incarnation of a young girl, Amy, she has herself disappeared, now into the Amazon jungle, now into the Nevada desert. She counters the possibility of her own demise by accepting it without reservation; for her, death becomes a step in a new direction. For example, she finds consolation in the mingling of her own atoms with the atoms of pebbles. Through the eyes of one stone "she can see back to the beginning, to a time before the Earth became a millstone around the neck of the Sun."

I still have her phone number stored on my mobile. I wish it would ring, though it could only be by some kind of error.

Translated by David Short (2015)

Hana Andronikova was born in Zlín, Czech Republic in 1967, and studied English and Czech literature at Charles University in Prague. She turned to writing full time after many years of working in the corporate financial sector, and won instant acclaim for her first novel, *The Sound of the Sundial* (Knižní klub, 2001) receiving the Czech Book Club Literary Award and the Magnesia Litera Award for Best New Discovery in 2002. Her book of short stories, *Heart on a Hook* (Petrov, 2002), cemented her national literary reputation, and in 2007 she was sponsored by the U.S. State Department to attend the International Writing Program at the prestigious Iowa Writers' Workshop. She was particularly noted for her use of time as a structural element in the narrative, and her skill at conveying intimate and dramatic moments using terse sentences and fragments. She was diagnosed with breast cancer shortly after her return home. Her book *Heaven Has No Ground* (Odeon, 2010) is a personal chronicle of her fight with illness and the looming possibility of death. For this work she won the Magnesia Litera again in 2011, but lost the battle for her life at the end of that same year. She was 44 years old.

David Short graduated with a BA in Russian with French from the University of Birmingham (United Kingdom) in 1965 and spent 1966–72 in Prague, studying, working, and translating. He taught Czech and Slovak at the School of Slavonic and East European Studies in London from 1973 to 2011. Among his literary publications are *Bohumil Hrabal: Pirouettes on a Postage Stamp* (Prague: Karolinum, 2008) and *Vítězslav Nezval: Valerie and her Week of Wonders* (Prague: Twisted Spoon Press & Jeppe Press, 2005). He has translated a wide range of literary and academic texts and has won awards both for translations and for his contribution to Czech and Slovak studies. In 2004, he was awarded the Czech Minister of Culture's Artis Bohemicae Amicis medal and the Medal of the Comenius University in Bratislava.

Lightning Source UK Ltd.
Milton Keynes UK
UKHW02f0725060218
317414UK00004B/298/P